A shadow blotted out the sky as a tremendous green roc landed with a boom upon the pub roof. The roof supported the roc's weight for a full second before collapsing.

Ace, riding the saddle atop its neck, cursed and yanked at the reins. "Damn it! What's wrong with you?"

The roc shrieked and squawked then calmed suddenly and scanned the crowd until his eyes fell upon Never Dead Ned. Then his beak parted, but instead of a shrill warble, out came a voice.

"Ned."

"I didn't know they could talk," observed Private Elmer from the crowd.

"They can't," said Ace.

"Never Dead Ned," said the roc with his newfound human voice. But it wasn't his voice. It was the voice of a dead wizard, and Ned's blood ran cold. Belok was back.

The roc ruffled his feathers and clucked the deep, thoughtful clucks of a roc enchanted with a will other than his own.

"Kill Never Dead Ned."

PRAISE FOR *GIL'S ALL FRIGHT DINER*

"Something Evil (with a capital E) is stalking Gil's All Night Diner in Martinez's terrific debut. . . . Fans of Douglas Adams will happily sink their teeth into this combo platter of raunchy laughs and ectoplasmic ecstasy."

—*Publishers Weekly* (starred review)

"[A] laugh-out-loud comic fantasy that should appeal to fans of Terry Brooks's Landover novels."   —*Library Journal*

"Do you know a young man twelve-to seventeen-years-old who hates reading? Does he love gory subjects, especially when action-packed sex, danger, horror, and fantasy are included? Then this is the book for him! . . . A fun-fest of ghouls, zombie cattle, ghosts of various kinds, and lots of battles featuring decaying flesh and body parts. . . . Reads like the work of Douglas Adams."   —*Voices of Youth Advocates*

"Delightfully droll, this comic romp will be a crowd-pleaser."

—*Booklist*

"The story finds its footing through its personable, likable characters and the absurdly awkward fight they put up against increasingly bizarre supernatural terrors. . . . *Gil's All Fright Diner* really goes the extra mile to distinguish itself from the pack, creating a unique mythology and canon rather than relying on preestablished guidelines for its various creatures. . . . It's an appetizing snack perfect for devouring quickly over a hot cup o' joe."   —*Fangoria*

"It's horror both humorous and grisly, a twisted take on small-town America and buddy adventures."   —*Locus*

IN THE COMPANY OF OGRES

A. LEE MARTINEZ

TOR®

A TOM DOHERTY ASSOCIATES BOOK
NEW YORK

This is a work of fiction. All of the characters, organizations, and events portrayed in this novel are either products of the author's imagination or are used fictitiously.

IN THE COMPANY OF OGRES

Copyright © 2006 by A. Lee Martinez

A Tor Book
Published by Tom Doherty Associates, LLC
175 Fifth Avenue
New York, NY 10010

www.tor.com

Tor® is a registered trademark of Tom Doherty Associates, LLC.

ISBN-13: 978-0-765-35457-0
ISBN-10: 0-765-35457-8

First Edition: August 2006
First Mass Market Edition: April 2007

Printed in the United States of America

0 9 8 7 6 5 4 3 2 1

A short list of acknowledgments and/or dedications:

For Mom, one of each.

For Michele. (Insert clever in-joke here.)

For the DFW Writer's Workshop, where I learnt me to be a gooder writer.

For me, because I was stupid or stubborn enough to get here.

And for Jim Varney.

ONE

His name was Never Dead Ned, but it was only a nickname. He could die. He'd met his death forty-nine times, and forty-nine times he'd risen from the grave. Although, after his reputation spread, people stopped bothering to bury him. They'd just throw his corpse in a corner and wait for him to rise again. And he always did. But every death took a little bit away from him, put another ache in his joints, sapped a little more spring from his step. And Ned learned the hard way that there were worse things than dying.

There was dying over and over again.

Ned didn't have much interest in living, but he did his damnedest to avoid perishing again. Not until he could do it right. Not until he knew with absolute certainty that he would stay dead. For a soldier, fearing death was usually a career ender, but Ned found a position in the bookkeeping department of Brute's Legion. It wasn't much. Just counting coins. It didn't pay well, but it was relatively safe. As safe as it ever was when your supervisor had a strict policy of devouring anyone whose books were out of balance more than three times a month.

War was the Legion's business, and business had been good until four hundred years earlier, when the various species of the world had finally managed to put aside their differences. The Legion's accountants had predicted a swift and irreversible downward spiral in profits. And sure enough, the following three decades had been rough. But what everyone should've known was that paranoia doesn't vanish with peace. Soon every kingdom, every country, every hamlet with two pieces of gold to rub together suddenly needed a military force. For protection, of course, and to deter the benevolent military forces of their neighbors from getting any ideas. Never mind that most had gotten along just fine without an army before. Never mind that most didn't have anything worth taking. The Legion was only too happy to lease its armies to the world. War had been good for business. But peace was far more lucrative.

Gryphons never stopped growing, and Tate, well over three hundred years old, was a giant beast. His impressive black wings spanned twenty feet when spread, but he didn't spread them often in the confines of his office, a literal nest of ledgers dating back to the very beginnings of the Legion. Back when it had been a handful of orcs, a few dozen mercenaries, and a pair of dragons with a vision. Back before it'd become the most successful freelance army on three continents.

Tate spoke. He rarely looked at who he was speaking to. This was a blessing, since his cold, black eyes focused with an unblinking, predatory stare. They always made Ned worry about becoming lunch, even when his books were perfect. He wasn't interested in coming back from the dead after a trip through anyone's digestive system.

Tate glanced through the ledger slowly, methodically. He turned the delicate pages with his long, black claws. He missed nothing, not the slightest detail. Especially since he was always hungry. His sharp beak bent in a frown. His great black wings flapped once.

"Very good, Ned. Impeccable as always."

"Thank you, sir." Ned adjusted his spectacles. He didn't need them. In fact, they blurred his vision, but they made him look bookish, which was a look he very much wanted to cultivate.

Tate handed back the ledger. He swept the chamber with his gaze, never quite settling his eyes on Ned. "For a soldier, you make an extraordinary bookkeeper."

"Thank you, sir." Ned adjusted his spectacles again in an effort to look even more bookish, but his flesh wore the reminders of forty-nine grisly ends. The scars crossing his arms and face, particularly the long, nasty one across his right cheek down to a red slash around his throat, made a far greater impression than his eyeglasses. And of course, there was his missing eye, his cauliflower ear, and his bad arm. All the marks of a man who should've been dead long ago. For a bookkeeper, he'd made a barely adequate soldier.

The gryphon cleared his throat, and Ned took this as his dismissal. When he turned to leave, Tate spoke again.

"When you were first assigned to me, I assumed you would be my dinner within the week." He ran a black tongue across his beak. "Instead, you've become one of the most trusted members of my staff."

"Thank you, sir."

"Pity I have to lose you."

Ned, taken aback, stared into those merciless eyes. Tate's gray and black feathers ruffled, and he sneered.

"I've just gotten the news today. You're being transferred."

"Transferred, sir?"

Tate nodded very slowly. He smoothed his feathers back with a talon. "I tried to talk them out of it, but this comes straight from the top. Upper, upper, upper management." He rummaged through his nest of paperwork and pulled out a blue scroll.

Ned swore under his breath. Blue scrolls were irreversible, unstoppable. As inevitable as death or, in Ned's case, even more inevitable than death. Tate handed over the blue scroll, but Ned refused to unroll it and take a look at his new orders just yet.

Tate cocked his head to one side, then another. His lion's tail swished lazily. He cleared his throat again, and again. Before Ned could leave, the gryphon spoke up.

"It's a promotion. You've earned it."

Ned snapped his teeth together softly, as he often did when irritated. "Thank you, sir."

"Congratulations. Upper management must have a great deal of faith in you."

"Thank you, sir."

He held the blue scroll tightly in his right hand, while his bad left arm tried to pry it free. In one of his more unpleasant demises, the left limb had been severed. The arm had come back to life without him, and though a medic had stitched it back on, it still had a mind of its own, with obnoxious tendencies in tense situations. Given a chance, he knew the bad arm would throw the scroll at Tate. That might get Ned eaten, and he had enough worries already.

He turned to leave once more. Tate cleared his throat, and Ned stopped.

"Sir?"

"You're dismissed. Send in Yip. Very sloppy work lately. I suspect disciplinary action is in order." Tate clicked his beak with a grin. "And tell him to stop by the commissary and bring up some bread, cheese, a bottle of wine, and a dinner salad. Something zesty, but not too filling."

Ned walked from the office, feeling very much like a condemned man. A blue scroll was supposed to be a good thing. It meant upper management had taken special notice of him. But it was like being noticed by the gods in the heavens. More often than not, it was a one-way ticket to a tragic fate. Up to now, he'd done a fine job of being unexceptional. Except for not staying dead, but that wasn't his doing.

His fellow bookkeepers avoided looking at him as he walked through the halls. And everyone averted their eyes from the blue scroll clutched in his hand. Rumor had it that blue scrolls were enchanted to strike all but their intended reader blind. This was mere conjecture, since almost no one had actually ever seen a blue scroll. But no one was willing to take the chance of looking directly at it.

Ned returned to his office, a small chamber he shared with two others: Yip, a ratling, and Bog, the slime mold. Yip was counting a stack of gold coins. He'd shove one in his pocket once in a while. Ned and Bog always pretended not to notice. Neither liked the ratling, and they weren't about to discourage anything that might get him eaten. Bog was busy weighing bars of silver. Yip glanced up from his work just long enough to grin and chuckle.

"Tough luck, Ned."

"Have you read it yet?" asked Bog.

Ned shook his head.

"It could be good news," offered the slime mold.

"Betcha it's a transfer to the wyrm farm." Yip clinked two coins together. "Up to your neck in dirt and manure all day. And those wyrms stink. Oh, boy, do they stink."

Ned sat, laid his head on his desk, put his arms over his head. His bad arm yanked at his hair.

"Glad I'm not you," said Yip.

"Tate wants to see you." Ned didn't have the energy to raise his eye to glimpse Yip's face, but he heard the ratling swallow hard. That made Ned feel a little better.

Bog's eyes bobbed in his transparent flesh, floating to look at Ned from slightly different angles. "You should read it before you start panicking."

"I'm not panicking."

"He's moping," said Yip.

"It's probably not as bad as you're imagining," replied Bog.

"Probably worse." Ned held the blue scroll down on his desk as if it might jump up and attack him. "I don't have a very good imagination."

"Give it to me." Yip bounded from his desk and snatched the scroll. Ned held fast, and they commenced a brief tug-of-war.

"Just give me the damn thing already!" The ratling snapped at Ned's hand, and he let go.

"You'll be struck deaf," said Bog.

"Blind," corrected Ned.

Bog adjusted his eyes with his tentacles. "I suppose that makes more sense."

With the same fearless stupidity that was soon to make him a gryphon's dinner, Yip unfurled the ominous document. Both Ned and Bog lowered their heads (or head-like protrusion in the slime mold's case), expecting something terrible. But there was no flash of lightning, no torrent of shrieking phantoms, no unholy blackness to fall upon the office. Not even a single cackling imp or cold snap.

"Well?" asked Bog. "Are you blind?"

Yip rolled up the scroll and set it back on the desk. "Sorry, Ned."

Ned opened the scroll. "They've given me a command."

"That's not so bad," said Bog with feigned enthusiasm.

"It's Ogre Company."

Quiet descended, a silence so consuming that even the drafty corridors ceased whistling. Bog wasn't certain where to look, so he solved the problem by plucking out his eyes and sticking them in a drawer.

"Tough luck, Ned." Yip strolled from the office with a frown, stopping in the door on his way to the belly of a monster. "Glad I'm not you."

TWO

GABEL THE ORC slammed his mug against the table. "I tell you, it's racism. That's what it is."

Regina slammed her own mug twice as hard because Amazons made it a policy to do everything twice as well as any male. "The Legion has nothing against orcs. Hell, it's built on them."

Gabel remained adamant. "Sure it is. Angry, hot-blooded, grumbling orc idiots. But exhibit a little intelligence, bathe regularly, avoid dangling participles, and suddenly you're not orc enough."

"That's ridiculous." Frank the ogre slammed his mug as well because it seemed the thing to do.

"Is it?" Gabel leaned forward and whispered so none of his fellow orcs in the pub would overhear. "All my life I've had to deal with this. Do you have any idea how many promotions have passed by me? Meanwhile, every mumbling, malformed, drooling moron gets to climb the ladder."

"Maybe it's because you're short," said Regina.

"Goblin short," agreed Frank.

Gabel glared ruefully at his mug and took another drink. "Still racism. Not my fault I was born a little short."

"Goblin short," reasserted Frank.

Gabel narrowed his eyes. He'd gotten used to this. Orcs and goblins, despite their size differences, bore a passing resemblance. It was mostly in the shape of their skulls, their sloping foreheads, their wide mouths, and the ears that sat high on their heads. Scholars hypothesized that the two species shared a common ancestor. Both goblins and orcs found the notion absurd. But Gabel, having wrestled with this handicap his whole life, had little tolerance for it.

"I'm not a goblin."

"Are you sure?" asked Regina. "Maybe the midwives had a mix-up."

"In the first place, orcs don't have midwives. In the second, I'm not a damn goblin."

Frank bent close and squinted. "It's just that you look an awful lot like a goblin."

"Orcs and goblins look alike. They're related specimens."

"Yeah, but every orc I've known was grayish blue. Whereas you're more of a grayish green."

"And your ears are very big." Regina illustrated the size with her hands apart.

"Not to mention there's not a hair on your body," added Frank.

"I shave."

"Well, that's not very orcish either."

Gabel jumped on the table. Even standing on it, his five-foot frame wasn't especially impressive. Though he was in fine shape, his was a lithe muscularity. Orcs generally had great, dense bodies. And not one stood under six feet.

Gabel put his hand on his sword. "The next one who calls me a goblin gets run through."

"Is 'through' a participle?" asked Regina. "Did he just dangle a participle?"

"I don't know," admitted Frank.

" 'Through' is a preposition." Huffing, Gabel hopped off

the table. "Not that I'd expect anyone else in this pub to know."

"It's not racism," said Regina. "It's sexism. I should be in charge, but men are too threatened by a powerful woman." She flexed her bulging bicep, then drew her knife and jammed it handle deep through the thick wooden table with one strike. "It doesn't help any that I'm flawlessly beautiful. That only threatens them more."

Frank and Gabel chuckled.

She sneered. "Do you disagree?"

"Oh, you're beautiful," said Gabel, "but I think it's a little much to say you're flawless."

"Someone's got a high opinion of herself," Frank pretended to say to a passing soldier who hadn't been privy to the conversation.

Regina's cold, black eyes darkened. "What's wrong with me?"

The orc and the ogre glanced at one another. "Nothing," they said in unison.

"It's just, well, you're a bit . . . how do I put this?" asked Frank.

"Manly," said Gabel.

Regina threw her mug at him, but he ducked out of the way.

"Do these look manly?" She arched her back to emphasize her ample bosom. "Or this?" She undid the knot atop her head, and a golden cascade of silken hair tumbled past her shoulders. "Or this?" She pulled back her skirt to show her long, perfectly proportioned leg. Some of the nearby soldiers leered.

She grabbed the closest orc by the neck and drew him close to her snarling lips. "Am I not a vision of feminine magnificence?"

He nodded and gulped.

Her sneer deepened. "Would you not give both your eyes for a single hour alone with me?"

He hesitated, and she tightened her grip.

"Maybe one eye," the orc answered.

"Only one?"

He winced apologetically. "I prefer brunettes."

Regina tossed him across the pub. She shouted to the room. "Who here thinks I'm the most beautiful woman they've ever seen?"

The pub fell silent. Finally a soldier dared raise his hand. She stalked over, thanked him, and knocked him out with a brutal uppercut.

Frank chortled. "Not manly at all."

"I'm an Amazon warrior, not some barmaid to be ogled."

"First you get upset that we don't notice how beautiful you are," said Gabel. "Then you get upset when we do."

"Now that's more like a woman." Frank snorted. He helped himself to a leg of lamb being carried past the table, and as he was very large, even for an ogre, no one protested. "You're half right, Gabel. There's racism at work here." He bit off half the leg, chewing with loud crunches. Bits of mutton and bone spewed from his mouth as he spoke. "If you think orcs have it bad, try being an ogre."

Gabel eyed the lumps of meat floating atop his ale. With a shrug, he drank it down. It wasn't bad, although he could have done without the ogre spit.

Frank ran his thick, black tongue across his thick, gray teeth. "Do you know how many ogres have command positions in the Legion? None."

"Surely you don't think you deserve the promotion?" Regina struggled to put her shimmering, flaxen hair back up.

"And why not? I'm the highest ranking ogre here. And this is Ogre Company."

"Only ogres can command ogres? Is that what you're saying?" asked Regina.

"That sounds a little racist," said Gabel.

"It's not about that." Frank belched, and something sailed from his throat to land across the room and slither away into the darkness. "It's about demonstration of advancement opportunities."

"Let's just agree we're all getting screwed." Gabel sighed. They banged their mugs together.

"So who's the new guy?" asked Frank.

"Never Dead Ned."

"I thought he was just a story."

"Apparently not."

Frank grumbled. "How are we supposed to kill a guy who can't die?"

Regina gave up on her hair, letting it fall back down. One scarred soldier couldn't help but stare at her beautiful locks. She rose, walked over, and broke his nose, then sat back down. "He can die."

"Are you certain?" asked Frank. "I mean, it's right there in his name. First two words: Never Dead."

"He's a man." She spat out the word. "All men are mortal. Hence Ned must be mortal."

"Not to fault your syllogism," said Gabel, "but I've looked over his file."

"What's a syllogism?" asked Regina. She was in a quarrelsome mood and not willing to overlook a chance to be offended.

"A syllogism is a deductive scheme of formal argument consisting of a major and minor premise and a conclusion."

Frank squinted skeptically at Gabel. "You're making that up."

"No, I'm not," said Gabel. "It's basic philosophy. I read it in a book."

"Reading," said Frank. "Not very orcish."

Gabel pretended not to hear that.

Regina's hard eyes glinted. "No man, mortal or immortal, is a match for an Amazon. He'll die. We'll find a way."

The officers shared a chuckle.

Gabel stood. "I better get going. New commander arrives in fifteen minutes. His trusted first officer should be there to greet him."

They shared a chuckle over that too. After he'd left, the remaining officers ordered another round.

"Syllogism, indeed. I still say he's a goblin," remarked Regina.

Frank shrugged. "Some people can never be comfortable with themselves."

"Poor fools."

Then the Amazon knocked a troll flat on his ass for daring to glance at her breasts.

Putting harnesses on rocs and using them as transports was an experiment in Brute's Legion with mixed results. Gabel would've used titan dragonflies. They were easier to tame, easier to ride, even a little faster. The Higher Ups, whoever the hell was in charge of such things, wanted the regal, reptilian birds with their vibrant red and gold plumage, their fearsome shrieks. And that was how a perfectly good idea had gone to hell.

Rocs just weren't tamable. The most that could be done with them was to keep them fed and try not to irritate them. When they weren't hungry or annoyed, they mostly behaved. Unless it was mating season. Or they heard a loud noise. Or something shiny drew their attention. Or they smelled a chicken. Or they thought they smelled a chicken. Or they just felt like stomping something under their tremendous feet. For such immense creatures, they were terribly jumpy.

Gabel glanced through the sky. The flight was ten minutes late. Might be a normal delay. Might mean the transport had gotten hungry and stopped for a snack. This wouldn't be the first new officer to be devoured before he reached the fortress.

Goblins staffed the roc program and nearly every other project that required personnel equally fearless and expendable. Their bold obtuseness was fortunate. Otherwise, the way they bred, they'd have overrun the world long ago.

Gabel stopped a goblin passing by. This one wore a helmet with the crest of a pilot squadron. Gabel didn't recognize the design. Either *The Flying Brunches* or *Stubborn Chewables*. This particular pilot had three scratches on his helmet, signifying he'd successfully flown a roc into the air and back again three times without perishing. That qualified him as a seasoned veteran.

"Yes, sir!" The pilot saluted sloppily, but Gabel ignored that.

"Any news on the commander?"

"No, sir!" The pilot shouted. "But I'm sure he's fine, sir!"

Gabel looked to the pens. Four rocs paced about. Their long serpentine tails whipped up clouds of dust. Their merciless eyes glared. The biggest bird, about thirty-five feet high, nipped at another. The attacked roc shrieked and nipped back. Instantly all four monsters were busy shrieking and tearing at one another. Stains of dried blood and immense feathers from previous squabbles littered the pen.

Three goblins rushed into the pen with their long barbed sticks. "Calmer Downers" in roc-handler terminology. One handler was crushed beneath a bird's clumsy step. A second was snatched up and swallowed. Several more handlers replaced them, and after about a minute of furious screaming and terrified yelping, the rocs relaxed. The two goblins that hadn't been eaten or mashed in the process exited the pen with wide, satisfied smiles.

They'd never get Gabel near one of those damn things.

The pilot sensed his trepidation. "One day, roc flight will be the safest form of travel, sir!"

There wasn't the slightest trace of doubt in his words. Gabel admired the eternal optimism of goblins, even if he hated being mistaken for one.

"I wouldn't worry about the commander, sir! Ace is our best pilot, sir!"

Gabel stepped back. The goblin's shouting was beginning to bother his ears. "How many flights has he had?"

"Seven, sir!"

Gabel was impressed. "He must be good."

"Yes, sir! He really knows what he's doing! Plus, rocs don't really like the taste of him, sir! Swallowed him three times, sir! Spat him out every time, sir!"

"How lucky for him." Gabel waved the goblin away. "You're dismissed."

The pilot saluted again. "Thank you, sir!"

By the time the ringing had gone out of Gabel's ears, the

roc finally appeared in the sky. Its flight was surprisingly smooth, its tremendous wings beating with power and grace. But the landing was the hardest part. Its grace in the air was countered by its clumsiness on the ground.

The pilot whipped the reins, spurring the roc into a sharp dive. Just when it looked certain the bird would crash into the earth, it pulled up and set down without a stumble. Handlers threw a rope up to the pilot, who tied it around the roc's collar. He slid down the rope with a grin.

Ace was short, even for a goblin—a little over two feet. Nonetheless, he cut a dashing, carefree figure. Almost heroic. He raised his goggles, threw back his long scarf. One of his ears was missing, probably having been snipped off by a roc. Or maybe something else. Goblins lived dangerous lives.

"Sir." He didn't salute, only drew his knife and cut another notch into his helmet. The pipe clamped between his teeth stank of some foul herb Gabel couldn't quite place. Whatever it was, it reeked of rotten flesh and spoiled fruit. Little wonder rocs didn't want to eat him.

A voice called from the bird's back. "Excuse me? How do I get down?"

"Well, you could jump!" shouted Ace. "Or you could use the ladder! Your call."

A rope ladder descended one side, and Ned started down. He was halfway to the ground when a scampering squirrel darting past startled the roc. The beast twisted, lost its balance, and tumbled over. Gabel and Ace were well out of squishing range, but Ned wasn't so lucky. The crash of three tons of bird flesh cut short his fearful yelp. The roc took some time before wobbling to its feet.

Gabel approached the crushed commander. "Damn, what a mess."

"He looked like that before," said Ace, "except his neck didn't bend that way."

"Sir?" Gabel prodded Ned. "Sir?"

"Pretty sure he's dead." Ace kicked the corpse.

"But this is Never Dead Ned."

"Guess they'll have to change his name to Distinctly Dead Ned." Ace booted the body a second time, hopped on its chest a few times, and waggled the broken neck. "Yep, that's dead a'right."

Gabel frowned.

Then he smiled. It was nice when problems solved themselves.

THREE

COPPER CITADEL DIDN'T have a proper graveyard. Its population consisted mostly of ogres, orcs, and goblins, all of whom considered a corpse, at worst, something to trip over and, at best, ammunition for a stimulating game of Catapult the Cadaver, a popular orc drinking game. But a few humans were stationed at the citadel, and as it was official policy of Brute's Legion to respect all cultures, even the absurdity of humans, there was a rudimentary cemetery set aside in a useless patch of dirt.

Two ogres, Ward and Ralph, were the official gravediggers. The position added a few coins to their wages. They could've done a poor job of it, and none but the dead would've cared. But Ward took some small pride in his work, and that rubbed off a little on Ralph. They were both typical ogre specimens: tall, wide, ruddy, hairy creatures with broad mouths and tiny, close-set eyes. Ralph was a little hairier than Ward, and Ward was a little taller. That was the biggest difference between them.

Ralph scooped out another shovel of dirt and glanced at the setting sun. "It's getting dark. That's deep enough."

Ward shrugged. "I don't know. Doesn't look as deep as the last commander."

"That's because I liked that guy."

"You might've liked this guy, Ralph."

They studied Ned's corpse with its bulging eye and purplish tongue hanging from blue lips.

Ralph frowned. "Looks like an asshole to me."

"They all look like that when they're dead."

Ralph picked Ned up by one leg and dangled the corpse. "Yeah, but what kind of idiot calls himself Never Dead Ned, then goes and dies?"

"Asshole," they said as one.

Ralph tossed the body in the hole. It didn't take long for the heavyset gravediggers to finish the burial. Dark clouds spread overhead. A few heavy drops of rain fell. Ward jammed a simple tombstone into place.

"That's nice," complimented Ralph. "When did you make it?"

"Soon as I heard the new commander was coming. Didn't think I'd have to use it so soon."

In the unadorned cemetery, ten graves stretched beside Ned's. Each stone bore the name of a dead human commander of Ogre Company. There'd been other casualties of the job, but only the humans needed to be buried. The orcs had been used as roc chow. An elf had been burned on a pyre. There'd been a dwarf too, but he'd been torn to so many pieces that no one wanted to bother picking them all up. So Ralph and Ward had never learned how dwarves liked their corpses handled.

"Is it me, or are we going through these guys faster than we used to?" asked Ralph.

"It's you. Although this one's got to be the record. Hold on a second. I've got to fix something here." Ward pulled a chisel and mallet from his belt and chipped an X through the "Never" in Never Dead Ned.

"Should we say some words?" asked Ward.

"Do we have to?" asked Ralph.

"Humans seem to like that kind of thing."

The approaching storm thundered. "Fine. But let's make it quick." Ralph's nostrils flared as he sniffed the air. "I smell rain. And magic. Dark magic."

Rare ogres were born with a talent for smelling magic. The gift had never been proven to any of the other races, but ogres accepted it as fact.

"What's dark magic smell like?" asked Ward.

Ralph drew in another snort. "Strawberries and cream." He wiped the rain from his eyes. "Get on with it."

Ward started to say something, then stopped. He started again and stopped.

"Well?" asked Ralph.

"I didn't know the guy."

"I'll do it." Ralph sighed. "Here lies another human. I didn't know him, but he didn't do anything to me so I guess he was all right. He was still a human though, and most of them are jerks. Except that one guy whose name I can't remember now."

"Oh, yeah," said Ward, "the fat one."

"Not that one. I'm talking about that short one."

"They're all short."

"True, but this one was especially short."

"Oh, yeah, the short one. He was a good guy," agreed Ward. "Too bad about that guy."

"Anyway," continued Ralph, "I doubt this guy was as good as that guy, but maybe he was. Probably not. Probably was an asshole. But maybe not."

A clap of thunder ended the ceremony.

"That was beautiful, Ralph."

The two ogres loped their way toward the citadel to escape the threatening rain. The rumbling clouds swirled in the blackened sky. The wind howled, but the downpour never came, only a few drops.

The woman stood by Ned's grave. She might've appeared there. Or just as possibly, she'd walked up unnoticed. She was a small, wiry figure with a bent back, dressed all in red.

Her cloak was crimson, her dress a sharp scarlet. Her long hair was sanguine, and her skin a pale cerise. A vermilion raven perched on her shoulder. She clutched a gnarled maroon staff in an equally gnarled hand. She raised it over her head and gathered the magic necessary to raise the dead.

Ned had been raised so many times that it was absurdly simple. One day, he might even rise without her help. For now, he still needed a nudge.

"Get up, lazybones."

It wasn't much of an incantation, but it was all that was required. The Red Woman stamped her staff on Ned's grave. The clouds dissolved, and the air grew still. She waited.

An hour later, she still waited.

"He's not coming up," said the raven.

"He's just being stubborn. He'll get tired of sitting in the ground soon enough."

Another hour later, he did. Ned had some experience digging himself out of graves, and it didn't take long once he finally decided to claw his way to the surface. He wiped away the moist earth clinging to his clothes.

"Took you long enough," remarked the raven.

Ned rubbed his sore neck. There was a crick in it now. That'd probably never go away. He always ended up with some such reminder after dying. There were so many now, one more didn't make much difference.

The Red Woman smiled and walked away.

He called after her. "Why don't you just let me die?"

She turned her wrinkled face in his direction. Her red cheeks glowed in the faded twilight. "Because, Ned, I've had a vision. One day, some far-off tomorrow, the fate of this world and every creature that walks its lands, swims its waters, and soars through its skies will depend upon you and the decision you will make."

He hadn't expected the answer. She'd never given him one before. He felt a little better hearing it, to know there was a reason for his suffering. He puffed out his chest with a proud smile.

"I'm just screwing with you, Ned."

Ned's chest and ego deflated, and he slumped.

"Some people knit. Others play cards. I raise the dead," she replied. "A girl's got to have a hobby. Otherwise I'd sit around my cave all day talking to zombies. Have you ever tried having a conversation with a zombie? They're very dull. And it doesn't matter how many times you tell them you don't mind the smell, they just keep apologizing. Over and over again. They're so bloody self-conscious."

"Sorry." He wasn't sure why he apologized. "But I was hoping you could just stop."

"Give them the silent treatment, you mean?" She scratched her nose with a long fuchsia fingernail. "Hardly seems fair to discriminate against them just because they're dead."

"No. I meant I was hoping you could stop bringing me back to life."

"That's a fine thank-you," she said to her raven. "Most men would consider themselves fortunate to have cheated death as many times as this one."

"It's just . . ." He struggled to find the right words. "Look. It's not natural for a man to keep dying."

She leaned on her staff. "What are you saying? You'd rather be dead? Is the grave so appealing?"

"It's not that. But a man shouldn't have to die more than once."

She shook her head very slowly. "That's your problem, Ned. You keep mentioning the dying. As if that's the most important part. Has it occurred to you that perhaps you'd do better to think more upon the time you spend among the living and less upon those brief moments in the company of the dead?"

"Certainly not," taunted the raven. "Ned isn't a very bright boy."

Ned reached for the dagger on his belt. It was gone. Over the years, he'd stabbed the woman with a variety of blades in a variety of points, but so far, she'd never seemed to care. He hadn't tried the raven yet. He didn't imagine it would work.

Even if he killed the damned bird, she'd probably just resurrect it.

"All things die, Ned," said the Red Woman. "Everything must molder in the ground sooner or later. You are no exception . . . probably. But while we live, whether by nature or magic, we'd do well to appreciate the experience."

"I don't know why you bother," squawked the raven. "Clearly he's an idiot."

"Perhaps." She stepped into the night. Despite her bright rubecundity, the blackness absorbed her. "See you around, Ned."

She was gone. He couldn't say whether she walked away or vanished into nothing. For a moment, he considered her advice, but before he could give it much thought, a faint odor of strawberries and cream reminded him how hungry he was. Returning from the dead always gave him an appetite.

Copper Citadel was a dim beacon in the gray night, and he headed for it. It was an irksome journey. He couldn't see well and kept tripping over the uneven, rocky ground. He'd had a lightstone in his pouch when he died, but it was gone along with his knife and money. He'd been robbed. Dead men had no use for gold. But now he wasn't dead, and he was broke and blind, stumbling through the dark. He half expected to fumble his way into a booby trap and perish again. He was even more annoyed by the time he reached the citadel, and his teeth were positively grinding.

The front gates were open, and the ogre sentries were asleep at their post. The light wasn't much better inside the citadel walls. The only illumination at all came from a few sizable lightstones that had yet to be stolen from their fixtures. Soldiers slept on the ground. Others milled about in drunken gangs. None noticed or cared about one stranger walking through their fort. Ned had heard Ogre Company was undisciplined, but this was an absurdity of a fortress. He was glad he didn't have to worry about dealing with security.

He found the pub without any trouble. He just followed the sounds of carousing. The harsh blare of the bonehorn, a vile orcish instrument capable of producing only three notes, assaulted his ears. The player kept tooting those notes in the same sequence. Ned recognized the tune: "Skullcrusher Boogie." Not his favorite orcish composition, but it beckoned him.

The pub was dark, musty, and crowded. Mostly ogres, as Ned expected. He kept his eye to himself and strode purposefully to the bar.

He caught the barkeep's attention. "Doom stout."

The barkeep, a short ogre easily a head taller than Ned, pursed his lips. "You sure you want that?"

Ned nodded, and the barkeep went to fetch a mug.

"Excuse me, but are you Never Dead Ned?" asked a goblin on the next stool.

"No."

Ace leaned forward. "Are you sure? You look like him."

"All humans look alike."

Ace frowned. "Yeah, but this guy was distinctive, even for a human. He was full of scars. Like you. And he had only one eye. Like you. And his left arm, it looked a little gangrenous. Like yours." He squinted. "Yeah, you're him a'right."

Ned admitted defeat. "Yeah. I'm him."

"Thought so. I flew you in. Remember that?"

"How could I forget?"

The barkeep set a mug of thick, black liquid before Ned. "I'd advise you not to drink this, little guy. Likely to put you right in your grave."

"Wouldn't be the first time," said Ned.

He gulped some of the doom stout. He had to chew to get it down, and swallowing was a feat of will. His gut burned. His tongue sizzled. His throat constricted so tightly that it cut off his oxygen for about a minute. His eye watered. After all that, a cool pleasantness filled his head. In an hour it'd be replaced by a crushing headache and a bloody nose, but an hour was a long way away.

"Never knew a human that could stomach doom stout." The barkeep smiled. "That one is on the house."

It was a good thing, because Ned didn't have any money. But he was commander here, and he'd just risen from the dead. That should've been worth a free drink at the very least.

Ace lit his pipe. A fly caught in the toxic yellow cloud retched audibly and fell to the floor dead. "Guess they call you Never Dead Ned for a reason, eh, sir?"

"Guess so." Ned bit off another gulp of ale.

"Hey, Ward, Ralph!" shouted Ace. "Look who's back! Guess you didn't bury him deep enough!"

Ned swiveled and scanned the pub. His gaze fell across the only two ogres who couldn't look him in the eye. Both held a mug in one hand, a shovel in the other. Ned rose and stomped across the room on wobbly legs. Ace, grinning, followed. The pub fell quiet.

"Did you bury me?"

Ward nodded. "Yes, sir."

"You're not supposed to bury me." The muscles of Ned's bad arm tightened. His hand balled into a fist.

The gravediggers gulped. Even sitting, they were taller than Ned, and there wasn't a human alive who could take an ogre in a bare-knuckle brawl. But any man who could return from the grave and drink doom stout was worthy of some respect. Since ogres weren't used to either respecting or fearing humans, they weren't sure precisely how to feel. They ultimately decided on awkward unease.

The doom stout bolstered Ned's courage, lessened his reason. He had no fear of death, merely a general dislike for it. He was capable of anything right then, and even he wasn't sure what he might do.

"My money."

Ralph dropped Ned's pouch on the table. "We didn't think you'd be needing it anymore, sir."

Ned belched loudly enough to nearly knock himself off his rubbery legs. "My knife. My sword."

The knife was given over.

"Someone got to the sword before us," said Ward.

Ned hunched over the table to keep his balance.

"We were just following orders," said Ralph. "Sir." He grunted that last word with obvious disgust.

Ned's bad arm swung out hard and fast and collided with Ralph's thick jaw. A terrible crack filled the air. Whether it was Ned's hand breaking or the ogre's teeth slamming together, Ned couldn't tell. But he knocked Ralph out of his chair and onto the floor. Ned spun around on the follow-through and, if not for a steadying arm from Ace, would've ended up beside the ogre.

The pub cheered. Every one of these soldiers appreciated a good, solid punch as an art form. Ned would regret it in the morning. His knuckles were swollen and red, but he didn't feel the pain. The stout kept him nice and warm.

Ralph stood. He rubbed his jaw. A trickle of blood showed on his lip. Not much, but more damage than any human had ever done. Actually he'd never been punched by a human. The peculiarity of the situation took away his anger, leaving him with only profound confusion.

"Here's a new order." Ned jammed his finger into Ward's chest. "Don't ever bury me again."

He turned and tripped his way back to the bar. When he'd settled back into place, the pub filled with noise again. The bonehorn player launched into a rousing rendition of "Broken Bone Blues," a tune consisting of the same notes in the same order as "Skullcrusher Boogie," but a little slower.

"You've got guts, sir." Ace slapped Ned across the back.

Ned's bad arm seized the goblin by his ear and tossed him into the bonehorn player. He hadn't meant to do it, but his arm always got extra nasty when he drank. The patrons chuckled with much amusement. Ace dusted himself off and found a seat at the gravediggers' table.

Ned swallowed another drink and wiped the sweat from his brow. The higher the fever, the better the stout. He ordered a steak, bloody rare. Nothing else agreed with a tall mug of doom stout.

A woman slid beside Ned. "So you're our new commander."

He glanced at her. She was pretty, not beautiful, with

short, simple blond hair. She was vaguely familiar. Something about her stirred his animal lusts, and it was unusual for anything to stir his lusts so soon after rising from the dead. And a hearty stout never helped.

"Have we met before?" he asked.

"No, sir." She smiled. A dimple appeared on her left cheek. He knew her. He just couldn't place where.

"Name's Miriam, sir." She ran her fingers up and down his bad arm. The limb warmed at her touch. "Can a lady buy you a drink?"

Across the room, Ralph dabbed at the blood on his chin. "Told'ja he was an asshole."

"Yeah." Ace puffed on his pipe with a grin. "I like him."

FOUR

THE RED WOMAN HAD amassed a great many responsibilities over her years. Whereas men existed six or seven paltry decades, she just kept on living, gathering tasks like a shambling sludgebeast gathered flies until the poor creature must eventually smother under the weight of a billion insects. But the Red Woman didn't smother easily, and when Never Dead Ned spoke of the peace of the grave, she understood more than she ever let on.

One of her tasks was the tending of a godling. This particular godling manifested as a phantom mountain. It wasn't much of a mountain, nor much of a god. But it was young, and gods aged at their own pace, some coming into being and passing away within an hour, others taking millennia to find form. The mountain was little more than a faithful puppy. It followed her everywhere, existing in some shadowy realm between the heavens and earth. Few could sense it. Even fewer could find it. But to the Red Woman, it was as real as anything else and never far away in the metaphysical illusion of distance. So she'd made it her home.

She stopped to catch her breath. She was very, very old and felt every bit her age on days like this.

Her raven flew ahead and called to her. "Come on now. Just a little farther."

She nodded as if she needed the encouragement, as if she hadn't taken this climb countless times before.

"I don't know why you don't just move to one of the lower caves," said the bird.

"I'm comfortable in my cave."

"Maybe so, but one of these days you aren't going to make the climb."

She silently agreed. Though nearly ageless, she was still flesh and blood. And flesh, even enchanted flesh, withered beside the antiquity of stone. She hoped with a decade or two the mountain might understand enough to provide her with stairs. It'd already given her something of a path to work with. Not much of a path, and there were portions she had to scramble over stubbornly. But it was a sign that this burgeoning godling understood something of her comfort.

The Red Woman reached her cave with some effort. The mouth was deceptively small, and a bend in the tunnel gave the impression of shallowness. But the cavern was exceptionally large, and she needed all the space for her various duties. It would've been too much for her to handle if she hadn't taken to drafting the dead. Dozens of zombies milled about their appointed tasks. Some were nearly indistinguishable from the living, but most were obviously deceased. One lurched to her side and took her cloak. Another handed her a glass of brandy. A drowned maggot floated in the beverage, but she'd grown accustomed to the sight. One couldn't work with walking corpses day in and day out without a strong stomach, and she'd developed a taste for maggots and worms and flies out of convenience. She sipped down the brandy and tucked the white speck under her tongue with a pleased smile.

She went to her cauldron and checked the corpse stirring the brew. Then she reviewed the jeweler's progress in sorting precious stones. Then she inspected the shroud weaver's latest work before checking the smithy's newest batch of swords, not one of which was worthy of the slightest enchantment. So many things to do, she mused. But she limped her way over to a stool and had a seat, resting her staff against her shoulder. Her raven was right about the climb, but none of the other caverns had the correct atmosphere.

A zombie maiden stopped sweeping. In life, the maid had been pleasant-looking, if not exceptionally beautiful. Now her skin hung from her bones, unliving proof that while perhaps one could never be too rich, one could certainly be too thin. "Did you do it?"

The sorceress nodded.

"He dies a lot, doesn't he?"

The sorceress nodded again.

"He must be very clumsy," said the maiden.

The raven cackled. "He's a buffoon."

"Death doesn't favor idiots," said the Red Woman. "She simply favors Ned. Oblivion doesn't surrender her prizes easily, and she never forgets those held, however briefly, in her loving embrace."

"She doesn't seem to care about reclaiming me," said the maiden, her sallow skin and yellowish eyes drooping.

"That's because you're only half alive. Death is far too busy to be concerned with the trivialities of whether your corpse continues to walk about."

"Let's hope he can go a while longer before expiring again," said the raven.

She smiled. Though her caretaking of Ned was her greatest duty, these journeys still consumed much of her valuable time, and she hoped Ned would stave off his next demise by at least a month or two.

The zombie maiden sniffed the air. Had her nose not fallen off long ago, her nostrils would have flared. "Do you smell that? Is that me?"

"I think it's me," said a gooey corpse mixing potions.

A dead knight raised his helmet visor. "Well, it's not me." He was a fresh addition to her staff. He was still in denial, though a spear clearly pierced his chest.

The legless torso of a deceased jeweler paused in his task of sorting gems. "It's not me. That's for sure. My flesh is almost all gone."

The rest of the zombies grumbled. When all the flesh fell from the bone, a zombie's conscription ended. A small scrap of skin clung to the jeweler's elbow, and several flies busily worked at it. His freedom was soon at hand, and his fellow drafted dead couldn't help but resent him. The Red Woman disliked this as well. She'd have to find another jeweler soon, yet another task she didn't have time for.

"Then it has to be me," said the maiden.

"No, it's me," disagreed the cauldron stirrer.

The raven cawed loudly. "Oh, for the heavens' sake, it's all of you, you decaying idiots!"

The zombies hung their heads and muttered.

"Not me," grunted the knight. He subtly raised his arm and sniffed himself, but his creaky, rusting armor drew attention to the maneuver.

The Red Woman sipped her brandy. Frowning, she shot the evil eye at some buzzing flies. They perished, falling into her glass. She took another drink and found this more to her liking.

The mountain rumbled, and she sensed an impending arrival.

The wizard materialized slowly with a great deal of pomp. He'd always been more concerned with the form of the magic than the function. A black tower of smoke billowed in the center of the cavern. Phantom women, absurdly proportioned with impossibly ample bosoms and preposterously thin waists and welcoming hips and long lithesome limbs, spun around in the air, droning in a demonic chant.

"Belok, Belok, Belok, Belok, Belok . . ."

One of the phantoms hovered before the Red Woman. The ghost's features peeled away to reveal a shining green skull. Her flowing hair turned to scorpions. Her gown fell to tatters. "Belok has come to call upon you. May the gods grant you mercy, for he certainly shall not." The phantom's appearance returned to her pretty state.

The smoke sank back into the ground, and a tall, thin figure stood in its place. His eyes were two golden pearls, his tunic a shimmering silver. He literally glowed with power. But his most striking features were a gray duckbill, a dome of short brown fur spreading from the top of his head to just below his eyes, and webbed, clawed fingertips.

The Red Woman was unpleasantly surprised to see him. She rarely entertained visitors, and this was one she could do without.

"Hello, Belok. Care for some brandy?"

The singing phantoms settled around the wizard's shoulders. They moaned musically.

With eyes that were still as sharp as in her youth, she spied a new hair sprout on the wizard's chin. The mountain godling brimmed with magic, and even merely breathing the enchanted air here brought on Belok's accursed allergies.

He reached into his tunic and held up a gleaming diamond. "By this shard of the Splendid Orb of Truth, I compel you, witch! May you speak only with ultimate veracity!"

"Veracity, veracity!" sang his phantom paramours in melodious glee.

Belok's golden eyes gleamed. His aura drew all the light to it, thus shining brighter and darkening the cavern at the same time. The gem clutched in his hand bathed the Red Woman in a pure white beam.

"Speak, witch!" shouted Belok. "I command you, speak!"

"Speak, speak, speak," chanted the chorus.

The Red Woman supposed a wizard allergic to magic shouldn't make such a production of it. But for all his power, Belok had never been particularly bright. She sat down again and waited for him to finish. It went on for another minute, although she stopped paying attention to the details. By the end, the fur on Belok's face had advanced its march to cover another fourth of an inch.

"Where is he?" demanded the wizard.

It took a moment for her to realize he was done with his spell. She'd nearly drifted off to sleep.

"Answer unclear," she replied. "Try again."

She thought he snarled. It was hard to read such expressions on the wizard's accursed bill. "But I wield a Shard of Truth. You can't keep a secret from me."

"You overestimate yourself, Belok. And your stone." She hobbled over to his side and plucked the diamond from his hand. "May I?"

He nodded curtly.

She tossed the stone to her jeweler, who examined it for a moment. "This isn't a Shard of Truth. It's just a diamond. And a poor quality one at that."

"You must be mistaken," said Belok. "I bought the stone from an alchemist in Minetown, and he assured me—"

"He bilked you," replied the jeweler.

"I am Belok. I am the greatest wizard in all the lands. I cannot be bilked." His phantoms shrieked mournfully at the very notion.

The Red Woman took the stone from the zombie and gave it back to the wizard. "Fine. Just take your worthless shard and leave me be. I don't know why we keep having to go through this. Orb of Truth or not, you haven't the strength to compel me. These visits of yours change nothing. Nothing except you."

"Damn you, witch. I should rip out your hollow soul and feed it to my minions."

The phantoms licked their lips.

"Spare me your threats. I'm every bit as powerful as you. Certainly my defeat is a possibility should we duel, but I would not fall easily, and the victory would cost you dearly, wouldn't it?" She leaned on her staff. "Have you grown that tail yet?"

He frowned. "A little one."

"Ah, well, I see the transformation is coming along smoothly then. You know, you needn't ever worry about it if you'd stop using magic."

"I am Belok! I am magic in the flesh! Vengeance is

mine!" His phantoms howled terribly, shaking loose a few of the smaller stalactites. They crashed to the ground, shattering. The zombie maiden sighed while sweeping the pieces into a pile.

"Be off on your vengeance then, but I can't help you. I can only offer my sympathies toward your plight." In truth, the Red Woman had absolutely none. He'd earned his curse, and she considered it mercifully short of the punishment he deserved. But there was some irony in it, she supposed. For Belok could've lived a perfectly peaceful life had he the wisdom to put aside his magic. Something he could never do. The punishment was only the form of his undoing, while his own mad obsession with arcane power was the true cause. In that way, the curse was quite poetic.

"Shall we continue this discussion?" the Red Woman asked. "I haven't the time to spare, and neither, I suspect, do you."

"You can't hide him forever."

"And neither can you stave off your transformation forever. Not so long as you insist on casting spells that will not work and visiting enchanted mountains."

"I'll be back." He snapped his duckbill. "And next time, you'll tell me what I want to know."

His exit wasn't the presentation of his entrance. It never was after one of these unsuccessful visits. He and his phantoms simply vanished.

"I thought he'd never leave," said the raven.

A fly nibbled away the last particle of flesh on the jeweler's elbow. The skeleton chuckled, falling into an inanimate heap. The rest of the workers glared enviously at the pile of bones.

"You'll be dead evermore soon enough." The Red Woman smacked the sweeping maiden lightly on the backside. "Now get back to work."

The sorceress eyed the jeweler's remains and shook her head with a sigh.

five

CONSCIOUSNESS ATTACKED NED like a thundering beast. Given a choice, he'd have stayed asleep. Forever. It was the next best thing to being dead. But he didn't have choices. He just had things he had to do, and waking up was one of those things.

His brain throbbed, pushing against the cage of his skull. He thought for sure it must've been oozing out of his empty socket. His left arm was stiff and unyielding. Any attempt to move it met only with a terrible ache, so he let it lie. Blood crusted under his nostrils. All these he expected, but there was something new: he tasted fish.

He hated fish. Even drunk on doom stout, he couldn't imagine willingly putting it to his mouth. He ran his tongue across his lips. It was fish all right. Salty, not horribly fishy tasting, but indisputably fish.

He smacked audibly and moved the pillow from atop his head. Furious light flooded in, and he put the pillow back with a groan.

"Good morning, sir," Miriam purred, "or should I say, good afternoon?" Her silken voice stirred those animal lusts, but his hangover and the peril of daylight kept him from responding.

He was too achy to smile, but he remembered now. A vague recollection of a night spent with her in his arms. It'd been magic. At least, he thought it'd been magic. The stout blurred the details. Still, he'd gotten laid. That counted for something. Maybe Ogre Company wouldn't be so bad at all.

Something scaly slipped between the covers to touch his shoulder. He pulled away.

"I have to get going, sir," said Miriam. "Kiss before I'm off?"

Eye closed, he lifted the pillow and puckered. Soft, cool lips met his. They tasted like fish. She tasted like fish. Reflexes kicked in, and he tumbled out of bed. For a minute, he struggled against the covers entangling him and the burning heat of daylight. When his vision cleared, he glimpsed a creature, a woman covered in golden scales, standing over him. She spoke with Miriam's voice.

"I guess this means the honeymoon is over, sir."

Ned covered his eye. "How drunk was I?"

"Very drunk, sir. But that really doesn't have much to do with it. I tend to appear to all men as the woman of their innermost desire. Hazard of being a siren."

He recalled how she'd looked last night. Pretty, yes, but nothing supernaturally appealing.

"Think about it," she said. "Is there anyone you've ever desired who you couldn't have?"

He didn't feel like running through the list right now. It didn't matter. This wouldn't be the first time he'd left a tavern with a beautiful girl and woke up to a woman with webbed toes. He swore this time it'd be the last. Although he'd sworn that the last time, so he couldn't pretend the promise counted for much.

Now that the shock had worn off, he noticed Miriam's shape was distinctly feminine. More so than he'd seen last night. She had long, supple legs, a narrow waist, and noteworthy breasts. Her face, resting someplace between a cod and a woman, left a lot to be desired. But her scales glinted beautifully, and the fins atop her head were tall and regal.

"Why don't you look like you did?" he asked.

"Like this?" She whistled a few pleasant notes. His vision blurred, and she transformed into a tall, dark-skinned woman. Not the same form as last night, but still very familiar. Yet another woman on his list that he couldn't quite place.

She stopped whistling, and the illusion fell away. "Sharing a bed has given you some tolerance, sir. Now it only works when I sing. That's why I seduced you. So we could get past it right away. Better for both of us."

He winced and felt sick. It wasn't Miriam. He was okay with that. Not happy about it, but okay. Remnants of doom stout congealed in his stomach, coated his throat. He felt like throwing up, but the stout wasn't letting him off that easy.

She smiled. A nice smile, even framed by plump, purple lips. "Admit it. You had fun."

He couldn't really remember. A night with the woman of his dreams and all he could recall was the morning after.

"Permission to leave, sir? If I don't take a dip, I'll start flaking."

He granted it. She slipped into her uniform, offered a casual salute, and left his quarters. He lay on his bed for a while, dredging up blackened bits of sludge from his throat. In a little over fifteen minutes, he'd half filled his chamber pot with a revolting brackish paste.

Someone knocked on his door. He grunted an approximation of "Come in."

Gabel entered and saluted. "Sir, first officer reporting for duty."

"Can I help you?" asked Ned, then remembered he was in charge here. "What is it?"

Gabel bowed. "Sorry to bother you, sir, but I was wondering when you'd like to do your first inspection."

"Never," said Ned honestly.

Gabel's brow furrowed curiously. "Sir?"

"Later. I'll do them later."

"And the address, sir?" asked Gabel.

"What?"

"The introductory address, sir? To introduce yourself to the troops."

"Later." Ned yawned. "Much later."

"Yes, sir." Gabel coughed softly to fill the silence while he organized his thoughts. "Might I ask you a question, sir?"

Ned groaned. "Yes, I was dead last night. And yes, I know they call me *Never Dead* Ned. But I guess that's only because *Occasionally Dead* Ned isn't nearly as catchy. Does that answer your question?"

"It's true then. You can't die."

"Actually, I die very well. In fact, I dare say I'm the undisputed grand master of the art of perishing. It's the staying-dead part that I'm not very good at."

Gabel coughed again to cover an awkward silence.

"I've never met an immortal before, sir."

"I've never met such a tall goblin."

Gabel frowned. "I'm an orc, sir."

Ned frowned. "Are you sure about that?"

An edge entered Gabel's voice. "Quite certain, sir."

Ned rubbed his face and studied Gabel for a few seconds before deciding he didn't give a damn. "Permission to leave."

Confused, Gabel looked around the room. "These are your quarters, sir."

"I was giving you permission."

The first officer saluted. "Thank you, sir. I'll alert the men to expect your address later this evening."

Ned mumbled something that was neither an affirmation nor a contradiction and rolled over in his bed. He disappeared under his blanket, but before Gabel could leave, Ned grumbled from under the covers.

"Do you know of anything that's good for washing out fishy tastes?"

"I believe the general consensus is a tall glass of warm grog works best, sir."

"General consensus?"

"Miriam has known most of the other men here, sir. In the most traditional sense of the word." Gabel grinned wryly. "Shall I fetch that grog for you, sir?"

The blankets bounced up and down in what Gabel took as a nod. He left the room, slamming the door shut. Ned groaned loud enough to hear through the walls. Gabel's grin vanished.

"Well?" asked Frank.

"Is it him?" asked Regina.

Gabel nodded.

"I thought you said he was dead," said Frank.

"He was."

"Are you certain it's him and not just some other human?" asked Frank.

"I can tell one human from another, thank you very much." Gabel's long, goblinlike ears wilted. "And this one is very distinctive. No one would mistake him for anyone else."

"But how is it possible?" asked Frank.

"Obviously it's some sort of magic," said Regina. "Is he a wizard?"

"He doesn't look like a wizard," said Gabel.

Frank leaned low, which still made him very tall, and whispered, "Maybe he's a secret wizard."

Gabel's voice boomed in comparison. "A secret what?"

Frank picked up the orc with one massive hand and clamped the other over Gabel's mouth. The ogre's meaty palm covered all of Gabel's face. He flopped around and re-sisted, but there wasn't much he could do. Frank nodded to-ward the far end of the hall, and he and Regina tiptoed away from Ned's door. Frank released Gabel.

"I could have you court-martialed for that," said Gabel.

"I didn't want him to hear you." Frank tapped the patch on his shoulder. "Besides, I outrank you."

"No, I outrank you." Gabel tapped his own patch with a sneer.

"No, you're first officer. I'm organizational lieutenant, first class. That puts me above you."

"No, it doesn't."

"Will you two stop bickering?" Regina folded her arms across her chest and stood ramrod straight.

"You can't tell us what to do," said Frank.

"Yeah," agreed Gabel, "we outrank you."

"No, you don't." She pointed to the insignia stitched to her robe just above her left breast. Frank and Gabel took note of it, but were wise enough not to stare too long and risk receiving a brutal right hook. "As archmajor, second stratum, sixth class, I'm the highest-ranking officer here." She tapped her temple with her finger. "At least, I'm pretty sure I am. I know I outrank at least one of you."

"Damn, the Legion made this complicated." Frank scratched the mane of thick red hair atop his pointed head. "Makes me wish I'd signed up with a smaller army sometimes."

Gabel said, "We can go back to my office and check the flowchart."

"Ah, forget it. Doesn't matter." Frank leaned in once again and whispered, "What I was getting at was that maybe our new commander is actually a secret wizard."

"What in the Grand Goddess's name is a secret wizard?" asked Regina.

"It's like a wizard. But secret." Frank bent lower until his head was level with Gabel's. "They're very dangerous."

"I've never heard of such a thing."

Though the Amazon and the orc kept their voices normal, Frank continued to whisper. "Very few have. That's why they're called secret wizards."

"Well, what's the point of being a wizard if you're going to keep it secret?" asked Gabel.

"Exactly."

Frank smiled wide and nodded very slowly, but he didn't supply any further explanation. Gabel was content to let the subject drop, but Regina couldn't help herself.

"What makes these secret wizards so dangerous?"

Frank leaned forward until his comrades were certain he'd fall on them. His voice was barely audible.

"Nobody knows."

Gabel sighed, and Frank stood straight and frowned.

"Don't you understand? They're like wizards, but secret. They're not like proper sorcerers living in floating castles and consorting with demons and mixing potions. Those kind are bothersome, but you know what to expect. There's protocol. Some nasty bugger raises an army of the dead or decides to forge an accursed ring or some other such nonsense, you can always dig up a magic sword or find some prophesied hero or just assemble a huge army and take care of them.

"But secret wizards walk among us. Nobody knows how many there are. Nobody knows what they're up to. And that's what makes them so dangerous."

"Fine. Let's pretend there is such a thing." Gabel grunted skeptically. "If Ned were a secret wizard, then returning from the dead would blow his secret."

Frank nodded with that knowing grin of his. "It's just the sort of thing a true secret wizard would never do. Which is precisely why it's just the sort of thing a very clever secret wizard would do."

"That does make a certain sense," admitted Regina. "It'd certainly throw off suspicion."

"Let me get this straight." Gabel paced in a small circle. "Never Dead Ned may actually be a secret wizard because secret wizards don't go around showing off their power in public, except to convince people that they aren't really secret wizards, which very few people suspect even exist in the first place."

"It's a very clever ploy," said Frank.

"Ingenious," agreed Regina.

"It's ludicrous." Gabel's voice rose, though he successfully resisted the sudden urge to shout. "It's absolutely absurd. That has to be the stupidest thing I've ever heard."

He stared down the ogre. Frank picked something out of the hair on his thick forearm, sniffed, and ate it. When Gabel stopped panting with annoyance, Frank mumbled, "Or it might just be the cleverest thing you've ever heard of."

Gabel ground his teeth. "Even if he were, which he isn't, he wouldn't be that clever."

By now, the Amazon was entrenched in the subject. She began to whisper too. "Anyone could be a secret wizard. And the more unlikely the suspect, the more likely they could be. What could they want?"

"Nobody knows," said Frank. "And few are willing to speculate."

Gabel threw up his hands. "When you're ready to talk about something more important than imaginary secret societies of hypothetical diabolical wizards, you can find me in my office. Oh, and Regina, the commander asked for some grog. You should get on that."

"Why me?"

Gabel struck on a plan that was very likely to put Ned back in his grave. Or at the very least, get Regina demoted. Since Gabel wasn't truly certain he outranked her, he couldn't lose either way. "The commander asked for a leggy redhead. I told him we didn't have any redheads, but he said a blonde would do in a pinch."

Regina scowled. "Swine."

"And he said to hurry up your pretty little ass."

With a guttural growl, she clutched the sword at her side.

Gabel, his back to her, chuckled before heading off to his office to consult the ranking flowchart.

Regina drew the weapon a few inches from its sheath and slammed it back into place several times. She glared at Frank. Her black eyes simmered with disgust for all males in general and one in particular. Even the very large ogre felt a trickle of fear down his back.

"I wouldn't suggest killing him unless you can be sure he'll remain dead. Even if it didn't upset him, he'd probably have you written up."

"Yes. You're right, of course." But her eyes didn't soften, and her grip on her sword tightened. "If you'll excuse me, I've grog to fetch."

Frank stepped aside, and she stalked her way across the citadel to the tavern. Every soldier knew well enough to stay out of her way by her burning gaze, clenched fists, and the hard kick of her step.

Regina's temperament had gotten her transferred to Ogre Company. The logic was, as ogres were large and fearsome, she'd be less likely to pick fights with them. It'd worked so far, but this was mostly because no ogres had gotten on her bad side yet. "An angry wife is good for life," went an old ogre adage, and had Regina been an ogress, she would've been very popular. But she was human, and ogres preferred human women to be delicate and cuddly, thinking of them more as pets one could fornicate with than as lifelong mates.

Regina did have frequent tussles with the humans and orcs stationed at Copper Citadel, but in Ogre Company, as long as no one lost a limb, such incidents rarely found their way into a soldier's permanent record.

She brought the grog back to Ned's quarters. Pausing outside the door, she drew her sword. Perhaps she couldn't kill him with it, but she might be able to teach him a lesson in respect. Frank's warning came back to her. He'd made a valid point. Ogre Company was the last place left her. If she blew this, she blew her career in the Legion. She didn't want to start over in another army.

"He's not worth it," she told herself. "He's just another worthless man."

Wrapping herself in Amazonian superiority, she sheathed the blade and pushed open the door without knocking.

Ned, obscured beneath blankets, groaned.

"Your grog, sir."

A scarred arm poked out from under the covers. It looked a little gangrenous. The fingers grabbed at the air until she put the mug in his hand. The limb retracted, and heavy gulps issued from beneath the cloth.

"Thanks. That is better." He belched and tossed the empty mug to the floor.

"Anything else, sir?" she asked.

"What?"

She swallowed hard. Her hand toyed with the dagger on her belt. "Is there anything else I can do for you, sir?"

Ned lowered the blanket, exposing his face and shoulders, a lattice of ugly discolorations. She'd seen healthier corpses. She expected a leer, perhaps an open ogle of her womanly perfection, but Ned barely glanced at her before rolling over, allowing her a glimpse of the slashes and scabs along his back. She found herself mesmerized, staring at the history lacerated upon his skin.

He turned his head to look up at her with his one eye, and she smiled at him without realizing it.

"Are you still here?" he asked.

She frowned. "Sorry, sir."

She saluted, turned, and left the room. In the hall, she stopped, feeling suddenly short of breath. She leaned against the wall as her legs were inexplicably shaky. She closed her eyes, and the slashes and scabs along his back flashed through her mind. There'd been a sword wound and, beneath that, a dagger's mark. Beside that, a purple welt that had to have come from a crushing mace blow. Claws of some terrible beast raked across his shoulder blades. And there was more than this. So much more. It was beautiful.

He was beautiful.

Regina had never felt this way before, and she didn't like it. She fingered her sword, contemplating removing the object causing her discomfort. But this was Never Dead Ned. She couldn't kill him.

And maybe, she considered with a snarl, she didn't want to.

SiX

NED HADN'T CARED about bookkeeping, nor soldiering, nor anything he'd done before that. Nor did he care about his new command position. If there was passion to be found in life, Ned was still looking. He did what was expected of him and very little else. And inspections were expected. After he'd slept off his hangover, he'd realized that. He roused himself from his nice, cozy bed, got dressed, and set about on his duty.

Seeing Copper Citadel in the light of day for the first time, Ned decided his initial assessment of the fortress had been too kind. The whole place was in terrible shape. The walls were crumbling. The buildings were in the middle of slow-motion collapse. Nothing had been cleaned or polished in a very long time, and garbage had been heaped in out-of-the-way corners—and in not-so-out-of-the-way corners. The cobblestones were cracked and uneven. The walls were held up only by the braces of garbage piles. And the front gate was too rusted to even close.

The soldiers of Ogre Company assembled before their new commander. Ned scanned the rank and file. The sun was near setting, and details were hard to pick out. In addition, the soldiers milled about in disorderly fashion, more a disoriented throng than a disciplined military unit. He estimated about three hundred ogres, one hundred orcs, seventy-five humans, a few elves and trolls here and there. There were goblins as well, but too many to bother counting.

Ned walked from one end of the courtyard and back again. He decided that was enough of a show.

"Dismissed," he grunted.

"Back to your duties, you pathetic wastrels!" shouted Gabel. "Makes me sick to look at the lot of you, undisciplined scum!"

The courtyard began to clear out, although no one seemed to have any particular place to go. A handful of soldiers remained.

"Sir." Gabel saluted. "I believe you'll want to have a look at our more singular personnel."

Ned wanted no such thing, but it seemed the kind of thing a commander was supposed to do. "All right."

"The archmajor has the files for your convenience, sir," said Gabel.

Regina stepped up, carrying an armload of scrolls.

Ned waved her away. "Just show me."

Regina and Gabel exchanged shrugs.

"Very well, sir." Gabel led Ned to the first in line.

The short, wiry soldier had a worn face, and a long red beard hanging to his belly. Even in the light of dusk, Ned could see the soldier's eyes were white and glassy as pearls. Ned barely glimpsed the image of a setting sun tattooed on the soldier's forehead.

"So you're—" Ned began.

"Yes, sir, I am." The soldier saluted. "Owens, oracle division."

"I didn't know the Legion still—"

"The program was discontinued, sir. Not cost effective."

"Are you—"

"Completely blind, sir."

"Do you have—"

"Yes, sir. Very annoying, I'm aware. But it's a difficult habit to break."

Ned rubbed his eye. "Are you—"

"I'm very good. Top of my class."

"Well, that's impress—"

"Thank you, but I feel I must acknowledge a limitation."

Ned opened his mouth, but the impatient oracle answered the question before it was asked.

"Since losing use of my eyes, I can only hear the future." The oracle flashed a proud grin. "But I hear it with an eighty-nine percent success rate."

This information had barely reached Ned's brain when the oracle spoke again.

"It still itches, sir, but a little ointment should take care of it. And thank you for your concern."

"What?"

"My rash. That was what you were going to ask, wasn't it?"

"No."

"Are you sure about that? Often we think we're going to say one thing when in fact we end up saying another."

Ned replied, "I'm positive."

"My mistake, sir. When you're right eighty-nine percent of the time, you're wrong the other eleven percent." He pointed to his nose. "I do smell the future with ninety-eight percent accuracy."

Owens answered before being asked. "No, so far it hasn't proven very useful. Gods bless you, sir."

"I didn't sneeze."

The oracle dug in his ear with his finger. "You will."

Ned moved to the next in line, a towering two-headed ogre. Such twins were rarely born, and they even more rarely survived adolescence, the tender formative years when ogres inclined toward their most perilously obnoxious. Puberty for the ogre race was a terrible ordeal involving gushing boils, boundless carnivorous appetite, and dangerously psychotic mood swings. Ogre youths were given lots of space during this stage, but two-headed specimens had little choice but to remain side by side. It didn't take long for one to kill the other—and himself—in the process.

The twins stood nine feet high if an inch and were nearly as wide. Their body was redder and hairier than those of single-headed ogres. The faces were similar but not identical. The one on the right had a fearsome overbite, and the one on the left had high-set, drooping ears. Still, it would've been obvious, even if they didn't share one body, that the ogres were related.

"Private Lewis and Corporal Martin," said Gabel.

They saluted with quick, military precision. They both began to speak, but stopped. Started again and stopped.

Lewis nodded to his brother. "After you."

"Oh, no, after you," replied Martin.

"Please, dear brother, I insist."

"Not to be difficult, Lewis, but it is I who must insist."

"Don't be foolish." Lewis bowed his head. "Clearly you were speaking first before I rudely interrupted. And it would be unseemly to speak before a ranking officer."

"Oh, no no no." Martin put his hand to his side of their chest. "It's perfectly obvious to me that you were the one interrupted. To which, rank or no rank, I can offer no valid excuse. Mother taught me better than that."

"Shut up," commanded Ned. The words sounded odd attached to his voice. The curtness of it struck him strangely. But he was in charge here. He supposed it only appropriate that he started acting like it.

Neither Lewis nor Martin seemed offended. Ned guessed their mother had taught them better than to question their superiors as well. The twins both tried speaking once more, but neither dared talk before the other.

"You." Ned pointed to Lewis. "What is it?"

Lewis saluted crisply again. "I just wanted to say, sir, that it is an honor to serve under the famous Never Dead Ned."

Ned nodded to Martin. "Now you."

"As you wish, sir, but I see no need to reiterate what my dear brother has declared with such eloquence. Though I myself would've preferred the word 'privilege' over 'honor.' "

Lewis smacked his forehead. "Of course, how presumptuous of me. As always, dear brother, you have demonstrated your superior understanding of language."

"Don't belittle your own grasp," replied Martin.

"You're too kind, but it is obvious that I have overstepped myself with my poor word choice."

"Now, now, I'll hear none of that."

Ned understood now why the twins had never gotten around to killing each other. They were too damn busy apologizing all the time. He left them to their atonements and moved to the next in line. The goblin was bright, leafy green, not the usual gray-green. And he had a shaggy red beard. Goblins didn't grow hair normally.

"This is Seamus," said Gabel. "Faerie blood in his family, isn't that right, Seamus?"

"Yes, sir. My great-great-great-great-grandmother had a fling with a leprechaun. Quite scandalous. We don't like talking about it."

"Seamus is a shapeshifter," said Gabel. "Give the commander a demonstration."

The goblin disappeared into a blue cloud. When the cloud faded, a large, white cockatoo stood in his place. A green fog swallowed the bird, and Seamus became a fat, brown rat. A burst of yellow smoke later, he transformed into a boot. Then a skillet. Then a trumpet. Then an apple. And finally a bucket.

Ned stood before the bucket a few seconds, but Seamus didn't change into anything else.

"I think he's stuck, sir. Happens sometimes. Nothing to worry about." Gabel nodded to the bucket. "Carry on, Seamus."

Fourth in line stood a long, white reptile. She was serpentine in form, fifteen feet long stretched out, but her body was coiled to a more reasonable six-foot height. Her limbs were short, four pairs in all. She stood on two pairs while her other two were folded. She radiated warmth, and the air shimmered around her. Her face was more like a cat than a reptile, and her two blue eyes sparkled in the dusky light. Little puffs of fire rose from her nostrils with each breath.

Ned said, "I thought all the salamanders were destroyed after the Terrible Scorching."

"No, sir." Flames erupted from her mouth as she spoke. Ned stepped back to avoid having his eyebrows charred. "Not all."

"What's your name, private?" It wasn't that he cared, but he was starting to feel like a commander, despite himself. And a commander should know his soldiers.

"You couldn't pronounce it with your thick, lumpy tongue, sir. They just call me Sally." Salamanders changed colors with their moods. Ned knew the basic color codes. Red for anger. Purple for vanity. Green for envy. She turned a golden orange, and he had no idea what that meant. He made a mental note to check her file later to see if it listed the more obscure shades.

"Good to have you on board, private," said Ned with enthusiasm that surprised him. He nearly slapped her on the shoulder, but caught himself in time to avoid a nasty burn.

She glowed a light purple. "Thank you, sir."

Next to last in line waited a short, treelike creature with a full head of yellowing leaves. The tree's bark was scarred. Some of the carvings looked like old wounds, but most appeared intentional or decorative. Only one caught Ned's eye. It read, "Don't pick the apples." A few arrow shafts were buried in the tree's trunk. He was amusing himself by plucking the petals from a fresh, young rose. Most striking to Ned was the burning cigarette pursed between the tree's lips.

"Private Elmer, sir," said Gabel.

Ned glanced the private up and down. It took him a moment to spot the tree's eyes, two dark spots that might be mistaken for knots.

"I didn't know we had En—"

"Treefolk, sir," interrupted Elmer.

"Treefolk. But I thought you called yourselves En—"

"No, sir. We aren't allowed to say that anymore."

"Why not?" asked Ned.

"We just aren't. A wizard put a spell on the word, so we don't say it anymore."

"A spell?" said Ned. "But it's just a word. Why would anyone want to put a spell on a word? What happens if you say it?"

Elmer drew a puff on his cigarette. "You don't want to know. Nothing too troublesome, but it's just easier to avoid it."

"But *treefolk*?"

"Well, we're trees and we're folk. Isn't too imaginative, but it gets the job done."

Ned shrugged. "I'm surprised there's any treefolk in the Legion. Didn't think they'd take up the soldiering profession."

"Why is that, sir? Because I look like a bush, I gotta be all lovey-dovey, kissy-wissy. Is that what you're saying, sir?"

"No, it's just . . ."

"I was told the Legion didn't believe in racial profiling, sir. I was told I would be judged by my ability to slaughter my enemies, not the texture of my bark."

"That's not what I meant . . ."

"Then what did you mean, sir?" Elmer plucked another petal from the rose. "What, pray tell, could you have possibly meant by that ill-informed, insulting remark?"

"I didn't mean to offend you," said Ned.

"Oh, I suppose that makes it all right then. You didn't intend to verbalize your ignorance. As long as the slur was unintentional, I guess we needn't worry about it. I guess I won't need to file a grievance with my union then." Snarling, Elmer dropped the flower to the ground and stomped on it with his roots.

He turned to Sally. "Disgusting mammal stereotyping." His leaves brushed the salamander's scales, and he plucked the smoldering bits of foliage before the flames could spread.

Ned moved on before he could say anything else he might regret. "I didn't know there was a treefolk union," he whispered to Gabel.

"Yes, sir. Only four of them in the whole Legion, but they've strong connections to the Troglodyte Brotherhood and United Siege Engine Operators. Best not to offend them."

"I'll keep that in mind."

Next was an elf. White stubble covered her shaved head. Her eyes were pink, her skin smooth and chalky. Although Ned had never found elves especially attractive, she might've been beautiful if she weren't quite so chubby. It didn't help that she was picking her nose.

"This is Supply Sergeant Ulga, sir," said Gabel.

She wiped her finger on her sleeve and nodded to Ned. "How's it going?"

"Could be better," he answered honestly.

"Ulga is part of the conjurer division, sir," said Gabel.

"Any good, sergeant?"

"I get by, sir. If I do say so myself." She reached into the air with a flourish and produced a plate of biscuits, which she presented with a smile. "Help yourself, sir."

Ned took a bite and instantly regretted it. It wasn't that the biscuit tasted bad. It actually had no taste at all. But it was so dry that it sucked all the moisture from his mouth. He swallowed. The morsel scraped its way down his throat and landed hard in his stomach.

Ulga clasped her hands before her, slowly spreading them to reveal a tin cup. She pointed her finger, the one that'd been up her nostrils only moments ago. Wine dripped from her fingertip to fill the cup, which she then offered to Ned. "I call it Ulga's Special Vintage. Have a taste, sir."

He took a gulp and retched. The warm drink took away his dry mouth, only to replace it with a slimy dampness. It was less a beverage and more a parasite clinging to his tongue.

Ulga read the disgust on his face. "Begging your pardon, sir, but it ain't all that easy to make the good stuff out of thin air. I ain't heard a man complain yet when nothing else was available. And it might not taste so good, but it'll get you drunk pretty fast."

"It will?"

"Yes, sir. Pure magic in a cup. There ain't nothing quite like it. Except maybe doom stout, but not many fools around who'll drink that."

Ned forced another swallow and emptied the cup. He did feel a little light-headed. "How much can you make?"

"About five pints a day, sir."

"Make as much as you can, and have it sent to my quarters."

"Yes, sir." She grinned proudly. "I can see you're a man of discriminating tastes."

He ran his tongue across his teeth, trying to scrape away the aftertaste. But free booze was free booze.

"And, sergeant, wash your hands before you do it," he added, moving down the line.

Miriam the siren waited next. Dusk was now upon the citadel, and the shadow of her body was very appealing. Although that was probably the enchanted wine at work.

"And, of course, you've already acquainted yourself with our morale officer," said Gabel.

The rest of the line chuckled except for Seamus, who had worked his way from bucket to potted petunia. Sally the salamander turned a bright blue.

Ned couldn't quite look Miriam in the eyes. But she didn't seem the least bit uncomfortable and winked at him with a slight smile. Maybe it was the wine, maybe her innate siren charm, maybe just ordinary indiscriminate animal lust, but he smiled back.

"Is that it, Number One?" he asked.

Gabel nodded. "Yes, sir."

Ned looked the line up and down. Ogre Company was the last stop in a failing career in the Legion. Even ogres didn't end up here unless they'd screwed up somewhere. But overall, they didn't seem a bad bunch. He didn't see why they couldn't be made into something worthwhile.

Too bad he wasn't the man for the job. He just wanted to put in his time and avoid getting killed again.

A huge, shrieking shadow soared over the courtyard. The

soldiers ran for cover. Except for Seamus, who was now a battle-ax, and Ned, who, lacking the reflexes, didn't realize what was happening until nearly being crushed beneath a roc's talons. The great bird craned its long neck downward to within a few feet of Ned's face. Sharp teeth lined its jagged beak, and its tongue was long and blue. Its breath was hot and sweet, like ripening honeydew. He'd never been close enough to the maw to notice before.

The roc snorted, and he thought for sure it would devour him. But Ace slid down its neck and kicked the bird on the back of its head. The creature barely noticed, but hissed and turned away.

"Sorry about that, sir. Long flight. Morena is a little hungry." Ace hopped to the ground. In one hand, he held a small pouch. In the other, he clutched the roc's reins, seemingly unaware that Morena could catapult him a good mile or two with a casual whip of her head.

"What the hell are you doing?" asked Gabel. "You can't land one of these things in the citadel proper."

"Beg to differ, sir." Ace puffed his pipe through grinning teeth. "I can land a roc pretty much anywhere. Mind you, getting them back in the air can be tricky. Especially Morena here. She likes a lot of room."

The roc beat her wings, and Ned expected her to fly away with the goblin wrapped in her reins.

"Quiet down, girl." Ace hopped in the air, yanking the tether with all his weight, which was about half as much as one of Morena's feathers. "Got to keep a firm hand with them, sir. Can't give them an inch."

Morena's serpentine tail thrashed wildly. Being crushed once was more than enough for Ned. He stepped back very slowly so as to not draw the roc's attention. She shrieked in a warbling, ear-splitting cry.

"Oh, shut up, Morena." Ace picked up a stone and hurled it at the monster. The rock bounced off her beak. She quieted, turning her hungry gaze upon the goblin. She licked her beak, splashing puddles of drool.

"Get that thing out of here," commanded Gabel.

"In a second, sir. But I was told to give this to the commander without delay."

Ace tossed Ned the pouch. The courtyard lightstones were burning now, and Ned glimpsed the wax seal with a symbol painted in blood: a scale encircled by a winged serpent atop a single, demonic eye. In all of Brute's Legion, there was no more dreaded division, no section more coldly ruthless, no battalion as unforgiving or merciless.

Accounting.

Ned shivered.

The roc jerked its head, lifting Ace in the air. The bird snapped up the goblin in her beak. Ned, pouch in hand, almost envied Ace.

The roc ruffled her feathers and shuddered. She gagged and spat up her morsel. Ace landed beside Ned. The goblin rose, wiped the saliva from his goggles, wrung the moisture from his scarf.

"Where's my pipe?"

Morena belched it up. Ace clamped it in his teeth and puffed, though the flame had been doused by the roc's copious saliva. "Keep it up. Just keep it up, and maybe I'll eat your damn dinner myself."

Morena shook the ground with two thuds of her tail.

"A'right already. A'right." He tugged on the reins. Morena lowered her head, and he climbed aboard. He whipped the reins. The roc hopped five times, nearly falling over every time. Once she teetered close to falling on Ned, but he didn't bother to move. Couldn't really see the point. Finally, Morena managed to stay airborne.

"Can't give 'em an inch," muttered Ace.

Morena offered a throaty growl and flew away.

Ned stood there awhile not moving.

Regina, her arms still full of scrolls, strode up to him. "Sir? Are you well?"

He nodded. Then turned and walked away, swallowed by the shadows.

"You'd better return those scrolls to records." Gabel held up a calico kitten. "And you'll have to look after Seamus for a while."

Seamus mewed apologetically. Ogres considered cats a delicacy, and his life was never in more danger than when he was stuck in kitten form. Shapeshifting was a complicated business, but Regina often wondered if this was an accident. She usually took care of him when it happened.

Gabel tossed the kitten onto the scrolls. Seamus curled up on the heap to rest his head between her breasts. By her code, she should've beaten him to a pulp. But he was so damn cute.

"If I ever find out you're faking this . . ."

Purring, he swished his tail.

She kissed his head. ". . . I'll grind you into furry mush."

With a soft, feline smile, Seamus batted his big green eyes.

seven

NED FOUND HIS OFFICE with some effort. He didn't bother asking directions. He just wandered through the citadel until he discovered a door marked Commander's Office. It was right next to his quarters, which made a lot of sense after the fact.

He sat in the room behind a small desk and stared at the pouch. Stared as if it might explode or dance around or some such thing. The contents of the pouch by themselves were harmless. Yet he knew their meaning too well.

He'd been a bookkeeper in the Legion's accounting division. Balancing ledgers. Checking expense reports. Filing and alphabetizing. An audit every so often. Grunt work. But the true terror of the accounting office rested in that small pouch.

He found a half-full bottle of liquor and took a long swig to discover that it contained either very good whiskey or very bad whiskey. He broke the seal on the pouch. Inside he found a lump of green and black coal with a slot in it, and a small coin wrapped in cloth. The coin was half gold, half platinum. On the gold side, a grinning, devilish visage was imprinted. On the platinum, a fat demon balanced the world on a scale against a pile of coins. Around the edges, the simple motto of the dreaded ninth circle of Hell was inscribed: "Better Evil Through Profit."

The ninth circle was where Hell did its accountancy. The demons within were ruthlessly efficient. All they cared about were profit and cost-effectiveness. Everything was a debit or credit, a gain or a loss. Their ultimate goal was to reduce the universe to a calculation, a final heartless equation in which every soul, living and dead, divine and damned, would serve in the Glorious Ultimate Dividend. They were evil incarnate, but they were the best at what they did, which was why the Legion subcontracted much of its troubleshooting work their way.

Ned drank the rest of the bottle before getting on with it.

He ran the sharp edge of the coin across his thumb, drawing blood. The coin absorbed the offering, gaining a crimson glint. Then he dropped it in the slot. The air sizzled. The unholy lump broke apart, hatching a devilish little creature, eight inches of stringy, red demon. The homunculus looked very much like a man, save the scales, wings, tiny horns, hooves, and long pointed tail. The creature was balding, though he had tried, with no success, to disguise this by brushing his thin hair across his shiny scalp. He wore a tunic stitched together from the cursed flesh of the damned, and he stank of moldy ledgers and burning dung.

The homunculus adjusted his thick spectacles and twitched his crooked nose. "Never Dead Ned, I presume."

Ned nodded.

"Excellent. Shall we get down to it?" The homunculus glanced around. "Where are your ledgers?"

"I don't know."

The homunculus frowned. "This is quite unacceptable. Time is money, after all. Every wasted second is another expense against the Final Profit. You should've been prepared."

"Sorry."

"Mortals." The demon sighed. "Just as well, I suppose.

We can skip the consultation phase. Saves time. Frankly I've looked over this case and already sent ahead my recommendations. Anything you said would've been summarily dismissed. I wouldn't even have listened. I would've just nodded my head until you were finished speaking and said what I'm going to say anyway. I did expect more from a fellow accountant though. Must say I'm disappointed."

"Sorry."

The homunculus kept on talking as if he hadn't heard Ned. "There is no business like war. Yet Ogre Company has never produced a profit for the Legion. This is unacceptable. It's a blasphemy, an unforgivable heresy against the Dark Ledger. There was talk, very serious consideration, of dissolving this particular venture and allocating its resources to a more productive end."

Ned didn't consider that a bad thing. If Ogre Company disbanded, he might get sent back to bookkeeping.

"However, it all comes down to the numbers," continued the homunculus. "The numbers reveal all. Profit exists throughout the universe. If we cannot find it, then we have let the numbers down, not the other way around. As such, I see no reason to abandon this project just yet."

The demon beat his wings and hovered in the air. He snapped his fingers, and a scroll materialized, floating before him. "I've drawn up a fiscal battle plan, which I can assure you is spelled out with such thorough magnificence that anyone should be able to follow it." He pushed his spectacles to the end of his nose and arched his brows in Ned's direction. "And I do mean anyone."

The scroll unfurled. It slithered across the desktop. When Ned reached for it, the parchment slapped at his fingers hard enough to leave a pinkish bruise. The budget shook, drew near Ned's face, and snarled.

"Careful," said the homunculus, "she bites. Perhaps it would be wiser if I explained some of the finer points. Just to be certain you understand." He snapped his fingers, and the scroll, growling in an obscenely affectionate manner, fell obediently into his grasp. "The plan is simple. It's broken into seven hundred and seventy-seven subsections." He cleared his throat. "Which I will now go over in detail."

Ned slumped in his chair. He wondered if Ulga would ever get here with that wine.

The homunculus droned on for hours. His squeaky voice grated on Ned's ears and stood his hair on end. The demonic bookkeeper chanted his depraved dirge to the powers of infernal accounting, and an evil spell settled on Ned's office. The scroll unfolded, filling the floor with line after line of cost cutting and expense trimming. The walls melted. Cruel imps cavorted in the shadows. The hourglass on the desk ran backward. And Ned could almost hear the distant howls of the damned.

The homunculus grew. The demon fed off Ned's suffering, and his agonizing boredom fed the homunculus well. By the end, he'd grown a foot taller, his skin had turned a brighter shade of red, and his tiny horns had curled into impressive ornaments. Ned hunched in his chair, drooling, with debits and credits poking at his brain with wee pitchforks.

"In conclusion," said the homunculus, "I believe this project can be redeemed. Providing Ogre Company can finally be whipped into a functional military unit. But that's not my end. I'm the accountant, and I can assure you the accounting is flawless."

Ned wiped the tears from his face with trembling hands. His flesh felt clammy and cold. The demon's lecture had leeched Ned's already diminished will to live. He'd have gladly fallen on his own sword then to end it all. He had no such option. Such were the disadvantages of immortality.

The ferocious budget slithered around his office, under the desk, across the floor, tightly coiled around his legs, cutting off his circulation. It alternately purred at its creator and grumbled at Ned.

The homunculus said, "It was my recommendation you be transferred to this post. There was some resistance to the idea. Your military record is nothing exceptional. But I pointed out that all the previous commanders had been fine officers and not one had been able to make anything of Ogre

Company. From a logical perspective, it would be a waste of resources to throw another distinguished soldier into the slavering jaws of almost certain death. But here was a man, by which I mean you, who had the necessary bookkeeping experience to understand the situation as most soldiers could not. A man blessed with a curious talent for thwarting death over and over again. Most importantly, a man who, should this talent fail him, was ultimately expendable."

Ned tried to stand. The budget wrapped around his waist, holding him to his chair.

A satisfied smile crossed the homunculus's face. "It took some convincing. I think they were just hoping I'd recommend scrapping the whole project. But I convinced them to give it one last shot. You've six months to turn this company around. More than enough time if you follow my counsel."

Ned couldn't remember any of the demon's recommendations. He couldn't remember anything of the last few hours except the infernal dirge, a hum without words, a song of the fiscally forsaken.

"Just follow the budget, and do your end, and things should work out fine, Commander."

The budget raised up and threatened to slice into Ned's face with a nasty paper cut. He didn't want to antagonize it, but his bad left arm had other ideas. It grabbed the empty whiskey bottle and brandished it at the parchment. The budget hissed and spat as it fought with Ned's arm.

"What if I can't make it work?"

The homunculus chuckled. "A consideration I've already taken into account. Profit knows the numbers never fail, but men are prone. In which case, Ogre Company will be dissolved, and its personnel reassigned per my recommendation."

"Where would I be going? Back to bookkeeping?"

The homunculus drank up Ned's anxiety. The demon's eyes simmered with red flames. "Oh, no. Your position in that department has already been filled. And it's a waste of your talents in any case. I believe you'd be of more use in the Berserker Program."

Ned's jaw tightened.

The homunculus grew another inch. "Berserkers have such generally short careers, I thought it obvious to assign someone who found death less inconvenient. I'm sure you can see the logic."

Immortal or not, Ned knew he'd make an abysmal berserker. Berserkers were supposed to rush headlong into battle, mindless raging warriors eager to meet death and drag as many souls as they could along with them. Ned was good at the dying part. He'd had a lot of practice. But he stank at the killing end of it. In his whole military career, he'd killed only one person. And that had been an accident. And someone on his own side. Every other time he'd stepped on a battlefield he'd always been among the first slain.

The homunculus nodded to Ned. "My work is done here. Best of luck, Commander." The demon shrank into himself and disappeared. The room brightened. The walls stopped melting. The sand in the hourglass started going the right way again. The imps vanished into their purgatory. But the budget remained.

It'd gotten hold of Ned's bad arm and was doing its best to yank off the limb. Ned wouldn't have minded if it succeeded, but he didn't feel like waiting around. He drew his dagger and stabbed the budget, pinning it to his desk. With a ghastly howl, it shuddered and fell limp. It wasn't dead. He could still see it breathing, the soft rise and fall of the numbers on its pages. Maybe if he drove a stake through its bottom line.

There weren't any stakes handy. So he grabbed one end and rolled it up. The budget didn't go quietly, but most of the fight seemed gone out of it. Someone knocked on the door. He stuck the free end of the budget in a drawer, slammed it shut, and leaned a chair against it. Reasonably constrained, one end stuck in the drawer, the other pinned by the knife, the parchment growled. Ned picked his way across the room, avoiding any entangling loops of biting paper. He opened the door.

On the other side, Regina held two jugs in her hands, two more under her arms. "Your wine, sir. Would you like me to put it in your office?"

"No." Ned slipped into the hall and slammed the door shut. He had no intention of ever going back in there again. And if the circumstances should arise that he couldn't avoid it, he'd be wearing a full suit of armor, armed with a very long spear, and with Sally the salamander and her fiery breath by his side. A terrible clatter came from the office. Good bet the desk had been overturned, and the budget was busy hunting expense accounts, feeding off them, growing stronger and hungrier at the same time.

He nodded to the room next door. "My quarters."

They put the jugs in a corner of the commander's apartment. Ned put his ear to the door adjoining his office. He couldn't hear the budget, but it was in there. He wedged a chair under the doorknob.

"Anything else, sir?" asked Regina.

He glanced back at the tall, beautiful Amazon and the kitten rubbing against her long, long legs. The budget thumped in the other room. Ned sat on the end of his bed and, slouching, scratched the kitten behind its ears.

Regina squinted downward. "Anything else, sir? Anything at all?"

"No."

She put her hands on her waist, thrust her impressive bosom forward. "Are you quite certain there's no way that I might be of some further service to you?"

A shadow slipped back and forth in the doorjamb. "Maybe something to nail the door shut." He lay back on the bed and closed his eye.

Regina stammered. She snatched up Seamus and stomped into the hall. The Amazon whirled on her heels. A forced smile replaced her frown.

"I've never had conjured wine before, sir. Might I trouble you for a drink?"

He grabbed one of the jugs and handed it to her. "Here. Enjoy." He shut the door.

Regina dropped Seamus, who mewed sadly as he brushed against her legs. She kicked him away roughly, and Seamus bounced off the wall. In a puff of smoke, the calico transformed back into his goblin self.

"Ouch." He rubbed his head.

Regina's black eyes darkened as she stared down the goblin.

"I guess the blow must've knocked me back into my original shape." He smiled sheepishly. "What a stroke of luck, huh?"

She didn't smile back. "Perhaps next time you're stuck, I should start knocking you around until you're unstuck."

Seamus scratched his beard. "Don't be mad at me just because you're a bad flirt."

"I'm not a bad flirt."

He arched his back and ran a hand up and down his thigh. "Is there anything I can do for you, sir? Anything at all?" He batted his eyes, puckered his wide, thin lips, and made loud kissing noises. "Not very subtle. Although some guys like the direct approach. Guess the commander isn't one of them."

Regina grabbed him by the throat and squeezed until his green face turned blue. "Amazons do not flirt. We do not kiss. And we certainly do not throw ourselves at the first handsome man we see."

Seamus, choking, managed to gasp, "You think he's handsome?"

With an unpleasant grunt, she hurled him away. Seamus became a silken scarf and slid harmlessly to the floor. He turned back into himself and followed her as she stalked down the hall.

"The guy looks like he took the scenic route through a dragon's innards," he said.

She didn't reply.

"Hey, I'm not judging. Sometimes I like to get a little goat action myself." One burst of purple smoke later, he transformed into a billy. He bleated once and turned back into a goblin. "Don't knock it until you've tried it. Anyway, this isn't about me. This is about you. So you really like this guy?"

"No."

"Oh, come on. It's obvious."

She stopped and put her hand on her sword. "I don't like any man."

"Is it me you're trying to convince?" he asked. "You don't really believe all that Amazon propaganda, do you?"

"It is my code."

"Some code. Men bad. Women good. Bit simplistic, don't you think?"

"The truth is simple."

"They really drilled that stuff into you, didn't they? Suppose I can't really blame you for not being able to get rid of it, though I do find it distasteful. All that bigotry." He shook his head. "Nothing makes a pretty girl uglier."

She drew her sword.

"Go ahead. Kill me." He raised his hands. "It's what an Amazon would do. Or a man."

Regina exhaled through gritted teeth. Reluctantly she put away the weapon. "Remember this, private." She lifted him by his long ears. "I. Do. Not. Like. Ned."

"Whatever."

They strolled through the courtyard toward the pub.

"How do you Amazons reproduce anyway?" he asked.

"That's a private matter."

There was an edge in her voice. Someone else might've shut up. But Seamus was a goblin, and goblins were blithely casual about danger. They expected to die at any moment and saw no point in fretting over it.

"I've heard the rumors, but I've always wondered."

Regina had heard the rumors too. And there were many. Dozens upon dozens. Depending on whom you asked, Amazons kept sex slaves locked in boxes in their bedrooms. Or they had mastered the esoteric art of removing and preserving key bits of male anatomy for later use. Or new Amazons simply sprang from the earth, grown right beside the cornfields. The theories ranged from the practical to the absurd, more concerned with creativity than truth.

"Do you really raid villages and kidnap young women?" asked Seamus.

"That practice created too much political tension amongst our neighbors and was abandoned long ago. Sometimes we do capture prisoners of war. Or buy criminals and exiles. If a male is of truly exceptional stock, we've been known to use him for our purposes."

"Sounds erotic." Seamus leered. "Is there a secret seduction ceremony? A glorious feast where the condemned man is treated to a thousand sensual delights before being brought to the height of passion until, utterly sexed to death, he expires with an eternal smile on his face?"

"Not exactly. Although there is a procedure."

The word "procedure" removed much of the fun from the fantasy for Seamus, but he'd come too far to turn back now. "What's it like?"

"You don't want to know."

"Is it a secret?"

"No, but you'll just be disappointed."

He grabbed her skirt. Yet another perilous act he did without a second thought. "Oh, come on."

She yanked her skirt away and kicked him to the ground. "We tie them to a bed, have sex with them, then do away with them."

Remaining sitting, the goblin's eyes gleamed with obscene possibilities. "What kind of bed?"

"A normal kind of bed."

"What kind of sex?"

"Functional, efficient sex."

He was unwilling to abandon the fantasy just yet. "How do you kill them? Some kind of poisonous kiss? Or do you squeeze the life out of them between your powerful thighs?"

"We usually just stab them with a dagger." She grinned. "Sometimes we behead them."

"Does the executioner wear a black hood and nothing

else? Her naked body glistening with dewy perspiration. Her heaving breasts jiggling as she delivers the deathblow."

"Eunuchs handle Amazon executions."

"Oh." Frowning, he rose. "Isn't as sexy as I'd hoped."

"I warned you. That custom isn't common anymore. Too impractical. We've no way of guaranteeing the child produced will be female, and if it's male, you end up wasting nine months.

"Now we mostly purchase young girls, ages five to seven, and initiate them into the nation. Many of our neighboring countries breed girls specifically for our needs. It's the fourth largest industry in the region."

"Sound very . . ." Seamus sighed. "Mercantile."

They walked a while more.

"So if you don't live with men, and you don't capture men, then what do you do for companionship?"

"All Amazons share the strongest bonds of sisterhood."

"Great, great. Sisterhood. Beautiful thing." He leaned forward and clasped his hands together. "But I'm talking about companionship. Y'know?"

"I don't understand the question."

"Y'know. Affection. Intimacy. Of the physical sort?" He ran through a rapid series of obscene gestures, half of which Regina didn't recognize. But she got the idea.

"We Amazons abandoned that ridiculous preoccupation centuries ago."

"You can't just abandon it. We all have needs." Seamus waggled his eyebrows. "You can't tell me it hasn't ever crossed your mind. Especially after you've spent a hard day slaying those oh-so-wicked men, and you're huddled in a tent with a couple of your Amazon sisters. Their trembling bodies sticky with sweat as they cling to you. Moist, hot, nubile skin. One of your tentmates pulls you close. Her warm breath is soft on your neck. Her long, red hair brushes across your pert bosom. Her nimble fingers move across your taut thighs to find your quivering—"

He never saw the punch coming. It succeeded in knocking

him a good distance but failed to wipe away his grin. Regina, sword drawn, stood over him.

She'd heard these rumors too, and there was some truth in them. Not all her sisters were as strong as she. Many had succumbed to the pleasures of the flesh, but Regina knew carnal desires as the supreme distraction they were, whether found with a man or a woman.

"You'll never mention any quivering parts of my anatomy again if you want to keep on living."

"Okay, okay. Can't kill a guy for having a fantasy. It's healthy to daydream."

She put her foot on him and pressed. He gasped but smiled. "Y'know, I can see up your skirt from this angle. Right to your quivering—"

He narrowly avoided being skewered through the face by transforming into an anvil. Her sword clanged loudly. Regina tapped the flat of the blade against him.

"Come out, you vile little coward. Face me as a man."

Seamus took on his natural form again. "Firstly, I'm not a man. I'm a goblin. Secondly, I thought all men were supposed to be cowards."

She tried to slice off his head, but he was quicker. Her sword bounced off a granite replica of the goblin, his tongue sticking out. Regina circled him, but he remained stubbornly immobile. He was either trapped, as sometimes happened, or just too fearful.

She picked him up and whispered in his stone ear. "Listen well, you little beast. If I ever catch you speaking such disgusting ideas, if I even suspect you are merely daydreaming of such base heresy, I'll chop off all your loose little goblin bits. Am I making myself clear?"

The statue of Seamus only leered. She suspected he was defying her right now, his stony brain playing degrading images of steamy Amazonian bathhouses and naked pillow fights. She pondered teaching him a lesson by chipping away his tongue. But her temper settled as quickly as it flared, and she wasn't in the mood to bother. Instead, she dropped him in the citadel well. She waited for some time, seeing if the cold water might spur him into taking on a more vulnerable form.

In the meantime, she uncorked her jug of conjured wine and drank heartily. The horrible brew comforted her. It tasted much like the special concoction young Amazons imbibed to make them big and strong.

She considered Seamus's absurd notion of the value of sex. She didn't see the purpose. Her time was better spent training her body and mind in the art of war. And while occasionally an Amazon might take a lover under very special circumstances, this was not one of those circumstances. Ned was just a man. A beautiful, immortal man. But that was not enough.

Yet the mere thought of him, of his scarred, disfigured flesh, sent a tremble through her. And certain parts that she avoided thinking about did indeed quiver.

"Damn it." She took another tug of wine.

Nothing came out of the well. Not even a fly. Although she didn't know if Seamus could become a fly. Regina tossed the jug over her shoulder, and it shattered on the cobblestones. Scowling, she continued on her way.

A little while later a tarantula crawled cautiously out of the well. Seamus looked around for a moment before shifting into a goat, bouncing amorously toward the meadows.

EiGHt

NED, WHO'D NEVER been concerned with courage or honor, still didn't have a taste for desertion. He had thought about it. He was only human. Even during boot camp, he wasn't sure a soldier's life was for him. Even so, he didn't like the idea. He'd planned on waiting for his Legion contract to expire. Four more years and he'd walk away from his military career. He could suffer his many deaths along the way. He could keep his end of the deal.

But the deal had changed. The Berserker Program was just asking too much of Ned. When the training succeeded, a soldier transformed into a mindless killing savage. When it failed, a soldier just became mindless. Either way, a berserker was taught to embrace death, but embracing death had never been Ned's strongest point. He was left with only one choice.

Two choices, technically. He could put all his military and accounting experience to use, and turn Ogre Company around with some luck. The only problem with that was while Ned was a damn fine accountant, he'd never been much of a soldier. Nor much of a leader. His one and only previous position of authority had been commanding a platoon in a skirmish against some troublesome brownies. The memory still haunted him.

To most everyone, brownies were tiny furballs. It was the name. It made them sound cuddly, harmless. But to anyone who'd ever faced them in combat, they were four inches of bloodthirsty terror. Their hideous battle cries still haunted him. The profane insults as they hurled their small spears. The weapons weren't sharp enough to break the skin, but they stung like hell. Worse than the spears were their harsh claws and vicious teeth. Brownies didn't play around. They pulled hair, bit ears, clawed at eyes, stuck their spears up any available orifice. A good codpiece was essential when fighting brownies.

They'd come without warning that night, swarming from the overgrown brush. There was chaos. Soldiers screamed. Brownies swore. All those tiny voices raining down profanities. They particularly delighted in assaulting one's parentage. He recalled with fresh terror the fuzzy enemy clamped onto his nose. Ned had been struggling to pull the creature off his face when one of his own men, in a careless flailing fit, had stabbed Ned in the back. As Ned lay dying, the brownie screamed a particularly hurtful remark about Ned's mother. Ned had never known his mother. Nor could he remember his childhood. But the remark seemed unnecessary and just plain wrong.

Ned had come back to life to find his platoon decimated, having killed each other in their panic. A victory for the enemy and a black mark on Ned's record. It wasn't easy to explain, and he hadn't bothered to try. The brutal savagery of brownies was something to be experienced directly. He'd hoped for a discharge. It hadn't happened, though he couldn't say why. His only guess was that the Legion still believed an immortal soldier worth having, if only for the novelty value.

The incident had been covered up to preserve the Legion's reputation. Teams of elementalists were called in to scorch the monsters and their woodlands to the bare earth, to wipe away all traces of the slaughter. Ned hadn't forgotten. Most of his deaths meant little to him. He'd grown inured to perishing. But this one still bothered him. It'd been a year before he could stand the sight of small rodents. He still broke out in a cold sweat at the sight of jackrabbits, with their resemblance to brownie warbunnies, and gerbils, a dead likeness to brownies themselves if standing upright.

Ogre Company would be better off without him, and he would be better off without Ogre Company. It might've been cowardly, but it was the truth. It was time to run, dig deep, and hide away. He hoped his novelty value wouldn't encourage the Legion to dispatch retrievers. But one problem at a time.

He waited until midnight and slipped away under cover of darkness. He traveled light, just the clothes on his back and a pack with a jug of Ulga's wine and some bread. The faster he was out of here, the better. As expected, the citadel's sparse, undisciplined night sentries were busy sleeping, drinking, or sleeping off drinking. He sneaked away, right through the front gates of Copper Citadel, without the slightest difficulty.

He passed by the graveyard on his way and stopped to read the headstones of the previous commanders, including his own beside his open grave. He didn't feel so bad about doing this.

A crimson lightning bolt arced from the shadows and struck Ned in his chest. He died before he'd even realized it, falling upon his own grave.

The Red Woman stepped from the darkness. Her staff glowed.

"Why'd you do that?" asked her raven.

"I have my reasons," she replied.

The Red Woman had resurrected Ned many, many times, but she'd never before killed him. She waved her staff over him, and Ned gasped. He hadn't drawn in his first breath before she zapped him with another bolt. He died before he could open his eyes.

The raven hopped to her other shoulder. "What was the purpose of that?"

"No purpose. Just seeing how it was on the other end of things."

"And how was it?"

"Oddly satisfying."

She turned and walked away, leaving Ned to rot atop his grave.

NiNe

It wasn't until late morning that Ned's absence was discovered, and it wasn't until late afternoon that his corpse was found by the gravediggers Ralph and Ward. In addition to planting bodies, they were also responsible for keeping the cemetery tended. They were prepared for their weekly weeding, and instead found their new commander sprawled across his own plot. Neither knew what to make of it.

"Is he dead?" asked Ward.

Ralph nodded. "Yup."

"What's he doing out here?"

"I don't know."

"Looks a little bloated, doesn't he?"

"Yup."

"Should we scare away that vulture?"

The large scavenging bird atop Ned picked at his flesh. It'd just found the meal and hadn't done much damage yet.

"Do what you want." Ralph rubbed his jaw. "I've got weeding to do."

He went to work. Ward watched the vulture chew on Ned's ear a while. He'd raised a vulture as a boy and had grown to love it. Then came the Feast of Saint Carrion, a revered ogre holiday, and his mother had slaughtered Mister Nibbles and served him for dinner. This vulture resembled Mister Nibbles only in passing. It was a thin, gawky sort of buzzard. Not the healthy fat bird he'd cherished. But it had the same spirit, the same boldness, to not fly away as he approached. He patted it once on its head. Then raised his shovel to brain it. He loved buzzards. Especially in cream sauce.

Ward hesitated, and the bird could've easily fled. Instead it glared back at him with its cold, black eyes. Eyes like polished glass. Merciless and cruel and hungry.

He lowered his shovel. "Go on, little fella. Have another bite."

The vulture smiled—at least it seemed so to Ward—and pecked some more at its breakfast.

"How do you think he died?" asked Ward.

Ralph sniffed the air. "I smell magic. Maybe that's what did him in."

Ward shooed away the buzzard. It hopped only a short distance away. Ward bent over and turned Ned on his back. A small burn mark showed on his chest. It didn't look like much, but it must've been enough to kill him. The face had been spared the vulture's sharp beak, but Ward blanched at the body's puffy grimace. "He sure dies a lot for a guy named Never Dead Ned."

"Yup."

Ward turned Ned facedown. He ignored the corpse for a while and joined Ralph at work. The vulture hopped over cautiously and tore off pieces of Ned's flesh, which it gobbled down its snapping beak. After they'd plucked the last of the weeds, Ward asked, "Should we bury him?"

Sneering, Ralph rubbed his jaw. "We're not supposed to bury him. Those were his orders."

"Maybe he changed his mind," said Ward. "Maybe he decided he was ready to be buried, and that's why he's out here. Only he didn't time it right and died before he could get back in his grave."

"Sounds pretty stupid to me."

"Why else would he be out here?"

"I don't know. And I don't care." Ralph pulled back his leg to kick the corpse, but thought better of it. "Orders are orders. If he wanted to be buried, he should've told us."

"We can't just leave him out here," said Ward.

"Why not?"

"He'll get eaten by wolves or vultures or something."

"So what?"

"He is our commander, Ralph."

"He was our commander." This time Ralph kicked Ned, though not too hard for fear of perhaps shocking the corpse back to life. "Now he's just a dead asshole. Let him rot, I say."

Ralph had been rubbing his jaw since finding Ned. He hadn't forgotten Ned's punch. The jaw was fine, but it was still a wound to his pride. Ward, on the other hand, had developed a begrudging admiration for this human. Ned hadn't seemed like such a bad guy, and after that drunken punch, Ward deemed the human either very brave or very stupid. Both qualities were well appreciated by ogres. Bravery for obvious reasons. Stupidity because it was just plain amusing.

Scowling, Ralph ran his fingers along his chin, and Ward smiled.

"What's so gods damned funny?" growled Ralph.

Ward ignored the question. "Dead or not, I like the guy." He scared away the vulture and threw Ned over his shoulder. "I'm taking him back and seeing what Frank wants to do with him."

They started back, and the vulture followed. Ward stopped and smiled at the scavenger.

"Oh, no," said Ralph, "we're not keeping him."

"But look at him. How can you turn away that face?"

Ralph looked into those black eyes set in the featherless, wrinkled pink head. The vulture spread its wide black wings with sparse feathers and screeched. Ralph shook his head slowly. "Fine, but you clean up after him. I'm not doing it."

Ward peeled off some loose bits of Ned's skin. He was sure the commander wouldn't mind. Then he fed them to the bird. It hopped onto his empty shoulder. Its talons drew blood, just like Mister Nibbles used to, and Ward, a tear in his eye, smiled.

The gravediggers headed back to the citadel. They passed the installation's command center, which had long ago been taken over by goblins and converted into a recreation room. No one knew exactly what went on behind those closed doors, what sort of depravity goblins enjoyed in their spare time. And no one over four feet high wanted to know. One of the previous commanders, a man of storm and fury, had tried to reclaim the room from the goblins. Three minutes behind the doors, he'd emerged pale and shivering. He never uttered a single word of what he saw, but there'd been madness in his eyes ever after. And two months later, when he'd been crushed beneath an avalanche of mead barrels, he'd died with a thankful grin on his face.

"Applesauce," he'd wheezed with his final breath. "Dear gods, the applesauce."

Since then the goblins had been left to their own. The center of power for Copper Citadel had shifted to the next most logical place: the pub. Ralph and Ward found Frank sharing a drink with the twins. They sat at one of the tables just beside the pub in the open courtyard.

Ward dropped Ned's corpse in an empty chair. "We found the commander, sir. He was in the graveyard."

Private Lewis held out an open palm. "You owe me a silver piece, Brother. I told you he hadn't deserted."

Corporal Martin, having command of the right side of their body, reached into his belt pouch and tossed a coin to his brother, who caught it and stuffed it back into the very same pouch.

"Serves me right, Lewis," said Martin. "Always think the best of everyone. That's what Mother always said."

"Surely she was a wise woman," agreed Lewis.

Ned fell over. His head cracked loudly against the table. Frank grabbed the body by the hair and glanced at the face. He let go, and Ned slumped. Frank swished his mead in his tankard. "Fragile sort, isn't he?"

"Must be all that practice he's had dying," remarked Martin.

"Practice makes perfect," seconded Lewis. "Such dedication is an inspiration to us all."

Gravedigger Ralph said, "He's your problem now, sir. I'm getting a beer." Muttering and still rubbing his jaw, he disappeared into the pub.

"That's a scrawny buzzard there," said Frank. "Not much good eating."

The vulture screeched, turning its head to glare at Frank.

"He's not for eating, sir." Ward help up his arm. The vulture traipsed down Ward's limb. Its talons dug shallow scratches in his thick ogre flesh. The bird spread its wings and affectionately pecked at its master's fingers with its pointed beak. "Once I get him healthy, I thought we might make the little guy into the company mascot. With your permission, sir."

"Just don't get him too healthy, private. Feast of Saint Carrion is right around the corner, and Legion supply might not send down enough vultures for the occasion." Frank pushed Ned aside so he could put his feet up on the table. "Got a name yet?"

"Yes, sir. Nibbly Ned. In honor of our commander."

"I'm sure he'll be touched by the homage."

Ward and Nibbly Ned went into the pub to fetch a drink. Several nearby ogres eyed Nibbly while licking their lips.

"Copper piece says Nibbly won't make it through the month," said Lewis.

"Ten days," said Martin. The twins shook hands to make the bet official.

"What, may I inquire, sir, do you plan on doing with the commander?" asked Lewis.

Frank eyed the corpse. "I don't know. In a normal situation like this we usually just bury the human. But this isn't a normal situation."

"Mother had a smashing recipe for human soup," said Martin.

"Dear brother," countered Lewis, "though I loved Mother's cooking every bit as much as you, I really must point out the impropriety of eating a superior officer. It simply isn't done."

"Of course, Martin. It was merely a recollection, not a suggestion."

"I've never eaten a human before," said Frank.

"They must be prepared just right, and even then it's usually not worth the trouble. Tastes like gopher."

"I hate to contradict you, Brother, but humans do not taste like gophers. Gophers taste like humans."

"Perhaps you're right, Martin. But in either case, gophers and humans are not very good eating."

Frank, having tasted neither, had no opinion and left the twins to their culinary discussions. He finished his drink, grabbed Ned by the hair, and dragged the body across the courtyard. Ned's boot heels thumped against the cobblestones. It didn't take Frank long to find Regina, who was busy with a training exercise.

Training in Ogre Company was voluntary. In truth, most everything in Ogre Company was voluntary in the sense that there were no consequences for skipping it. Discipline had long ago deserted the installation. But Regina rather enjoyed the martial arts, and she practiced for three or four hours every day, drawing a regular audience. The soldiers pretended to study, but they were really there to ogle her athletic form as she grunted and sweated in her two-piece training gear. It was the only time ogling was allowed since she took combat training too seriously to notice. Sometimes her students practiced alongside her. Sometimes they even learned something. And on occasion one or two would openly challenge her to a sparring match. She remained undefeated.

At present she was busy hacking away at a straw dummy with a scimitar. The blade was a whirling flash. It cut the dummy with dozens of shallow slashes. Straw flew in the air for a solid minute before Regina ended her demonstration and sheathed the blade.

"You must be losing your touch," said Frank.

"I was merely demonstrating the death of a thousand nips. You have to imagine all that straw is blood to understand the full beauty of the technique."

Frank had never developed a taste for fancy swordplay. Ogre tactics rarely grew more sophisticated than smashing opponents until they stopped twitching. As a very large ogre, his weapon of choice was a nice, solid tree trunk. The technique had never failed him. In a duel, Frank expected he could best Regina, but all that blood littering the ground (even in straw form) gave him pause.

"We have to talk to Gabel." He held up Ned.

"Oh, hell." She drew her sword, spun around, beheaded the training dummy, and put away her weapon in one fluid motion. Her audience applauded with much appreciation, both for her technique and the slippage of her top's neckline to reveal a tantalizing glimpse of her bosom. She toweled her glistening flesh, so distracted by Ned's corpse that she didn't notice the leering soldiers.

"Lesson over. Tomorrow we'll cover the pike with particular emphasis on gouging and impaling. If there's time, I'll demonstrate the proper way to mount a head." She threw a less revealing robe around her shoulders, and her students dispersed.

Frank, grasping Ned by the neck, shook the body. Its stiffened limbs flopped like a cheap marionette. "He's dead."

Regina cupped Ned's chin and stared into his single, glassy eye. "How?"

Frank lowered his voice. "You don't know?"

"What are you implying?"

"I'm not implying anything." He dropped Ned, who fell in a heap to the ground. "I'm asking you directly. Did you kill him?"

"No, I didn't," she replied. "Did you?"

"Don't be absurd. I know the agreement."

"So do I." She snarled. "None of us gets rid of a commander without first discussing it. That's the agreement that I've sworn to, and an Amazon never breaks her word."

They wasted a moment on an exchange of furtive, mistrustful glances.

"Gabel must've done it," Regina said finally. "Never trust an orc to keep his word. Especially an orc that's really a goblin."

Frank nodded. "I guess we should have a talk with him. This could be trouble."

She readily agreed. The three ranking officers of Ogre Company had taken a more active role in their advancement opportunities, but all their previous *accidents* had been neatly above suspicion. But Ned was dead with no clear cause, and that was sure to draw attention. Ogre Company's run of fatally poor luck might not stand against closer scrutiny. It wasn't like Gabel to make such a mistake, but perhaps he'd just grown impatient, they guessed.

On the way to see Gabel, Frank dragged Ned by his leg. Regina, marching directly behind, found herself staring at her commander. Some incomprehensible, alien sensation stirred within her. It wasn't pity. She had none for the dead. Nor was it guilt. Killing was her profession, and she had little moral qualm with slaying anyone who got in her way. All the previous commanders had been buffoons. She'd seen nothing in Ned to make her think he would've been any different. But as his head bounced against the cobblestones, she found that unidentifiable stimulation remained.

"Do you have to carry him like that?" she asked.

"Like what?"

"Like that. He's lost half his scalp."

Frank stopped and saw bits of hair and skin trailing behind them. "I don't hear him complaining."

She didn't know why she cared, but she did regardless. "Just let me carry him." She gathered Ned in her arms. He stank a little of decay, but she hardly noticed. She gazed into his bloated face and for some unfathomable reason, she smiled.

"Should I leave the two of you alone?" asked Frank.

Her only comment was a harsh grunt. She tossed Ned over her shoulder and proceeded to Gabel's office. He was busy filling out forms, something he did with clockwork precision. Brute's Legion was a never-ending struggle against a tide of paperwork, and to fall behind was to court disaster. Gabel was displeased by the interruption, but even more so by the reason.

"Which of you did it?" he asked at the sight of Ned propped in a corner. "Which of you idiots couldn't wait until the right moment?"

"Don't look at me," said Frank.

"I didn't do it," replied Regina. "We assumed you had."

"I had nothing to do with it," said Gabel.

"If you did, you should just tell us," said Frank.

Gabel slammed his palms against the desktop. A stack of requisitions toppled to the floor, and sighing, he gathered them up. "I'm telling you, I didn't kill him."

The trio exchanged glances of unspoken skepticism. Their alliance had survived thus far because no one had acted without the others' approval. Now that spotless trust wasn't quite so spotless, and they found themselves looking at a roomful of assassins. Regina put her hand on her scimitar. Frank clenched his gigantic fists. Gabel sat back down, reaching for a short sword he kept strapped under the desk. And Ned continued to rot in the corner.

"I swear I had nothing to do with it," said Gabel.

"Neither did I," said Regina.

"Nor I," said Frank.

"I guess that settles it then." But Gabel kept his fingers on the sword.

Frank cracked his knuckles. "I guess so."

"Agreed." Regina lowered her arms from her weapon, but her fellow officers knew she could draw it in a flash.

"It must've been an accident," said Frank. "A real accident."

"Poor timing for one," said Gabel, "and hardly believable. When the head office hears of this . . ."

"Why should they?" asked Regina. "He's Never Dead Ned. Shouldn't he come back to life?"

Frank exhaled with relief. "I'd nearly forgotten about that. I guess that's a lucky break."

Gabel nodded to the corpse. "Even a cat has only nine lives. Still, let's assume he'll return. I guess we should just put him back in his room until then."

"I'll do it." Regina hoisted the body across her back, and before either man could disagree (although neither had any intention) she was out of the room.

"Is it just me, or is she acting strange?" asked Gabel.

Frank didn't reply. He studied the orc with narrowed eyes.

Gabel met the ogre's stare. "For the last time, I didn't kill him."

Frank shrugged. "If you say so."

Regina laid Ned in his bed. She tucked his swollen tongue back into his mouth as far as it would go, closed his eye, and pulled his blanket to his chin. Then she stood by his bed for a short while and studied his bloated features. She sneered, but it was a halfhearted attempt to remind herself that this dead man before her was beneath her contempt.

She didn't understand this. Outside of an odd talent for resurrection, Ned wasn't anything special. As far as she could tell, he wasn't even much of a soldier. Yes, he was handsome in a scarred, disfigured way only an Amazon might appreciate, but that hardly seemed enough to warrant her reaction.

She hoped he would just stay dead this time and rid her of the problem.

The door opened, and Miriam stepped inside. "Oh, I'm sorry, ma'am. I just came in to see how the commander was doing?"

Regina stepped aside to allow Miriam to view the corpse.

"Still dead?" asked the siren.

"Still dead."

Miriam went to the bedside. Neither woman said anything for some time, lost in their own private thoughts.

"How long do you think it'll take for him to recover?" asked Miriam.

"It only took a few hours last time," observed Regina.

"I guess I'll wait then." Miriam sat on the end of the bed.

"You'll wait?"

"I'd like to be here when he wakes up."

"You like him?" Regina's already rigid posture stiffened. Her brow creased in a hard glare. "You like him?"

The three fins atop Miriam's head raised and flattened. "Yes, ma'am."

"Why?"

"I don't really know." She reached under the blanket and took his hand. "You know how soldiers are, ma'am. They're all bluster, always trying to impress each other with how drunk they can get or how long they can keep a badger down their trousers. But Ned doesn't put on a show. He's just himself. It's hard to find a guy like that. Especially around here."

Regina worked her way quietly behind the siren. The Amazon silently drew her dagger.

"It's not like he's much to look at, I know," continued Miriam, oblivious. "And he isn't great in bed either. Although he was pretty drunk. But I like him. I wouldn't expect you to understand, ma'am."

Regina, poised to slit Miriam's throat, hesitated. She had no problem killing when it suited her purposes, but there was only one reason to slay Miriam. And that reason, absurd as it seemed, lay decomposing on that bed. To kill her rival would be admitting she had a rival. She wasn't ready for that.

Miriam glanced backward at Regina, who was now picking her fingernails with the dagger.

"Sometimes I wish I were an Amazon," said the siren. "It must make life so much easier."

Regina forced a smile. The hostility within her eyes was not lost on Miriam, but as Regina's eyes were always full of seething fury, the siren had no reason to suspect some of that fire was directed at her.

"I'll wait with you." Regina plopped down into a chair. "Just to keep you company for a while."

Miriam put a tender hand to Ned's cheek and smoothed his hair.

Regina, caressing her long, sharp dagger, locked her stare onto Miriam's throat.

TEN

JUST BEFORE DUSK, a demon entered the citadel. No one bothered to stop him. There were few sentries, and only a tiny percentage of these were alert enough to have observed the demon if he hadn't been wearing his cloak of seclusion. And of these, even a tinier portion would've cared. But the demon was not one to take chances. He wore his magical cloak, though the garment was worn and stained. Only the seamstresses of the damned might repair the cloak's frayed edges, and only the River of Blood could wash out the blotches. It'd been centuries since the demon had been to the underworld, and if he had his way, it would be many centuries more. Even demons hated Hell. Ice demons in particular found the sweltering temperatures disagreeable. So he tolerated the loose threads, the huge blot of a wine stain smudged down its front. It seemed foolish to worry about a stain on an invisible enchanted cloak.

He strode across the cobblestones. He stopped by the well and removed a pendulum from his sleeve. He held it by its silver chain, and the pendulum pulled very slightly in one direction. Beneath his shadowy hood, the demon smiled. It wasn't much of a reaction, but it was stronger than there'd ever been before. He was very close.

"Hey, what's this?" asked a passing goblin.

"Looks like footprints," replied an ogre.

"Looks like they're made of ice."

The cloak's magic, like its stitching, was ragged and worn. Should an observer notice a trace of his passing and care enough to follow up on the clue, they might become aware of him.

"Hey, what's all this then?" asked the goblin suddenly. "Who're you?"

"No one." The demon turned to face them. "I am no one." His long, bony fingers tensed like a spider preparing to jump. Black icicle daggers, sharp enough to slice through tempered steel, materialized in his hands.

The goblin glanced at the ogre, who took a pull of wine.

"All right then," said the drunken ogre, "see you around."

They sauntered away. The demon was as coldly calculating as one might expect, and he weighed the appearance of two corpses against the chances these two would report his appearance to anyone who might care. He tossed his daggers into the well and continued on his way.

Elmer the treefolk stared into Ace's beady goblin eyes. No quarter would be given. No mercy would be offered in this clash of wills.

"Got any threes?" asked Elmer.

"Sorry, bud." Ace grinned. "Go fish."

Grumbling, Elmer drew a card and rearranged his hand, careful to avoid brushing against Sally the salamander's hot scales. The oracle Owens rounded out the quartet.

"I don't see why we have to play this stupid game," complained Elmer.

"We can always play War," suggested Owens. "That's a good game."

"Forget it," said Ace. "I lost half a month's wages last time we played that."

"I was thinking a more sophisticated game," said Elmer, puffing on his cigarette.

"Old Maid?" asked Ace.

"Crazy Eights?" proposed Sally.

"How about Super War?" said Owens.

"What's—" asked Elmer.

"It's like War," interrupted Owens, "but you slam the cards on the table a lot harder."

Elmer scowled, but the blind man was unaware. "Your turn, Sally."

The salamander, an unrevealing shade of white, sorted clumsily through her hand. It wasn't easy. Her fingers were thick and awkward, and the fireproof mittens necessary for her to avoid singeing the cards didn't help. While she considered her next move, she idly said, "I heard the commander is dead again."

Elmer puffed on his cigarette. "Guy's an idiot, just like the rest of the imbeciles the head office sends down."

"Oh, I don't know about that," said Ace. "He didn't seem like such a bad guy."

Sally fruitlessly asked for sixes and wound up drawing a card. "Regardless, we're not exactly rid of him. He is immortal."

"How do you think he does that?" asked Ace. As a goblin, he couldn't help but be curious. His race didn't fear death, but they would've preferred to avoid it, even if they rarely possessed the common sense to do so. But the benefit of immortality was getting to cheat death without having to worry about all that commonsense rubbish.

"Who cares?" Elmer grunted. "It's just a gods damned parlor trick, is what it is. Doesn't amount to much."

"I don't know about that," disagreed Owens. "Imagine an army of such men and what they might accomplish."

Elmer laughed. His leaves shook noisily. "Are you serious? He's been here less than a week, and he's died twice already.

As a rule, humans are worthless, and immortal or not, that's not going to change. Sooner we're rid of him, the better."

"Yeah, maybe you're right," said Sally. "The fates seem to agree with you."

They all chuckled. Everyone in the citadel had their suspicions about the "accidental" deaths plaguing their commanders. No one really cared, but there was etiquette about saying anything outright.

"Though the fates seem a trifle impatient," added Sally. "It's not like them to be so sloppy."

"I think this time it might not have to do with the fates," said Ace. "Lewis and Martin said the lieutenant seemed surprised by Ned's corpse. Got any fives, Elmer?"

The treefolk handed over a pair of cards. "You're suggesting this guy died twice by accident? Genuine accident?"

"Uh-huh." Ace grabbed a handful of unshelled peanuts in the center of the table and crabbed them in his mouth. His cheeks bulged, and as he spoke, shells spewed through the air. "If you ask me, they weren't accidents. I think—"

"It's an interesting theory," interrupted Owens.

Ace continued, "I think he wants to die."

"But why—" asked Sally.

"What sane person wants to be immortal?" replied Owens.

"Stop doing that," said Elmer.

"Sorry," apologized Owens.

"I think Never Dead Ned is just a clumsy oaf," said Elmer. "That's what I think. But if he wants to die, you'd think even an idiot could figure out how to do it. It's your turn, Owens."

"I know." Owens sorted through his cards, holding them before his sightless, white eyes.

"I bet if you chopped him up into a thousand pieces he wouldn't come back," said Elmer.

"Maybe. But what if he did?" Ace had yet to finish off his last handful of peanuts when he shoveled another into his mouth. He said something, but it was nothing but shells and spit.

Elmer leaned back in his chair. He had a hard time getting comfortable in human chairs. They never took into account the knots on his back. "Or fire. Fire pretty much kills everything."

Sally snorted. A small fireball burst from her left nostril. "Not everything."

"Most everything," corrected Elmer, as he blew out one of his smoldering leaves. "It's your turn, Owens."

"I know."

"Just ask for something already," said Elmer.

"Give me a minute, will you?" Owens pulled his cards close to his chest.

"Do you even know what you need?" Elmer snuffed out his cigarette and had Sally light another for him.

"I see the future. Of course I do."

"You hear the future," corrected Elmer. "Tell me what you've got in your hand right now."

"No."

"Name one card in your hand."

"Then you'd know what I had."

The other players chuckled. Owens held several cards in the wrong direction already, although no one bothered to point it out.

"At least one of us would know then," said Elmer.

By now, Ace had swallowed enough peanuts to be understood. "I bet if someone turned Ned to stone, he'd stay dead. Or boiled him in acid until everything dissolved. Even his bones."

"If I were trying to kill him," said Owens, "I'd tie him down with some heavy rocks and throw him in a real deep lake. I figure even if he didn't stay dead, he'd come back alive underwater and just drown again before he could free himself. Over and over and over, if need be. Not exactly killing him, but it'd be the next best thing."

Everyone agreed it sounded like a good plan, although Elmer still insisted that burning Ned to ash would be easier.

"Do you know how hard it is to burn a human to ash?" asked Sally. "They're not quite as flammable as treefolk.

Trust me, there's always stuff left over. The bones and heart and a couple of other choice organs."

She raised and cocked her head. Salamanders were especially sensitive to subtle changes in temperature, and a cold spot passed through the hall outside the room. She set down her cards.

"Where are you going?" asked Elmer.

"Deal me out." She stretched, uncoiling her long, serpentine body. "I've got to check something." She slipped quietly into the hall.

"What's gotten into her?" asked Ace.

"Who cares?" Elmer deliberately blew a smoke ring into Owens's face. "If you don't take your turn now, we're going to skip you."

Owens admitted defeat. He leaned over to Ace and asked for a suggestion.

"I'd go for sevens," replied Ace.

"Crap." Owens drew a card.

"You didn't ask," said Ace.

"Trust me," replied the oracle, "he doesn't have any."

Anyone else might not have given much thought to the frost along the hallway walls, but Sally knew underworld ice when she smelled it. Salamanders and ice demons were natural enemies. In addition to the innate conflict of their nature, there was a lot of bad history between the races. Her warm skin burned hot enough to simmer the air.

She turned the corner, and her adversary stood before her. He'd surely sensed her presence as easily as she'd felt his. Neither made a move right away, instead taking measure of the other.

The demon pulled back his hood. His face was long and angular. The horns growing from his brow curved back to touch the top of his bald skull. As she grew hotter with anticipation, he grew colder. As wisps of flame danced on the scales along her back like a sail of fire, frost crystallized on his blue skin. A chill mist slipped from his tight lips as he spoke.

"I'd heard your kind were extinct."

She paled a humorless gray. "I don't know what you're doing here, and I don't care. An ice demon killed my cousin, and I've always wanted to return the favor."

She snorted. Her scales brightened a bloodred shade. A sword and shield of blackest ice materialized in the demon's hands.

Sally darkened from murderous crimson to merciless ebony. She spat a fireball. The demon deflected the strike with his sword. Both the weapon and the flame dissolved in a blinding cloud of steam. The demon hurled jagged icicles without aiming. Sally twisted her serpentine body to avoid all but one. It struck her dead center but melted away almost instantly so that the worst of the damage was just a nick. She shrieked as a gout of flame poured from her jaws. It met the demon's frozen shield, and soon the entire hall was obscured with fog and the sound of battle.

Drawn by the noise, a nearby door opened. Regina and Miriam stepped out of Ned's quarters into the muggy, misty hallway. The siren was nearly impaled by an ice dagger that buried itself in the wall three inches from her face. Regina grinned, but her grin faded when a lick of flame shot close enough to sear the tip of her hair. They could see nothing else but shadows wrestling in the fog.

The demon struck Sally a hard blow with a frozen club that sent the salamander reeling. She tumbled from the fog to land at Regina and Miriam's feet. Before Regina could demand an explanation, Sally hastily saluted.

"Excuse me, ma'am. This won't take another minute." She sprang back into the mist.

In truth, it took just eleven seconds under a minute during which Sally hissed and shrieked and even howled three times. She spat enough fire to burn down two forests, and her skin blazed hot enough to smelt bronze. It was fortunate Copper Citadel was mostly stone and mortar, or else it would've been ablaze. Finally, she fell quiet. The steam gradually faded enough to reveal the salamander coiled around a large block of ice.

"Oh, damn. Decoy." She unwound from the block. Her tongue flicked out to taste the air, but the demon was gone. Like a fire burning too hot, Sally's rage was all but consumed. She settled into a more tolerable temperature, and Regina was able to approach.

"What's going on here?"

"Ice demon, ma'am. Caught him snooping about, but I'm afraid he got away."

Regina gave Sally orders to lead a few soldiers in a search of the citadel, but she expected the effort to be fruitless. Sally slipped away, leaving Regina and Miriam standing in the puddle of a melting ice block.

"I wonder what it was doing here?" asked Miriam.

Regina frowned deeply. She didn't like the idea of unauthorized visitors roaming the citadel. Murderous conspiracies aside, she was a thoroughly by-the-book officer.

The demon's cloak of seclusion would've failed him against a thorough search, but Ogre Company's lax discipline gave him plenty of time to slip away. He was out of the grounds and on his way before a proper alarm was raised.

Despite the troublesome salamander, he was most pleased. She'd not interfered before he'd gotten close enough to get a good reading off the pendulum. It'd even glowed. That could mean only one thing, and his frozen blood chilled in anticipation. Lost in his icy thoughts, he failed to notice the Red Woman until he'd practically run into her.

She saw him, of course. Even new, his cloak's magic couldn't hide him from her eyes. She nodded to the demon. "Hello."

"Hello."

"Fancy seeing you here."

"And you as well."

They shared a silent moment as they shuffled through their own private musings.

"What brings you down from your mountain?" asked the demon.

"Nothing of great importance," she replied. "And what of yourself?"

"Just a trifling matter. Nothing you'd be interested in, I'm sure."

They both offered forth empty, polite smiles.

"Must be off then," said the demon.

"Oh, please, don't let me keep you." The Red Woman stepped aside, and the demon walked off into the night.

Her vermilion raven flew down from the treetops to perch on her shoulder. "Do you think he knows?"

The sorceress shrugged. "If he doesn't, he soon will."

"What are you going to do about it?"

"Nothing."

"You could destroy him, couldn't you?"

"With a single wave of my staff." She demonstrated the simple gesture. "But they would sense that, and there would come more. They were bound to find Ned. It was only a matter of time."

"You could always hide him again," suggested the raven.

"I could. But this is where Ned belongs. It is time to see what he is made of, to hope that he is ready."

The Red Woman continued on her way to the citadel, which by now was on full alert. She had more potent magics at her disposal than old, enchanted cloaks. No one spotted her.

"Do you think Ned will be ready?" asked the raven as they walked through the front gate unmolested by guards.

A frigid wind swept across the fortress.

"No, I don't suppose he will be."

Phantom darkness fell over the citadel like the shadow of an unseen colossus, and a hard rain poured from a cloudless, starless sky.

ELEVEN

WHILE OGRE COMPANY RAN about in poor discipline, the Red Woman slipped into Ned's room. She walked in those moments between moments, those bridges between now and then, and none noticed her passing. Ned was the sole occupant of his room by that time. Miriam and Regina were off aiding in the search efforts. The sorceress stood at the foot of the bed and studied the corpse.

"What are you waiting for?" said the raven. "Just raise him so we can get out of here before someone spots us."

The Red Woman chuckled. She could be gone in an instant. Nor did she have anything to fear should she allow herself to be seen. She only sneaked about because it had been her habit for so long she'd lost patience for dealing with the living. But she'd tarried long enough. She walked to the head of the bed, and waved her hands over Ned. The corpse's bloat shrank. The burn on his chest faded to a less noticeable shade, not quite visible except under the proper light, but as he always carried a memento of his deaths, it would remain. After she'd lovingly tucked his tongue back in his mouth, Ned appeared to be merely dozing. His wounds were such that one could usually only be certain he was alive by his breathing. He wasn't breathing yet.

She paused. It was truly a shame he couldn't remain dead, forever frozen in this peaceful slumber. But death wasn't for Ned.

The raven flew to the headboard. "Just do it already."

She smacked Ned across the forehead. He jumped to life with a yelp. Returning from the dead was as normal as waking up, and there was a sense neither of wonder nor disorientation. Only disappointment, and even this emotion was slight.

"How long was I gone?" he asked the Red Woman. Her resurrections weren't always prompt. Once he'd been deceased for three months before she'd gotten around to raising him.

But the Red Woman wasn't there. She'd crept away in another of those "between" moments. This surprised him. She'd always been the first person he'd seen. Not that she ever told him anything useful, nor explained herself. But she'd never just run off before without sharing a few words. Ned didn't care, but the distinct impression she was avoiding him did cross his mind. Never one to take a lucky break for granted, he took advantage of this moment to lie on his bed and relax. Right now, the Red Woman was gone, and no one else in the citadel knew he was alive. For at least a little while, he could enjoy the quiet.

It didn't last very long. It never did.

The door opened. For a split second, he entertained the notion of sticking out his tongue, closing his eye, and pretending he was still deceased until whoever entered had gone away. He wasn't quick enough.

Miriam's large black eyes opened wider. "Oh. You're back."

He stared at the ceiling. "I'm back."

"Are you feeling better, sir?"

He didn't reply. That was a complicated question.

There was an awkward silence then. Ned was too involved in his own thoughts to notice as Miriam frowned and fidgeted a bit, tracing small circles on the floor with her left foot while, arms crossed, drumming the webbed fingers of her right hand on her left forearm. Had he any practice reading siren body language, he would've also noticed the fins atop her head flatten bashfully, and the tiny nervous gills just below her ears gulping down air. She tried to stop that. Outside of water, it'd only give her gas.

"It's good to have you back, sir. I . . . we missed you."

He raised his head and squinted quizzically. "Really?"

"Yes, sir."

He lay back and considered this. Currently he was too self-absorbed to understand the implications. Romantically speaking, Ned was rather dense. He'd never done well with women. His accumulation of scars and disfigurements hadn't helped. It wasn't a question of self-esteem. It was simply a question of experience, of expecting the world to behave in certain ways. That Miriam might find him desirable was as likely as the end table wanting to be his best friend. It just didn't make sense to him, and like anyone confronted with the unbelievable, he had two choices. He could make that leap of faith and believe. Or he could just not notice.

He chose the latter, although "choice" might imply the slightest conscious effort on his part.

Miriam moved closer but still remained a few paces from the bed. "Can I get you anything, sir?"

"No, I'm fine." He pursed his lips and blew out a long breath. "Thanks anyway."

For her part, Miriam was well aware of how she felt. She liked Ned and had absolutely no way of telling him. All she need do was sing a little song, and he could be hers. Ned had already succumbed once to her allure. He would easily do so again. Women had been seducing men since the dawn of time by employing their wits and natural charms, and singing enchanted melodies was as natural to a siren as breathing. Would it have been so wrong to employ a little musical charm at this moment?

Yes, she decided. Miriam had never seduced a man against his will, and she wouldn't start now. But more important than the moral question was the notion that singing would be a cheat. If she was going to have anything truly worthwhile with Ned, it couldn't start with guile or manipulation or base mesmerism.

But she had no idea how else to get started. Admitting defeat for the moment, though she hadn't given up yet, she saluted crisply and turned on her heel to leave.

"One second." He pushed himself up on his elbows. "I am a little hungry. Could you get me something to eat?"

She smiled and nodded. "Of course, sir."

"And a drink wouldn't hurt either."

"Anything else?"

He sat up. "Can you not tell anyone I'm alive yet? I'd really appreciate it."

"No one? Not even the officers?"

"Especially not the officers."

"As you wish, sir. I'll be right back." She left the room, but on the other side of the door, a few visitors confronted her. Several soldiers filled the hall. The corridor was barely wide enough for two ogres side by side, and all she saw was a pair of them before her, though she heard others behind them. Ace, all two feet of him, slipped between the ogres' legs.

"They're here to see the commander."

"They can't," she said. "He's dead."

"That's what I told them," said Ace, "but they want to make sure he's not faking it."

"Faking it?" asked Miriam.

The soldiers murmured among themselves. Ogre voices were deep and not made for murmuring, so it was quite a racket.

"They think it's all a hoax," said Ace. "They think the Legion cooked up this whole Never Dead Ned business as a public relations fabrication."

"But he's already risen from the dead once," said Miriam.

"That's what I told 'em." Then he shouted at the soldiers. "I told you idiots he was dead! Saw him with my own eyes!

There never was a man as dead as that! Ask Frank or Ralph or Ward. Lewis and Martin. They'll all swear to it."

The ogres continued to murmur skeptically.

"Most of you saw him too!" shouted the goblin.

"Only from a distance," said one of the front ogres. "Could've been a dummy filled with straw for all we know."

"Or some other guy!" said a raspy-voiced troll somewhere in the back. "All those humans look alike!"

"We do pretty much look the same," said a human soldier peering from behind an ogre's elbow.

"Almost exactly!" agreed another human, who just happened to be the first's twin brother. "Sometimes our mothers can't even tell us apart."

Miriam stood resolute. "I'm afraid the commander is not available for public viewing."

Ace stood beside her. More accurately, he stood in front of her, barely above her knee. "You heard the lady. Scram."

The soldiers murmured louder still. One of the leading ogres put a massive hand on Miriam's shoulder. "We'd really like it if you'd please step aside, ma'am." It was not a request.

She hummed almost inaudibly, and the gathered crowd stepped back.

"Now that's not fair." The ogre moved to clamp his hand over her mouth, but she'd already started singing. Siren songs weren't foolproof, and an audience developed resistance with each exposure. But ogres, for some reason, were especially susceptible, and since they didn't hear it often, the effects were nearly instantaneous.

Sirens were most famous for their beguiling melodies, but their enchanted songbook was chock-full of other useful tunes. There were songs to call down rain, songs to shake the earth, songs to shatter walls, and songs to encourage a seedling to grow into a mighty oak in a day, songs to open locked doors, and songs to summon spirits, and songs to cast them out. Miriam wasn't particularly adept. By siren standards, she was a little tone deaf. And while she'd never been good at seducing rivers to change their course or charming dragons, she did have a great talent for the most dreaded of siren tunes, the Dirge of Revulsion.

The dirge bubbled up from her diaphragm, boiled out of her lungs, steamed through her throat to burn on her audience's ears. The soldiers, tears in their eyes, dashed away in a scramble. Some resisted more than others, but in the end most succumbed before a dozen notes had escaped her lips. Only the goblins, curiously resistant to mesmerism of any sort, remained.

Miriam stopped singing and rubbed her throat. The dirge was hard on her voice, and she spoke with a rasp.

"Get out of here."

Without their ogre backup, the goblins reluctantly departed.

Ace said, "Nice trick."

"It gets the job done." She cleared her throat. "Can you do me a favor and watch the door until I get back?" She wasn't very worried about anyone besides goblins sneaking inside. The power of the dirge would cover this spot for a few hours, keeping most away.

"Sure." Ace sat and lit his pipe. "Make it snappy though. I've got a flight in twenty minutes."

Miriam went off to the pub to get Ned's meal, and it wasn't six minutes later that Regina approached his quarters.

"What are you doing?" she asked.

"Smoking." He offered her his pipe. "Want a puff?"

"Step aside."

"Are you authorized?"

She scowled. "What are you talking about?"

"I'm not supposed to let anyone in."

"You little beast, I outrank you."

"This isn't about me. It's about orders. Since I don't really know whose orders I'm following, I can't as a good soldier just allow you to pass." Ace puffed deeply on his pipe. The putrid yellow smoke slithered its way along the wall to gather at the ceiling. "Unless you happen to know the password."

"What password?"

"I don't know it."

"Then how will you know what it is?"

Ace removed his goggles and inspected them for specks, mostly for something to do. "Way I figure it, if you were authorized and you knew the password, you'd tell it to me straight out. And if you were authorized and there were no password, you'd just tell me to go to hell."

"Go to hell."

He smiled. "Nice try, but your first response is all that counts. And that tells me you aren't authorized."

She smiled back. "Very clever. Although there is one flaw with your plan."

"What's that?"

The Amazon snatched up the diminutive goblin by his scarf and hurled him down the hall and out of her way. He landed hard on the floor, but his race was innately bouncy so there was no harm done. By the time he'd gotten to his feet, she'd already gone inside. The magic of the siren's dirge had no power over a woman.

"Hadn't thought of that." With a shrug, Ace collected his pipe and went on his way.

On the other side of the door, Regina's dark eyes widened. "Oh. You're back."

In no mood to care about déjà vu, Ned said, "I'm back."

"Are you feeling better, sir?"

He didn't reply. That remained a complicated question.

There was another awkward silence, the second such clumsy hush to fall between Ned and a woman this evening. Ned, as usual, didn't notice, but for Regina this was agony. She no longer denied she felt something for him. She dared not give it a name. She wasn't ready for that. But this unlabeled emotion, this ridiculous and inappropriate desire, was nothing less than a blight on her proud Amazonian soul. At least she didn't have to worry about parental disapproval. Amazons had neither fathers nor mothers. They had only the code of their society to guide them, and the code was very specific and quite unforgiving.

In a situation like this, where temptation had somehow wormed its way into her iron breast, only blood could cleanse her spirit. Ned's blood. She had to kill him, and her code said to do so right now. She pulled her dagger quietly and edged toward him as he sat on his bed, his back to her. A dozen ends flashed through her warrior's mind. She could spear him in the heart, cut his throat, sever his spine, or forgo the dagger and break his neck with her bare hands. And though these thoughts should've brought a grim smile to her lips, instead they made her frown.

Goddesses despise her, she couldn't do it. And even if she could, it wouldn't have worked. Never Dead Ned was immortal. Her dilemma wouldn't be solved so easily, but she would have to find a way.

Ned turned his head slowly as if he'd forgotten her presence and was now just remembering. Dagger in hand, she glanced around the room and tried not to look murderous. No more murderous than usual.

"It's good to have you back, sir."

He tilted his head to one side like a goat trying its best to understand the workings of a catapult and failing. "Really?"

"Yes, sir." She tried to look casual with her drawn dagger, twirling it as if she were merely trying to keep her hands busy. "Can I get you anything?"

"Thanks, but Miriam is already doing that."

Regina's dark eyes reddened. "Miriam." She spoke the name like a curse called down from the heavens. Not the glowing heaven of glorious goddesses, where grand feminine divinities dwelt in righteous splendor, but the lesser, forsaken heaven of gluttonous and useless gods, where the masculine deities wasted all their time getting drunk and peeping down on virgins in earthly bathhouses.

The door opened, and Miriam, carrying a tray full of food and drink, entered. Ned didn't have the energy to rise from the bed, and instead he lay back down. "Put it on the table."

"Yes, sir," said Miriam very pleasantly.

But the siren and the Amazon locked stares. Regina twirled her dagger faster. Balancing her tray on her hip, Miriam put her free hand on the short sword at her side. Ned remained steadfastly oblivious.

Miriam addressed him, but her eyes never moved from Regina's. "I've brought enough for two if you'd like some company, sir."

Regina squinted. Her brow wrinkled. "An excellent suggestion. You're dismissed, Miriam."

Miriam's full, fishy lips tightened into a forced smile. "I think that's really up to the commander, isn't it, ma'am?"

"I suppose it is." Regina stopped twirling her dagger. She grasped it in tight fingers, ready to slash open Miriam's face at only a moment's opportunity.

Ned stood and went to the tray. He uncorked a bottle of wine and took a long drink. "Thanks, but I'd rather be alone."

Miriam frowned at the rebuke. Regina frowned at the rebuke too and scowled with the hard acknowledgment that she cared about his rebuke.

"As you wish, sir," spat the Amazon through clenched teeth. "Come along, Miriam."

"After you, ma'am."

The women exited, drawing close enough to attack each other, but Ned's proximity held them in check. On the other side of the closed door, they quickly put some distance between themselves. Neither said anything, but both were plagued with doubts.

To Miriam, her Amazon rival was a vexing obstacle. True, Regina was unskilled in the art of seduction, but she was flawlessly beautiful, tall, and well-proportioned, with smooth, soft skin. And there was her hair, that shimmering, flaxen mane. A bald, scaly siren couldn't compete against any of that. Not without her songs, which she was determined not to use.

She didn't have a chance.

Regina saw Miriam as a creature of exotic undersea loveliness. Her scales glimmered even in the dim hall light, and her natural grace was undeniable. Worse than that, she was a siren. Enticing men was second nature to her. And Regina, as an Amazon, knew absolutely nothing about wooing a lover.

She didn't have a chance.

Either woman might've leapt upon the other to end their rivalry the only way they could think of at the moment. But fate flipped a coin, and the moment passed.

Regina sheathed her dagger. "If you'll excuse me, I've duties to attend to."

"Yes, me too." Miriam lowered her hand from her sword. "Perhaps we should go attend to our duties together."

"I was thinking the same thing," agreed Regina.

Both glanced at Ned's door. Then, smiling sweetly at one another while plotting each other's death, they went on their way.

TWELVE

NED COULDN'T STAY in his quarters forever, but he dared not leave. For one thing, he'd never been terribly motivated. He wouldn't have minded lying in his bed under his covers, having his food brought to him and doing nothing else except the occasional turn to prevent bedsores. He knew it was an impossible dream. He'd have to get up sometime to relieve himself, and a bath every so often seemed more necessity than luxury. But if he was going to live forever, then he could live forever here just as easily as anywhere else.

It was just a dream, and an unrealistic dream at that. Even Ned wasn't that lazy. A century or two—providing he couldn't finally die of old age, which he didn't know—and he'd get bored. He lowered his goal to a more reasonable few hours of peace and quiet before life assaulted him again.

What really held him under his covers was fear. Not fear of death, which he'd lost long ago. Nor fear of resurrection, which he begrudgingly accepted. What haunted him was the unknown. He couldn't remember how he'd died. All he re-

membered was getting his stuff together and stepping out of
his room on his way to desertion.

And then . . .

Waking up. How he'd died, who had killed him, or if it'd
merely been another accident. All those details escaped him.
Without some idea of what had done him in, he had no idea
how to avoid it again. So far, Ned had never died the same
death twice, and he had no intention of starting now.

He'd noticed the faint, almost invisible burn on his chest.
It must've had something to do with it. For once, he wished
the Red Woman had stuck around after raising him. He
could've asked her without much embarrassment. He refused to ask anyone else. It would just be too embarrassing,
too preposterous. He'd rather not know.

But that left the question of the door and what terrible
doom awaited him on the other side. The riddle bedeviled
him for a few hours, but Ned's mind wasn't possessed of the
determination to hold on to any single obsession for long.
Eventually he ran out of wine, and the comforting call of
booze was one of the few things capable of pushing him into
action. He got out of bed and paused at the door. And then,
heedless of whatever nameless death awaited him, he
opened it.

He didn't die, and he wasn't surprised. That would've
been too easy. No, the fact of the matter was that each time
he'd died, it had always come as a shock. It was only natural
to assume a man who'd died so many times would get a
sense of it. But so far, he'd never seen it coming. Which
made him wonder why he ever bothered worrying. If he
couldn't predict it, if dangerous things didn't always kill him
and harmless things sometimes did, and just as often the
other way around with no perceptible pattern, then worrying
was pointless.

Still he worried as much as he worried about anything: not
very much. Worrying implied control or, at the very least,
the illusion of control. Ned had long ago abandoned that illusion. He often skipped worrying entirely and went straight
to acceptance, with only a brief stopover in annoyance.

When he stalled in this process (as he sometimes might), he used booze to kick-start the journey.

He stepped into the hall. The door shut behind him, and a moment after, Ned realized he didn't need that drink after all—at least not enough to go out in public or deal with other drunks. He turned back, but something, some overwhelming dread, kept him from touching the handle. He didn't know about Miriam's dirge, but he knew he dared not go back inside that room.

Laughter and obnoxious shouts filled the hall. Soldiers were coming. Rather than stick around and face them, he ascended a nearby staircase in hopes of escape. He followed the spiral all the way to the top, where he opened a trapdoor and stepped out onto a watchtower and into the cool night air. There were supposed to be sentries posted, but the place was deserted. Relieved, Ned sat down low so that no one below might spot him (not that anyone was that alert) and didn't think of anything at all.

It wasn't much later that someone else climbed those stairs. Ned slumped into the shadows as best he was able, hoping to avoid detection and knowing the hope was futile. A small figure, too big for a goblin but too short for an ogre, rose from the trapdoor. It was a dim night, but his long beard gave Owens the oracle away. He walked to the opposite edge of the tower, and though he was blind, he seemed to gaze down on the surrounding countryside. Ned tried not to breathe too loudly, and for a minute he succeeded admirably. Then a tickle worked its way into his nose, and Ned felt the germ of a sneeze developing. He shuddered. He choked it back. He held his breath. But it was only a matter of time before he lost the battle with his traitorous nostrils.

Owens kept staring off into the horizon. Without turning his head in Ned's direction, the oracle remarked, "I told you you'd sneeze. Gods bless you, sir."

Ned wiped his nose on the back of his hand. "Thanks."

Owens's only reply was a nod.

Ned noticed a small jug hanging from Owens's belt. He wondered what was inside it.

"Ale, sir," answered Owens.

Ned was about to ask for a drink when Owens threw the jug. His aim was off by a good yard. Ned had to get to his feet to retrieve it. He uncorked it and took a sip. Before he could thank Owens, the oracle said, "You're welcome, sir."

Ned took another drink and frowned. "That's really—"

"Yes, sir. I know."

Ned gave back the jug, and Owens enjoyed a draught.

"I love coming up here at night, sir. Wonderful view, don't you agree?"

"Too dark to see anything."

Owens chuckled. "That's one of the advantages of being blind. The view's always the same."

Ned opened his mouth to ask how long ago the soldier had lost his sight.

"Seven years," the oracle replied.

It was then that Ned noticed something, and since he rarely noticed anything, he was taken aback. Observations were a sure sign of a sober mind. He almost asked for another drink, but he decided to ride it out this time. He could always get drunk later if it became too unpleasant.

"You hear the future, don't you, Owens?"

"Yes, sir."

"But how can you hear a question which, by your very act of hearing it, never gets spoken?"

"I'm afraid I don't understand the question, sir."

"What day is—"

"Wednesday, sir."

"See what I mean?" said Ned. "I was going to ask you what day it is, but you answered before I finished asking, which means I never did ask, which means you couldn't have heard the question because it was never actually asked. You heard a future which doesn't exist."

Owens contemplated this. "Bit of a paradox, isn't it?"

"A bit," said Ned.

A few quiet minutes passed.

"Mind if I ask you a question, sir?"

"Go ahead." Ned already knew the question as surely as if

he could hear the future. How did he cheat death? As if immortality was some grand prize.

"How the hell did you get this job?" asked Owens.

Ned hadn't expected that, and that made it a pleasant surprise.

"Not to offend you, sir," added Owens.

"It's okay." Ned chuckled. "I'm here because I don't have any other place to go."

"Same as the rest of us, eh?" Owens tilted his head in Ned's direction. "Welcome to Ogre Company, last stop in your illustrious Legion career. Well, I suppose it's nice to have somewhere to belong."

Ned didn't have the heart to tell Owens the company was careening wildly toward dissolution.

"You don't want to be here, do you, sir?"

"No. I want to balance books."

"Seems a waste of talent, if you ask me. What with your immortality and all, sir."

"Immortality isn't a talent," replied Ned. "It's a gimmick."

"Maybe so," agreed Owens. "Maybe so."

They were quiet again.

"Could I offer you some advice, sir?"

Ned didn't reply aloud. But he thought of his answer and pictured himself saying it. Owens, true to form, heard the unspoken words.

"As long as you're here, you might as well make the most of it."

"You don't understand. I'm a terrible soldier, and I'm a worse leader. The only thing I've ever been really good at is dying, and even that I can't get entirely right."

"I know what it's like to feel sorry for yourself." Owens pointed to his useless eyes. "But life doesn't always go the way you want. You can either grumble and moan about it, or do what you can with what you're given."

Ned took another drink. "I think I'll just stick with grumbling and moaning."

"Always play to your strengths, I suppose."

Ned gazed down at the citadel. In the gloom of night, the

courtyard was full of darkened soldiers lost in drunken carousing. His citadel. His courtyard. His soldiers.

He hadn't asked for this job. This was all the workings of cruel fate, of forces beyond his ken. And those forces certainly didn't give a damn about his whining. Since they enjoyed tormenting him so much, it was a good bet they probably relished his suffering. But hell, he had a right, didn't he? Moping might not accomplish anything, but accomplishing things was overrated. Everything always fell apart in the end. So why bother?

He hadn't intended to pose the question, but somehow or other, Owens heard it.

"What have you got to lose?"

Ned let the question sink in. He didn't really think about it, but he didn't completely ignore it either.

"When I went blind, sir, I thought I'd lost everything. The Legion was my life, you understand. In addition to seeing the future, I was a damn fine soldier. Then it all went away. I went back home, grew potatoes, and felt sorry for myself for three years. And then one day I realized something. Two things, actually."

"What—"

"I hate potatoes. I despise their taste. I despise their skin. I despise digging them up. I despise them mashed. I despise them boiled. I absolutely despise everything about them. Damned potatoes. A pox on whatever god created them." He spat over the watchtower edge and made an obscene gesture toward the heavens.

"The other thing I realized was that going blind wasn't the worst that could happen to me. There are always men worse off. And the way I see it, there are a lot more terrible tragedies in this world than an oracle who hears the future and a man who can't die."

"You—"

"Oh, I understand. None of us wants to be here, sir. But we are. And maybe while we are, we should give it a go." Owens started toward the trapdoor. "You can keep the jug, if you like."

Ned uncorked the ale and put it to his lips. But something made him hesitate. He wasn't a good commander. He couldn't save Ogre Company. But what did he have to lose? He could always get drunk later. And there was no rule saying he couldn't do his job and still feel sorry for himself. Anyway, how badly could he screw it up?

He stopped Owens, who had already started down the steep steps.

"Thanks, but I won't be needing this."

Without thinking, he threw the jug. It sailed through the air to smash into Owens's face. He crumpled over and tumbled loudly down the stairs. Ned winced with every thud, flinched with every curse shouted by the crashing soldier. After a brief pause, a weak voice echoed through the trapdoor.

"I'm okay. I think I broke my arm, but I'm okay."

Never Dead Ned glanced to the heavens but kept his rude gestures to himself. It was going to be a long, long six months.

THiRTeeN

LATE THAT NIGHT Regina received a summons to Ned's office. She was quite pleased for she felt certain that at this late hour there could only be one reason. Obviously Ned had noticed her incredible beauty—of course, couldn't help but notice—and had only been hiding his growing attraction to her. But that attraction must surely have grown too strong to ignore any longer. She admired that he'd resisted for as long as he had, but now he planned on announcing his affections in a quiet meeting behind closed doors. She hadn't decided how she would deal with this. Even her culture couldn't completely deny the worth of men, and there were provisions set down for how an exceptional man might prove himself worthy of an Amazon's love. She doubted very much Ned was such a man, but she didn't care about that right now.

Before reporting, she changed into her finest garment, a suit of ceremonial armor she hadn't worn in years. It wasn't intended for battle, a fact made apparent by the plunging neckline of its chain-mail bodice and the shortness of its metal skirt.

She had a devil of a time putting on the thigh-high, polished leather boots. They'd always been skintight, and her thighs, loath as she was to admit it, were not as perfectly shaped as they once were. She studied herself in a full-length mirror for five minutes, adjusting buckles, shifting straps, and alternately pushing up her breasts and tucking them back until achieving just the right amount of cleavage. She went through her many capes, settled on a flowing crimson cloak, then decided she didn't like it after all, and went with a shorter black one that complemented her shoulders without hiding her butt.

Next she sorted through her many weapons. Amazons collected armaments like dragons collected the bones of heroes, and Regina was especially guilty of this habit. She searched for just the right one to wear on her hip. A huge silver claymore was her best sword, but it was too awkward and would remove the grace from her walk. A short sword would've been comfortable, but too comfortable. She didn't want to appear easy. She considered and discarded a pair of sabers. Too showy. And she deliberated briefly on something unconventional, like her trident or maul, but decided it might seem as if she were trying too hard. In the end, she went with her standard, Legion-issued sword. Not her best weapon, but the best for the situation.

Studying herself in the mirror, she decided that there was no doubt she was a most beautiful and irresistible creature. Miriam, for all her otherworldly siren charms, could never match the flawless magnificence of an Amazon warrior in her prime. Regina smiled with no small pride.

Then she saw them, and her confidence waned. Crow's-feet. Almost imperceptible wrinkles around her eyes. She frowned, and the wrinkles deepened.

She leaned closer to the mirror, and this tiny flaw grew larger. She wasn't that old. She shouldn't have these. She leaned closer still and ran her fingers along the hideous chasms in her flesh. Touching her skin, she noticed the dryness. And her eyes, they were too close together. Or possibly too far apart. Either way, they were at an imperfect distance. And had her nose always been so pointy? Her blond eyebrows could use a good plucking. And was that a mole just below her left earlobe?

She wasn't flawless. On the contrary, she was covered with flaws. Hundreds, she observed. Thousands she probably hadn't yet. But Ned would notice. He must have. That was why he hadn't announced his feelings. He didn't have any. He couldn't possibly care for such a ghastly beast, such an imperfect thing as she. Why hadn't she taken better care of herself? Why had she been so neglectful?

Because she was an Amazon, and Amazons weren't supposed to care about those things. But now she did, and she scowled. Those wrinkles tore their tainted path across her offensive face, and she scowled even more so with the realization that she cared.

Miriam didn't need to worry about these things. Her accursed golden scales were as smooth and wrinkle-free as ever, and probably would be until the day she died. And while it was true Miriam's fishlike face wasn't the most ravishing, Regina couldn't justly call herself superior. Not so long as those imperfections in her own face mocked her. She couldn't bear to look upon herself anymore. Regina grabbed her mace and smashed the mirror with one enraged strike.

It didn't make her feel better. If this was what came from attracting men, she'd been better off without them.

Her door opened, and a goblin stuck his head in. "Are you okay, ma'am? I heard a noise."

Regina's only answer was an annoyed huff.

"The commander sent me to check on you," said the goblin. "He wanted to know what's keeping you."

She huffed again. "Tell him I'm on my way."

The goblin shut the door.

Regina made a few more last-minute adjustments. Her limited experience assured her that men liked breasts, and this was one area in which she surpassed Miriam. She pushed her bust forward until it threatened to spill forth from her breastplate. Hair was another area where that scaly aquatic female couldn't compete. Regina undid her bun and let the shimmering blond mane cascade across her left shoulder. But perhaps that was too obvious. She threw it behind her back. With a little more time she might do something with it, although she had no practical experience with hairstyles.

The door opened, and the goblin poked his head in again. "Ma'am?"

Snarling, she whirled on him. "Come here."

He swallowed a gulp and stepped just within the threshold of her room. "Yes, ma'am?"

"Do you desire me?"

"I'm sorry, ma'am?"

She stood straighter, hands on her waist, her hip cocked to one side. "Do you find me desirable?"

He cupped his weak chin and chewed his heavy lips. His long ears twitched thoughtfully.

"Well?" she asked impatiently. "Be honest."

"No, ma'am."

"No? Look at me!" She advanced and bent over until her breasts were practically in his face.

The goblin stared into her cleavage with mild interest. "It may surprise you, ma'am, to discover that not every species worships the human female form."

She straightened and stared down at him. "Are you saying you wouldn't have sex with me?"

"Oh, sure, I'd have sex with you, ma'am, but we'd have to put out the lights first. And I'd be thinking of an ogress the whole time."

If her mace had been within easy reach, Regina would've caved the goblin's skull in. But she was already late for her date, and she refused to fret over this nonsense any longer. She was beautiful, perhaps not flawless, but close enough. And if Ned didn't see it, she'd pummel him until he did.

Ned's office was a short walk from her quarters. She crossed paths with several soldiers who couldn't help but leer. Normally she would've scorned such attention, but she was reassured for once by this affront, and since she was late, she had no time for even a short beating. At the office door, she paused to recheck her straps. She shifted her sword, put a slight smile on her lips, and stepped inside.

"Sorry I'm late, sir."

Ned hunched over his desk. He didn't look up. "That's fine, Archmajor. We started without you. Hope you don't mind."

She suddenly realized there were others in the room. First Officer Gabel and Organizational Lieutenant Frank sat on the couch in one corner. Both smiled knowingly at her formal armor.

"I'm sure she doesn't mind at all," said Frank.

"Yes, Archmajor," said Gabel. "Why don't you have a seat?"

"Thank you, but I think I'll stand." She stiffened.

Ned had yet to glance up from his paperwork. He scribbled on his infernal budget. The angry parchment shook and hissed as he moved numbers around, but several daggers pinned it securely to the desk.

"I'm sorry for the late hour of this meeting," said Ned, "but I couldn't sleep, and I was hoping to get some work done." He scratched something out, and the budget growled. "I'm good with numbers, but there's not much to work with here."

"May I ask what this is about, sir?" inquired Regina.

"The commander was just informing us that Ogre Company has been given six months to improve itself," said Gabel, "and he was asking us for any suggestions to do that."

Regina's surprise pushed aside her annoyance. "Sir, are you asking for our advice?"

He glanced up finally, and she was quite pleased when his eyes paused, however briefly, on her chest before turning back to his paperwork.

"That's right, Archmajor. Is that a problem?" asked Ned.

"No, sir," said Regina. "It's just that none of the previous commanders ever asked for our advice."

"You are supposed to be my advisors, aren't you?"

"Yes, sir." Frank shifted, and the couch groaned under his bulk. "But all the other commanders thought they knew better."

"And now they're all dead," said Ned. "Right?"

Gabel, Regina, and Frank exchanged paranoid glances.

"Isn't that right?" asked Ned once more.

"Yes, sir," replied Gabel. "All accidents of course."

"Terrible misfortunes," added Frank.

"They were great men, and they deserved better," said Regina.

"Without a doubt," said Gabel, "but let's not dwell on the freakish, yet perfectly explainable, mishaps that ended their lives, but instead on the glory of their deeds."

The three conspiratorial officers exchanged another round of guilty looks. Ned, as usual, was wholly oblivious.

"You three have been here a long time," he said, "and if I'm going to turn this company around, I'll need your support." He put down his pen and leaned back in his chair. "To be honest, I don't have any idea what I'm doing. It'd make a lot more sense for one of you to be in my position, but nobody asked us, right?"

They nodded.

"You must have a few ideas," he said.

"Yes, sir." Regina smiled, felt the wrinkles around her eyes, and went perfectly blank.

"Good. Let's get to it then."

They passed the following two hours offering up suggestions. Each couldn't help but be skeptical at first, assuming Ned already had his own ideas how to proceed and was merely putting on a show, pretending he valued their opinions. But within a few minutes, it became clear that he really did want their advice. Once they recovered from their shock, both Frank and Regina shared their ideas freely. Gabel remained silent, submitting nothing useful. He sat on the couch, his arms folded, his eyes narrowed, his long ears tilted back.

As they worked, Ned continued to scrawl his adjustments

to the company's budget. Slowly the infernal document changed more to his liking. The budget was tamed by the time the meeting was over. It purred and rubbed against its new master's legs. Ned, with no small pride, ordered it to furl itself up, and it obeyed.

"I guess that's enough for tonight." Yawning, he handed the budget to Regina. "See that this gets to the head office for approval, would you, Archmajor?"

"Yes, sir." She saluted, and for the first time she actually meant it.

Ned rose from his desk, stretched, and opened the door adjoining his office to his quarters. "See you in the morning." He shut the door, leaving them alone in the office.

None said a word. They waited until they'd delivered the budget to the roc facility for rush delivery and had a round of drinks at the pub before they spoke of what had just happened.

"That settles it," said Gabel.

"It certainly does," agreed Regina.

"So we're all agreed then?" said Gabel. "We have to get rid of him as soon as possible."

Regina sneered at the orc. "We can't do that."

"We can find a way. Immortal or not."

"That's not what I meant."

"What did you mean?" asked Gabel.

"I'm not so sure Ned has to die anymore."

Gabel barked a harsh laugh that quieted the pub for a moment. He leaned forward and spoke in a hushed whisper. "He's obviously up to something. Why else would he put on that charade tonight?"

Regina leaned forward, not very easy to do in her tight bodice. A purely decorative strap popped loose. "Maybe it wasn't a charade."

Gabel was so focused on the argument, his glance didn't stray to her breasts, slipping another three-quarters of an inch closer to freedom. "Don't be naive, Amazon." He plopped back into his chair. "What do you think, Frank?"

Frank shrugged. "I don't know."

"I do know," countered Gabel. "I know that Ned's planning something. And I'd wager every coin I've got that he has suspicions."

"Of what?" asked Frank.

"Of us, you dolt."

The ogre's massive fists tightened. He was a good-natured sort, but Gabel recognized that Frank had his limits. Gabel plastered a pleasant grin across his face and bought the next round to cool Frank's temper.

"Why should he be suspicious of us?" said Regina. "We haven't even tried to kill him yet. Have we?"

By now the officers had much practice with furtive glances, and so they exchanged another round among themselves.

"Of course not," said Gabel. "But he has died twice already, and that's got to look suspicious. Even if they were accidents this time. Which they were, we all agree."

"Yes." Regina narrowed her eyes. "Accidents."

"Unfortunate spots of bad luck," agreed Frank, but he didn't sound quite convinced. "Maybe Regina's right. Maybe we should wait a little longer before we decide."

"And give him more time to piece things together?" Gabel shook his head violently. "I say the sooner we kill him, the better."

"And I say we shouldn't kill him at all," replied Regina.

"You would, Amazon." The last word he mumbled with derision.

"What do you mean by that, orc?"

"Nothing. I just never thought I'd see the day an Amazon warrior would throw herself so brazenly at a man." He muttered into his tankard. "But what can you expect from a woman?"

Regina exploded into action. She kicked the table to one side and shoved one of her leather boots across Gabel's cheek. He tumbled from his chair and skidded to a painful stop.

Frank sighed.

"Get up." She growled, drawing her sword. "Get up and die, you pathetic male!"

Gabel rose and drew his own weapon. "I've always wanted to teach you some respect, you lesbian bitch."

"I am not a lesbian!"

"Oh, that's right. How could I forget?" Gabel smirked. "Lesbians don't wave their tits around in front of boys."

Regina howled a fearsome battle cry that sent alternate waves of fear and excitement through the pub. Before she could launch herself at her foe, Frank smashed her over the head with a jug of wine. Moaning, she fell to the floor.

"Why did you do that?" asked Gabel. "I could've taken her."

Frank slammed one giant fist down upon Gabel's skull, and he joined the Amazon on the floor.

"All right, folks. Nothing to see here. Carry on."

He scooped up the stunned orc under one arm, the dazed Amazon under the other, and walked from the pub. He searched for a secluded, darkened corner. This wasn't easy. Most of the shadowy spots were already occupied by slumbering drunks or soldiers engaged in prohibited activities that Frank didn't bother investigating. When he finally found the empty pool of shadow he sought, Gabel and Regina had come to their senses. Frank set them down.

Regina punched him. He barely felt the blow, but that he felt it at all spoke well of the Amazon's strength.

"How dare you!" She cocked back her fist.

"I know you think I deserved that, so I'll let you have the first one for free." The ogre inhaled, puffing out his thick chest. "Second one will cost you."

Her hand dropped to her empty scabbard. If her sword hadn't been left in the pub, she would've tried her luck. Instead she turned her wrath back to its original source. She glowered at Gabel. He glowered back.

Frank leaned against a wall. "Go ahead. Kill each other if it'll make you feel better. I just wanted you to do it someplace more private. With your fists."

Gabel adopted the stooped posture of traditional orcish wrestling. "I'm so sick of your precious Amazon superiority. It's time to show you what a man can do."

Regina laughed. "You push a quill across paperwork all day. You're not a warrior. You're a file clerk."

"Watch her left," Frank advised. "She leads with her left."

Howling, Gabel charged. Saliva and foam sprayed from his lips as he dove, his outstretched hands reaching for her neck. She darted to one side and chopped him in the throat. Gagging, he fell to his knees.

"She's not bad with her right either," added Frank.

Regina circled her choking opponent until he could get to his feet.

"Lucky shot," sputtered Gabel.

He rushed her again. Regina spun and thrust her heel into his gut, knocking the wind from him.

"Gotta keep an eye on the legs," said Frank.

Gabel used a wall to steady himself. "Now you tell me." His breath was ragged. His green face paled in the moonlight. This time he moved forward cautiously. He was still unprepared when she grabbed him by the wrist, and with a pivot and a jerk, he was down on the ground.

"Okay." Gabel sat up. "I definitely spotted a flaw in her technique that time."

Frank closed his eyes and listened to the sounds of combat, consisting of one orc being tossed around, thumping against the stony ground, bouncing off the brick walls, and once smashing into a couple of empty mead barrels. Frank was positive he'd heard Gabel break something. When the racket fell silent save for the orc's ragged breaths, Frank opened his eyes again.

"All done?"

For Regina, battle in all its forms was a calming exercise, as close to meditation as an Amazon ever got. Beating Gabel had taken her edge off. "I'm done if he's done."

Gabel lay on the ground where he'd fallen and wheezed a noise that might be taken as surrender. "What are we going to do about Ned?" he asked between gasps.

"Whatever we have to," said Frank. "But the rule is none of us acts unless we all agree. And since none of us agrees—"

"We wait." Regina ground her heel into Gabel's gut as she walked away.

He waited until absolutely, positively certain she was out of earshot before pushing himself up on an elbow. "Her judgment is impaired."

"What are you saying?" asked Frank.

"I'm saying maybe she's become a liability."

Frank seized Gabel in one huge hand, lifted the orc to his feet, and didn't let go. "I don't want to hear talk like that." He tightened his grip.

Gabel winced. His legs buckled, but Frank kept him from falling.

"What's the big deal?" asked Gabel. "We've taken care of problems like this before."

"We stick together. If we turn on each other, it'll all fall apart."

Frank squeezed tighter.

"Okay, okay. I get the point."

Frank let go.

Gabel staggered a bit, nearly falling over again. "But you have to admit she's not thinking clearly. What do you think she sees in him?"

"I don't know. She deserves a lot better."

"Deserves? What do you mean by that?"

"She could do a lot better."

Gabel looked up at Frank, and Frank looked down.

"You didn't say that," remarked Gabel. "You said 'deserves.'"

"So?"

"It's a funny word to use," said Gabel.

"Funny how?"

"Just funny."

"I don't see what's so funny about it," said Frank.

"Forget it." Gabel attempted to limp away, but Frank clamped his hand back on the orc's shoulder.

"Funny how?"

"It's nothing really. Just the context. Just the way you said it."

"How did I say it?"

"Like it meant something."

Gabel would've been happy to leave it at that, but Frank exerted a tad more pressure upon the orc's bruised, swollen shoulder.

"It just sounded like maybe you liked her," Gabel said.

Frank let go. "I don't like her. I mean, I do like her, but I don't like her. Not like that. I don't *like her* like her, if that's what you mean."

"Of course, you don't. Even the mere notion of an ogre and an Amazon together is perfectly ludicrous."

Frank scowled. "Yes. Ludicrous."

"Absolutely laughable," said Gabel. "Totally ridiculous."

"I wouldn't go that far," said Frank.

"I'll admit she's nice to look at, but that personality doesn't help much."

"I like her personality," mumbled Frank.

"Can you imagine what she'd be like in bed? Probably telling you what to do all the time. 'Move here! Put that there! More to the left! Too far left! Oh, you're doing it all wrong, maggot! Pleasure me properly, maggot, or it's a thousand sit-ups!' "

"I like a woman who knows what she wants," mumbled Frank, though Gabel didn't hear.

"And even her taste in men is preposterous. Hundreds of stout, worthy soldiers in this citadel, and she picks the one guy who can't go a day without dying? Women . . . who can figure them out?"

"Yes," agreed Frank softly. "Women."

They started back to the pub. Battered and sore, Gabel limped along, holding his right arm stiffly.

"You might want to get that looked at," said Frank.

Gabel snorted. "It'll be fine until I get a couple drinks in me."

They walked a bit farther.

"It's not perfectly ludicrous," said Frank, mostly to himself.

"What?"

"You said that an Amazon and an ogre together would be perfectly ludicrous."

"Yes?"

"So it's not perfectly ludicrous."

Gabel came to a sudden stop. Frank bumped into the orc and nearly knocked him off his feet again.

"What are you talking about?" asked Gabel.

"Nothing really," said Frank. "It's just, I don't think it's right to say it's a perfectly ludicrous pairing. We ogres have many qualities an Amazon might find desirable. We're big. We're strong. We fight well. We're grand drinkers and passionate lovers. And we like to cuddle."

Gabel shook his head. "Fine. It's not perfectly ludicrous." He turned to walk but halted when Frank didn't follow. "Are you coming or not?"

Frank folded his arms and nodded thoughtfully to himself. "We agree then. It's just ludicrous. But not perfectly so."

Gabel forced a smile. "No, not perfectly so."

"Very good."

"So do you like her?"

"Don't be stupid," Frank replied. "Although she's a fine woman. If she were an ogress, she'd make some lucky ogre a fine wife." He smiled wistfully.

"You do. You do like her!"

"No, I don't."

"Yes, you do."

"No, I don't."

"Yes, you do."

The ogre lowered his voice to a whisper. "Okay. Maybe I like her a little. But only a little bit."

Gabel chuckled. The laugh rattled a cracked rib and brought tears to his eyes. "What's so funny?" asked Frank.

Gabel continued to chortle and groan.

Frank spat. "I don't really like her that much. Hardly at all actually." He put a finger to the sore spot under his collarbone where Regina had punched him. In the moonlight, there were indications that it might turn into a small bruise. He smiled.

"But if you think about it, it's not that ludicrous at all."

"Whatever you say." Gabel started back, determined neither broken bones nor lovesick ogres would keep him from a tall, stout ale.

FOURTEEN

NED DRAGGED HIMSELF out of bed twenty minutes before sunrise. He wasn't a morning person, and he nearly rolled over and went back to sleep. But he managed somehow to get dressed and haul himself into the main courtyard. Gabel, Regina, and Frank were waiting for him. Gabel and Frank looked just as put out, but Regina, having kept a strict regimen despite Ogre Company's lackluster discipline, was keen and alert. A goblin bugler was also present. The little fellow slept, sprawled out across the hard cobblestones. Ned wanted to lie down beside him.

He noticed Gabel's severely bruised condition. His left forearm was tightly bandaged, and he used a long mace as a walking stick.

"What happened to you?" asked Ned.

"I tripped," said Gabel.

"Must've been some fall," said Ned.

"I've had worse, sir."

"Shall we get started, sir?" asked Regina.

Ned nodded.

Regina kicked the snoozing goblin awake. The bugler sat up, rubbed his eyes, yawned. He remained sitting as he put the bugle to his lips and blew the call for morning assembly. He completed the tune in three minutes, then immediately went back to sleep.

The courtyard was empty.

Regina prodded the slumbering bugler again. He turned heavy eyelids in her direction.

"Sound the call," she commanded.

"Again?"

She picked him up by his long ears.

"All right, all right." He blew into his bugle once more. Again, after the call was finished the courtyard remained empty.

Ned ordered the call sounded over and over again. Twenty minutes later, soldiers began to show. None seemed any happier to be there than Ned did. It was forty-five minutes from the arrival of the first soldier to the last, but eventually the courtyard was filled with drowsy, grumpy personnel. Most hadn't gotten properly dressed, and while it was true ogres were formidable creatures, it was hard to take them seriously in their underwear. The soldiers hadn't managed a correct formation of rank and file, and were milling about in a griping mob.

"Sound the call to attention," Ned told the bugler.

The goblin put the instrument to his lips, but after a pause he lowered it. "What's that sound like? I forget."

Ned strained his memory. It'd been a while since he'd heard it himself. "I think it goes da-da-da-dum, da-dum, da-dum, dum-dum-da-dee."

"Begging your pardon, sir, but that's the dismissal song," said Frank. "Call to attention has more pep. Da-dee-da-dee, dum-dum-dee-dum, dee-dee, I believe."

"I thought it was more like dee-dee-dee-dee, dum-dum-dee-, dee-dee-doh," said Gabel.

"You're both wrong," countered Regina. "It's dum-dum-dee-dee, dum-dum-dee-dum."

"That's the orcish wedding march," said Gabel. "Call to attention has more *ooomphh*."

"What's *ooomphh*?" asked Frank.

"It's half the pep," said Gabel, "and about three-quarters more pizzazz."

"There's no pizzazz in the call to attention," said Regina, "and if you ask me, he's already overdoing the pep."

The insulted bugler balked. "My pep is always dead-on, I'll have you know. My pizzazz is nearly perfect. I'll grant you my *ooomphh* isn't always on target, but I'd say a touch more *shebang* and a healthy dose of *zing* is what's required here. I could throw in a little *wawawa* as well. That never hurts."

"There's no place for *wawawa* in legitimate military music," said Regina.

"Yes," agreed Gabel. "Just stick with the *ooomphh*."

"No *shebang* either?" said the bugler.

"I guess you could put in a little *shebang*," said Gabel, "but if I even hear one note of *wawawa* I'll have you thrown in the brig."

Though small, the bugler's slight chest was mostly lungs, and he unleashed a long blast of musical improvisation. The discordant tune filled the citadel. The orcs and goblins nodded along appreciatively, while everyone else covered their ears. The powerful sound floated all the way to the roc pens where the giant birds proceeded to tear at each other in panicked alarm. Caught up in the performance, the bugler kept on playing until Ned gave the order to stop, and Regina yanked away his instrument.

The sweaty bugler gasped. "How was that?"

"Too much *zoop*," said Frank.

"Not enough *zing*," added Gabel.

"No *bop* at all," said Regina.

The goblin snatched back his bugle. "Everybody's a critic."

Ned surveyed his company. Half wore snarls on their haggard faces. The other half grimaced. The worst soldier here could kill him, and he knew it. Any ogre could crush his skull in one hand. Any orc or human could run cold steel through his heart. Even the lowliest, most clumsy, drunken goblin armed with a frozen sturgeon and enough incentive could pose a serious danger. He'd already died once beneath the spoiled flounder of a pissed-off gnome, and to go like that again would just be embarrassing. But he'd grown accustomed to embarrassment, particularly in death, so he ignored the sea of murderous eyes.

He wasn't a good speaker, and opening his mouth would only get him in trouble. He was only too happy to delegate the morning address to someone else and just stand aside, doing his damnedest to appear commanding. Mostly he stared at his boots and avoided the seething gazes of his lethal band.

Gabel stepped forward. He passed his eyes over the company with undisguised contempt for a full minute. Then he started shouting.

"For far too long, Ogre Company has suffered from lax discipline! No more! Brute's Legion is the greatest freelance army in three continents, and you, each of you, are a member of that army! It is time for us, for all of us, to take that responsibility seriously! Your wages come with certain expectations! Starting today, you will meet those expectations! No, you shall exceed them! You will wake up at sunrise! You will train! You will sweat and you will scream and you will push yourselves to your physical and mental limits until you have nothing left to give! You'll have blisters on your eyeballs and scars under your fingernails when Ned's through with you!" His voice dropped to a softer roar. "You'll beg for his mercy, but he'll give you nothing but the heel of his boot!"

Ned began to wish he'd asked to check Gabel's speech beforehand. It was too late to interrupt now, but he tried clearing his throat to let Gabel know he should tone it down. Gabel was too absorbed in his own shouting to notice.

"You are all worthless! Worthless, fat, and lazy! Stupid and worthless and fat and lazy and pathetic! Commander Ned will have no more of that! He will see you molded into the finest fighting unit in this army! Many of you won't make it! In fact, I daresay some of you will perish in the process! And the survivors will envy those lucky dead bastards!"

Ned inwardly winced. He was beginning to envy the dead himself. More so than usual. He cleared his throat again, but Gabel paid no mind.

"And in the end you will hate Commander Ned! You will despise him as no other man! Because he despises you! He is revolted by your weakness, your ineptitude, your pathetic natures! You sicken him! Every man here fills him with gut-churning disgust! It's all he can do to not vomit at the merest sight of you!"

Gabel followed this up with a long string of varied and colorful insights. He made sure to include traditional slurs of every race present. He belittled the ogres' love of their mothers and the orcs' ability to urinate at a distance. He assaulted the humans' lack of efficient government, the goblins' talent for dying pointlessly. He even threw in a few offhand remarks about shrunken genitalia, which greatly annoyed the few elves in the company. After about two minutes, Ned ran over and finally cut Gabel's speech short. "Thank you. That's quite enough."

"Yes, sir." Gabel saluted. "Just trying to instill a little respect in these disgraceful cretins, these utterly useless slobs!"

A single audible growl rose from the entire company. It echoed through the courtyard, boring its way into Ned's thumping chest. The Red Woman was going to be very busy the next few days. He retreated to Frank's side. The huge ogre was where he felt safest, although even Frank couldn't hold off the entire enraged company.

At the front of the mob, gravedigger Ralph raised his hand. Gabel stalked forward, and the short orc shouted into Ralph's navel, as close as he could get to the ogre's face.

"Excuse me, private! Did I ask you for your opinion? Did our hard-ass, cruel commander give you the indication that he actually cared what you thought, that he gave a damn for any measly, worthless ideas running through that thick skull of yours? Because I can assure you, he does not!"

Ned stepped forward and pushed Gabel politely aside.

"Yes, private?" Ned asked. "What is it?"

"I think that training would be a waste of time, sir."

"You would, lazy maggot!" bellowed Gabel.

Ned pulled Gabel aside and whispered. "Thank you, officer. Good work. I'll handle the rest of it."

Gabel saluted and took his place in line with the other ranking officers.

"Very subtle," mumbled Frank. "Why don't you just stuff him with candy, hang him by his ankles, and give the company ax handles?"

"I don't know what you're talking about." Gabel chortled. "I'm just doing my job."

Ned smiled as widely as possible. "Please continue, private."

"I'm not saying the others couldn't use some exercise. But ogres don't really need to train. We're already better than everyone else."

The ogres grunted their agreement while the non-ogres muttered their disapproval.

A scarred orc at the front of the line spat. "What makes you think you're better than me?"

Ralph chuckled. "Oh, come on. It's obvious, isn't it?"

A goblin said, "Just because you're bigger than us, doesn't make you a better soldier."

A human in the crowd shouted. "What a load of drakeshit! You ogres are so full of yourselves! It makes me sick! Your skin isn't thick enough to repel a spear point. Especially when I thrust it up your ass!"

"Big talk from a brittle-boned runt!" shouted back an ogre.

Waves of hostility rose from the mob. While Ned appreciated that the rage was no longer directed at him, he didn't like where this was heading.

"Everybody knows that one ogre is worth fifteen humans on the battlefield!" said an ogre.

"Twenty-five is more like it!" added another.

"And ten orcs!" said Ralph. "And fifty goblins!"

A contingent of goblins approached him. Ned recognized Seamus the shapeshifter at their head.

"Now just hold on one minute there," said Seamus. "There's more to being a good soldier than size."

Ralph grabbed Seamus in one hand. "I've got fleas on my ass bigger than you."

Ned called on his sternest commanding tone. "There's no need for that kind of talk, private."

From somewhere in the middle of the mob, Elmer the treefolk shouted, "Ogres, orcs, goblins, bah! You're all just fleshies!"

"At least we can sit by a campfire!" shouted someone else.

Ned screamed at the top of his lungs. "Everyone, shut up!"

Much to his surprise, the company fell quiet.

A few awkward moments later, Ralph spoke up. "I'm just telling the truth." He smirked at Seamus, still clutched in his hand. "Tough for them if they can't take it."

"The problem with being the biggest," said Seamus, as he sucked in a deep breath, "is that there's always someone bigger."

A flash of red smoke exploded around him and Ralph. The cloud dispersed to reveal a twelve-foot-tall cyclops with bulging muscles, and fists the size of an ogre's thighs. Seamus held Ralph in the air by one arm.

Ralph gulped. "I didn't know you could become something that large."

Seamus spoke with the booming resonance of his new form. "I'll be sore as hell in fifteen minutes." He cocked back his massive fist. "But I won't be the only one."

Seamus threw a powerful uppercut, and Ralph sailed into the mob. Even before Ralph hit the ground, several ogres had tackled Seamus. He staggered back into the crowd, colliding with soldiers all about him. A fat orc tumbled, accidentally butting skulls with a tall elf. The elf crumpled to the ground, but not before smacking a goblin with a flailing limb. The goblin, in undirected retribution, sank his sharp teeth into a troll's thigh. Several other goblins, impelled by species loyalty, pounced on the yelping troll, who staggered about in a howling whirl. In his attempts to lose the snapping pests, he wound his way through the crowd, striking down anyone close. Soon a tidal wave of rage ricocheted through the mob, and within scant seconds the brawl was in full swing.

"At ease, men!" shouted Ned.

The furious roar swallowed up his orders, but even if he'd been heard, he'd have been ignored. This particular battle had been brewing a long, long time. It had nothing, if anything, to do with interspecies conflict. Ogre Company hadn't seen combat in many years, and five hundred irritated, restless soldiers were a fight waiting to happen.

At first the battle lines were drawn along race lines. Orcs battled humans. Humans battled goblins. Goblins battled ogres. Everyone knocked the elves around. Soon enough that fell apart, and everyone began pummeling anyone within reach. It was fortunate that no one was armed properly, or else the citadel grounds would've run red with blood. But no one fought to kill, and the only casualties were a few dozen goblins crushed underfoot, which no one gave much thought to.

After nearly having his head knocked off by a flying goblin not once, but twice, Ned gave up on order and let them have it out. He stepped a safe distance away, beside his officers.

He watched the melee with passing fascination. "That could've gone better."

Regina put a hand on his shoulder. "Look at it this way, sir. At least they're training."

"Thanks, Archmajor. That's something, I suppose."

"Please, sir," she said, "it's Regina. I insist."

He smiled at her, and she smiled back.

Frowning, Frank clenched his fists. A desire to snatch Ned up and rip off his arms and legs came to Frank. Rather than do that, he waded into the melee and proceeded to beat a path of destruction.

Ned gazed deep into Regina's dark eyes, and she into his.

She was beautiful, he suddenly realized. Before he could think anything else, he was knocked flat by a hurtling goblin bugler.

"Sorry about that, sir," apologized the bugler to his dazed commander. He put his horn to his lips, blew a charge, and dashed back into the fight.

Regina bent down on one knee to help Ned up. "Are you okay, sir?"

"I'm fine." He gazed up into her dark eyes. As his vision cleared, her beauty struck him again. She was quite stunning. He preferred redheads, but there was no denying her appeal. Especially now that she was smiling.

"Allow me, sir." She easily hoisted him to his feet, and he noticed too for the first time that she was three inches taller than he was.

"Please, Regina, call me Ned."

"If you insist, sir."

"I do."

She still held his arm. It didn't mean much to him, but it was the longest she'd held any man's arm without attempting to break it. Frank, in the midst of the brawl, deliberately hurled a goblin at Ned again, but an orc jumped on Frank's back and threw off his aim. The shrieking, green projectile arced over Ned's head and smashed into a wall. The orc soon followed.

Owens, his left arm wrapped in a splint, approached.

"How's the arm?" asked Ned.

"Not bad, sir. Only a sprain. Should be good as new by week's end."

"Sorry about that again."

"Don't worry about it, sir. Accidents happen."

"Why are you so late for morning assembly?" asked Regina.

"I didn't want to be here when the fight broke out."

"You knew about this?" asked Ned.

"I had an inkling." Owens pointed to his ear. "Heard it last night."

"You could've warned us," said Gabel.

"I meant to. Wasn't sure exactly when it would happen. And I forgot."

Ned decided the only thing worse than an oracle who couldn't see the future was an absentminded prophet.

"Do you have any idea when it'll end?" asked Ned.

"My foresight is rarely that exact," explained Owens. "Sometimes I hear a few seconds into the future. Other times it can be days or months or years. Centuries on occasion. It isn't easy to pinpoint."

How do you handle all that information? asked Ned mentally, having adapted to Owens's talent for answering unspoken questions.

"It's tricky, sir," replied Owens. "Probably why so many on the oracle project went mad. Nine out of ten ended up completely insane. The rest tended toward eccentricity. I'm fortunate enough to have avoided . . ." His voice trailed away, and a dopey grin spread across his face.

Ned waved his hands in front of Owens's milky eyes, and then realized the pointlessness of the test. He took Owens by the shoulder and shook him. Owens continued to stare dreamily. Ned turned his attention back to the melee and left Owens to sort through whatever extranormal input he was receiving.

"I guess we should break it up before someone gets seriously hurt," he said.

"Yes, sir," agreed Gabel. "Just how do you propose we do that?"

Ned studied the escalating sea of violence before him. Three hundred enraged ogres were definitely going to be trouble. Once they got through the other soldiers, he wondered if their bloodlust would abate. He didn't consider ogres stupid. Well, he didn't consider them especially stupid. Not stupider than most anyone else, although Ned had a generally poor opinion of the mean intelligence of the soldiers of Brute's Legion in specific and the civilians of the world in general.

Miriam gently nudged her way between Ned and Regina. Regina moved the smallest distance to allow the siren to pass.

"Allow me, sir," said Miriam.

"Can you handle that many men?" asked Gabel.

Miriam glanced back through half-closed eyes. The large black eyes struck Ned as surprisingly beautiful. They caught the morning light, holding it in shimmering depths. That same light glittered off her scales in a heavenly glow.

"Oh, I'm sure our dear Miriam has handled many more men than that in one sitting." Regina's voice boiled with frozen acid. Everyone noticed except Ned, who was fairly new to noticing things at all.

"We can't all despise men with such admirable inflexibility," said Miriam.

Gabel chuckled. Regina drew the dagger behind her back. An Amazon infant could hurl the blade into Miriam's exposed throat. Much more creative targets passed through Regina's mind. Before she could choose the most agonizing point to plunge her dagger, Ned moved a step to the left and put himself in harm's way. She still considered risking a throw. She was an excellent aim, and Ned would just come back again if she accidentally killed him. He'd probably be upset just the same, and her time in Brute's Legion had taught her the quality of patience. She could always kill Miriam later. She was confident of that.

The siren turned to the brawl, closed her eyes, and focused her enchanted voice. Her lips parted to send a soft hum across the courtyard. Too light to be heard, the hum vibrated in the air, and the soldiers of Ogre Company proceeded to beat the hell out of each other with subtly less enthusiasm.

She hadn't been as confident as she pretended. She'd enthralled dozens before, but never a crowd so large. There was enough hostility and frustration present to devour any weaker enchantment cast into the audience. A single missed high note or slip in concentration could blow the whole thing. She wasn't sure if she was up to it, but there was only one way to find out.

She sang. Her voice danced a delicate, crystalline melody. She wove her spell for a full minute without much effect and was ready to give up when the wind, enticed by her supernatural aria, lifted her off the ground in its loving embrace. The sun caressed her tenderly with its warm, gentle rays, while all the nearby flowers uprooted themselves and ran closer to hear her better. Spurred onward, Miriam sang louder. One by one, soldiers ceased their brawling. They lowered their fists, and wide, goofy grins spread on their faces. The same type of grin that Owens wore.

The goblins, being immune, got the chance to throw in a few cheap shots on their helpless opponents. But they quickly lost interest. It wasn't very much fun sinking teeth into the ankles of enemies who just stood there grinning. Even kicks in the crotch, dropping soldiers to their knees without removing their smiles, lost much of their satisfaction.

Ned felt the magic too, but Miriam had deliberately avoided enchanting him. She couldn't shield him from the entire spell, but he remained relatively uncharmed. He just tilted his head slightly and smiled softly, feeling quite pleasant. At the moment Miriam looked like a petite, raven-haired beauty to him—a woman he'd never met in person, who might not even exist except for a fountain statue he'd seen once. "How lovely."

Regina scowled. "I've heard better."

Ending the song would be the trickiest bit. To just stop singing would unleash the hostility all the stronger. Miriam had to dispel that aggression. She took her time disassembling it, though the strain of the enchanted song wore on her voice. It took another two minutes. Slowly, her melody trailed away, growing softer and softer. The wind set her down. The sun paid her no special attention. And the flowers grew disinterested enough to scamper back to their cracks in the cobblestones. She half expected the brawl to start up again when her voice finally gave out with a harsh crack. Instead, the soldiers stood in a residual daze.

Ned surveyed his troops. He was feeling grand, and so were they from the looks on their faces. He dismissed them while the happy feelings remained. The soldiers dispersed in a mild, yet harmless, stupor.

Miriam, no longer singing, resembled herself again, but was no less beautiful.

"Excellent work, officer."

The strain of the magic song had reduced her voice to a whisper. "Thank you, sir."

"Please, call me Ned," he said. "Could I buy you a drink?"

"I would be honored, Ned."

"The honor is all mine."

They headed toward the pub, leaving Regina, Gabel, and Frank behind. Miriam glanced over her shoulder to bat her lashes at the Amazon. The lashes were far too dark and long to belong on that scaly face, mused Regina.

"Isn't she swell?" said Frank of the siren.

"Exquisite," agreed Gabel dreamily.

"You idiots," said Regina, "you've been entranced."

"We most certainly have," said Frank.

"Entranced by such intoxicating grace and charm," said Gabel.

They both sighed wistfully.

Two passing goblins disagreed. "Aw, she's not so great," said the first.

It was nice someone still had their senses, thought Regina.

"Oh, yeah," agreed the second, "take away the magic voice and what do you got? Nothing but a sexually adventurous, exotic seductress."

"With a great ass," said the first.

"And limber too," said the second as they passed out of earshot.

Regina growled, harsh and guttural, like an angry mountain cat. She'd lost this battle, but she was determined not to lose the war. Neither her burgeoning sexual desire nor competitive Amazon training allowed for that possibility.

FiFteeN

THE IRON FORTRESS of the demon emperor Rucka was, strangely enough, made of stone. But to Rucka's ear, "Iron" carried a more ominous ring than "Stone." And as he was the most powerful demon in all the Ten Thousand Hells, there were none who cared to argue the accuracy of the title. Regardless of its erroneous name, Rucka's fortress was truly a terrifying presence. Carved from blackest obsidian, it was adorned with glittering jade battlements, and decorated with dozens of fearsome gargoyles chained to their perches to leer down upon any timorous creature below. The fortress wasn't very large as fortresses went, but its defenses were formidable, its infamy awe-inspiring, and its inhabitants unimaginable. It could also outrun every other roaming citadel and ambulant stronghold on the continent, though this was admittedly a very small group.

The Iron Fortress had only lost once, being soundly outpaced by a galloping cottage. The loss bothered Rucka's pride, and if he should ever set his multitude of eyes upon that cottage again, he intended to see it scorched from the earth. But the cottage and its witch had wisely scampered away before he'd gotten the chance, and the demon had more important concerns than the pursuits of damaged pride. These concerns set Rucka to restlessness, and because he couldn't leave its walls, the Iron Fortress paced sympathetically.

Currently it strode with great, earthshaking stomps through a lush forest, leaving deep craters and dust clouds in its wake. Occasionally it might crush a village with casual indifference, which mattered not at all to Rucka except for the inconvenience of having to stop every other week to have the mashed peasants cleaned from between the fortress's toes.

In the meantime, he waited for news from his advance scouts that he might unleash his horde upon the earth and claim the one last thing he needed. He dallied this afternoon in his harem room, surrounded by fifty-one adoring succubi. And he gazed out the window down upon the world that he would one day see cleansed to ash. He had to stand on a stool to enjoy the view as Rucka stood exactly nineteen inches tall.

He wasn't a particularly terrifying demon at a glance. Stocky and purple with three black horns, four gray wings, four arms, and a long, long tail. He was covered in eyes, each a different shape and shade. They spread down his face, across his chest and back, running along his limbs. When Rucka blinked, his lids scraped audibly against his dry eyes, and those who knew him trembled at the sound.

"What's wrong, sweetie?" asked a dark-haired demon. She was one of his favorites, though he couldn't be bothered to remember her name. Or anyone's name. He just called his minions by whatever name struck his fancy, and should they fail to answer, he usually destroyed them for their insolence.

"Nothing."

"Come here and let Momma make it all better."

She took him in her arms, cradling him like a swollen, deformed infant to her ample, heaving bosom. This particular succubus had a talent for bosom heaving, and he smiled despite his ill humor.

"What's wrong?" She poked his tummy playfully. The red eye where his bellybutton should be blinked and watered, and Rucka chuckled.

"What is always wrong?" he replied.

"The war," cooed a blond demon who had a special talent for cooing her dialogue. "Always the war."

"But you've won, haven't you, sweetie?" asked his dark-haired favorite.

"I'm winning. I've not won."

"It's only a matter of time, my love," consoled an orange-skinned concubine.

Rucka leapt to his feet. His many eyes glared venom, and the consort tried to apologize. Before the words could come, he snapped his fingers, and she dissolved into a festering puddle.

"Time I have enough of. It's patience I find myself lacking."

His remaining consorts paused. Then the favorite spoke up.

"How many more, dear, dear master? How many more do you need?"

His glare passed over her, and he was but a gesture from destroying her when he reconsidered. Rucka had a special fondness for heaving bosoms, and she prudently heaved hers as never before.

All of his eyes burned and smoldered with hunger. Black clouds choked the air of his harem chamber, and his demon lovers, accustomed to sooty air, still gagged.

"One."

Rucka flapped his wings, and the smoke blasted through the window and soared, screaming, into the atmosphere, where it devoured a flock of migrating ducks—feathers, bones, and all.

The demon king sighed. His irritation was spent for the moment, but it would return soon enough. He dropped into a mound of pillows made of the tender skin of elven nobles.

His concubines crowded around. His favorite stroked his horns and whispered sweet blasphemies in his ear to keep him calm. No one liked a rankled demon emperor, especially not his minions.

The chamber doors opened wide and several barbed imps entered, crawling on their hands and knees, their heads held low, their noses scraping the floor. Rucka was in just pleasant enough temper not to destroy them outright for their interruption.

"We beg your forgiveness, oh cursed and merciless sire."

Rucka pushed away his harem. His eyes darkened. His tiny claws dripped venom onto the bare floor. The Iron Fortress trembled painfully. "This had better be important. Your death shall be one of agony."

The imps crept aside, and an ice demon came in. He knelt low before his master, and the news he gave was of such importance that Rucka, much to everyone's surprise including his own, didn't destroy anyone. Although he did maim several imps just to stay in practice.

And the Iron Fortress ceased its aimless meandering and strode with inexorable purpose toward Copper Citadel.

Belok's fortress didn't move. It stayed firmly put atop an inaccessible mountain peak. It had seen better days. Once it'd brimmed with magical artifacts and fantastical creatures, but his curse demanded their relocation to the dark, dank basement, far from the high tower where Belok sulked.

The wizard spent a great deal of his time sulking. When he wasn't scouring the world for objects of ancient power in his vain quest to get the Red Woman to speak her secrets, he was usually sitting on his throne, drinking wine and moping. He liked to think of himself as brooding sinisterly, but more accurately, he pouted.

He was very good at it. Like many powerful wizards, he had a great deal in common with spoiled children. He could focus his inflated sense of entitlement into a sulk so heavy and impenetrable not even light could escape its surface, and time could barely seep its way out around the edges. He could waste weeks in one of these moods, though to the outside world it might appear only minutes. But even the ill temper of wizards had its limits, and eventually it would pass.

The darkness brightened, and Belok noticed a vermilion raven perched on his windowsill. The wizard didn't get up, but he was surprised. The Red Woman had never before paid him a visit.

"Come to taunt me, have you?" he asked.

There was no reply. He glanced around the room, but he didn't see a hint of the sorceress. Even if she were invisible, he would've sensed her presence in his inner sanctum. He turned his head in the raven's direction.

"Where is she?"

The bird raised its wings in a shrug. "This doesn't concern her. This is business between us. I'm here to apply for a job."

"Don't you already have one?"

The raven ruffled his feathers. "Frankly, I'm a little bored with it. It's not much fun being her familiar. All she does is mix potions and restore idiots to life—and walk. And walk. She doesn't just teleport anywhere. It's always a walk. Even if her magic makes everything a ten-minute journey, it's still a bit tiresome."

Belok studied the raven, but it was difficult to read a bird's face. Even for a wizard. "You want to be my familiar?"

"Why not? You've got style, at least. And you don't walk a lot, do you?"

"No. Not much. But I already have familiars."

His ghostly maidens became visible by his side. They poured Belok another glass of wine and cooed in his ear.

"Spirits aren't proper familiars," said the raven, "and while I can't caress you, I'd be infinitely more useful."

Two of the ghosts floated forward and hissed.

"We ravens don't fear spirits. We show them the way from the netherworld, and when they annoy us, we snatch them in our talons and send them back."

The bird cawed, and the maidens dissolved into two piles of phantom bones on the floor. The raven chuckled. "I told you spirits aren't worth much."

Belok pushed away his paramours. "Why should I believe you?"

"Why shouldn't you? But I can offer you a good-faith gesture. I can tell you where he is."

Belok scanned the raven's face but found nothing to confirm or dispel any suspicions. He was suspicious by nature, but he was also offered the one piece of information he desired more than anything.

"If this is a trick—"

"Why would I bother to trick you? What would I have to gain? He's in a place called Copper Citadel. It's in the Eastlands. I'm sure a powerful wizard such as yourself doesn't need directions. Go and see for yourself. What do you have to lose?" The raven turned back to the window. "I'll be in touch."

He flew away. At the foot of Belok's mountain, he perched atop the Red Woman's staff.

"I don't know if he believed me."

"He doesn't have to believe you," said the Red Woman. "His desire for revenge will lead him to investigate regardless."

"I don't see why you just didn't tell him yourself," said the raven.

"He would've suspected something."

"I thought you said it wouldn't matter if he suspected something."

"It wouldn't. But I just wasn't in the mood to deal with him."

"Why are you sending him after Ned now anyway?" asked the raven.

"Because it's time."

"Time for what?"

"I'm not certain." She smiled. "But it's time for something."

She turned and started back to her mountain.

"Can't we just teleport?"

"Oh, but it's such a nice night for a walk."

The raven sighed.

sixteen

REGINA STOOD IN one dark corner, studying Miriam at the opposite end of the pub. The siren stood brazenly beside Ned. Occasionally he'd say something Regina couldn't hear over the crowd, and Miriam would laugh as if he'd just pronounced the most marvelously entertaining utterance. She'd put a hand on his shoulder and sometimes "accidentally" brush her breasts against his arm. It was disgusting. And Ned seemed to be falling for it. He was an idiot and a fool. Like all men. Unworthy of Regina's affections.

The more she despised him, the less he seemed to notice her and the more she wanted him. And she would have him. She knew it well enough. She just had to get rid of the damned siren.

Regina's eyes strayed to the table. For the past ten minutes, unaware, she'd been gouging her dagger into the wood. Ugly gashes tore deep into the planks, almost coming out the bottom.

Ulga the chubby elf conjurer and Sally the salamander passed near the table. Regina grabbed the elf by the arm.

"Ma'am?" asked Ulga.

"You must hate men," said Regina.

Ulga's pink eyes narrowed. "Beggin' your pardon, ma'am?"

"Well, look at you."

Ulga did indeed look herself over. "Yes, ma'am?"

"You're fat."

"I do got a few extra pounds on me, ma'am."

"So men must treat you very poorly."

"Some," admitted Ulga. "But others do enjoy the extra portions." She made a show of adjusting her bountiful chest.

"You don't hate men?" asked Regina.

Ulga shook her head. Regina released her and took up her table carving again.

"Something troubling you, ma'am?" asked Ulga.

Regina missed the question, obsessed with watching Miriam blatantly rubbing Ned's shoulders.

"I wouldn't let it trouble you none, ma'am." Ulga sat at the table. "Ain't met a man worth dying over yet."

Regina quite agreed. No man was worth dying over. But she was beginning to think some just might be worth killing over.

Sally slipped into the chair next to Ulga. The reptile put her elbows on the table, and it smoldered. "I can't say I understand these human mating rituals. Far too much conflict. We salamanders resolved that problem long ago."

"How so?" asked Ulga.

"It all goes by length. The longest female in the village gets the first pick of any male she wishes. Then the second longest. Then the third. And so on and so on until everyone is paired off. No arguments that way."

"But what if the male doesn't like who picked him?" asked Ulga.

"No one asks him. Salamander males are drones. They have no drives other than to eat, defecate, and procreate.

They can't even speak properly or bathe themselves. Like stupid children. Or clever dogs."

"Sounds like every male I've ever met," muttered Regina.

"They must be very dull company," remarked Ulga.

"Yes, but it's for the best," said Sally. "After all, if they were smarter, it would only make it more disconcerting to eat them."

A portion of Regina's attention drew away from Ned and Miriam, though her eyes remained locked on the pair. "You eat your mates?"

"What else are you going to do with them once you're finished?" Sally snorted a fireball. "Good gods! Otherwise they just crap all over the place and chew on the furniture. My sister kept one mate around for a few years, and it was a devil of a time getting him housebroken. And she had him declawed, which I always felt was inhumane." She took a sip of beer, which bubbled and steamed as it touched her lips. "Much nicer to just bite their heads off before you get sick of them."

Regina and Ulga grinned.

"You might have a point there," agreed Ulga.

Seamus the goblin approached the table. "Mind if I have a seat?"

"Ladies only," said Ulga.

"No problem." With a burst of pink smoke, he shifted into a feminine form. Since goblin females resembled goblin males almost exactly, save for larger eyes, fuller lips, and smaller ears, Seamus looked nearly identical to her old shape. The most noticeable change was the loss of her beard.

"Isn't that uncomfortable?" asked Ulga.

Seamus pulled up a chair. Her voice was now an octave squeakier. "Naw. This is just going from outie to innie. Now if you want to talk about tough shapes, try becoming a dictionary sometimes. After 'aardvark,' I'm nothing but blank pages. So what are we ladies talking about?"

"Men," said Sally.

"Who needs 'em?" Seamus raised her glass. "Am I right or am I right?"

Chuckling, they banged their drinks together.

"Of course, goblin society sidestepped that whole mess," said Seamus.

"I wasn't aware goblins had a society," remarked Ulga.

"We don't. That's how we avoided it." The goblin raised her glass again. "Am I right or am I right?"

No one bothered to toast this time. They shared inconsequential chatter for a few minutes as Regina continued her single-minded surveillance.

"I say if he doesn't want you, he isn't worth your time," consoled Ulga.

"Yeah," agreed Seamus, "especially since you can't really compete against Miriam anyway."

Ulga smacked the goblin on the back of her head hard enough to leave a slight bruise.

"Hey, we were all thinking it," said Seamus. "I just had the guts to say it."

This time Sally slapped the goblin across the pate, leaving another bruise and a minor burn.

"That's outie talk," said Sally.

"It's the truth, isn't it? She's a siren. They have powers over men. What's the archmajor got?"

They thought about this for a moment.

"She's a mammal," said Sally. "That should count for something."

"Aren't sirens mammals too?" asked Seamus. "Like dolphins?"

"I'm pretty sure they're amphibians." Ulga pointed to a spot behind her own ear. "They've got gills after all."

Seamus put down her ale. "As a male most of the time I think I've got the best perspective here. And I'm telling you it doesn't matter whether she's fish or fowl when the lights go out."

Sally hissed and turned a sickened green shade. "Maybe it wouldn't be so hard to bite off your head."

"We all know what Regina has to do if she's going to win Ned. She's got to employ her Amazon strengths." Seamus winked, not once but twice. "Shouldn't be too hard to put the siren down. I've never seen her pick up a sword."

Miriam and Ned shared another boisterous guffaw. Regina pulled her dagger from the table and stood. She was ten leaping paces away from plunging the blade into Miriam's face.

Ulga grabbed the Amazon by the elbow. "Hold on there, ma'am. You don't want to do that."

"I don't?"

"No, ma'am. You can't kill a siren. I hear tell that when they sing their death rattle, their slayer dies with them."

"That shouldn't be a problem," said Sally. "The archmajor is a woman, and siren songs have no effect on females."

"You willing to take that chance?" asked Seamus.

Regina cut off two strips from her skirt and stuffed them in her ears. She tried to take another step, but Ulga held tight. The elf was stronger than she appeared.

"Beggin' your pardon, ma'am, but I don't think you should."

Regina pulled the plugs from her ears. "What?"

"This goes against the rules of courtship," said Ulga.

"There are rules?" asked Sally.

"Yes, and unlike salamanders, it's not as simple as who's tallest."

"Sounds needlessly complicated," said Sally.

"It can be tricky," agreed Ulga, "but it's the way it's done among us mammals."

Sally's long ears flattened. "And yet my species is the one that's nearly extinct."

"Seduction is like war," said Ulga. "And war has its rules."

Seamus laughed. "War doesn't have rules."

"Everything has rules. The trick is to know which rules you can ignore, and which you can't." She pulled Regina back into her chair. "Let us help you, ma'am."

"You'd help me?" she asked, eyes wide.

"Sure," said Ulga. "I never much cared for that blasted siren."

"Nor I," seconded Sally. "Besides, it will be interesting to get a closer look at how you mammals do this."

"I'm in," said Seamus.

Sally lowered her head to stare into the goblin's eyes. "No one invited you."

"Hey, it's a girls-only project. And you can't be picky where you get your girls around here, or you aren't going to get many."

The salamander and the elf exchanged skeptical glances. Finally Ulga said, "All right. But you stay a female for the duration of the project."

"Deal." Seamus frowned and wiggled in her chair. "Guess I'm going to have to buy some new underwear."

Regina was taken aback. Despite the bonds of feminine sisterhood, she'd never felt close to any of the women in the company. Even in the Amazon army, she'd been very much a loner. That shock, more than any other reason, was enough to cool her murderous rage.

Across the pub, Frank stood in a darker corner. He watched Regina watching Ned. And Frank wasn't happy about it.

Gabel occupied a stool beside the ogre. "I wonder what she sees in him," he said.

Frank grunted.

"I bet she'd notice you if he were gone," said Gabel.

"I know what you're doing, Gabel, but I'm not going to kill him."

Gabel's eyes widened. "Heaven forbid. I wouldn't suggest anything of the sort."

Frank ground his teeth. The noise was enough to smother nearby conversation. All the soldiers within arm's length of the very large ogre, including one ogre nearly as large, discreetly moved out of reach of his thick, bone-crushing hands. Gabel patiently waited for Frank to quiet down.

"Anyway, I don't think you could kill him," said Gabel, "even if you wanted to."

Frank glowered down at the orc. "I don't want to."

Gabel mumbled with mimicked indifference. "Why would you?"

Frank took a long drink. As a boy, he'd chewed glass

whenever nervous or upset or bothered. He'd broken the habit years ago, but tonight he ran his tongue along the mug and scraped his teeth along its edges.

"She's not thinking clearly," said Gabel. "Maybe Ned's mesmerized her. That would explain it, wouldn't it?"

Frank clenched his fist. He closed his jaws, and a hairline crack split down the mug. Beer dribbled down his chin.

"He can't mesmerize anyone," said Frank.

"I would think a secret wizard could do all sorts of unnatural things."

Frank wiped his chin. "I thought you didn't believe in secret wizards."

"I don't. Not really. But sometimes things happen. Strange things without any reasonable explanation. It just makes me wonder. Maybe there really are secret wizards. And if there are, I wouldn't put it above such duplicitous sorcerers to use their powers for so base and vile a purpose."

Frank sucked in a deep breath. "You're just saying that. You don't really believe it."

"No, not really," admitted Gabel. "But it's not like I know everything. I could be wrong. Or I could be right even if it is a ludicrous theory I don't believe myself." He waved his drink in Regina's direction, then in Ned's and back again. "But it's an absurd situation in the first place if you think about it. So maybe, when things don't make sense, the logical mind has no choice but to consider absurd alternatives."

Frank nibbled on his glass. "But it doesn't make any sense at all. If he's using magic to entrance her, why is he ignoring her?"

"Maybe he's just playing hard to get," said Gabel. "Or maybe he's just an asshole."

"He doesn't seem like an asshole."

"He doesn't seem like a secret wizard either. But you can't always rely on first impressions when it comes to secret wizards." Gabel grinned. "Or assholes."

With a disgusted snort, Frank chucked his entire mug in his mouth. He crushed the glass between his powerful jaws.

Gabel jumped onto his stool and reached up to pat Frank's

shoulder. "Oh, what difference does it make? Secret wizard, asshole, whatever else he might be. We can't kill Ned until we all agree, and even if you and I know it's the best thing to do, we can be assured Regina won't. Maybe she's be-witched. Maybe she's just got bad taste. I guess that's just the way it is."

Frank swallowed loudly. He ran his shard-studded tongue across his blistered lips. "Yeah. Guess so."

"We are honorable soldiers after all. Without that, what are we?" Gabel nodded to Regina. "Shame though. You might have a shot at her otherwise."

"You really think so?"

"Who's to say? Big, handsome ogre such as yourself and a mighty Amazon warrior. I've seen stranger things."

Across the pub, Ned and Miriam shared a chuckle. Regina glowered while twisting her dagger into the table. And Frank, with a contemplative frown, tucked the mug into his left cheek and chewed.

seventeen

NED HAD HOPED TO get training under way immediately, but his better judgment said it would be wiser to wait one more day. The company needed time to adjust to their new schedule. But by morning they'd be up and ready to forge themselves into a dedicated, organized fighting unit as battle-worthy as any in the Legion. That was what Ned told himself anyway, and he chose to believe it despite his cynical nature.

He wasted the rest of the morning in the pub, sharing drinks with Miriam. He didn't drink much. Not much for him. He'd set aside the joy of warm inebriation for the time being, but he hadn't given up the pleasures of a nice mug of watered-down mead.

Miriam had a nice smile and an easygoing appeal, and once he'd gotten used to her more aquatic features, he had to admit she was surprisingly lovely. It was probably her natural siren powers on his groggy perceptions on this early morn, but she was quite charming. And while he preferred redheads and didn't like the taste of fish, once or twice he recalled what she'd looked like naked, and he wasn't repulsed by the idea of seeing her that way again. It didn't hurt that the crowded pub kept forcing her to press her breasts and hips against him. The clumsiness of ogres in tight quarters surprised Ned. It didn't seem like three minutes could pass without some oaf brushing against her, sending her squeezing against him.

She'd apologize each time with a playful smile on her lips. Lips that were full and moist and probably not nearly as fishy-tasting as he dimly recalled, and even if they were, was that such a bad thing? He definitely would've considered bedding her again under different circumstances, but he was commander. He'd made a mental list of things he couldn't do anymore. Though he hadn't bothered to prioritize that list, fraternization had to be somewhere near the top.

He'd never been good at self-discipline, which was just one of the reasons he'd been a poor soldier. But it wasn't hard to abstain when female personnel were sparse and most of his command consisted of hairy ogres, brutish orcs, malodorous trolls, and reckless goblins. Ogresses were even hairier than the males of the species, and even if he'd found that appealing, any carnal attempts would assuredly lead to a crushed pelvis. Orc females in the throes of passion were notorious biters, and he liked having all his fingers. He'd heard troll women got all drippy when aroused. He hadn't asked what that meant, but he was pretty sure he didn't want to hear the specifics. And while he liked petite women, goblins were just too short.

There were only a handful of women in the company that might tempt him. Although Ulga was nice, she was both chubby and an elf, neither of which he found endearing. Regina was beautiful, but she was an Amazon, so there was no point in considering that. Miriam was the only temptation. She had the sweetest smile and a lovely laugh and an enchanting figure and splendid grace, but she was also a fish. That was a lot to get around.

It wasn't a tremendous obstacle. He'd hated the taste of

broccoli once, and he'd gotten over that. And Miriam was infinitely more tempting. But he was commander. He kept reminding himself, and for now, it was enough. It wasn't a dilemma anyway. He couldn't imagine that Miriam was actually interested in him. She was just being friendly. It was her job as morale officer. The rest was merely siren charm and wishful thinking. Still, every time she touched his arm or laughed at one of his weak jokes or batted those big, black eyes at him, he couldn't help but wonder. He might've even pursued it, despite his determination not to, except he had other things he needed to do.

He finished his mead and excused himself. "Company business," he explained vaguely, and Miriam seemed satisfied to leave it at that. He walked across the pub, stopping before Frank and Gabel.

"Can I speak to you a minute, Lieutenant?" asked Ned of the ogre.

"What about, sir?" said Frank, crunching some silverware between his teeth. The pub staff had stopped bringing over mugs after he'd devoured his fifth.

"It's a private matter." Ned walked away, and Frank, casting a suspicious backward glance at Gabel, followed. Ned led Frank out of the pub to a quieter section of the courtyard where no one else was listening.

"I need your help," said Ned.

"Yes, sir?"

Ned leaned forward. "I can't fight."

"Sir?" Frank squinted skeptically. Maybe Gabel had been right. Maybe Ned was playing some sort of mind game.

"I can fight," Ned continued. "But not very well." He grimaced. No point in denying it. "Not well at all." He shrugged. It wasn't so hard to say after all. It felt almost freeing to admit aloud.

"I don't understand, sir," said Frank.

"I need a tutor. A war tutor."

Frank's skepticism waned but lingered. "You're commander, sir. You don't need to know how to fight."

"But I should be able to," said Ned. "At least a little bit. I want to set a good example for the staff."

"You do?"

"Yes. Shouldn't I?"

Certainly, you should, agreed Frank silently. But he'd never met a commander yet who followed this philosophy.

"I thought I might train with the rest of the soldiers," said Ned. "But I was hoping to get some pointers first. I don't mind looking like an idiot, but I'd like not to look like a complete incompetent."

"Why me, sir?" asked Frank.

"It was you, Regina, or Gabel. I was going to ask Regina first, but she's gone off somewhere. And Gabel isn't in the best of shape right now. I trust I can count on your discretion."

If this was some sort of trick, Frank couldn't think what it might accomplish. And Frank, despite himself, found himself liking Ned. It took a strong character to admit one's faults and an even stronger character to try and improve them when one didn't have to. Thinking on it, Frank had never seen any of the previous commanders demonstrate the slightest degree of martial prowess. They'd all been too busy barking orders and strutting around.

"Will you help me?" asked Ned.

Frank saluted. "When do you want to get started, sir?"

Ned decided there was no time like the present, but his embarrassment kept him from wanting to train in the open. Copper Citadel had a private garden set aside for its commander's use. No one had tended it in some time, and it was a sorry sight. Half the plants were overgrown, the other half dead or dying. Ned hadn't chosen it for aesthetics, but for its high walls and enough open space for sparring.

"How should we start?" he asked.

"Always start with the basics," said Frank. "Come at me. Let's see what you've got, sir."

Ned already knew what he had. Or didn't have. And he knew that he didn't stand a chance against a small ogre, much less one Frank's size.

"Should I use my sword?" asked Ned.

"If you want."

"I don't know if I should. I don't want to hurt you."

Smiling, Frank shook his head. "You won't, sir."

"I might."

"Then come at me without the sword if you think that's safer," said Frank.

Ned hesitated. On the one hand, he wasn't much of a threat to ogres without some sort of weapon. On the other, he'd hate to wound Frank. He didn't expect to. Not on purpose. But accidents happened.

"Whenever you're ready, sir."

Ned drew his sword, but the sharpened edges put him off. He wasn't a good fighter, but he considered himself unlucky, almost supernaturally so. The one time he wouldn't want to kill someone would very likely be the one time he did. He put the sword away and instead picked up a heavy limb fallen from a half-dead tree. It was thick enough to inspire confidence without posing much danger to Frank. Ogres were notoriously thick-skinned. Pointed things might kill them, but most maces and warhammers just bounced off.

Ned raised his club over his head. He took a step forward, but Frank made no move to defend himself.

"Uh, I'm starting," said Ned.

"I noticed." But Frank remained in a perfectly relaxed posture.

Ned took another step. "Here I come."

"Yes, sir. Although I would point out that in a real battle it's unwise to announce your attack beforehand."

"I know that." Ned lowered his club. It was heavier than it looked, and he took a second to rest his arms. "Okay. Now I'm ready."

Frank, hands behind his back, said nothing. Ned charged with a primal scream. He whipped the club up high, aiming a blow at Frank's head, but reaching only as high as the ogre's shoulder. Frank blocked with his forearm, and the club cracked in two. The force rattled Ned's hands. He dropped the club and staggered off balance. Frank extended his index finger and pushed Ned over. He landed on his butt with an embarrassing thud.

"Not very good," said Frank. "But not entirely bad."

Ned remained sitting. "It wasn't?"

"Not at all, sir." Frank rubbed his forearm. "I felt that. So you've got some power. Of course, your offense is weak, and your defense is nonexistent. But no one is born knowing how to fight properly." He pulled Ned to his feet. "Let's try again, shall we? Use your sword this time."

Ned rushed Frank. He aimed his blade at his opponent's side, hoping to score a glancing blow for the sake of his pride. Frank simply knocked Ned aside again. It happened so fast, Ned couldn't say how.

Somebody laughed.

Ned glanced around. "Who's there?"

Elmer stepped forward. The short treefolk had blended in among the trees.

"How much did you see?" asked Ned.

"Enough to know you need a lot of work"—Elmer struck a match against his side and lit a cigarette—"and that this ogre isn't going to be much help."

"What do you mean by that?" said Frank.

"It's just a fact." Elmer blew a gray cloud that hovered over Ned's head. "Ogres fight like ogres. Which is fine if you're an ogre. But in case you didn't notice, Ned is a human. And he needs to learn to fight like one."

"I was going to ask Regina," said Ned.

Elmer chuckled. "She wouldn't do you much good either. Amazons aren't human."

"They aren't?"

"No. They're grown in melon patches. Or possibly carved from enchanted stone. Either way, they aren't human. Can't teach a human how to fight."

Easily discouraged, Ned saw Elmer's point.

"I've seen enough humans fight to understand the rudimentary concept," said Frank.

"Such as?" asked Elmer.

Frank paused to think about it. "Well, there's a lot of screaming. And squishing. They're very squishy."

"So as far as your experience goes, the basic technique of human warfare is to scream and be squished."

Frank frowned. "Squishing avoidance was the first thing I planned on teaching Ned."

"And then what?" asked Elmer. "The finer talent of crushing one's opponents beneath tree trunks? When is the last time you even picked up a sword?"

"Just last week. I used it to pick my teeth."

Ace, who'd been perched silently on the garden wall for the entire conversation, finally spoke up. "Squishing avoidance is a lot harder than it looks. Take it from an expert."

So much for his private training session, realized Ned.

"Oh, please. What can a goblin teach about fighting?" asked Elmer.

"Fighting? Not much," admitted Ace. "But I'm three years old. I think I know a thing or two about survival."

It was true that the average goblin's life span was measured in months, not years, and that Ace's old age was an excellent recommendation.

"When it comes to the art of war, no fleshie matches the prowess of the plant world. Take a look at this garden." Elmer swept his arms wide. "All around is a constant battle. The rosebushes struggle against the ivy. The ivy strangles the flower beds. Nature is in a constant conflict, and only the smartest, most persistent flora wins."

"Ned is not a plant," said Frank.

"He isn't an ogre either," replied Elmer. "Or a goblin."

Ace hopped off the wall and onto Frank's shoulder. "That doesn't mean a goblin can't teach him a thing or two."

"Or an ogre," said Frank.

"Or a treefolk," said Elmer.

"It's agreed then," said Ace. "We'll take turns tutoring him."

They shook hands on it. Ned wasn't entirely sure it was a

good idea, but since no one bothered to ask him, he decided to go along. What was the worst that could happen?

A little under an hour later, his three tutors stood over Ned's corpse splayed on the ground. His crushed limbs with their shattered bones bent in unnatural angles.

Ace lit up his pipe and exhaled a putrid yellow cloud. "I told you squashing avoidance was harder than it looked."

EiGHTEEN

NED'S TUTORS DECIDED that it would be better to leave Ned in the garden. He'd wanted his training to be secret, and trying to sneak his corpse back to his quarters seemed like more trouble than it was worth. If they were caught (which they probably wouldn't be) and if someone cared enough to ask for the details (even more unlikely) a story would have to be invented as to how Ned had perished once again, and no one wanted to bother. Neither did they wish to wait for Ned to rise from the dead. So he was thrown into an overgrown flower bed and left for his latest resurrection. And there he stayed, quietly enjoying the agreeable state of death.

Birds descended on Copper Citadel at early evening. Flamingos and ibises, robins and red bishops, peacocks and finches, seagulls and drongos, figbirds and buntings, shrikes and woodpeckers, and a single bony ostrich. They covered the citadel like a fog. Not one soldier could remember seeing them arrive, but there they were. And every bird, regardless of species, was as bright red as fresh-spilled blood and deathly silent.

The soldiers whispered about dark powers at play, and gravedigger Ward had to stop up his nostrils to hold back the overpowering stench of magic. Aside from this, none gave it much thought. In Copper Citadel, everything was always someone else's problem, and everyone left it for someone else to handle. "Let Ned deal with it," was heard more than once, to which others nearby would nod their heads and get on with their business. Only Gabel paid special notice to the birds, and that was only long enough to fill out a Suspected Thaumaturgical Incident Report, which he dropped in his stack of outgoing mail before heading off to the pub.

The Red Woman's magic was generally a subtle art. She had little use for fearsome explosions or howling winds. Such effects were merely pandering to an audience, the realm of courtly wizards and sideshow conjurers. Spectacle was contrary to her nature and her duties. Magic both preceded and followed her, and there were always signs of her passing. Little things that only the keenest eye might spot, or the most superstitious soul might fret over. But today she was annoyed, and today her magic showed itself. Though it was her power, albeit unconsciously, that summoned the monstrous brood, she found it more bothersome than anyone else. She was grateful to find the garden mostly empty of birds except for a pudgy scarlet penguin entangled in withering grapevines.

The Red Woman circled Ned's body three times, casting only casual glances at it. He was dying far too often these days for her taste, but this wasn't the sole cause of her annoyance. More troublesome dilemmas plagued her. She prodded him in the chest with her staff.

"Get up, get up."

Groaning, he stirred to life. She walked to a bench and waited.

He rose. He glanced at the sorceress with mild interest, but said nothing as he dragged his stiff limbs to the bench and had a seat. He and the Red Woman were quiet for some

time, neither having much to say. He was every bit as annoyed with these constant deaths as she was, but neither
deigned to comment on it just yet.

After a few minutes, he stretched the last bit of stiffness
from his bad left arm and said, "Thank you."

This surprised the Red Woman, but she hid it well. "Have
you decided then that it would be better to be alive than
dead?"

He thought about it, and there was no easy answer. "Not
really. But for now, I think I'd rather be alive."

"And why is that?"

Ned thought about this and found the answer a little easier. "I don't know." It was unclear but honest.

The Red Woman reached out with her gnarled hand and
ran her fingers along the scars on Ned's neck. There was ten-
derness in the caress beneath the scratchy, pointed nails. He
was taken aback. She'd touched him before, but only briefly
and never with any hint of affection.

"I don't like you, Ned," she said quietly as her hand fell to
her side. She stood. "I don't like who you were, and I don't
care much for who you are. But I believe it is possible that
one day I might like who you will become."

Having no idea what she meant, he just nodded.

The Red Woman simultaneously hobbled and glided her
way across the garden, where she patted the scarlet penguin
on its head. "I'm going to tell you a story. It's a story about
you. Let me just say that right out. But though you won't understand much of it, I advise you to listen closely. And perhaps you'll be able to explain it to me, since even I don't
understand it all.

"Long ago, in another age of another universe, there was
a singularly powerful force of ultimate madness and boundless destructive might. This creature was unique in all the
universes, but it's easiest to just consider him a demon. But
there had never been such a demon before, and fates help us,
there shall never be another. Such was his awesome power
that every other lord of every other hell bowed before him.

There was no match for him in heavens, earth, or hells. So powerful was he that even the endless bickering of devils and demons fell away, and this supreme demon, having assembled the greatest unholy army in the memory of eternity, set his sights on casting his universe into chaos, of scorching his world to ash from the pits of the damned to the palaces of the gods."

"This is about me?" asked Ned.

"Let me finish. This demon, this Mad Void, succeeded in all these things. He did so without any trouble at all. There was some token resistance, a few minor battles here and there, a handful of heroic and futile last stands. But in the end there was never any question. The Mad Void laid low the gods, brought misery and pain to everything and everyone around him. He twisted his universe into an appalling mockery of agony and discontent. But though this had always been his goal, he found no satisfaction in the accomplishment. So in ultimate disgust he razed his universe into oblivion. Alone in the boundless darkness of his own creation, he sulked for untold millennia."

"Can't you just skip to the end?" asked the raven.

She could see he had a point. Ned's gaze wandered around the garden with a hint of boredom, but the Red Woman refused to be rushed. The story was far too important. Her staff floated across the garden and rapped him soundly on the knuckles.

"Pay attention," she commanded. "How long the Void brooded is difficult to say for time meant nothing to him, but eventually he discovered, either by design or luck, a whole other plane of existence awaiting his blessed touch. He wasted no time in invading this new universe. With even less difficulty than the last, he corrupted it, and finding himself again displeased, he destroyed it as well."

Ned rubbed his bruised fingers. "I still don't see what this has to do with me."

"You still haven't figured it out?" said the raven.

"I guess not," Ned admitted.

"Idiot, you're the Mad Void."

The Red Woman sighed. "I was saving that for the end of the story."

"Oh, a dramatic presentation is wasted on Ned," said the raven. "He's too simple for that."

"Perhaps," she agreed.

They gave Ned a moment to absorb this idea, but he utterly failed. "I'm an all-powerful demon?"

"Not exactly," she replied. "That's why I was saving that bit for the end. It's less complicated that way."

"I think there's been a mistake somewhere," said Ned.

"Obviously," agreed the raven.

"But I can't be the Mad Void. I've never even heard of it."

The Red Woman laughed. "There are many things which go unheard of. But that doesn't make them any less real."

"I think I'd remember destroying universes."

She laughed again. "You would, Ned, but you're a man. Or a reasonable facsimile of a man. But the Void existed only to destroy. For him, remembering all the realities he obliterated would be as reasonable as you recalling every ant you've ever stepped upon."

He felt sick. "I don't want to hear this."

"You don't," she confirmed, "but you must. Don't judge what you once were too harshly. The Mad Void devoured universes because it was his nature. One can't blame a wolf for springing upon a helpless doe or flames for consuming a forest. These are the trials of fang and blood that all things must endure in some form or another. The death of a universe is no less tragic, yet no less necessary in a grander understanding."

"Less metaphysical," said the raven. "You're going to lose him again."

But Ned heard every word, and he didn't like any of it. The Red Woman continued.

"In due course, the Void stumbled upon our realm of existence. By then he'd grown weary of his role in the great scheme. All his destruction, his slaughter and madness, had brought him no comfort. So he did the only thing he could."

She hobbled her way to Ned's side, laying a hand on his shoulder.

"He decided to change his nature. Understand, Ned, that this was unprecedented. In the history of our universe, and I assume nearly every other as well, no demon has sought redemption. I believe they all crave it in some form, though they'd never admit it. Just one of the reasons they're so unpleasant. But the Void wasn't just a demon; he was something more. And perhaps all his success and its related weariness allowed him a glimpse of his flawed character. Perhaps all demons might benefit from scorching a universe or two."

The Red Woman's voice trailed off, and she stared off into the distance. To Ned it seemed as if she wasn't looking through the garden's walls, but piercing the veil separating universes. Probably just his imagination, but he couldn't be sure of anything anymore. She turned her dull cerise eyes on him, and she seemed to look at him and through him at the same time.

"Once the decision was made, the Mad Void realized that, powerful as he was, he would need help. He sought out a cabal of gods who'd taken on guardianship of this realm, and though their combined magic was nothing compared to his, he asked for their help. This is where the story gets rather vague, I'm afraid. Forbidden magics were invoked. Many immortals perished in these experiments. Many more sacrificed their sanity. For it was acknowledged that if the Void couldn't be changed, then inevitably his malevolent essence would be turned upon our reality, just as thousands of doomed others before."

"Thousands?" interrupted Ned.

"No one truly knows. Possibly it was only a few dozen." Her voice trembled. "Possibly tens of thousands. Or millions."

Ned wasn't very imaginative, but the notion of even one destroyed universe filled him with dread. He couldn't handle the idea of millions. How many billions upon billions had the Mad Void—had he—cast into oblivion?

"They should've destroyed me," he said.

"They tried. They transformed the Void. Don't ask me how. I don't think anyone truly understood the process. It was mostly blind luck, overpowering magic, and a happy accident. The Void's memory was suppressed. They separated him from his dreadful might, laid aside in some secret place even they couldn't find, and he was made into a man. Of sorts.

"This was when they hoped to kill him. And so they did. Unfortunately the demon's immortality was beyond godhood. To kill him was only to slay his mortal transformation. Death only returned him to his all-powerful form. Once more, great gods perished until the accident was, through sheer temerity, re-created."

"Wait a minute," said Ned. "I've been killed dozens of times. I keep coming back as me, not some raging demon."

"A technicality was discovered," she explained. "If the Void was resurrected from a source other than his own, then he remained a man. A guardian was appointed to watch over the Void. Her sole purpose in this task was to restore the demon to life with her own magic whenever necessary. It was her job to keep the cage door shut by insuring he never found the motive to open it. In this way the Void was repressed, if not truly tamed."

As Ned considered this, he studied his hands. He balled them into fists and imagined crushing worlds, then solar systems, then whole universes as if they were old parchments full of scribbles he no longer had use for.

"I suppose you're wondering why they didn't lock you up?" asked the Red Woman. "Cast you in some pit where you could be kept safe from harm, properly tended until the end of time?"

He wasn't inclined to wonder, and he still hadn't adjusted to what he'd just learned.

"They tried that too. The Void grew irritated, and when displeased, you can do appalling things."

"Like what?"

"Do you really want to know?"

"No," he replied instantly.

She smiled with some hint of affection. "If it's any consolation it was a very small continent, and no one misses it anymore."

Ned sank. He slouched, defeated, burdened suddenly by a guilt so heavy it nearly crushed him into the earth.

"I'm not happy," he said, realizing the situation. "How come I'm not destroying things now?"

She sat beside him. "You have lived a thousand lifetimes, Ned, and only in these last few have you been you. In all the others, which you do not remember, you were someone else. You've been kings and peasants, warriors and milkmaids, assassins and priests. I've been beside you the entire time. I've been at the beginning and end of each incarnation. And each was unique except for one constant. Even when surrounded by wealth and power, or peace and quiet, or any and all things a man might desire in between, they were all quietly miserable."

Ned rose. "You think I want to feel bad? I know I deserve to suffer."

"I never said that."

"But you're thinking it." He pointed at her accusingly, as if this were all her fault somehow. "I'm punishing myself for all the damage I've done. It's like some sort of penance. Endless, pointless, aching penance."

"If that's the case," she said, "then it's more a matter of what you think than I, isn't it?"

"Why did you have to tell me this?"

"You wanted to know."

"I've changed my mind."

"Too late for that. Besides, you already knew it. You've always known, deep down inside yourself. I've merely forced you to finally admit it."

"I thought you said you were joking when you said the fate of the world depended on me."

"I was. It doesn't depend on you. It depends on something inside of you."

"Can't you just erase my memory? That shouldn't be too hard."

She stood, leaning heavily on her staff as if her legs could barely support her, and put her fingers to his forehead. "It could be done, but it must be known. You must know."

Her face went blank. She hobbled away and spoke with her back to him.

"Because they're coming."

As one, the flock of crimson birds took to the air, darkening the skies over Copper Citadel. The fort became nothing but blackened shadows in the consuming gloom.

"Who?" he asked.

In the blackness the Red Woman spoke softly. "Your enemies, Ned."

"I have enemies?"

She chuckled. She waved her staff in a small circle, and the thousands of birds dispersed to the four winds, gone as if they'd never been there. Except for the penguin, who remained earthbound and had no choice but to waddle its way from the garden toward the citadel gates.

"You have had many, accumulated over a thousand lifetimes. But there are only two you need concern yourself with now. The first, most important one is a demon emperor. He comes for your power, hoping to take it for his own. Whether he has any hope of success, I couldn't say. But he is still a potent force of destruction. I shudder to think what would happen should he find a way.

"The second is a trifling matter in the greater view. His name is Belok, an old wizard of some small talent. In a previous incarnation you were a wizard too, and the pair of you got into some sort of ridiculous affair of honor. The matter ended with your death and a curse upon Belok that he struggles in vain to break. He understands something of what you are, but not enough. It could make him troublesome."

A cold wind swept across the fort. The Red Woman pulled her cloak tighter around her shoulders.

"And I do believe he has finally arrived. A touch later than I expected."

The wind died down, but the air grew frigid. Ned's breath crystallized as he spoke. "Now? He's coming now?"

The Red Woman didn't bother replying. She pointed her staff skyward, and a contingency of ghostly maidens poured from the clouds. They screeched and howled, chanting the name of their master.

"Belok! Belok! Belok!"

The Red Woman groaned. It was always such a production.

The phantoms formed a column of writhing bodies and tangled hair. Their spectral forms turned to dragons, then tigers, then serpents. They sparkled brilliantly, and Ned covered his eyes. When he could finally look, he saw a fur-faced, duck-billed wizard standing before him. His ghostly paramours caressed him tenderly as others broke away and floated absently around the garden. The plants withered and died at their touch.

Ned stood frozen. He pretended to believe it was some ghastly enchantment that held him in place, but it was nothing of the sort. Neither was it fear nor awe. It was shock, not for the wizard, but for the way everything in his life had suddenly become infinitely more incomprehensible.

"Hello, Belok," said the Red Woman.

Belok snapped his bill. "What are you doing here?"

"Just visiting."

He snapped his bill again for good measure. "What tricks are you devising, witch?"

"No tricks. Just a test."

"Come then. Test my might and die."

"I didn't say I was testing you," she replied, seating herself at the bench.

Belok turned his beady eyes on Ned. The wizard raised his hands, and boiling lava dripped from his fingertips. "Break my curse. Break it, or suffer eternally."

Ned swallowed a gulp. "I don't know anything about curses."

"Don't lie to me." The phantoms seized Ned by his collar and sleeves and carried him to their master.

"I'm not." Ned shuddered in the cold embrace of the ghosts. "I'm not a wizard. Or a demon. I'm just a man."

The Red Woman smiled.

"Your body may have changed," said Belok, "but you can't change your true nature." The phantoms carried Ned to the Red Woman and deposited him harshly at her feet. "Change him back," commanded Belok of the sorceress. "Find the wizard inside him, and change him back."

"I can't."

"Don't give me that. You're his keeper."

"Just because I keep him alive doesn't mean I can force him to do anything. The magic at work is beyond my ken. And yours. You'd do best to leave it alone."

Belok ignored the advice, as she knew he must. Just as the Mad Void couldn't change his nature, neither could the wizard.

"If you're not going to help me, step aside," he ordered.

The Red Woman waved her hand at Ned. "As long as you do not kill him, I don't care what you do to him."

Belok's phantoms snatched Ned into the air again. He struggled vainly. His hand grabbed hold of the Red Woman's staff.

"You're supposed to watch over me," he said. "It's your job."

"For heaven's sake," said the raven, "have some dignity, man." The bird pecked at the straining fingers, and Ned was tossed through the air by the malignant spirits.

"Do try and take care of yourself, Ned," said the Red Woman.

The phantoms held Ned by his ankles. Upside down, his head filling with blood, his ears thundering, and his vision blurred, he watched the Red Woman hobble from the garden, leaving him to his fate.

"I can't do anything," he said. "I don't know any magic."

Belok gestured and his phantoms raised Ned high enough to peer into the wizard's golden eyes. "It's inside you. Somewhere it's all inside of you. Everything you've ever been. If I dig deep enough, if I strip away every other false skin, I think I can find what I'm looking for." He raised a hand with blackened skin and webbed fingers and ran his sharpened nails across Ned's flesh. "I do hope this hurts."

Ned should've screamed then. He didn't. Something held him back. He still wasn't afraid.

He wasn't a man, he mused. He was the Mad Void. He was the most powerful destructive force in this or any other universe. He should be able to destroy Belok without even trying. So why didn't he? Why was he just floating there helplessly as the wizard prepared to skin him alive both physically and metaphysically?

Because he deserved it. He deserved every bit of it and more.

He could've called for help. He could've pleaded for mercy. He didn't do these things either. He just waited for his punishment. No matter how bad it was, it would never make up for what he'd done.

Belok raked his claws across Ned's forehead. Blood trickled down his scalp to drip from his hair. He winced. He cried. But he didn't cry out.

Then came the next thought. What if there had been a mistake somewhere? What if he wasn't the Void, but just Ned? What if he was paying for someone else's sins? Either way it all seemed so pointless.

"Hurting me won't solve anything," he said, surprised by his calmness.

"On the contrary," replied the wizard, "it will at least make me feel better."

The phantoms rotated Ned and planted his feet on the cobblestones but still held him tight. Belok licked the blood on his claws with a tiny purple tongue. "I may not be able to kill you, but I can do many distasteful things. Perhaps I'll start by removing your other eye. Perhaps knowing you're spending eternity in perpetual darkness would cheer me up." He moved a claw toward Ned's eye.

Ned cringed. He bit his lip in preparation for pain. Over and over the thought ran through his mind: he deserved this. At least he hoped he did. It was the only comfort he could find, and it'd be a terrible shame if a mistake had been made and the Mad Void was currently a thousand miles away enjoying a nice cup of tea.

A bolt of lightning knocked Belok away and sent his phantom entourage howling with rage.

"Who dares strike Belok?" moaned the phantoms in a musical shriek. "What fool dares clash magic against Belok?"

The Red Woman lowered her staff. "Really, Belok. Always so melodramatic." She swung the smoking staff in a few wide circles. Rumbling clouds swirled overhead. "You'd do well to get behind me, Ned."

He didn't have to be told twice.

"Are you sure you know what you're getting into?" the raven asked the Red Woman. "It's been a while since you've faced a wizard in battle."

She stamped her staff twice, and the earth rumbled. "It's like riding a horse. One never forgets."

"Have you ever ridden a horse?" said the raven.

"I don't recall."

The raven flew from her shoulder and perched on the wall. "Think I'll sit this one out over here."

Belok's golden aura darkened to a bloody copper. A small sphere of fire appeared between his outstretched hands.

"Fireballs?" The Red Woman held up her own wrinkled palm, and materialized a red and white fury. "Not very original, Belok."

"I don't waste my A material on piddling witches." Belok's flames grew larger and larger. He pitched one of his phantoms into it, and the blaze blackened, feeding on the ghost's agony as her screams darkened the air itself. The power struggled in his grasp, yet it grew larger still. As large as the wizard who'd created it. The Red Woman's fireball remained conveniently palm-sized.

"Is that all you've got to show me?" mocked Belok.

Chuckling, she balanced her magic sphere on one withered finger. Funny how most wizards, even one of Belok's experience and power, made the same mistake. They always thought it came down to who had the biggest balls.

Nineteen

AFTER LEAVING NED in the garden, Frank was invited to play a game of goblin crush. It was a favorite among those who enjoyed equal parts skill, violence, and luck in their sports. Teams of goblins were arranged on a playing field with miniature terrain. They were given equipment to emulate different military units. And then the players (or generals, as they were called) took turns maneuvering their goblins, either jockeying for the high ground, or attempting to reach a flag, or often just beating the hell out of the other army until all the soldiers on one side were eliminated or the goblins got bored and wandered off.

Goblins generally enjoyed the game. The armaments were largely symbolic, and rarely were casualties real. Although when fatal accidents happened, as they sometimes did, it was the goblins themselves who were most impressed. It took a great deal of skill to brain a thick-skulled goblin with a paper-thin wooden sword.

There were goblin crush courts in use by some royalty

that had actual miniature fortresses and rivers and simulated cities, but Copper Citadel's was an improvised affair. Barrels and plants were placed here and there. There was a high mound of rocks for a hill. It got the job done.

Frank was company champion. He rarely lost. Part of this was due to a natural talent for tactics, partly due to the generally poor skill of his opponents. But the most important part was that Frank bought the drinks for his winning army, which granted his goblins just enough incentive to fight a little better, a little longer. And it held their attention so that usually the other team was the first to wander off.

Presently he engaged Gabel in heated combat, though the game had experienced a brief timeout when all those birds had appeared. Gabel was no slouch in the game. Frank's army was pinned down behind some barrels, and he was having a devil of a time getting them out of there. He was considering his next move when Gabel observed, almost as if the thought had just occurred to him, although Frank knew better, that Ned had been curiously absent for the past few hours.

"I wonder what happened to him?" said the orc.

"Must be off somewhere," said Frank.

"Last I saw him, he was wandering away with you, wasn't he?"

Frank grunted.

"I hope he's okay," remarked Gabel.

Frank grunted again. He ordered a unit out in the open, two strides toward more cover. One of the enemy archers aimed true, and a padded arrow socked the unit right in the eye. Frank shrugged. He hadn't expected it to work. He still had his Ace though.

Ace was a good player, but only if he got to play a behemoth hound or a giant or some other titanic creature. He now sported a pair of wings and a horn strapped to his head to symbolize his current stature as a fire-breathing dragon. He lurked, reptilian, behind some trees, waiting for the order to strike.

Gabel skipped his turn, holding his army in place. "You wouldn't have any idea what happened to Ned, would you?"

Frank scowled. "I killed him, okay? I killed him. But it was an accident."

"I'm sure it was," said Gabel.

Frank turned his attention to the game. He suspected Gabel was only bringing this up to distract him, but it worked. "He wanted my help. So I helped him. And then I accidentally crushed him."

"Is that so?" asked Gabel, smiling innocently.

"It wasn't on purpose. Humans are very easy to crush."

"I'm sure they are."

Frank glowered. "Are you saying I crushed him intentionally?"

"I don't believe I'm saying anything," replied Gabel. "It's your turn. The armies are getting bored."

Ace slinked impatiently behind the tree. He uttered a low, grumbling imitation of a hungry growl. When he played a dragon, he played it very well. But Frank kept Ace safely behind cover and moved a cavalry unit. The goblin took a hit, which according to the rules reduced him to infantry. With a great show of disappointment, he threw aside his hobbyhorse.

Gabel made a show of studying the field this time. He never took his eyes off it as he spoke. "But some people might think it's an awfully strange coincidence that the man your woman likes should be crushed by you. It does look suspicious. If one were of a suspicious sort."

Frank mumbled, "She's not my woman. And I don't care if she does like him, although even if she did, it would surely be a mild attraction, a passing fancy. And even if I did care, I wouldn't crush Ned for that reason alone. If I'd wanted to crush him. Which I did not."

"Of course." Gabel's artillery units tossed several rubber balls into the air. The rounds pinged off several of Frank's units, removing them from the game. Except for the berserkers, who took off their blue "calm" hats and put on their red "angry" ones. Which was exactly what Frank had been waiting for.

He should've smiled, but he was too distracted by other thoughts. Try as he might, he wasn't convinced he hadn't killed Ned on purpose, even if he had done so subconsciously. As a young recruit, he'd slain a handful of soldiers in boot camp. Orcs, thick-boned, didn't crack easily, and trolls, naturally squishy, usually just popped back into shape. But humans were far less hardy, and elves, they snapped like twigs. But Frank had learned how to handle these delicate species, and it'd been years since he'd squished anything by accident—except for goblins, who hardly counted. If Ned's death was an accident, it was inexcusable. And if it was on purpose, it was even more so because Frank liked Ned, and Frank had a strict "No Friend" squishing policy.

"It's your turn," said Gabel in a singsong voice.

Frank wasn't sure if Gabel was a friend or not anymore, and put him on the indeterminate squishing list for the moment.

"Where did that storm come from?" observed Gabel as angry clouds spread over the citadel.

"Stop trying to distract me."

The ogre waved his hand. His army knew what to do. The berserkers, shouting, battle-ax-shaped cushions held high, actually foaming at the mouth, charged forth as Ace, flapping his arms and thrashing his artificial tail, soared in from another direction. Gabel's catapults were empty. His archers were useless, as arrows had no effect on berserkers with red hats or on roaring dragons. Gabel's knights stepped forward to meet the enemy. And Ace, with a terrible roar—terrible for a goblin's throat anyway—swallowed half a jug of wine, put a funnel to his lips, and prepared to breathe fire.

Then Copper Citadel exploded. Not the whole citadel, just the garden. In a tremendous, seething blast its walls were blown to dust. The force of the explosion knocked everyone except Frank off their feet. The towering ogre first wondered just what had been in Ace's wine, then marveled at the clouds of ash and heat where the garden had once stood, and then noticed a screaming figure plummeting earthward, coming straight at him. All Frank had to do was sidestep with open arms to catch it, which he did.

Ned, covered in black and singed around the edges, sputtered in the ogre's arms. "Thanks."

"You're welcome." Frank smiled, feeling perhaps he'd made up for killing Ned earlier. Although he did wonder, had he known it had been Ned, if he would've bothered to catch him at all.

A barrage of fireballs erupted from the smoking garden. Most of the projectiles went into the air, but a wall, a roof, and a small gathering of soldiers were blown to pieces. That was all it took to send most of the other soldiers scurrying for cover. Only Frank, Ned, Gabel, and Ace remained. And Gabel cowered behind the tall ogre.

Clouds boiled overhead. With a deafening thunderclap a blast of blue lightning sizzled through the sky to strike the garden. A shaft of purple flame followed. It shot upward and burned away the cloud with a demonic howl.

And then, only quiet.

"What was that?" asked Ace.

Ned dropped to the cobblestones. "Wizards."

The vermilion raven flew down to perch on his shoulder. "Wow! Didn't think the old bird still had it in her."

"Is it over?" said Frank.

"Probably not," replied the raven. "They're both very powerful. I imagine they'll have to kill each other several times to get it right."

Belok strode from the gray haze. He seemed shorter now. And hairier. He rubbed his shoulder. An expression of minor discomfort crossed his face. His phantoms had taken on ghastly appearances, gaunt and corpselike with hollow eyes and bony limbs. He raised his hand in Ned's direction, and the cackling specters poured forward to snatch Ned up. Frank and Ace swung wildly at the ghosts, but their blows passed harmlessly through the phantoms. They dragged Ned to the wizard.

A black sphere shot from the smoke to strike Belok on the head. He lurched forward. His phantoms released Ned, who scrambled back to safety by Frank. Not that there was much the ogre could do against this magic, but he was still the largest, toughest thing around. Instinct alone compelled Ned to Frank's side.

The Red Woman limped her way from the smoke. Milky white blood ran down a gash across her face.

Belok rubbed his head. "You're tougher than I thought."

"Perhaps you're weaker than you think," she replied. Strange energies gathered on the tip of her staff. The magic pulsed and throbbed. By now the cloudless sky had gone a dark, consuming gray, and the magic cast a brilliant beacon in the gloom.

Ned pondered running away, but this wasn't something he could retreat from. These two wizards were deciding his fate, and there wasn't a damn thing he could do about it.

Belok grew into a large, reptilian beast: a dragon with giant wings and a single, jagged horn protruding from his forehead. With disgust, Ace threw away his mock wings and horn. Even in dragon form, Belok had his bill and his furry head. And his tail was the round, flattened appendage of a beaver, proportionately large enough to pulverize three healthy ogres in one swat. He drew in a deep breath. His cheeks bulged. And Ned noticed a line of fur advancing down his back and across his shoulders.

The dragon exhaled his gout of fire, which the Red Woman parted with a wave of her glowing staff. She burst from her skin into a long, crimson serpent. She hurled her staff away as the two massive reptiles snapped and wrestled. The staff, still radiant, clattered at Ned's feet.

"I don't know if that's a good plan," said the raven.

"What plan?" asked Ned.

"I wasn't talking to you," replied the raven, turning his attention back to his telepathic discussion. "I don't know if I'd rely on Ned myself." The bird cocked his head to one side. "You're the boss. Ned, pick up the staff."

Ned hesitated. The staff glowed with dangerous sorceries. "Uh . . . I'd rather not."

"It won't hurt you."

"Are you sure?"

"Fairly certain." The raven sighed. "I told you this was a bad plan."

The Red Woman shrieked.

"Don't yell at me," shouted back the bird. "Yell at Ned."

Regina appeared by Ned's side. She held a long, long spear topped by a three-foot blade, a weapon designed for dragon slaying from her personal collection. She never thought she'd have use for it. But having studied combat with all manner of man and beast, she knew its use well, and she was quite excited by the possibility of wetting the blade with actual dragon blood. Had there been only one beast, she would've waded into battle immediately, but now it made more sense to let the monsters fight it out and then take out the weakened victor. Less sporting perhaps, but the raging behemoths were enough to give pause to even Regina's courage.

Everyone was so intently watching the fight that it was some time before Ace glanced up and noticed a difference in the Amazon.

"What happened to your face?" he asked.

She glared down at the goblin but pretended not to hear the question over the howls of monsters. But once the detail was called to attention, Frank noticed as well.

"What's that stuff?" His curiosity compelled him to reach out, cup her chin, and lift her face up to him.

"It's nothing."

She turned her back on him to study the battle. The dragon's beaver tail brushed against a wall, reducing it to rubble. The serpent spat some sort of acid that sizzled on the dragon's scales.

Ned glanced over at her, his eyes wandering from the spectacle. "Is that makeup?"

"No, sir." Regina shaded her face, a half-finished application of powders and paints. "It's ceremonial war paint."

"Amazons don't wear war paint," said Ace.

"Yes, we do."

"I've never seen you use it," observed Ace.

Regina clutched her long spear. Effective as it was against dragons, it was far too unwieldy for goblin slaying. "We only wear it when we kill dragons," she lied.

Ace appeared skeptical, but didn't care enough to explore the topic.

The dragon Belok spewed flames hot enough to set a stone construction ablaze. Scorched and bloody, the serpent managed to twist around and bury her fangs in her opponent's rump. Belok roared, and the grappling beasts rolled from one end of the citadel to the other, leaving wreckage, fire, and blood in their wake. The phantoms cheered on their master, while the raven coached the Red Woman.

Ace's sifting nostrils discovered a strange scent lingering among the smoky odor. "Is someone wearing perfume?"

Before Regina could swing her spear into a workable goblin-skewering position, the dragon sank his fangs into the serpent's neck. A great fountain of white blood gushed into the air. The Red Woman hissed. Her coils loosened, allowing Belok to slash her all the more.

The Red Woman became a flock of cardinals and soared her way free of Belok's fangs. He swallowed the birds that hadn't escaped his snapping jaws with a satisfied slurp. He roasted another portion with his flaming breath. The handful that remained settled down to earth and returned to the Red Woman's familiar shape. She bled badly; drenched in her own pale blood, she could rightly be called the White Woman.

Belok laughed. His voice rumbled like two mountains grating against one another. He gazed down upon her withered, wounded form. She showed neither fear nor defiance. Only quiet acceptance as he raised a clawed hand to grind her into dust.

"It's now or never, Ned," said the raven. "By all the gods, she's sacrificing herself for you. Don't let her die in vain."

Ridiculed into action, Ned grabbed the staff without thinking. He felt the power running through it, sending shivers up his arm.

"Now use it," said the raven.

"How?"

"Don't ask me. I'm just a talking bird."

Belok's hand fell. Ned heard every one of the Red Woman's bones crunch, every nauseating squish of every pulped organ. The staff still vibrated with seething, unharnessed magic. Belok turned, lowered his head to look Ned in the eye, and stalked forward. Gabel bolted, but Frank and Ace remained with Ned. He held the staff forward at arm's length, waiting for something to happen.

Regina charged with her spear angled to pierce the dragon's heart. Despite her inexperience, it was a flawless maneuver and would've worked on any ordinary dragon. But Belok snatched the weapon by its shaft and hurled it away without breaking stride. Regina refused to release the spear and was tossed away with it. She landed a few feet away, slightly bruised but unharmed. Belok could've crushed her with a single step, but she was disregarded by the wizard as beneath his notice.

He laughed one of his earthshaking chuckles into Ned's face, nearly knocking him over. "Is this all that has become of the Mad Void? Is this weak little immortal the ultimate end of his quest for redemption?"

The phantom maidens, ridiculously lovely once more, tittered. They tousled Ned's hair and pinched his cheeks.

"Use the staff, Ned," said the raven.

Belok agreed. "By all means, Ned. Use it. Find a spell. Bring your wrath upon me."

The staff vibrated in Ned's grasp. He felt the power, but he couldn't access it to form it into fireballs or lightning bolts. He wasn't a demon. Or a wizard. He was just a soldier now, and he could think of one thing to do.

He prepared himself to be roasted alive and smacked the dragon across his bill.

There was a burst of light. Bits and pieces of magic hopped from the staff into Belok. The wizard roared and stumbled back. More silky brown fur sprouted on his scaly skin.

"Again, you dolt!" shouted the raven.

Ned struck the dragon, narrowly avoiding being flattened by Belok's flailing tail. More of the staff's magic infected the wizard, and he diminished. With each blow, the staff's glow faded, and Belok, growling in agony, shrank and shrank. And as the chances of getting crushed shrank, Ned continued to beat the writhing, hissing wizard. When Belok was very small and no longer dangerous, Ned held the staff near the wizard until all the magic emptied out, and he was left standing before an enraged platypus.

"Isn't he the cutest thing?" observed Ace.

The irritated little beast dove for Ned's shin, but Frank caught it by the tail. "Careful, sir. They're poisonous." He pointed to the spurs on the hind legs. "Not lethal, but painful as hell."

The platypus Belok snarled and wiggled in Frank's grasp. The phantom maidens glanced at one another, shrugged, and soared off into the clear blue sky.

"I'll be," said the raven. "It worked."

"Did I do that?" asked Ned.

"In a roundabout manner," explained the raven. "The curse upon Belok was slowly turning him into a platypus with exposure to magic in any form. The mistress basically threw all her magic into her staff, and gave it to you because she knew it was the only way to get him to lower his guard. Typical wizard mistake, really. His arrogance was the ultimate source of his undoing."

"I don't get it."

"I thought I explained it simply enough that even a dullard such as yourself could understand," said the raven.

"Not that." Ned glanced at the white puddle. All that remained of the Red Woman, and it was evaporating quickly. "Is she really dead?"

"Relatively."

"What's that mean?"

"It means death isn't so black-and-white when it comes to wizards. She's certainly more dead than I've ever seen her. Whether or not that means she's irreversibly so or not is another matter."

"Why would she do that? She didn't even like me."

"You'd have to ask her. Personally I'd have left you to Belok."

Ned felt more confused than ever. He stared into the shrinking white pool until it disappeared completely, leaving him with an unenchanted staff, one very angry platypus, and too many unanswered questions.

TWENTY

NED BEAT A hasty retreat before too many soldiers dared reveal themselves in the aftermath of the wizards' duel. He locked himself in his office, where he sat behind his desk and wished for something hard to drink.

"Poor old Ned, feeling sorry for himself again," said the vermilion raven perched upon his window. "You really are a pathetic wretch."

Ned, still carrying the Red Woman's staff, got up and swung the stick at the bird, hoping to shoo it away. But the raven hopped inside, landing atop a bookcase.

A glance out the window showed soldiers milling about, in much discussion. Several nearby ogres pointed to Ned and whispered to each other.

"They do go on," said the raven. "The rumors have already started."

"What rumors?"

"Oh, the standard speculations. Some say you're a witch. Others a warlock. And some others say you're cursed by the gods themselves, damned to walk the world forever, bringing plagues and misfortunes wherever you wander."

"But this wasn't my fault," said Ned.

"That's beside the point," replied the raven. "Somebody must be blamed. And since you are responsible, even if only indirectly, you're as good as any."

The soldiers cast disapproving glances toward Ned. His blood ran cold at the thought of hundreds of ogres, who already didn't like him, finding one more reason to do him in.

As if reading his thoughts, the raven said, "Right now, they're considering stoning you to death, quartering the corpse, burning it, and possibly stoning it once again for good measure. There are other proposals, but that's the most interesting in my opinion."

Ned shut the window, locked it (as if that could keep a single determined ogre at bay), and drew the curtain. He sat down at his desk, still clutching the staff.

The raven paced from one end of the bookcase to the other. "I certainly wouldn't want to be you, Ned. If ever there was a man with a run of bad luck. At least all the other poor wretches of this world get to finally perish. Maybe there's some truth to the rumors. Maybe you are cursed by the gods."

Yes, he was cursed, agreed Ned. But the gods had nothing to do with it. It was himself, or the thing he used to be. Some part of him wanted to suffer. He knew that. Not just because it made sense, but because of this vague guilt he felt, had always felt without realizing, so accustomed to it he'd grown. Even if he wasn't the Mad Void anymore. Even if he was just a man now. It wasn't enough punishment. Eons of tedious existence liberally sprinkled with a hundred thousand horrible, agonizing deaths could still not be enough. Nothing could wash away the blood of merely one obliterated universe, much less hundreds.

It didn't seem fair.

The raven flew from the bookcase to perch atop the staff. "Well, who ever said life was fair?"

Ned glowered. "Stop reading my mind."

The raven chuckled. "It's not your mind I'm reading. It's your face. You wear your thoughts, Ned. Can't hide them at all."

Ned willed his expression blank, but the bird continued.

"If life were fair, you wouldn't exist in the first place. What right do you have to redemption? What cruel, contemptible destiny allows you the possibility of happiness while otherwise good souls who've done no wrong to anyone suffer from fate's cold indifference?"

"Shut up." Ned shook the staff, and the raven hopped onto the desk.

"It doesn't matter anyway. Not now. Within the year, this harsh, unbalanced universe shall be nothing but ash and smudge. Good riddance, I say."

"What are you talking about?"

"The way I see it," replied the raven, "you'll get yourself killed within the passing of a day or two. You'll stay dead for a while, awaiting my mistress to raise you to life. But she won't come, and eventually you'll get impatient enough to raise yourself, which will restore you to your old self. And the Mad Void will go about his business, and that will be that."

"But there has to be a backup plan. She couldn't have been the only one watching over me."

"I'm afraid so, Ned."

"But that's just poor planning. What if something happened to her?"

The raven pecked at his wing. "How could anything happen to her? She was practically immortal. She could only truly be killed by her own consent."

"But what about the gods?"

"What about them? Do you think any of those divine blowhards would risk intervening in these affairs? They're afraid of you, Ned. Gods aren't much different from men. They fear things they don't understand. And of course, most of them are too busy demanding tribute and worship to be of much use for anything important."

Ned laid the red staff across his lap. "But why would she

sacrifice herself? If she's dead, then doesn't that put the universe at risk?"

"Undoubtedly. Especially since your survival skills are highly questionable. But look on the bright side. You've still got her staff. Maybe there's some magic left in it. Now all you have to do is find a new wizard who has mastered the forces of life and death itself to be your keeper."

Ned ran his fingers along the staff, waiting for that tingle, that pulse of a whisper of the faintest particles of forbidden sorcery. He felt nothing. The wood was not only cold, it also seemed to be peeling beneath his touch.

"Mind opening the window?" requested the bird. "It's been ages since I've had a day off, and I'd like to find a nice female raven to while away the days before the impending death of the universe."

Ned complied, eager to see the raven go. The bird paused on the sill. "Take care, Ned. And do try to stay alive as long as possible." He spread his wings, but stopped. "Oh, one more thing. I nearly forgot, but she gave me a message for you right before she died."

"What was it?" Ned wasn't interested, but he hoped in vain it would offer him some insight into how he should handle his future.

"Beware of demons."

The raven flew away. Ned watched it go, thinking how damned useless a sorceress's advice could be. He still had no idea what to do or expect. Only one thing was certain. He needed to avoid dying. He wasn't going to destroy another universe if he could help it.

Like the raven, Ned doubted he'd last more than a week. He'd gone longer without perishing, but since arriving at Copper Citadel, his luck had taken a turn for the worse. He took some small comfort in that, since commanding Ogre Company had a reputation as a dangerous job. Justifiably so. But that would have to change now, and he gathered up what little determination he had into one tight knot of resolution in his gut. It was unpleasant, but he felt certain. He had no doubt—not much, anyway—that he could do it.

A fat vulture landed on the windowsill with a screech. Its sudden appearance sent Ned recoiling in shock. The staff found its way between his legs and tripped him up. He fell backward, banging his shoulder against the sharp point of his desk. A few inches higher and to the left and the blow would've cracked open his skull. This was going better than expected since he didn't die. Not much of an accomplishment for most people, but Ned grabbed all the little victories he could.

The black vulture squeezed its way through the window, hopped onto a chair, and stared down Ned with its merciless, ebony eyes. Its head bobbed sideways. It opened its hooked beak, rasping quietly. Black wings spread, casting a shadow of death over Ned.

Luckily for him, he didn't believe in omens.

He rose, rubbing his sore shoulder, and used the staff to encourage the cruel bird back out the window. The vulture wasn't so easily discouraged. It snapped at the staff's tip. Ned gave up after a minute. He locked stares with the forbidding harbinger.

"Get lost."

The bird ruffled its feathers and swayed side to side on the chair. It didn't go anywhere. Nor did he expect it to. He shrugged, feeling a twinge in his shoulder.

"Fine. But if you're looking for a meal, I'm not going to be it."

The vulture shrieked once, then settled in as if perfectly willing to wait. Ned sat back at his desk, resolving this time not to move until absolutely necessary. Hard to get yourself killed just sitting around, he reasoned. He wasted a minute trying to stare down his unwanted guest, but abandoning that, he leaned back and closed his eye.

Someone knocked on the door.

"Come in."

Frank stepped inside. He carried a canvas sack in one hand. The contents squirmed. "Ah, there you are, Ned."

"Where else would I be?" asked Ned.

"Not you, sir. I was speaking to the vulture."

"His name's Ned?"

The vulture screeched, flapped its wings, nearly tipping over its chair.

"Nibbly Ned," said Frank. "We usually just call him Nibbly to avoid confusion. Sort of the company mascot, sir. Ward's been looking all over for him. Worried sick. Thought the poor little guy might've been killed in the confusion. He'll be glad to know otherwise."

"Grand bit of luck," agreed Ned.

"You shouldn't be in here, Nibbly. Go on. Get out, get out."

The vulture flew back to the sill, cast one last hungry glance at Ned, and jumped out the window. Ned was simultaneously pleased and annoyed to see it go. Glad to be rid of it, but irritated that nothing in this citadel, not even the mascot, took him seriously enough to follow his orders.

"Something I can do for you, Lieutenant?" he asked.

"Yes, sir. I was wondering what you'd like me to do with the platypus." Frank placed the squirming canvas sack on the desk.

"Get rid of it, I guess."

"Is there a special way you'd care to have that done?" asked Frank somewhat vaguely.

"You can eat it for all I care."

The platypus made a fearful noise and struggled all the more in the sack.

"Is that safe, sir?" asked Frank.

"I don't know. I've never eaten a platypus."

"Not that," said Frank. "I mean, is it safe to eat a wizard? Even in platypus form?"

"Hadn't thought of that," said Ned. "I guess it'd be safer to destroy it."

"Yes, sir. Shame. It's been years since I've enjoyed a good roasted platypus." He threw the sack over his shoulder and moved toward the door. He paused as he touched the handle. "And don't worry, sir. Your secret is safe with me."

Ned almost didn't ask, but some small voice, some stifling masochism compelled him. "What secret?"

"You don't have to pretend with me, sir. I already knew all

about secret wizards. I just never thought I'd meet one. Well, actually I did think I'd meet one. I just assumed I'd never know."

Ned considered correcting Frank but didn't see any point in it.

"But you needn't worry, sir," added Frank.

"Glad to hear it."

"And I'm sure the others won't let anyone know either."

That spurred Ned's attention. "How many people know?"

"Oh, just myself, Regina, and Gabel. They didn't believe me either when I first told them. But I knew all along. But mum is the word, sir. You can trust us. Rely on our confidence."

Ned nodded. So his ranking officers thought him a wizard. He couldn't see the harm. It might even get him some respect.

"Although I'm not too sure about Ace," said Frank. "Hate to say it, since I like the little guy, but he might let it slip."

"Ace knows?"

Frank held up his hands. "I didn't tell him anything, sir. But it was kind of hard not to notice, what with your talking to birds and turning dragons into platypuses. Goblins are a chatty bunch, sir. I'd offer to squish him for you, but I don't squish friends. Maybe you could have one of the other ogres do it."

"That won't be necessary."

"Oh, I see. Going to erase his memory, eh, sir?"

"First thing in the morning, Lieutenant." Ned tapped the maroon staff twice on his desk.

Frank winked, and Ned winked back. Although with one eye, it was difficult, if not impossible, to distinguish his winks from his blinks. But Frank seemed to get it, and he left to dispose of the platypus.

Ned passed the next few minutes quietly not dying in his office, and was pleased with how well it was going. He'd stayed alive longer, but now that he was concentrating on it, it felt more like an accomplishment. Although he still couldn't make a bit of sense of the Red Woman's sacrifice, which seemed utterly pointless. Ned couldn't die, but the universe could. So why bother to save him?

"Why?" he wondered aloud.

"Why not?" someone replied.

Ned jumped, toppling out of his chair and rolling onto the floor. The chair jostled a polearm leaning against the wall. The weapon swung down and buried itself just above his head. An inch to the right, and it would've split open his face. He wondered if his office was such a safe place after all. He viewed the world with a new eye now. Everything was sharp and pointy and eager to drive itself into his brain apparently. He considered cowering under his desk, but he wasn't quite ready to throw away all his pride.

A quick glance confirmed that the office was empty. "Is someone here?"

"Someone, no," said the new voice. "*Something* would be more technically accurate."

"Where are you?"

"Here."

Ned stood, bracing himself on the desk. "Where?"

"Here."

"Where?" he asked.

"Why don't you ask again? Because if you ask the same question three times, you're sure to receive a more accurate answer."

"Where?" asked Ned again.

"I was being sarcastic. Of course, if you'd like to ask me again, go right ahead. But as I can't see nor can I feel, I can't really help you out. Or instead of asking the same ridiculous question over and over again, you could try another."

Ned, who'd grown tired of being mocked, sat back down. "Are you a ghost?"

The voice chuckled. "No. If I'm anything, I suppose I'm a memory."

"What's that mean?"

"I don't know."

"You don't know?"

"I don't know." The voice sighed. "Must you insist on asking every question more than once? Do it again, and I won't reply. In fact, I don't think I'll bother with any pointless questions from now on."

"You won't?" asked Ned.

No reply. The voice before had seemed to be right in his ears. He waved his hands around his head and felt nothing. Not a cold spot or invisible speaker or chatty horsefly.

"Are you still there?"

No reply.

"Hello? Still there?"

"Yes, I'm still here." The voice sounded outright irritated now. "Where else would I be? I can't move on my own now, can I?"

"You can't?"

The voice grunted, but said nothing else.

"I must be going mad." It seemed time for that. A trifle behind schedule. He considered searching his office but just didn't care enough to chase phantom hecklers. He decided to ask one more question, and if that didn't work, he'd give up.

"What are you?"

The voice exhaled with much relief. "Finally. Was that so hard? I'm the staff."

"The staff?" asked Ned.

The speaker grumbled. "Yes, the staff. You're really quite thick, aren't you?"

Ned snatched up the staff. Now he needn't worry. Now he could relax, let death take him. The well-being of the universe was somebody else's problem.

He clutched the Red Woman's staff close, clinging to it the way an amorous, drunken troll might cling to an amorous, drunken elf with a lazy eye and an open mind.

"How did you get in there?" he asked.

"I'm not *in here,*" replied the staff. "I am."

"What's that mean?"

"Everything must be thoroughly spelled out for you, mustn't it? I take it back. You aren't thick. You're patently ample-skulled."

"Huh?"

"Well put," said the staff. "I am not what you think I am. Neither spirit nor preserved soul, I'm all that remains of my former owner. A memory imbued with a touch of magic. I possess no true life, merely the nuanced simulation of such. I can't even speak unless spoken to, and only in reply to a question."

"You can't?" asked Ned.

The staff ignored him, and he silently agreed it should. He did have an annoying habit of asking questions over again.

"Why?" he posed.

The staff deemed this worth answering, but the irritation in its voice was obvious. "An echo can't exist without a sound. Though the magic that created me allows me more creativity in my replies, an echo is still what I am."

"Why are you here?"

"I don't know."

"Did she leave you on purpose?"

"I don't know."

"Did she leave you to help me?"

"I don't know."

Ned frowned at the staff. "What do you know?"

"I don't know."

"You don't know what you know?" he asked.

"Someone or something must be aware to know, and I'm not aware. I only reply. If in my replies information can be found, that is not the same as possessing the information myself."

"I don't get it," said Ned.

He waited. The staff didn't respond. It took him a moment to realize he hadn't asked it a question.

"Why don't I get it?"

"Because you're a dull-witted jackass. Even I can see that. And I'm not self-aware, nor can I see."

Ned almost yelled back at the staff, but he refused to trade insults with an inanimate object. Especially since he seemed to be losing the battle. And he couldn't come up with any

new questions. Only new wording for old questions. He put
the staff on the desk and turned to more productive tasks. If
his office was going to be his haven, he needed to make it
safer. His first act: removal of all the sharp things. Then he'd
take care of the hard things. Eventually he'd get rid of
everything in the room. Even the chair to play it safe. And he
could sit on the floor for at least twelve hours a day. It wasn't
much of a plan, but it was the best he had.

He'd gathered up the swords and axes littering the office,
presumably left by former commanders, when someone
knocked on his door. The next step in his haven would have
to be the addition of a Do Not Disturb sign.

"Come in."

The door opened, and in stepped Miriam and Regina. It
took some time for the women to enter as they struggled to
squeeze through the door frame simultaneously, each digging her elbows into the other's ribs. Ned, his back turned,
was hunched over a bundle of blades and didn't notice.

"What is it now?" he asked.

"Just checking in, sir." Regina saluted sharply.

Scowling at the Amazon, Miriam saluted just as sharply.
"And making sure you're feeling well, sir."

"Obviously Ned can take care of himself," said Regina.

"Expressing concern over the commander's well-being
doesn't insinuate assumption of weakness," replied Miriam.
"Perhaps you'd understand that if you were more in touch
with your feminine side."

Regina balled up her fists. Miriam didn't seem to care.
The women glowered, and Regina noticed that sirens had
fangs. Small ones, not too damaging (especially once they
were knocked out of Miriam's jaws). Before it could come to
blows, Ned turned around, holding an armload of swords,
axes, and one spear.

"Just getting rid of a few things," he explained.

"Let me help you, Ned." Miriam grabbed some of the
weapons.

"Allow me." Regina snatched up the rest. "That's a heavy
load. Wouldn't want you to hurt yourself, Miriam."

"What are you implying?" Miriam's large black eyes narrowed.

"Merely expressing concern." Regina's not-so-large black eyes narrowed. "Which doesn't insinuate the assumption of weakness." She grinned. "Can I get that staff for you, Ned?"

"No, leave it." He didn't think it was good for much, but he hoped the Red Woman had left it behind on purpose. And even if she was well and truly dead, he still liked having it around. He felt safer somehow.

"Is there anything else we could help you with, Ned?" asked Miriam. "Anything I could help you with?"

"No. I got it. Thanks."

"Nothing?" The siren shifted her load of weapons under one arm so she could suggestively caress her own neck, running the fingers down between her breasts as she bit her lip. "Nothing at all?"

"Are you deaf?" Regina slammed her hip into Miriam, who nearly toppled over. "He said he doesn't need anything from you."

"I just wanted to make sure he understood the question," growled Miriam.

"Are you saying he's stupid?"

"I said no such thing."

Slouched over his desk, Ned rubbed his temple. "You're dismissed," he mumbled.

"You heard him," said Regina. "Get lost."

Ned raised his head and gave the women his first glance since they'd entered the office. Both looked different.

Regina's changes were more obvious. She still had on her war paint. Thick, unflattering, and even a little clownish, it appeared very un-Amazonian to him. But he didn't know much about Amazons. Her hair, normally knotted in a tight bun or let loose to flow down her shoulders, was now puffy with thick braids. And she stank of flowers and cinnamon. As he became aware of it, the malodorous perfume burned his nostrils and brought tears to his eyes.

Miriam's differences were subtler, but not so subtle as to completely pass him by. For one thing, there appeared to be some sort of glistening gel applied to the scales of her face and shoulders. If it was supposed to make her striking golden skin more appealing, it only succeeded in making her appear more slimy and fishlike. And she wore the remnants of a uniform, most of which had fallen beneath a pair of shears, leaving behind only a very short skirt and a midriff-exposing top. Not very regulation.

Both females possessed a natural sexuality, though Regina's wasn't always as easy to spot, and spotting it was often a way to end up with a broken jaw and a black eye. They were now buried beneath an avalanche of effort. The right man would've understood this, would've even been flattered by the attempts, unsuccessful though they were. But Ned wasn't the right man. It wasn't that he held to some higher standard of natural beauty. He just preferred things simple and straightforward, including his women. He had enough riddles in his life.

The Amazon and the siren smiled eagerly at him. They didn't know how to tell him their feelings, and he didn't know enough to consider they had those feelings at all.

"You're both dismissed," said Ned. "And tell everyone I don't wish to be disturbed again."

The women kept their smiles, although both their thumping hearts dropped from their throats to land hard back in their rib cages. For Miriam at least, this was less a metaphor, as siren hearts wandered a bit through their bodies depending on their mood. But to be accurate, hers hadn't risen all the way to her throat, stopping as high as her sternum before sliding its way down and resting on her bladder, thus adding a need to urinate to her disappointment.

"Yes, sir," said Miriam.

"Yes, sir," said Regina.

Both saluted, less crisply this time, and trudged from the office with slumped shoulders. Ned picked up the staff and sat behind his desk.

"What's wrong with them?" he wondered aloud.

The staff replied, "They like you."

TWENTY-ONE

COPPER CITADEL HAD always been rundown, a victim of negligence. Hence the terrible mess left behind by a couple of powerful wizards wasn't especially noticeable. There was generally more rubble lying about, and that rubble was more charred and blackened than usual. The garden was now a crater, and a crumbling tower that had leaned dangerously close to falling over was now fifteen degrees closer to collapse. The improvised wooden braces creaked and groaned under the pressure, but they held. A dozen ogres had been assigned to lean against the tower until maintenance could get around to shoving a couple more braces in place. Or the tower collapsed. Either way the problem would eventually solve itself.

There were only a handful of facilities in Copper Citadel that held any concern in the average soldier's mind: the pub, the mess hall, and the barracks, in that order of importance, with the last two a far distance from the first. The dragons had knocked a hole in the mess-hall roof and smashed open one wall of the barracks. Both of which seemed improvements, adding ambient moonlight and sunlight to one's dining experience. The barracks doors had always been a tad narrow for broad-shouldered ogres, who could now enter three abreast without difficulty. The pub was untouched, and it was still the focal point of activity within the citadel. This came as no surprise to Frank. He remembered vividly the time, not many months previous, when he'd seen the pub ablaze yet still bustling with thirsty soldiers.

He stopped off for a drink himself, seeing no rush in his platypus-disposing orders. Ned hadn't seemed worried about the ex-dragon, and as a secret wizard Ned should know. Frank laid the sack on the table and ordered an ale to slake his thirst. He considered how to execute his orders.

There were many ways to kill a wizard, each and every one with its own disadvantages. Frank collected such lore as a hobby, and while he didn't entirely believe them, he couldn't safely dismiss them regardless of how absurd. Magic made all things possible. Especially the absurd.

He could burn the platypus, but inhaling wizard ashes cursed one with eternal hay fever. Hanging a wizard would afflict the tree used with evil that might crawl down into the earth through the roots and infect the very soil unless the tree was immediately chopped down. Too much fuss and toil in Frank's opinion. Clubbing wizards led to thirteen years bad luck for every broken bone, and it was impossible to brain a thing without crushing the skull at the very least. Skewering spilled blood, and wizard blood had a tendency to behave oddly, springing into giant scorpions or angry skeletons or noisy harpies. At the very least, it tended to leave a stain behind that never, ever disappeared.

There was only one safe way to dispose of wizards. They needed to be drowned. Everyone knew wizard spirits couldn't swim. They might fly right through the air and pass through the earth, but they sank like stones in the water. The spirit and all its evil magic remained forever trapped at the bottom of a pool. It was even better if a river was used so that the spirit was carried away to the ocean where all that salt water dissolved it.

A river ran near the citadel, but it was a little over four miles away, a longer walk than Frank cared for now that he'd gotten comfortable. But he was under orders, so he did the only thing an officer in his position could do. He delegated.

Ralph and Ward were sitting at the nearest table, thus targets of opportunity. He tossed the sack to them. "Throw this in the river." He added, "Commander Ned's orders," then turned his back.

Ralph sneered. He was in no mood to walk either, but he was in even less of a mood to get into an argument with an ogre of Frank's size.

Sighing, he threw the sack over his shoulder and started toward the river. Ward accompanied him. Nibbly Ned perched on Ward's shoulder. The vulture tended to stick with Ward since he was the only ogre in the citadel who didn't lick his lips at the sight of the bird. Nibbly had been well fed over the last two days but was still scrawny enough not to be worth fighting Ward over. But it was only a matter of time.

"This place isn't the same since Ned got here," remarked Ralph as they passed through the gates. "There didn't used to be so many orders."

Ward shrugged. Nibbly teetered, digging his talons deeper into the ogre's flesh to avoid falling. "I don't know. I think I like it. Used to be rather boring around here. Now we've had demons and brawls and dueling wizards. I can hardly wait for tomorrow."

Ralph grumbled. "I didn't join the Legion to be ordered about all the time. I joined to crush things."

"Yes, crushing things is fun," agreed Ward, "although I prefer smashing myself."

"Smashing? How could anyone enjoy smashing once they've discovered the joy of crushing?"

"Oh, I'll grant you," said Ward, "that crushing is great fun. Particularly elves, what with that popping sound they make. Or humans in armor. A good club gets a great ping.

But smashing is a lost art, if you ask me. Orcs were just made for smashing. And trolls, they're terrific fun to smash. Isn't that right, Nibbly?"

The vulture shrieked.

"Regardless," said Ralph, "I didn't join up to dig graves and throw sacks in rivers."

"It's a decent wage."

It was Ralph's turn to shrug, although he elected not to and continued to sneer. He was particularly ill-tempered, as only an hour ago he'd finished up a four-hour shift of tower holding-up. His shoulders and legs ached. The river seemed very far away.

He stopped suddenly. "I've got an idea. Come on."

The ogres veered off to the roc pens just beside the citadel. It was near dusk, a time of day when the giant birds displayed some semblance of calm. They paced about their cages, uttering low growls and snapping at each other. The biggest beast cocked its head to one side and studied Ralph and Ward as they approached. It licked its beak and pressed its eyes against the heavy chain mesh of its cage, which already had several holes and was in need of repairs. The mesh wasn't strong enough to contain a full-grown roc, but they were conditioned from hatchlings to respect it. Goblins were always on duty, with long spears to poke the monsters with should the rocs try to test the mesh. Escapes still happened, but only because a clumsy beast might trip and accidentally topple into the chains, tearing them down. The rocs would dash about like colossal, shrieking chickens until the goblins managed through sheer persistence to get them contained. This usually happened after the monsters had devoured enough goblins to fill their bellies, and they'd wander back to their pens.

Neither Ward nor Ralph nor many of the company's ogres enjoyed being near the roc pens. As ogres, they were used to being the biggest, most dangerous creatures around, and the green roc that eyed them, in his own separate pen due to his size and disagreeable nature, clearly surpassed them in these qualities. A sign hung on his pen named him Kevin. Beneath that, another sign warned:

Always Hungry.

Do Not Look Directly in the Eye or Make Any Sudden Moves.

No Sneezing or Loud Breathing.

Below, another sign read:

Eats Anything. This Means You.

And below that, in bold red letters:

Please Refrain from Stepping in Maw. Thank You.

There was one last warning posted, no doubt for those who couldn't read. It was a series of pictographs showing a careless goblin's journey through Kevin's digestive tract from beak to rectum. The artist had done a thorough job of showing the unpleasantness of the experience, even painting a frowny face on the pile of dung at the very end.

The warnings might've seemed excessive and unnecessary, but for goblins (who stubbornly ignored peril as a mark of general pride) it illustrated how dangerous this particular roc could be considered.

Eager to be on his way, Ralph prodded a trio of goblins snoozing nearby. They jumped to their feet with spears at the ready to jab into a roc's eyes or groin or other sensitive area.

"Sir, yes, sir!" shouted the female at the front.

"At ease," said Ralph.

The goblins, seeing nothing worth jamming their spears into, slouched. The female yawned. "Something I can do for you, sir?"

Ralph dropped the sack at her feet. "Commander Ned ordered this thrown into the river."

"The river, sir?" said the second goblin, a tall male barely reaching an ogre's knee. "But that's a forty-minute walk. Don't need a roc for that."

"Are you questioning orders?" asked Ralph.

"No, sir. But it's just that it's an awful lot of trouble to get a roc saddled up. They're all put away for the night."

"Just do what you're told," said Ralph.

The goblin female saluted. "Yes, sir."

"Very good, soldier."

Ralph, Ward, and Nibbly walked away, leaving the sack with the trio. They studied it for some time.

"I'm not getting a roc out just for that," said the third goblin, a fat little one.

The female nodded. "Agreed, but we have to do something with it."

"We could always walk it to the river," said the tall goblin.

This idea was quickly dismissed. The journey seemed even more arduous and unappealing than to the long-legged ogres.

Kevin shrieked. He clawed at the earth, raising a cloud of dust. The goblins exchanged sly grins, and the sack was tossed into Kevin's pen. Instantly he gobbled it down. Then with a gruesome retch, he spun around and collapsed. His agape beak allowed a glimpse of the sack lodged in his throat. It wasn't quite suffocating him, but it had cut off enough oxygen to reduce the great monster to a pitiful, wheezing heap.

"Oh, terrific," moaned the fat goblin. "I've seen him devour four hogs in one swallow, but one sack kills him."

"We should do something," said the female.

Though not particularly dutiful, each had been working with rocs long enough to develop a certain affection for the beasts. And Kevin was the oldest roc and so possessed a great deal of sentimental value. He'd eaten so many goblins in his years that his normally golden red feathers had taken on the mottled green hue of their species. This inspired even more fondness since goblins were just happy for the existence of something that large and threatening that happened to share their coloring. Unofficially he was a goblin, if not by birth then by dietary concentration. The three agreed something must be done to preserve him.

The tall goblin entered the pen, and attempted to push the sack down Kevin's throat with the blunted end of his long spear. It didn't work. He laid down the spear and rolled up his sleeves. "Guess I'll have to do it the hard way."

"You're not supposed to step into the maw," observed the female, pointing to the sign.

"Do you have a better plan?" he asked.

The others shrugged.

The tall goblin entered Kevin's jaws. He leaned his shoulders against the sack and found it slid in easily.

"This isn't stuck," he observed. "It's not stuck at—"

Kevin slurped down the goblin and the sack with a satisfied squawk. He rose to his feet and paced hungrily in his cage.

"He was faking," said the fat goblin.

"Imagine that," said the female.

Both smiled, feeling some pride that Kevin was not only the world's biggest goblin but very likely the cleverest as well.

The roc collapsed again, flapped his wings once, and wheezed.

"Nice try, Kevin," said the fat goblin. They both returned to their posts, where they drifted off to sleep.

Ever ravenous, ever cranky, Kevin ambled around his cage as restlessly as ever. But there was something new in his pitiless eyes. As he absorbed the hue of his latest goblin snack, he absorbed something much more malign from the digested platypus: the beginnings of a gnawing hunger, fueled by hate and a last spark of dying magic. He turned his gaze on the citadel, past the leaning tower and toward the office where Never Dead Ned hid away.

TWENTY-TWO

WHEN REGINA REPORTED the failure of makeup and perfume to attract Ned's affections, Ulga wasn't discouraged. She had Regina, Sally, and Seamus gather together in one of Copper Citadel's small kitchens. Since Ned wasn't attracted to glamour, Ulga's next plan was to try the domestic type.

"I can't cook," said Regina.

"You don't have to," explained Ulga. "You just have to fill his belly with some good food, properly presented, and he'll be yours."

"Are you sure?"

"Pretty sure," replied Ulga as she chopped potatoes, steak, and bell peppers and skewered them on rapiers. "There's no guarantee on precisely what it'll take."

Regina wondered about Ulga's expertise. She didn't seem to know how to get a man's attention at all.

"There's a lot of guesswork," admitted Ulga. "But it's the only way."

"Not the only way," said Seamus.

"I suppose you have a better suggestion." Ulga handed the shish kebab to Sally, who roasted it slowly in a steady flame blown from her left nostril.

"As a matter of fact, I do," said Seamus. "You could just tell him you like him, rip off your clothes, and have sex with him."

Ulga frowned. "That's not how it's done."

Seamus shrugged. "Maybe that's how it should be done."

"I agree," said Sally. "All this maneuvering and strategizing seem ridiculously ineffective."

"Don't listen to them, ma'am," said Ulga. "They don't know how this works."

"It doesn't seem to be working at all," observed Sally as she roasted the second kebab.

"It's working fine." Ulga slapped Regina's shoulder. "Everything we learn that doesn't work is one step closer to finding what will."

Seamus flattened her ears. "Or you could just skip all the hard work and go with a plan that's guaranteed. As a mostly male, I'll tell you right now that nothing gets a man's attention like a naked woman rubbing against him."

"Not every species approaches mating like your unsophisticated race," said Ulga with obvious disgust.

"And not every species makes sex into such a production as yours," said Seamus.

Regina agreed with the goblin. This was a great deal of work for something she wasn't sure she wanted. No wonder Amazons had abandoned sex so long ago.

"You can keep arguing," said Ulga to Seamus, "or you can make yourself useful and cut those radishes into flowers."

"Can we at least keep the rubbing strategy as an option?" asked Seamus.

"Fine. We'll call that Plan Z."

Seamus grabbed a radish. "You want roses or tulips? I can do both."

Ulga had Regina wash away all her makeup and put on something a little more comfortable. Ulga failed to convince Regina to abandon her armor and wear something considered more feminine. The Amazon would hear nothing of that, but she did finally change into some hardened leather breeches and a shirt made of very light mail. She absolutely refused to abandon her sword, and instead added a sash of throwing daggers and a hatchet on her hip to counter her sense of vulnerability.

"Not very domestic," said Sally.

"It'll have to do," said Ulga.

"It's a start," said Seamus. "You can almost see her nipples through the vest."

Regina scowled. "I'm changing back."

"Do you want this to work or not?" asked Ulga as she added the finishing touches to the kebabs.

Regina sniffed the offering. It smelled delicious. Except for the thick, greenish fluid congealing on the mashed potatoes. It stank of old linen and stale garlic.

"Had to conjure the gravy," explained Ulga.

Regina stuck her fingertip in the sludge, which burned to the touch like the acidic vomit of a spiked bogspitter. "Is it safe?"

"Sure. Might give you gas though. Or explosive diarrhea. Probably better not to eat it if you want to keep a romantic atmosphere." Ulga put the lid on the platter and handed it to Regina.

The Amazon didn't know why she was bothering with any of this. The more she thought about Ned, the less sure she was she cared for him at all. He seemed a good enough man but hardly worth casting aside her ethics. Ethics that had served her well, kept her life simple.

"You'd better hurry," said Sally. "You can bet Miriam isn't just sitting around."

Regina tensed. She'd worry if Ned was worth having after she'd gotten him. But Amazons never walked away from a fight, and she wouldn't lose this one. Especially not to a singing fish.

"Good luck, ma'am," said Ulga.

"And remember," called Seamus, "if all else fails, it never hurts to rub against him until he gets the message."

Regina stalked from the kitchen and across the compound. She turned a corner and nearly collided with Miriam. The siren wore a goldenrod sundress, and she carried a covered dish. The women attempted to stare each other down, but neither gave in.

"What have you got there?" asked Regina.

"Smoked salmon," replied Miriam.

Regina grimaced. "Smells like it has gone bad."

"It's fresh." Miriam turned up her nose. "What have you got there?"

"Shish kebab with mashed potatoes and gravy. Garnished with radish flowers."

"Roses or tulips?"

Regina smirked. "Both."

Miriam held up a bottle. "I've got wine."

They stood there for a second, saying nothing.

"I guess we'll let Ned decide which he likes better," said Regina.

"I guess so," agreed Miriam.

They offered up gracious smiles and continued the rest of the journey side by side in deathly silence.

At their destination they ran into an unexpected obstacle. A lean ogre and a thick orc stood guard at the door.

"Step aside," said Regina. "We've brought the commander's dinner. And some spoiled fish."

"No one enters," said the orc.

"Commander's personal orders," added the ogre.

"He's got to eat," said Miriam.

"He was very specific," said the orc. "He said no visitors unless he asks for them."

"No visitors for no reason," said the ogre.

The women shared annoyed glances.

"Why don't we just ask him if he'd like some fresh fish?" said Miriam. "Or some overdone kebabs?"

"Sorry, ma'am," said the ogre. "But we knocked once earlier when the first officer tried to drop by for a visit, and the commander yelled at us."

"He yelled at you?" Regina was surprised. Ned didn't seem the type to shout. Not that he was calm or rational. More quiet and lethargic.

"Not exactly, ma'am," answered the orc, "although he did raise his voice."

"And he threatened to transform us into newts if it happened again," said the ogre.

"He did?"

"Yes, ma'am," said the orc.

The ogre cleared his throat. "Not exactly, ma'am. But he did imply he might."

"How so?" asked Miriam.

The guards searched their memories but fell short of an exact recollection of his words.

"He might not have said it," said the orc, "but you can be sure he thought it."

"You know how wizards are, ma'am," said the ogre. "And since we'd prefer not having a tail, I'm afraid you'll have to take your overdone kebabs and spoiled fish elsewhere."

"This is ridiculous." Regina reached toward the door.

The ogre latched onto her wrist, and the orc drew his sword halfway from its scabbard. Regina would've drawn her own except her other hand was occupied balancing her platter against her hip.

Regina stepped away from the door. The ogre released her, and the guards unsheathed their weapons. She was in poor temper, and she didn't like being ordered around by a couple of grunts. Miriam hummed to herself, warming up her enchanted voice. But Regina would be damned if she let the siren solve this problem. Before blade or song could be unleashed, the door opened, and Ned stuck his head into the hall.

"Is there a problem here?"

"No, sir," said the orc. "We were just getting rid of them."

Ned glanced at the women, both of whom smiled and held up their meals.

"We brought your dinner, sir. Fresh smoked fish." Miriam lifted the cover.

"And steak kebabs," said Regina, "with potatoes and gravy."

"We told them you weren't hungry, sir," said the orc.

"Please don't turn us into newts," said the ogre.

Ned's glance passed over the offering and across the women's eager smiles. He made a peculiar popping sound with his mouth.

"Thanks. Not hungry."

He withdrew into his office and shut the door.

"You heard the man," said the orc. "Now are you leaving, or do we have to get rough?"

Regina didn't respond well to threats. Her face went red. She ground her teeth. She was three seconds from disemboweling the guards when Miriam put a hand on her shoulder.

"Come on, Archmajor. Let's go."

Regina grappled with her temper, but in the end she chalked the experience up to another one of those failures Ulga had prepared her for. There was no point in killing these guards; they were just doing their jobs. And if Miriam was walking away too, Regina could live with a draw this round.

The Amazon and the siren retreated in defeat.

"Your kebabs smell delicious," said Miriam.

"Thanks." Regina nodded to Miriam's platter. "I love salmon. And what kind of wine is that?"

"Care for some dinner, Archmajor?"

They shared a smile that, if not outright friendly, was passably civil. Then they found an empty room with a table.

Miriam set aside the platter of devoured kebabs. "Did you cut those roses yourself, ma'am?"

"Yes."

"Beautiful. So how was the salmon?"

"Delightful." Regina took the last mouthful and pushed away the plate. "You didn't try the potatoes."

"I'm stuffed." Miriam rubbed her stomach.

"At least have some of the gravy," said Regina.

"Maybe later."

They sat across the table, saying nothing, lost in their own thoughts, and enjoying their glasses of wine.

"What are we doing?" asked Regina.

"Ned, you mean?" Miriam hunched over the table and ran her fingers around the platter rim. "I don't know. He doesn't seem worth it, does he?"

"Look at us." Regina glowered. "We're two well-respected, intelligent women. We're better than him."

"He's a bit of a loser actually."

"You're a siren, by all the gods of the sea and air. You can have any man you want."

"And you're a resplendent Amazon warrior. Any man would be grateful to share your bed."

They clinked their glasses together.

"So what are we doing?" asked Regina again.

"I don't know," answered Miriam again. "Maybe I should just give up and let you have him."

"Or maybe I should just give up and let you have him," said Regina.

Miriam chuckled.

"What's so funny?" asked Regina.

"Oh, nothing." Miriam leaned back in her chair and put her feet on the table. "It's just amusing how you still think you have a chance against me."

"What?" Regina leaned forward and put her elbows on the table. "Are you implying I couldn't seduce Ned away from you?"

"I'm not implying it. I'm saying it."

"I thought I was a resplendent Amazon warrior. I thought any man here would be grateful to share my bed."

"Oh, sure. As long as they couldn't share mine."

Regina's voice took on a grave edge. "You're a gods-damned fish."

"And you're a wrathful, man-hating she-wolf," replied Miriam. Her fins raised into an aggressive posture.

"You're lucky you're not an Amazon. Or I'd teach you a lesson right here."

"Don't let that stop you, ma'am."

They jumped to their feet. Miriam kicked the table aside, spilling food, utensils, and wine across the floor. Huffing and snarling, they stepped closer until there was less than an inch between them. Regina was taller by a good six inches, but Miriam hardly seemed intimidated.

"You don't have a sword," said Regina.

Miriam grinned through bared teeth. "I don't need one."

Bodies tense, eyes locked, they stood ramrod straight. Every breath was a snort of rage and disgust.

"What are we doing?" said Miriam. "Are we really going to kill each other over Ned?"

"I don't know." Regina heaved a weary sigh. "This is so confusing."

Miriam shook her head and laughed softly. "Men. They make women do stupid things."

Regina righted her chair and sat. "Do they always?"

"Almost always."

They shared a giggle.

"I say screw him," mumbled Regina.

"Yeah. Screw him!" shouted Miriam.

"Screw him!" they cheered in unison.

They righted the table and began cleaning up the mess.

"I mean, why are we fighting?" said Regina. "We're sisters. No man should come between us."

"That's right."

"And besides, it wouldn't be right to fight you. I'm an Amazon, trained for combat. You're just a siren."

"Am I now?"

The humor drained from Miriam's face, replaced by cool rage.

"Oh, yes," said Regina. "Now if we were to settle the matter with a singing contest, perhaps a glee of some sort, I'm sure you'd have the advantage."

"I'm sure," agreed Miriam as she picked up a platter, raised it over her head, and crept up slowly behind Regina.

The door opened, and Ulga entered the room.

"There you are, ma'am. I guess it didn't go so well."

"No, not very well. Isn't that right, Miriam?"

"No, ma'am." Miriam set the platter on the table with an innocent smile. "Not very well at all."

TWENTY-THREE

THICK CLOUDS ROLLED over Copper Citadel the next morning, and dawn was dull and gray. Gabel, Frank, and Regina stood in the empty courtyard. The goblin bugler lay snoozing across some rubble.

"Where's Ned?" asked Regina.

"He's not coming," replied Gabel. "He said he wouldn't be coming to these morning assemblies anymore."

"Why?"

"I don't know. He just said he wouldn't. He didn't bother explaining."

"That doesn't seem like Ned," said Regina.

"How would you know?" said Gabel. "How would any of us know? He's only been here four days. Can you really claim to know someone that well that soon? People are complex. You can't just go by your first impression."

Frank snorted.

"I suppose you have an opinion," said Gabel.

Frank shrugged. "Just doesn't seem like Ned."

Gabel smirked. "We can't all have the amazing insight of an ogre."

"Just because we're big that doesn't mean we're dumb. I believe it was the great ogre philosopher Gary who observed that complexity is, generally speaking, an illusion of conscious desire. All things exist in as simple a form as necessity dictates. When a thing is labeled 'complex,' that's just a roundabout way of saying you're not observant enough to understand it."

"Oh, and I infer that you understand everything then."

"No, but I know enough to know that when I don't it's generally a flaw in me and not whatever I'm observing. But when it comes to Ned, there's not a lot to observe. He's pretty straightforward."

"He doesn't seem the deceptive type," agreed Regina.

"Have you both lost your minds?" asked Gabel. "I don't know what's so special about him. He's just someone in our way. Or have you forgotten that we all agreed to keep getting rid of these fools until one of us gets the promotion?"

"I don't know," said Frank. "I didn't have any problem knocking off the other guys, but they were all jerks. Ned seems like a genuinely decent guy."

"He's an idiot."

"Maybe," agreed Frank. "That doesn't mean I can't like him."

Gabel knew any appeal for reason from Regina was doomed. Rather than waste the effort, he went over and kicked the bugler. The goblin jumped to life, and after shaking himself to semi-alertness, he blew the call to assembly just as it started raining. Distantly, thunder rumbled. The rain grew harder, the wind colder. Gabel resented being exposed to this while Ned sat cozy and warm in his office.

It seemed out of character for their new commander, Gabel had to agree. He prided himself on being a good judge of men. He was at least as good as any ogre. And he had a fair idea of what Ned was like. His opinion didn't differ much from Frank's. Ned was decent, even likable in an unassuming way. But whereas Frank was easily fooled,

Gabel was wisely wary. Ned was too unassuming, too plain. But Ned was also immortal at the very least and possibly a secret wizard as well. It didn't add up. He was too damned unremarkable, too obviously mediocre to not be up to something. Regardless, he was still in Gabel's way. He'd worked too hard, assassinated too many people to give up now.

Ogre Company still wasn't used to getting up this early, but they were ready for it this morning and managed to shave five minutes off their previous assembly time. They didn't appear happier for the effort. The hard rain didn't do much to improve their mood, except for Miriam and Elmer who enjoyed a little extra moisture. Sally looked absolutely wretched, having taken on a pallid gray shade while raindrops steamed on her scales. Though still dangerously warm to the touch, she shivered noticeably.

Gabel addressed the company briefly. For his own amusement he threw in an offhand remark about Ned wanting to behead every soldier just to study their twitching bodies. Then Gabel handed the company over to Frank, who started the soldiers running laps around the citadel, slipping and sloshing through the soggy earth while Gabel went to consult with the commander.

The sentries currently posted at Ned's office weren't nearly as devoted as the previous pair, and they allowed the officer to knock on the door. It opened, and Ned stuck his head out.

"Yes?"

"Excuse me, sir," said Gabel, "but I was wondering if I might have a word with you."

Squinting, Ned appraised his first officer. "Just you?"

"Yes, sir."

"Make it brief."

Gabel stepped into Ned's office to find it stripped to the walls. There was nothing in it except a mound of cushions. Gabel already knew this, having carried out the orders to have everything removed, but it was strange to see. The commander clutched a red staff, the same staff he'd used to transform the dragon wizard into a platypus.

Gabel hadn't taken the time to dry off and stood in a puddle growing larger around his feet.

"Why are the men running in the rain?" asked Ned.

"Just whipping the company into proper fighting shape, sir. As per your instructions."

Ned went to the window and glanced at the churning, gray sky. "But it's awfully wet out there, isn't it?"

"They don't mind, sir."

"They don't?"

"There are some grumblings, sir. But you've got to expect that sort of thing with this lot. They haven't had much discipline lately, but they'll get used to it. I daresay soon they'll wonder how they ever did without it."

"Really?"

"Positively, sir." Or, Gabel thought with a cheerful grin, they'll storm your office and tear you to pieces. That should slow Ned down a bit, immortal or not.

Ned sat on the pile of cushions. It looked quite comfortable, but he was clearly uneasy. He wrung the staff. There was something different about Never Dead Ned, but Gabel couldn't quite decipher it.

"What did you want to speak about?" asked Ned.

"Some of the others were wondering how much longer you planned on staying in here, sir."

Ned wrung the staff tighter with whitened knuckles. His forearms tensed into knots. "I suppose it can't be good for morale. Everyone out in that weather while I'm dry and warm in here."

Gabel scoffed. He made a show of it because Ned didn't seem particularly bright. "I wouldn't worry, sir. The men know the chain of command. They understand you have important business to attend to." He glanced about the empty room.

"I can explain this," said Ned. "I can. Really."

"Of course you can, sir." The orc's long, goblinlike ears tilted forward eagerly.

Ned hesitated. He got up and paced the opposite end of the room. "It's complicated, but believe me, I have my reasons."

"Of course you do, sir." Gabel frowned briefly. He'd hoped for an explanation but hadn't expected one. He was beginning to suspect that Ned had gone mad. If not full-blown insanity, then mildly unsound peculiarity. Gabel wouldn't have been surprised. Secret wizard or not, a man couldn't keep dying over and over again without being affected.

"Believe me, sir," Gabel added, "I would never dare to question your orders. I trust your judgment implicitly. But there are a few others—I'd rather not name names, sir—who don't believe in the strength of your command."

He paused, waiting for Ned to ask for those names. Gabel would of course insist he couldn't betray any confidences, and only after Ned ordered him would he relent with great reluctance. With a bit of a push it wouldn't be difficult to get Ned to turn on Frank and Regina, thus forcing them to their senses.

But Ned didn't ask, proving how difficult it could be to sow discord with a man who apparently lacked even the merest curiosity, much less suspicion. In all Gabel's military career he'd never met anyone of noteworthy rank like Ned. The commander was an anomaly in Brute's Legion, and probably in every army in the world.

Gabel didn't trust anomalies. Anomalies didn't happen. That was what made them anomalies. He scrutinized Ned more closely, trying to unwrap this puzzle. Everyone was up to something. There were no exceptions. Some might say this observation said as much about Gabel as anyone, but he knew better. The only difference between him and the rest of the world was that he didn't bother to hide it from himself.

"Anything else?" asked Ned.

"No, sir, I guess not. Shall I tell the men you'll be staying inside a few days longer?"

Something crossed Ned's face. Some alien emotion wrinkled his brow and darkened his eye. "Yes. Just tell them . . . tell them whatever you like." His hands twisted the staff still tighter, and he frowned slightly.

"Yes, sir. I've got some paperwork to take care of." Gabel saluted hastily and left. The image of Ned ran over and over in Gabel's mind. Halfway across the citadel he stopped dead in the pouring rain. And he smiled.

Never Dead Ned was afraid.

It was really quite obvious. Gabel only had trouble placing the emotion because he'd never seen Ned afraid before. His most reliable emotions tended to be indifferent annoyance, disinterested indifference, annoyed confusion, and confused disinterest. Even when the dragon had attacked him, Ned seemed more confused than terrified. And why shouldn't he be? What terror could force an immortal to lock himself in an empty office?

Thunder cracked the sky as Gabel stifled a sinister chuckle. "He's not immortal anymore."

The idea was certainly worth exploring, but he wasn't one to act on his own. He considered himself more of a plotter, the mind behind the muscle. He couldn't go to either Frank or Regina. They couldn't be trusted. He needed someone else, someone who disliked Ned. Ogre Company was full of soldiers who wouldn't mind seeing Ned dead, but Gabel couldn't pick just anyone. He needed someone he could rely on. Someone who would kill Ned in the blink of an eye. Someone who could take the fall if Gabel was wrong and Ned was still immortal.

A line of soldiers jogged briskly beside him. They all looked soggy and miserable and ill-tempered. But one in particular possessed that hint of murder in his beady ogre eyes. Gabel pulled that one out of formation.

"Yeah?" asked gravedigger Ralph. "What is it?"

"What would you say if I told you I knew a way to insure that you would never have to run in the rain again?"

Ralph wiped at the water cascading down his slanted forehead to dribble in his eyes. "Who do I have to kill?"

TWENTY-FOUR

IT RAINED THE next day as well. And the next. And the next. Ned grew restless sitting alone in his office, but the dreary weather encouraged him to keep to his plan. It wasn't much of a plan, but so far it'd worked. He'd gone four days without dying, a new record for him as commander of Ogre Company. He hadn't even come close to perishing. The worst incident had been some possibly undercooked chicken brought for his supper on the second day. He'd sent it back with a sense of grand accomplishment. Nothing could touch him while he remained safely tucked away within these four bare walls. Nothing but boredom.

He tried conversing with the speaking staff, but none of the talks went well. The staff seemed to get more bored and irritated as time passed. Ned's questions were met with snide insults. The staff, never particularly courteous, became downright obnoxious.

"How much longer do you think it'll rain?" he'd asked it on the third day.

"How should I know? I'm a speaking staff, you idiot, not a weather vane."

After that Ned stopped talking to it. He stuck the staff in the corner where he was positive it was glaring at him, though it claimed not to be truly aware. Nor did it possess any eyes. He'd turn it a few degrees every hour in hopes of getting rid of the feeling. It didn't work.

By the evening of the third day, Ned's boredom drove him to desperate ends to amuse himself: poetry. He'd never been artistic, not even to the slightest degree. He couldn't draw or paint or play an instrument. And he couldn't write very well either, but that was the great thing about poetry. It didn't really have to be good. It just had to express something. Heck, it didn't need to rhyme anymore, which meant just about anyone could do it. After an hour and a half of exhaustive inspiration, he set down his pen and read his defining masterpiece.

A heap of cushions,
The speaking staff mocks me still,
This poem is not good.

Ned cast aside his one and only work of literature. He whiled away the rest of the evening literally twiddling his thumbs and discovered, with mild interest, that one's thumbs could actually cramp after too much twiddling.

By the fourth day, he was so bored that he considered sending for someone to talk to. But he didn't really know anyone at Copper Citadel. Not well.

He thought of Frank. He seemed a pleasant, likable fellow. But he'd also killed Ned once already. Ned was pretty sure it'd been an accident. There'd been no reason for Frank to do it on purpose, but inviting a large ogre who had already proven how easily Ned could be crushed seemed a poor idea. He might just as well bash in his own head and get it over with.

Gabel occurred next to Ned, but was quickly dismissed. Gabel was a stand-up officer, but not the most interesting conversationalist. Plus it unnerved Ned that Gabel pretended to be an orc when he was obviously a goblin.

Regina and Miriam were natural choices. They were two engaging, attractive women. And they liked him, if the speaking staff could be trusted. That was the problem. He'd never been good with women. His strongest asset with the opposite sex was an assumption of complete and utter disinterest in him, which could be misinterpreted as a sort of relaxed confidence. He'd lost that now. Now he knew they liked him. Now he'd start trying. He'd say stupid things. Stupider things than normal. And he'd worry about those stupid things, which would lead to even stupider things. In the end he couldn't have a normal conversation with a woman if he thought she was interested in him. There was just too much pressure.

He glared back at the speaking staff. It hadn't a single piece of good advice to offer him, and the trivial observations it'd shared had only complicated his life. Too bad he didn't know anyone capable of dispensing sound advice.

Someone knocked on his door. He considered not answering, but he was too bored not to. He opened the door a crack, not even wide enough to stick out his head.

Owens saluted. "You sent for me, sir?"

"I didn't."

"You will, sir." The oracle held his salute. "Shall I wait here in the meantime?"

Ned contemplated the odd nature of fate. He hadn't planned on sending for Owens, but now that the soldier had arrived, Ned supposed it would be convenient to invite Owens in. Ned had found some guidance in their last conversation. True, his attempts to follow the advice had ended with him being crushed by an ogre, but that was as much Ned's fault as anyone's. If he wasn't going to blame Frank, Ned certainly couldn't blame Owens. The oracle was sure to be more polite than the speaking staff at the very least.

Ned invited Owens in, and Owens was polite enough to wait for the spoken invitation before stepping inside.

"How can I be of service, sir?" he asked.

"Don't you know?" Ned asked back.

He walked over to the corner and took up the staff. He still felt safer holding it, though he had no proof it had any magical powers besides the ability to point out how dumb he was.

"I'm an oracle, sir," replied Owens, "not a mind reader."

Owens had read Ned's mind on occasion, although that wasn't really what he'd done. Technically he'd heard words that were going to be spoken while they were still merely thoughts, thus transforming them into words that were never spoken except in some theoretical future that never came to pass. It was a paradox. The same sort of paradox that summoned an oracle to Ned's door before he'd thought of the idea himself, but giving him the idea to summon Owens, which Ned didn't need to do since Owens was already here. In other words, the past was a product of the future, and the future was rendered obsolete before it ever happened. Just thinking about it gave Ned a bit of a headache.

He stopped thinking about it. He didn't need to understand Owens's powers. He suspected Owens himself didn't understand them. Causality was far too fragile a thing to undergo deep inspection in certain circumstances.

Ned didn't care about whatever Owens might hear either. Owens's ability to hear the future was little more than a parlor trick in the end. Its only reliable use was in speeding up conversations. But Owens still had a level head and a good attitude, what little Ned knew of the soldier, and Ned needed the judgment of someone he could trust. Someone other than himself, whom he trusted least of all.

He composed his thoughts, deciding what to tell and what to keep to himself. He waited for Owens to reply, but the oracle just stood there smiling.

Ned cleared his throat and thought very deliberately about speaking the words this time. Owens still didn't respond.

"Is something wrong?" asked Ned.

"No, sir. Why do you ask?"

Ned plopped down in his pillows. Funny how irritating life could be. Owens, who usually answered questions before they were asked and interrupted constantly, was now oblivious. Which meant nothing other than slight frustration for Ned, who apparently had to actually say things to have the oracle hear them.

"Do you feel okay?" asked Ned.

"Very well, sir." Owens's smile widened. "Better than usual."

"You just seem off your game."

"Well, sir, I don't hear all the future. Just little bits here and there, and sometimes the reception is better than others, depending on probability matrixes and spatial juxtaposition and personal relevance. Basic oracle theory, sir. I'm sure you're not interested."

"And you'd be right," replied Ned. "I called you here"— although I didn't actually call you, he added mentally—"to ask for some advice."

"That's what I'm here for, sir."

"Terrific. You've probably been wondering why I've locked myself away in this room for the past few days."

"Not really."

"But it's been four days. Four days all by myself with the barest physical contact. That hasn't made you curious?"

"No, sir. It did seem a bit odd, but I assumed you had your reasons. Or perhaps you just went mad. It's happened before. With other commanders here, I mean. One took to calling himself Lord Dragonstrike and convinced himself he could summon thunderbolts. Pure nonsense." Owens stroked his long beard. "But then again, he was killed by a bolt of lightning, so maybe he was onto something."

Ned tried to lean forward on his perch of pillows but couldn't get the leverage. "Some of the other soldiers must be wondering."

"A few, sir, but for the most part it's not a topic of conversation that comes up often."

Ned felt vaguely insulted. And unimportant. It was one thing to hide away from the world. It was quite another to discover the world didn't miss you when you were gone.

"But I fought a dragon." He held up the staff, although the gesture was lost on Owens. "I defeated it with this stick."

"Yes, the staff." Owens nodded slowly. "There's been some discussion of that."

"But it's just a piece of wood."

"It slew a dragon, didn't it, sir?"

"I slew the dragon."

"Yes, sir. With the magic staff."

Ned scowled at the speaking staff. He could envision it smiling smugly. He didn't like thinking himself an accessory to the staff in the dragon incident, though that wasn't far from the truth. He propped it against his shoulder with a sigh of resignation.

"Here's the situation, Owens. I don't want to die again, but I'm tired of being in here. So I was wondering if you had any suggestions."

"Go outside."

"Is it safe out there?"

"Is it safe in here?" replied the speaking staff.

Owens cocked his ear in the direction of the new voice. "Is that the staff?"

"Yes, it is," said the staff.

Ned asked, "How did you know it could speak?"

"I didn't, but there's been some debate over whether it might. I guess Lewis owes Martin two silver coins."

Ned slouched. There'd probably been more discussion about this piece of enchanted wood than about him, and he was not only resentful, but a little jealous.

"The staff has a point, sir," said Owens. "The dangers of the world are many and varied. Just because you're hiding in here doesn't mean they still won't find you."

Ned rolled off the pillows and went to the window. It was a warm, sunny day. Soldiers engaged in various training exercises throughout the citadel. Regina was busy showing a class how to properly use a battle-ax, while Frank taught another group the finer points of wrestling. Everyone seemed busy, and it was probably safe to go out. For a few minutes at least.

"Do you really think it'll be okay?" asked Ned of either Owens or the staff. He didn't care which.

"I wouldn't worry about it, sir," said Owens. "Life's too short not to enjoy it while you can."

The observation didn't fully apply to Ned, an immortal. But he couldn't make himself hide in this office any longer. If he was really, really careful and retreated back to this sanctuary at the first sign of trouble, then how dangerous could things be? He thanked Owens for his advice and gingerly, with great care, stepped out the door.

The oracle felt along the floor until finding the pile of pillows and took a seat. He briefly wondered why Never Dead Ned cared if he died again. It was probably terribly inconvenient, he guessed. But Ned didn't need worry much longer. No one did.

Owens heard the future, and now he heard very little. The future was deathly quiet. As quiet and still as the grave. That silence, so loud in its inevitability, overwhelmed the whispers of possibility that he normally had to filter. It was why he was so happy. It'd been a long time since Owens had enjoyed a moment of true peace. It was only a shame that the world had to end for him to have it.

TWENTY-FIVE

A GRIM FOREBODING told Ned he'd made a mistake stepping out of his office. He expected the entire building to collapse on his head. He expected the floor to open wide and swallow him whole. He expected Death herself to be standing there, cradling his tombstone in her pointed, red fingers. But there were only the two posted guards.

One of the guards asked, "Is everything all right, sir?"

The foreboding left Ned. He had no reason to be nervous. The universe wasn't out to get him, and why should it be? His death was its death. If anything, the forces of fate must certainly have been doing their best to keep him alive. Ned didn't place much faith in higher powers. Gods were unreliable. Destiny was a hope found in the hearts of desperate men. But sometimes, if they believed strongly enough, desperate men could do great things. Ned was desperate. Desperate enough to believe someone somewhere was watching over him. He had no other hope to cling to.

"I'll be taking a brief constitutional," said Ned.

"Should we accompany you, sir?" asked the guard.

He dismissed it as unnecessary. All his deaths at Copper Citadel had been accidents, all preventable with some caution and a bit of common sense. He didn't see the need for a personal guard.

"No, stay here. I should be back soon."

Ned ambled carefully down the hall. Along the way he tapped the floor ahead of him with his staff, like a blind man feeling his way. By the time he reached the door leading outside he was more confident. Each step felt like a success; each second he lived was now nothing short of a miracle. He reached for the handle but paused. Maybe it would be better to call it a day. He could always try going outside tomorrow.

He glanced back at the guards. Both averted their eyes to look elsewhere, but they'd been watching him. He couldn't just turn around now without looking like some kind of idiot.

"Just a couple of minutes couldn't hurt," he mumbled as he turned the doorknob and stepped outside. His gaze met the cruel, black eyes of Nibbly Ned perched on Ward's shoulder. The vulture emitted a scratchy, rasping screech and spread his wings. Ned's sense of dread returned.

Ward saluted but Ned hardly noticed, so intent was his stare locked on Nibbly's. "Hello, sir. Good to see you about."

Ned swallowed his fear and mumbled something even he didn't understand.

"Are you feeling well, sir?" inquired Ward. "You're looking a little pale."

"Fine. I'm fine."

Ned broke his stare, and Nibbly folded his wings, snapped his beak, and shifted on Ward's shoulder. Judging from its fresh red scars, the bird had trouble finding a spot it enjoyed for long.

"Glad to hear it, sir. Frankly I was getting a bit worried. And Nibbly here has been as well. Hardly eaten a thing the last few days. Isn't that right, Nibbly?" He reached up to pet the vulture, only to have Nibbly's sharp beak clamp onto his fingers. The ogre chuckled amicably as he wrestled to free the digits. "See there? He's already back to his old playful self."

As Nibbly tugged, the vulture's eyes never strayed from Ned's. Ward's fingers were not the buzzard's meal of choice, Ned realized.

Ward saluted again. "If you'll excuse me, sir . . ."

"You're excused," said Ned. Just as long as the ogre took that damn buzzard with him. But as Ward walked away, Nibbly jumped from Ward's shoulders and flew to a perch atop a high rooftop. He glared down with unblinking focus on Ned.

"Not to worry, sir," said Ward. "He likes to be where he can see everything. It's funny though. He usually perches on the northwest corner."

The perfect spot, mused Ned, to stare into his office. Several times in his sanctuary he'd sensed the cold shiver of death stalking him. Now he saw it in this bird, this ugly caricature of a harbinger so obvious, so unimaginative, that he refused to take it seriously. But if Nibbly ever got close enough, Ned decided he'd brain the gods-damned bird with his speaking staff, if for no other reason than to get some use out of the worthless stick.

Ned toured Copper Citadel quickly. All about, soldiers were engaged in various training exercises. The main courtyard was divided into smaller classes. Surprisingly, Ogre Company seemed to be enjoying themselves. Not everyone of course. Ned caught a fair number of irritated glances, but the majority seemed not to mind the work, and a noteworthy percentage were going about their training with zeal. He guessed that once they'd accepted the idea, the soldiers were glad to have something to do other than sit around all day and drink.

Now they had games to play while they drank.

The soldiers had applied their creativity to combine the imbibing of drink and the art of war. In wrestling class, pinning your opponent won you a drink. Apparently so did getting pinned—though it earned you a smaller mug. A table was set to one side with six hearty mugs of ale, and whoever finished a lap around the citadel fastest got first choice. Any soldier finishing seventh or later had to go dry until his faster comrades, dulled by drink, slowed down a bit. Climb a rope while someone poured out a drink, and you could have whatever was left when you reached the top. Smack someone with a training club; have a drink of various stouts and ales in various servings depending on just where you hit your opponent. Pitch a spear into a straw dummy; have a drink. Shoot an arrow into a target; have a drink. One hundred push-ups; have a drink. The unorthodox approach appeared to be working, and while many soldiers were a bit unsteady on their feet, particularly the humans and elves by nature of size and delicate livers, Ned guessed an army that could fight drunk just might be a force to be reckoned with.

A large hand fell upon Ned's shoulder. "There you are, sir. Finally out of your office, I see."

Ned managed to wrench himself free of Ralph's tight grip. "Yes, private."

The ogre squinted and wobbled in place. He must have been training a little too enthusiastically this morning. His breath reeked of dozens of different alcohols, mixing into an unholy stench that nearly melted Ned's speaking staff.

"I've been looking for you, sir." Grinning, nostrils flaring, Ralph poked Ned in the chest with a finger. Ned nearly toppled over save for a quick brace from his staff. "I've wanted to speak with you."

Regina, walking by with an armload of javelins, stopped suddenly. "Ned, you're outside."

People had noticed his absence. He felt validated in some manner. And maybe the speaking staff had been right. Regina did seem pleased to see him, but that only made him nervous. He couldn't imagine what she might see in him, but he wasn't in a position to pursue romantic complications. He had enough trouble understanding normal women. An Amazon could only be more vexing, particularly since she could easily kick his ass if the mood struck her. He fumbled for a reason to leave her presence.

"You'll have to excuse me, Archmajor, but Private Ralph here wanted a word with me."

Ralph belched. "That's all right, sir. It'll keep." He stumbled away, swaying slightly.

Ned and Regina stood there quietly for an awkward moment that stretched into an uncomfortable half minute.

"Training is going well, I see," said Ned.

"Yes, sir."

He rocked on his heels. "So, uh, javelins, huh?"

"Yes, sir. I just finished practice. Taking them back to the armory."

"Oh."

Ned had never noticed how attractive she was. He'd noticed she was pretty, but she wasn't exactly his type. She was too tall, but in Ogre Company being under seven feet could almost be considered petite. And she was more striking, less cute, than he preferred. This quality was lessened again by the surrounding personnel. Anyone with all their teeth and not covered in shaggy hair had a lot going for them.

"Armory, huh?"

Regina nodded, frowning. "Yes, sir."

"Training is going well."

"You already said that." Her frown deepened to a scowl.

"Yeah, uh . . . so who thought of the drinking games?"

"I don't recall."

It was, in fact, Miriam's idea. Loath as Regina was to admit it, Miriam was actually a good morale officer, but Regina wasn't about to say that aloud.

"I don't want to keep you, Archmajor," said Ned.

Regina sighed. "No, sir, I suppose you don't."

He turned to leave.

"Have I done something to offend you, sir?" she asked.

"Beg your pardon?"

"I was just wondering if I've done anything to put you off."

"No. Why?"

She laid aside the javelins. All those rules Ulga had laid down about the art of seduction passed quickly through her mind, and were just as quickly discarded. She had had enough of this bizarre game. Subtlety wasn't an Amazon's way, and it certainly wasn't in her nature. She refused to play it any longer.

"Do you find me attractive?"

"No. I mean, yes. I mean, you're very pretty."

"Then you like me?"

Ned shrugged. "I dunno."

She stalked forward, hands clenched in fists, fists on hips. "What do you mean, you don't know?"

"Well . . ." He shrugged again. "It's just that I don't really know you very well."

Regina's face twisted into a grimace. "What does that have to do with anything?"

He was tired of shrugging so Ned rocked the staff back and forth. "I dunno."

Though only a few inches taller, she towered over him. He slouched under her icy stare.

"What's wrong with you?" Her voice raised, and nearby soldiers turned their heads. "You don't care about knowing me. All you care about is having your way with me. I'm naked flesh. I'm a serving wench, a cook, a nursemaid to your fragile ego. I'm an incubator for your worthless seed. But I am not a person."

"You're not?" He almost apologized, but he wasn't sure what he'd done wrong.

"I'm better than a person. I'm a woman. But you're a man, and you're not supposed to give a damn about that."

"I'm not?"

"So what's wrong with me?"

"I dunno."

She literally growled. He expected her to knock him out with a single right cross, but she snorted and stared him down.

"You're just a little . . ."—he didn't want to finish the sentence, but her intimidating presence overwhelmed his good sense—". . . manly."

She didn't raise her arms, but he still flinched. To his surprise the Amazon suddenly calmed. Her face fell blank.

"I suppose you need a woman weaker than you then."

"No. It's not your strength. That's admirable, and I'm pretty used to everyone being stronger than me. It's just—I guess I haven't really thought about it—you're a little rough. It can be scary."

Regina smiled suddenly. The expression seemed forced, and even someone as wholly unobservant as Ned could see the fury seething just beneath her surface. But there was always a little bit of quiet rage boiling in the Amazon.

"Ned, may I call you Ned?"

He nodded.

"Would you like to have sex with me?" She spoke the sentence slowly, as if speaking to a child. A dull-witted child at that.

He froze. The answer was obvious, but he sensed the wrong response could have terrible consequences.

Her forced smile widened, and she took his hand in hers. She stepped closer. He couldn't look her in the face. His gaze fell across her slender neck, pausing on her ample chest, sliding to her shoulder. Her creamy, kissable shoulder.

She whispered in his ear. "I don't know why, Ned, but I desire you. Honestly I don't think I even like you. You're not a bad sort, but you aren't truly worthy of what I offer. But that doesn't matter. None of that. What matters, Ned, is that I'm offering you my body, my tender, untouched by any man, Amazon flesh. Do you want it?"

Ned gulped. There was barely an inch between them. Her heat washed over him. Drops of sweat beaded on his face and neck.

"Do you?" she asked.

"Yes?" he replied.

"There. That wasn't so hard, was it?"

She planted her hands on his chest, and he thought for a moment that she was about to have her way with him right there, right now, in front of all these leering soldiers. She shoved him away. Caught off balance, he fell on his back. Regina's sword flashed from its scabbard. She adopted an offensive stance.

"Defend yourself!"

His eyes widencd. "What?"

"Defend yourself, Ned!"

He scrambled to his feet. "What?"

She swung the blade in a blur. His cheek stung. A trickle of blood leaked from a shallow cut. Before he could protest, she kicked him in the knee and then swept his legs out from under him so that he was back on the ground. She raised her sword to drive it through his heart.

"Wait! Wait! Wait!" He curled into a ball, holding out one hand in surrender. "What are you doing?"

She lowered her weapon. "I am an Amazon warrior, Ned. And there are certain rules I must follow. My code allows me to take a lover only if he can best me in a fight. Only then can he prove himself worthy of me."

"But I can't fight you."

"Apparently." She helped him to stand. "No man is my equal. But that is why you're perfect for me. You're immortal. No matter how many times I slay you, you can always try again. Eventually you should win. With a great deal of luck." She raised her sword again. "Now then, defend yourself!"

"Wait, you don't—"

She kicked him in the gut. He fell to his knees, huffing for breath, unable to explain anything.

"Better luck next time, Ned."

Disappointment etched Regina's face as she swung the blade to split open his skull. Steel clanged against steel. Ned's head remained whole.

Miriam stood between Regina and Ned. She'd parried the deathblow, and now the two women stood across from each other, swords in tightened fists.

The siren nodded to Ned. "Commander." Her large, black eyes narrowed to the tiniest slits and focused on Regina. "Archmajor."

Now every soldier in the courtyard had forgotten their training and their drinking. They crowded around, leering, grinning. Mock meows and hisses rose from the audience.

"Just what the hell do you think you're doing, Archmajor?" asked Miriam through gritted teeth.

"Stay out of this, Miriam," replied Regina coldly. "This doesn't concern you."

"You were about to kill our commanding officer. I think that concerns everyone here."

Ned felt he should say something, but he wasn't sure what to say. As commander, he still tried. "It's okay. This is all just a misunderstanding."

Regina glared at him. "I beg your pardon, Ned, but this situation was plain and simple until Miriam stepped in. I offered you my flesh, and you agreed to fight me for it."

Miriam lowered her sword and frowned at him over her shoulder. "Is that true, Ned?"

Guilt inexplicably fell upon him, although he was positive he hadn't done anything wrong. But the disappointment in Miriam's eyes had that effect on him.

"No . . . I mean, sort of. I agreed to the sex, but I didn't know I had to fight her."

"What did you think?" said Regina. "That an Amazon would surrender herself to any man who asked?"

"I didn't ask. You asked me."

"Semantics." Regina snorted. "Anyway, ignorance is no excuse. Now that you've expressed an interest in engaging me in carnal relations, you must fight me. It's the only honorable course of action." She raised her weapon and took a step forward. "Move aside, Miriam."

Ned held out the speaking staff, hoping some leftover spark of magic might transform the fearsome Amazon into a bunny or woodchuck or bear or dragon. Something less dangerous so he might stand a chance—or more dangerous so he wouldn't be so embarrassed being killed.

He didn't understand why nobody was helping him. He was their commander. Someone should've stood in his defense, but the soldiers merely hooted and laughed at his plight. Only Frank, standing at the front of the crowd, was silent. All the color drained from his red face, leaving it a pale pinkish shade. The ogre looked sad and angry at the same time, although Ned couldn't imagine what wrong he'd done to Frank.

"This is insubordination!" Ned shouted above the ruckus.

Regina stopped. "Actually it's not. As long as an Amazon slays a fellow soldier, regardless of rank, according to the customs and policies of her culture, it is allowed according to the Cultural Acceptance Policy of the Legion.

"And according to Brute's Legion's official Code of Conduct, a violent act is only considered an act of willful insubordination when it subjects the target to irreparable harm. It's like cutting off the arm of a troll. Unpleasant, yes, but since it'll grow back, the most you usually get is a written reprimand. And since you're immortal, killing you isn't much worse than that."

"But I'm not immortal," said Ned.

The crowd fell silent. His secret was out—although it was only a little bit of the secret.

"Is this true?" asked Miriam.

He scanned the crowd. He glimpsed nothing but bloodlust in the faces. Except for Frank, pale and rigid and frowning.

"Why do you think I've been hiding in my office these last few days? Because every time I step outside, I die, and I can't die again."

The audience grumbled among themselves, and from the snatches of conversation Ned caught, not many believed him. And those who did, still didn't care.

"It doesn't make any difference," said Regina. "You've stated your intention. Now you must live up to it."

Ned considered running, but all around was a thick wall of soldiers. They might part for him. They might not. Either way he wouldn't make it very far before Regina caught and killed him.

"If I die again," he said, "I'll destroy the universe."

A hush fell on the courtyard. Soon guffaws filled the air. Copper Citadel rumbled with laughter. Only Ned, Regina, Miriam, and Frank remained silent.

"Really, Ned." Regina rolled her eyes. "Now defend yourself, and let's get this over with."

This was going to be a stupid way to die. He'd died many times, and at least half had been stupid deaths. But this was also a stupid way to herald the end of the universe, and that bothered him greatly.

If he was going to perish (and he could see no way around it) he could at least put up a fight. He raised the speaking staff and hoped for a lightning bolt. It didn't come.

Miriam interposed herself between Regina and Ned. "No. If you want him, you'll have to take him." She scraped a line in the cobblestones with her sword. "From me."

"You have no right," said Regina.

"I have every right. According to Amazon law he's unclaimed, and if I want him too that means you have to beat me to take him."

"How do you know that?"

"It's my job to know."

"You can only fight for him if he agrees to be yours."

Miriam asked, "Ned, will you—"

"Yes!" shouted Ned.

"Very well. I question the wisdom of facing me in personal combat, Miriam, and I doubt you're worthy of the honor of dying by my blade. But if that's the way you want it . . ." Regina swung a few practice strokes.

Miriam smiled coldly. "Are you going to fight or talk all day?"

The audience hooted and hollered as the ladies warily circled each other. The muscular Amazon was a head taller than Miriam, if one ignored the siren's fins. Regina was a skilled combatant. Ned had seen enough to know that, but he hadn't seen Miriam touch a sword up to now. But she was his only hope. His and the entire universe's.

Regina lunged forward. Miriam parried the blow. Regina swung at Miriam's throat. Miriam knocked aside the strike and sliced at Regina's legs. The Amazon jumped back just in time, only to have her opponent rush in and stab for her gut. Regina blocked the sword, but wasn't ready for the foot that stomped on her toes. She stifled a yelp, only to be elbowed in the face and flounder backward.

Blood oozed from Regina's nose. She growled. Miriam

winked, a wry grin across her thick lips. The audience murmured approval and surprise.

Regina wiped her nose. "That's a cheap shot."

Miriam chuckled. "Oh, I'm sorry. I thought this was a fight. Not a fencing match."

The soldiers howled with delight.

Enraged, Regina charged. A whirlwind of steel, she slashed at Miriam. The siren beat back each furious blow. A hole in Regina's assault allowed Miriam to take the offense. Her strikes were batted aside with strength and finesse. And so it went, back and forth, for a frantic minute. Ned couldn't keep track of the action. It was just so much metal clashing against metal, angry roars from Regina, eerie concentrated silence from Miriam. They circled and whirled, advanced and retreated. Finally an upward sword thrust nearly disemboweled Regina who leapt out of the way, but not before her blade sliced off the very tip of Miriam's fin.

The women sucked in short, rapid breaths, neither wishing to appear weak.

"Where did you learn to fight like that?" asked Regina.

"Just something I've always had a knack for." Miriam tossed her sword into the air. It twirled three rotations before she caught it in her other hand. "Did I mention I'm ambidextrous?"

"So am I." Regina plucked a long knife from a sheath on her belt. "Shall we continue, or do you wish to concede now?"

Miriam curtsied, drawing her own knife. "I'd sooner see you dead, ma'am."

The warriors fell upon each other once more. This time though, there was a more cautious approach to their conflict as each took careful measure of her opponent, waiting for the right opportunity. It was still a rapid exchange, graceful in its skill and ugly in its rage. It led the combatants across the compound until the two women stood before the pub.

By now the audience had grown to include just about every soldier in Ogre Company. The soldiers in back couldn't see much of the action, but Ned had a front-row seat. Whenever a good blow was struck, whether by Regina or Miriam, the crowd cheered.

So far neither had landed a solid strike, though both were covered with nicks, scrapes, and bruises. Ned was getting tired of just watching them. Their breath was ragged. Sweat covered Regina. Sirens didn't sweat, but the sails atop Miriam's head, which she used to cool down, were fully extended. They were tiring, but neither was ready to surrender.

"Hundred gold on Miriam," said Martin.

"I'll take that bet, Brother," replied Lewis.

Ned really should've done something. He liked Regina. He liked Miriam. There had to be a way of ending this before someone died, and it was his job as commander to find a way. He still wasn't used to giving orders, but it was worth a try.

Before he could order the women to stand down, Miriam and Regina, locked in a combative embrace, fell through the pub window with a crash. Soldiers rushed after them as quickly as the slim doorway allowed. The pub couldn't hold all the soldiers, and the rest crowded around the windows eagerly. The clatter of battle continued inside.

Only Ned and Frank remained aside, not interested in fighting the crowd to get a better view.

"Destroy the universe, huh?" asked Frank.

"Yeah. It's complicated."

To Ned's surprise, the ogre didn't appear skeptical. "Why did you come out of your office then?"

"Got bored," said Ned plainly. "Guess I should've just sent out for a checkerboard."

"Guess so," agreed Frank.

The soldiers at the pub's second window, the unbroken one, parted suddenly as Regina and Miriam hurtled through it. They rolled around on the ground in broken glass with their hands around each other's throats.

"This is getting ugly," said Frank. "Somebody should stop it."

"Somebody should," agreed Ned, fully intending to step

up to his position of authority. But Frank brushed him aside and strode to the swearing, bloodstained ladies. He seized each by one arm and pulled them apart.

"That's enough."

Unable to reach each other, the ladies turned their aggression on the ogre between them. They bit and clawed at him without much effect until Frank hoisted them in the air and shook them until their skulls rattled.

"I said that's enough!"

The women stopped their wriggling and muttered and snarled instead.

"Now I'm going to set you down," said Frank, "and you are both going to behave like civilized officers. Or so help me, I'll break some bones in each of you. I won't specify which because I haven't made up my mind yet."

He set them down. Miriam and Regina still grumbled, but neither made any advance on her rival. It was plain to see that they were both exhausted, and Frank's threat had been the final smidge of motivation to give them pause. Ned wished he could be that assertive, but it didn't seem to be in his nature. He wasn't too hard on himself since Frank had all the motivational talents that came from being a very large ogre. And even a very large ogre was taking a chance standing between these two enraged warriors.

"She started it," said Regina with a huff.

"Oh, shut up, ma'am," replied Miriam.

"You shut up."

"Why don't you both shut up?" asked Frank. It was clearly not a question. "And stop acting like fools. I mean, look at yourselves. You're two of our finest officers, and you've reduced yourselves to this."

The crowd murmured as it milled about. The fight appeared over, and they were losing interest. Ned, on the other hand, was very interested. He hoped Frank could fix this problem. He didn't want anyone to die.

Ralph crept stealthily up behind Ned. It was difficult for ogres to attach the adjective "stealthily" to anything they did, but the mob of disinterested ogres all around offered just the right camouflage. Ralph palmed a blade in one of his hands and slipped closer to Ned's exposed back.

Frank continued his lecture. "You two really should be ashamed. What kind of example is this for the company?"

"She challenged my honor," said Regina.

"And she's just a bitch," countered Miriam.

They pounced on one another and got in a few good hits before Frank managed to separate them again. He shook his head and sighed.

"Is all this really worth it? Do either of you really like Ned enough to die for him? To kill for him?"

They both glanced at Ned, who just stood there and shrugged.

"I like him," said Miriam.

"Well, I love him," replied Regina.

"I love him more!" shouted Miriam.

"No, you don't," said Ned suddenly. He stepped forward just as Ralph was half a second from driving the knife into his back. The treasonous ogre cursed under his breath and quickly hid the weapon behind his back.

"You don't love me," said Ned. "You don't even know me."

Miriam said, "But I think I could love you."

Regina said, "And I think I could too."

"Maybe you could," agreed Ned, though he didn't believe it very possible. "But shouldn't you know for sure before you decide to start killing each other?"

Regina lowered her head. Miriam's golden scales darkened with a crimson blush.

"Good then," said Frank. "Then it's settled. Nobody dies just yet."

A shadow blotted out the sky as a tremendous green roc landed with a boom upon the pub roof. The roof supported the roc's weight for a full second before collapsing, and the soldiers of Ogre Company groaned. The roc thrashed, smashing everything in its attempts to get free.

Ace, riding the saddle atop its neck, cursed and yanked at the reins. "Damn it, Kevin! What's wrong with you?"

"Get that thing out of here!" shouted Frank.

"I'm trying, sir! I'm trying!"

Kevin shrieked and squawked. He calmed suddenly and scanned the crowd until his eyes fell upon Never Dead Ned. Then his beak parted, but instead of a shrill warble, out came a voice.

"Ned."

"I didn't know they could talk," observed Private Elmer from the crowd.

"They can't," said Ace.

"Never Dead Ned," said Kevin with his newfound human voice. But it wasn't his voice. It was the voice of a dead wizard, and Ned's blood ran cold. Belok was back.

Kevin ruffled his feathers and clucked the deep, thoughtful clucks of a roc enchanted with a will other than his own.

"Kill Never Dead Ned."

Ned didn't hear. He was too busy running away.

TWENTY-SIX

NED HAD NEVER been swift, and the mob broken into chaos all about him diminished his speed. The only reason he wasn't knocked to the ground and trampled to death was that many of the surrounding soldiers, realizing Ned was the great roc's target, shied away from him. Kevin would've easily overtaken him, except that despite the enchantment digesting in the roc's stomach, he wasn't a very bright beast. He was terrifically intelligent for a roc, which made him only slightly smarter than a keenly sensible boulder. In the panicked crowd he had a bit of trouble picking out Ned from all the other darting morsels. His vicious, barbed beak would pluck a prospective tidbit, and if by chance it turned out to be a tasty goblin, he'd slurp it down. If it were an ogre or elf or some other morsel offensive to his peculiar dietary preferences, he'd hurl it away in disgust.

His thundering footsteps crushed fleeing soldiers, and more than once he lost his balance and toppled over, crushing even more and growing irritated.

Swearing, Ace swatted the roc across the head with an iron club and yanked at the reins. Kevin ignored his rider and continued the search, scooping up three goblins in his maw, swallowing them whole.

"Neeeeeeeeeecced!" he howled.

A flash of recognition twinkled in the bird's enchanted brain. One speck, easier to spot because the other specks avoided it, rushed toward the safety of a building. Kevin spread his wings, hopped in the air, and sailed across the courtyard to land with a crash between Ned and his escape.

The monster stabbed at him with a pointed beak. Ned barely stumbled backward in time, but Kevin raised his head in a flash and struck again. Ace managed to hit a sensitive spot just above the eye. Kevin's head veered. His beak gouged the ground scant feet from Ned.

Kevin shook fiercely and jumped about in an effort to rid himself of his passenger. Ace held tight, cursing, his pipe clenched tightly in his determined jaws.

"Is that all you got?" he taunted. "C'mon, Kevin boy, I expected more!"

In his wild thrashing the roc spun around, and his long, serpentine tail thumped the ground again and again. Ned rolled to one side, barely avoiding a flattening. He rolled to the other without a second to spare. But the third swat fell with certain doom.

Lewis and Martin intercepted the strike. The twins, sharing one body with the strength of two ogres, sank to their knees but stopped the collision. They held the tail, struggling against its spasms. Kevin grew even more furious, with a goblin banging his skull and ogres grasping his tail.

Ned gaped when he should've been running. It'd been so long since death had been anything more than an inconvenience. His flight reflexes had atrophied.

Kevin finally snapped his head hard enough to send Ace flying. He sailed high in the air toward the other side of the citadel, probably to bounce on his rubbery goblin butt with only a bruise to show for it.

Ned turned and dashed toward the nearest building in the

opposite direction. He tripped over a goblin running around in panicked circles and was knocked down by a fleeing orc. These hardly stopped him, as he was too focused on escape to notice a few bruises and scrapes.

A new glimmer of intelligence flashed in Kevin's eye. He cracked his tail in Ned's direction. The twins lost their grip and were hurled to bounce twice on the cobblestones before landing atop Ned. Lewis was out cold, and Martin, stunned, could barely groan. Ned couldn't move at all as Kevin stamped his way over. The roc brushed aside the twins with a fresh, uncharacteristic delicate sweep of his talons. Ned, still not quite ready to lie down and die, crawled for it. His progress ended with a smashing roc foot in his path.

He curled up in a ball and waited for death. He presumed it wouldn't be a long wait.

Kevin laughed. Hot breath washed over Ned. He dared open his eye and look into the roc's face.

"It will not be an easy death for you, Ned," said Kevin. "No crushing jaws, no sudden end."

Ned stared down the roc's gullet. "You can't do this, Belok. Killing me won't hurt me. It'll only destroy the universe."

Kevin cocked his head to one side, then another.

"Who's Belok?"

The roc was the same color as goblins because he'd eaten so many, but he wasn't a goblin. And he had Belok's voice, his intellect, and his hate of Ned through a quirk of digestion and a bit of magic. But Kevin wasn't Belok, and where even the dark wizard might've hesitated to sacrifice the entire universe for his revenge, Kevin only knew Ned must suffer, must die for some very good reason that the monster couldn't quite remember. Kevin was still more roc than wizard, and so he was little troubled by subtleties of motivation.

He seized Ned by a leg, delicately so as not to break anything just yet, for Kevin wanted to enjoy every bit of Ned's suffering. The roc spread his wings to fly away to a less distracting location.

A javelin pierced his shoulder, quickly followed by another. The wounds weren't deep, but the pain pushed aside his higher reasoning. He shrieked, releasing Ned, who fell hard to the ground with the wind knocked from him. By some miracle nothing felt broken, but he could barely get to his knees.

Regina hurled a third javelin and held out her empty hand so that Miriam, carrying a bundle, could give her another.

Frank lifted Ned and passed the battered, bruised commander to a nearby ogre. "Get him out of here."

Ralph saluted. "Yes, sir." He roughly threw Ned over his shoulder and ran. Every thumping step rattled Ned's brain.

Kevin spread his wings wide. His green feathers ruffled. He lowered his head and charged his attackers. Frank held his ground. When the roc was about to tear him in half with a vicious swiping beak, Frank punched Kevin across the nose. The monster staggered, more shocked than injured. Nothing had ever challenged his charge before. He snapped again. Frank unleashed a solid uppercut that swayed Kevin, even buckling his knees and knocking loose a tooth, and Kevin's unfocused rage found a new target.

"Get out of the way!" shouted Regina. "I can't get a clear shot!"

"Can't get a clear shot?" said Miriam. "The thing's as big as . . . well, as big as a damned big roc."

Miriam was correct. Regina had plenty of target if she was interested in sticking dozens of javelins into the beast. But all the vital points were behind the very large ogre currently bloodying his knuckles on Kevin's stubborn chin.

"I don't see you doing anything," said Regina. "Other than carrying my spears."

"You're right." Miriam dropped the weapons. She closed her eyes and began to hum, and the air around the siren shimmered darkly. Regina got a bad feeling about that.

Frank did his part to distract Kevin. Regina had never seen him fight before. His intimidating size cooled most tempers. She knew ogres to be strong, and Frank, being an unusually large specimen, was even stronger. But she'd never imagined him capable of fending off a roc single-handed. That took more than strength. That took skill. Frank was remarkably agile. It wasn't a dancer's grace, a fencer's elegance. Ogres weren't built for that. It was the art of the brawl, the confident form of an extraordinary pugilist. Not a single wasted move. Every strike delivered with deadly precision. Whenever Kevin lunged, he received a hindering blow across his beak, over and over again.

Miriam opened her eyes. The black orbs were now literally blood red. Sanguine tears ran down her cheeks. The veins on her fins throbbed. Her body trembled. The cobblestones cracked around her feet. Whatever the siren was up to, Regina hoped it would be quick. Even with all his skill and strength Frank couldn't hold Kevin forever.

Tired of getting smacked across his sore beak, Kevin tried to crush Frank beneath his foot. The attempt pushed Frank on his back, where he strained his immense muscles to keep Kevin from pulverizing him. It was a losing effort. The foot fell inch by inch until it pressed down on his chest.

Kevin chuckled. "Die, Ned."

"I'm . . . not . . . Ned," he wheezed.

Kevin's brow furrowed. It was the first time a roc's brow had ever furrowed—in fact, rocs were incapable of the expression. Only the dark magic coursing through his veins allowed Kevin to do it. He shrugged. This too was a roc first.

"You'll do."

A javelin buried itself in his neck. Green blood sprayed from the wound. Frank's massive muscles discovered newfound strength and shoved the stunned beast off him. He clasped his hands together and clocked Kevin across the face. The force snapped the roc's head back and spun his entire body. His serpentine tail whipped around, caught the ogre. Frank was flung across the courtyard and hit a wall hard enough to smash through it.

"Frank!" called Regina, though she wasn't certain why.

Kevin, blood dripping from the javelins piercing his flesh, turned his attention upon the Amazon. Regina prepared to throw another, but it wasn't likely to stop Kevin.

"Whatever you're doing, do it fast," she said to Miriam.

There was a note hidden behind the scales of melody by

the twisted gods of harmony. It didn't belong in this world, but it was known by the siren race. Other races spoke of it in whispers. Sirens spoke of it not at all for fear a slip of their charmed voices might blast continents to dust. It could not be taught. It could only be found by a siren of sufficient desperation and skill. Miriam's voice was barely adequate by siren standards, but she was desperate. And she found it.

Her lips parted ever so slightly. The final note was silent, but none would've heard if she'd made a sound. For the earth rumbled and the clouds screamed. Miriam's song surged from her throat, blossoming from her mouth into a twenty-foot-wide blast of boiling air and slicing winds. The cobblestones heaved themselves into the air. The note poured over Regina, knocking her to the ground. It rushed into the roc, who struggled to remain upright against the gale. The blast continued on, disintegrating a small guard shack that had fallen into disuse. It carried past that, shattering a section of Copper Citadel's outer wall. Still it continued, scouring the grass from the earth, uprooting trees, and freezing the river miles away. By then much of its force was spent, and it surrendered to the wind, which snatched it away into the sky where it infected a fluffy white cloud. The cloud darkened and grew angry, and for the next six centuries it would roam the skies in search of weddings, harvest festivals, and other joyous occasions upon which to rain down bricks or flaming dog dung or dead beetles.

It was a good thing Miriam's voice was not even slightly more skilled or all of Copper Citadel would've been destroyed, blasted to a barren field without even a piece of rubber or single male corpse to remember her by. As it was, every male within the sound of her voice (which couldn't be heard in the first place) was stricken with headache, nausea, and bleeding ears.

Miriam collapsed as Regina rose. The Amazon's gender spared her from the onslaught.

The roc twisted his head to one side. Kevin appeared unharmed despite the awesome power directed against him.

He'd lost a few feathers from the trembling air and had been unsettled by the quaking earth.

"It should've destroyed him," Miriam croaked incredulously, barely audible. "Nothing can withstand the final note."

And it was hard to imagine anything short of a god not being obliterated by the siren's song. But the roc rose to steady feet and cackled.

"Kevin's a girl," realized Regina. "Those damn goblins misnamed her."

Regina considered running for it, but Miriam wasn't even able to stand. She should've left the siren to die, but it wasn't her way to abandon a sister-in-arms. They hadn't gotten the chance to finish their fight, and she would be damned if some rampaging beast would deprive her of her rightful victory. She'd rather die first.

She tightened her grip on her javelin, but Kevin thundered past. The roc had no interest in such distractions as those two nongoblin morsels below her. She'd found her focus again.

"Neeeeeeeeed!" she shrieked.

Paperwork occupied most of Gabel's day, so it wasn't unexpected to find him in his office when Kevin started her rampage. A glance at the pandemonium outside his window encouraged him to remain indoors. It wasn't uncommon for a roc or two to get loose. The handlers of the program usually got everything back in order without too much difficulty. One of the smaller buildings might get crushed, and it was expected that some personnel would get eaten or flattened. Since he had no desire to be either, he wisely tucked himself under his desk and waited for the noise to die down. He dared crawl over to his filing cabinet just long enough to pluck out a standard Petty Chaos and/or Minor Tumultuous Calamity report, which he filled out. No reason to wait until the last minute.

The sounds of disorder continued much longer than Gabel expected. Usually the escaped roc slurped down its fill, mostly goblins, for which Gabel was immensely grateful as the Legion didn't bother with death notices for the species. The sated bird could then be led in lethargic agreeableness back to the pens. Several times he heard someone shout Ned's name, and with a bit of luck the commander might've died in the incident. Gabel craned out his arm and opened the top drawer of his desk, where he kept the Accidental Expiration Notices. He had one all ready for Ned, with everything but date, time, and manner of death filled out. Gabel had another form recommending himself for promotion under that. The recommendation was worthless as no one of any rank had endorsed it. But he still liked to look at it.

Something green and huge lurched past Gabel's window, rattling the entire office with her terrific, thumping footfalls. "Neeeeeeed!" screamed the unfamiliar voice. The monster stopped and lowered her head to peer through the window with one eye, but she didn't see Gabel under his desk.

"Come out, Ned!" shrieked Kevin. "You can't hide forever!" She stomped away with a growl.

Gabel crawled to the window and closed the curtains. He didn't know where the roc had found her voice, but it was obvious Ned had something to do with it. Regardless of Never Dead Ned's leadership talents, dubious at best, he was definitely a man followed by ill fortune. Demons and wizards and dragons and rampaging, talking rocs were proof of that. Gabel hadn't liked any of the company's previous commanders, but he hadn't gotten rid of them for any other reason than personal advancement. When Ned was finally disposed of, regardless of whether Gabel received a promotion out of it, he would still breathe a little easier.

The office door opened before Gabel could creep back under his desk. He sprang to his feet. "Dropped my pen," he explained before even looking up.

It was Ralph and Ned. The ogre clutched Ned by the neck. One squeeze of those fingers would crush Ned's spine. Ned seemed to know, judging by how stiffly he squirmed in Ralph's grasp.

"What are you doing?" asked Gabel.

"We gotta talk," said Ralph. "About him." He lifted Ned like a kitten and shook the human's fragile form. Ned sputtered.

Gabel leaned on his desk. "You idiot. You were supposed to leave me out of this."

"That's what we gotta talk about."

Ned was turning blue. Ralph casually tossed Ned, gasping and choking, into a chair in the corner. "Stay put, sir."

"What's going on?" asked Ned breathlessly.

"Quiet, sir," said Gabel, "this doesn't concern you."

Ralph imitated the small orc's leaning posture. The ogre's weight threatened to mash the desk. "I've been thinking . . ."

Gabel groaned. He hated it when minions started thinking. When would everyone finally realize how much easier life would be if they left the thinking to him?

"What's in this for me?" asked Ralph.

"I would think that would be obvious," said Gabel. "You don't like Ned."

"Yeah, so? I don't like lots of guys. Killing one asshole doesn't really make my life easier."

Ned rose from the chair as if to bolt for the door.

"Don't make me break your legs, sir," admonished Ralph. Ned sat down.

"As I was saying, I'm taking all the risks here, and you're getting all the perks. Doesn't seem like a good deal to me. I think it's time to renegotiate."

Gabel chuckled. "You idiot. There's nothing to renegotiate now. Ned knows you were planning to kill him, and now he knows I'm in on it too. If he walks out of this office, we both hang. We're both in this together now, and you have every bit as much to lose as I do. The first rule of negotiation is you've got to have something of worth or at least the illusion of something of worth, and you've got nothing." He grinned smugly. "Now kill him like you were supposed to so we can figure out what to do with the body."

Ralph grinned back. "Oh, I've got something."

He grabbed the desk in both hands and with one swift motion, cracked it across his knee. The splinters exploded in the room, driving a few choice wedges into the walls, toppling books, knocking down the curtains, and splitting one of Gabel's collection of dwarf skulls. One shard nearly skewered Ned through the eye. Another came dangerously close to piercing Gabel's foot. Several shards drove themselves into Ralph's thick skin, piercing his cheek, neck, and brow. Blood trickled, but Ralph seemed not to care.

Gabel and Ned gulped.

Ralph dropped the shattered halves of furniture. "See, the way I got it worked out, I'm not going to be in more trouble for breaking two officer necks than one. So we aren't negotiating for Ned's life. We're talking about yours."

"You wouldn't dare," said Gabel.

"Hey, you said it yourself: I don't like Ned. And I don't like you either. Truthfully I suspect you're every bit the asshole he is. Probably a little more of one."

Gabel snarled. He bent and grabbed a Furniture Requisition from the paperwork lying all across his office floor. Bit of good luck that one happened to be on top. But Ralph's devious nature was a bit of bad fortune. Gabel would have to be more careful when choosing his minions in the future.

"What do you want then?"

"I want to stop digging graves, but I want to keep getting paid for it," replied Ralph. "And I want free beer. Maybe some new boots."

"Is that it?"

Ralph realized perhaps he wasn't the shrewd negotiator he'd first thought. He knew killing Ned for Gabel should be worth a lot, but Ralph was damned if he could put a solid value on it. And he was a very simple ogre with very simple needs. He would've been happy with all the previously mentioned items, but that Gabel seemed untroubled by their request told Ralph he hadn't asked for enough. The ogre plumbed the depths of his mind, but it was a very shallow metaphoric pool, and he struck his metaphoric head on the metaphoric rocks at the bottom and was momentarily stunned.

As for Ned, he was slightly insulted by the exchange. He

liked to think his life was worth more than a new pair of boots. The indignity spurred him to think of escape again. He wouldn't let the universe die over a bottomless mug of ale. He didn't move just yet. Ralph was poised too near the only exit. Ned hoped when an opportunity came he'd spot it in time.

"Anything else?" asked Gabel impatiently.

"No, I guess not." Ralph snapped his fingers, though the meatiness of the digits produced more of a loud slap than a snap. "Wait. I'd like a girlfriend. Can you requisition one of those?"

"I'll see what I can do. Are you satisfied now?"

Ralph considered asking for more things, but the only other request that came to mind was some sort of magic sword. He didn't know if Gabel could get one of those, and Ralph didn't feel right asking for it anyway. Killing Ned would be far too easy. He couldn't in good conscience demand much more for the job.

Ned dashed for the door. He attempted to duck past Ralph's iron grip, but the office was so small and the ogre so large that there wasn't enough room. Ralph caught Ned by the arm and tossed him back in the chair.

"What if you're wrong about this?" asked Ralph. "What if Ned comes back again?"

Gabel knew he wasn't wrong. Ned's fear was apparent, and an immortal had no use for fear. But Gabel had not advanced this far through sloppy assassination, and he couldn't be absolutely sure Ned would remain dead. That was why he'd wanted Ralph to slay the commander. If Ned rose again, Gabel would have plausible deniability. Now that wasn't an option.

"We'll bind and gag the corpse and hide it someplace private," said Gabel. "We'll feed him to the rocs if we have to. Shouldn't be anything left to rise after that."

"Works for me," agreed Ralph.

"Wait," said Ned. "You can't do this. If you kill me, I'll destroy the universe."

"Not that again," sighed Ralph. "You're going to have to come up with a more believable lie than that."

Ned shouted for help as the shadow of the ogre fell across him. It was no use. There was far too much racket going on outside. The thudding footsteps of Kevin alone were enough to drown out most noise. Ned kicked and punched at Ralph with no effect. The ogre wrapped his thick hands around Ned's face, muffling any screams.

"I bet if I rip off his head he'll stay dead," said Ralph.

"Don't do that," replied Gabel. "Too messy. Just break his neck and get it over with."

"That's not much fun."

Ned squirmed and twisted. His hands clawed at Ralph. His legs kicked out to bounce harmlessly off the ogre's ribs.

"You're not doing it for fun," said Gabel. "Just finish him off."

Ned's teeth found purchase in a meaty mound of flesh in Ralph's palm, one of the few sensitive areas in his thick-skinned body. Ralph yelped and dropped Ned. He ducked between the ogre's legs and scrambled for the door. Gabel jumped in the way and kicked Ned across the face. Ned crumpled, and Gabel drew his sword.

"For crying out loud, do I have to do everything myself?"

Ned glanced up at the sword raised to behead him. He didn't think Miriam would be saving him this time.

"Uh, Gabel," said Ralph.

Gabel refused to be distracted any longer. He didn't turn around, and so he didn't see what Ned and Ralph saw. A single roc eye glared through the window.

"Neeeeeeeeeed!" shrieked Kevin as she shoved her head through the wall. Ralph scrambled to one side of the cramped office, barely avoiding being skewered by the roc's barbed beak. Ned curled in a ball, the most effective means of defense at his disposal.

Kevin snatched up Gabel in her toothy beak and withdrew her head to get a better look at her latest morsel in the sunlight. She discovered with some disappointment it was not

Ned. But it was the largest, juiciest goblin she'd ever come across. Only after she'd slurped him down did she notice the unsatisfying orcish flavor. Her hideous face twisted into an unusually gruesome sneer, she shrieked and dragged her tongue across the cobblestones, scraping away the clingy bits of orc aftertaste.

Ned and Ralph had put aside their differences and now sought to take advantage of the distraction to escape. The roc's body blocked the hole in the wall, and a mound of rubble blocked the door.

Kevin thrust her head back into the office.

"Get out of my way!" Ralph shoved Ned aside and prepared to break down the door with a thrust of his shoulder. Instead he got his head nipped off by Kevin's clumsy beak. Ralph's ogre nervous system locked his corpse into instant upright rigidity, and the exit was rendered more blocked than before.

Kevin lunged and pushed harder, and the wall buckled and bits of ceiling fell as inch by inch she moved closer to Ned frozen in the corner. If the roc were only a bit smarter, she could've dropped to her belly and easily angled in to snag him. But it was only a matter of moments.

Ned laughed: a derisive cackle at the forces of fate that seemed so damned determined to see him dead. If he wasn't the Mad Void now, he was at least mad. But he was a madman with a purpose. He would be damned if he'd willingly slide down Kevin's throat. He'd fight all the way down, and if possible he'd give her a good kick in the ass as she excreted him.

Gabel's sword was lodged between two of her wicked teeth. The hilt pointed out at him, and it waggled as she snapped her jaws. Ned, heedless of any danger, reached for it. It came loose almost as soon as he touched it and seemed to fall into his hand. By some miracle he managed not to lose a limb to the crushing beak.

The blade wasn't long enough to reach the roc's vitals. Surprising himself most of all, Ned pounced on Kevin's beak between snaps. He took hold of one of her nostrils with his free hand, and growling, she pulled her head out of the office.

The beast's eyes were on the side of her face. She twisted her head side to side to get a better view of the prey stubbornly clinging to her beak. Ned raised the sword and hacked at Kevin's face. The angle was awkward; most of his strength was invested in tight, whitened knuckles. The blows penetrated the flesh only to bounce off the monster's thick skull. Finally through sheer luck and persistence he managed to plunge the blade into the roc's eye. The angle was just right and the sword just long enough to pierce Kevin's three-ounce brain.

The realization of her death took a moment to reach the rest of her body. Kevin swayed. She coughed. Her eye glazed. Her feathers ruffled, and her legs wobbled. With one last horrid gasp, the roc tumbled over and collapsed on the ruins of Gabel's office.

Buried, barely able to draw breath in the overwhelming, sooty darkness, Ned nevertheless chuckled. He was alive. He'd cheated death. For once the icy touch of oblivion had been put off. For once Ned had won. He might suffocate in the next moment, but that seemed someone else's problem just now.

He heard digging above him. A stone was flung aside to shine sunlight in his face.

"Is this him?" asked one of the shadows over him.

"The pendulum," said another. "See how it burns."

Hot stone pushed against Ned's forehead. His skin smoldered, and he smelled smoke, but he didn't feel any pain.

They lifted him roughly from the rubble. His eye adjusted. They weren't soldiers, but lanky, purple-skinned, winged creatures with small horns jutting from their brows.

Demons.

Ned was too tired to struggle. He had nothing left. Whatever last portions of vigor he'd possessed were buried somewhere under Kevin's ten-ton corpse. One of the demons tossed Ned over his shoulder. They spread their wings and took to the air.

Demons filled the sky. Dozens upon dozens of the flying monsters. He squirmed, but there could be no escape. And even if he did manage to slip free and avoid the dozens of hands that tried to catch him, he'd fall to his death. Either way, fate had beaten him. As it always did.

Ogre Company milled underneath him. Regina shouted his name, but he couldn't pick her out of the crowd. Soon the demons had taken him beyond the walls of Copper Citadel.

The last thing he noticed was Nibbly Ned. The vulture perched atop a tower, watching Ned's abduction with cold, black eyes and an almost clinical detachment. And Ned laughed. And he kept on laughing, though he couldn't say why.

TWENTY-SEVEN

THE DEMONS CARRIED Ned not very far. Copper Citadel had just disappeared over the horizon as their destination appeared. It was a fortress of black stone and glittering jade. He would've sworn Copper Citadel was the only outpost in a hundred miles, but then he saw this new fortress had great, stony legs like those belonging to a thousand-foot elephant. Flocks of demons orbited the Iron Fortress, and Ned expected to be torn to pieces by the hungry monsters.

The demons parted. A portcullis opened, and Ned was whisked into the darkened fortress. He couldn't see much, but he smelled a foul concoction of urine, smoke, and putrid flesh. It smelled of ugly death, an odor he knew all too well.

His captors threw him roughly to the floor. New hands seized him. Claws sank into his shoulder. Blood ran down his arm.

"Is this him?" The voice was deep and possessed a quality of diction as if the speaker had practiced the sentence a thousand times in front of a mirror to insure that every nuance of lip and tongue was absolutely flawless. The feat was all the more impressive because the monster who held him lacked anything in the way of lips.

The demon was a bulging abomination. Muscles squirmed atop its muscles, yet it was grotesquely fat at the same time. It reminded Ned of an ogre, though infinitely more repellent. It was entirely naked save for thick hair all over its body that gave it the illusion of clothing, and a black executioner's hood draped over its relatively tiny head. There was a hole cut to show its toothy, lipless mouth, but none for its eyes. How it saw, Ned couldn't fathom.

"Scrawny little thing, isn't it?" asked the executioner.

"Just throw him in the cell," said one of the purple demons.

The executioner dragged Ned into a darker part of the dungeon. Baleful green torches cast a dim light, and the flickering shadows had faces twisted in agony. There were things in the other cells. Ned heard them crying, screaming, growling, breathing. Scratching softly at their prison doors. He didn't speculate on what they might be. They reached his cell, a long thin room littered with bones, none of which appeared human. There was another green torch set high in the wall. Its light was cold, and Ned could see the frost of his breath. The executioner locked manacles around Ned's wrists. Ned slumped to the floor defeated. The short chains kept him from falling all the way. The demon lifted Ned's chin. "Don't look like much, do you?"

If the executioner's breath was rotten, it was no more rotten than the rest of the dank, fetid air. He snorted again and spat. The saliva froze in midflight and shattered against the floor. He lumbered away without saying another word.

Ned hung in the darkness. Occasionally his bad left arm twitched. Sometimes it yanked at its bonds. The chains rattled. The other prisoners cackled and whispered.

"What'cha in for, buddy?" asked the occupant of the next cell. His voice was dry and menacing. There was a small hole in the wall that allowed him to peep through with a single, bloodshot eye.

"Destroying universes," replied Ned. "You?"

"Littering."

Ned raised his head skeptically.

"Littering the ground with the corpses of my enemies," clarified the prisoner. His red eye glowed sinisterly.

"What are you?" asked Ned.

"I don't know. I think I used to know, but I've been here so long I've forgotten. You'll forget too. Eventually."

Harsh, humorless laughter filled the dungeon.

"I won't be here that long," said Ned.

More laughter.

"That's what I said." Something, perhaps a sword or claws or fangs, scraped against the wall. The eye vanished from the crack. "At least I think that's what I said."

At some point Ned fell asleep. Or maybe he just thought he did. Something touched his wounded shoulder. He didn't have the strength to even yelp.

"Sir, are you okay?"

Ned raised his head with considerable effort and came face-to-face with an ugly, big-nosed demon with pock-marked skin.

"Go away," mumbled Ned. "Or kill me. I don't care which."

The demon whispered. "Sir, it's me."

Ned squinted.

"It's me, Seamus." The demon leaned closer. "Private Seamus."

Ned couldn't place the name.

Seamus glanced around to make sure the coast was clear before transforming back into his goblin self.

"That's a neat trick," said the prisoner in the next cell.

Ned's addled memory worked slowly. He didn't remember Seamus's name, and all goblins looked alike to him. But shapeshifting was just enough of a distinction to earn some recollection.

"I saw them take you away, sir," said Seamus, "and I decided to follow, see what I could do. I was a little worried at first that I might not be able to fool them, but nobody pays much attention to grunts. Not even in demon armies, I guess."

He checked the chains around Ned's wrists. "These are pretty thick. I might be able to break them if I transform into something big."

"Don't bother."

"I'm sorry, sir?"

"And then what? Even if you freed me, you'd never be able to get me out of here." Ned struggled to hang his head lower. "It's all pointless."

"He's right," said the prisoner. "No one has ever escaped these dungeons. No one and no thing."

"I could get some help," said Seamus.

"Why bother?"

"Don't you want to be rescued, sir?"

"I don't know. I guess."

Ned wasn't against it, but he didn't see how it was possible. And he was through hoping for impossibilities, or even improbabilities.

The dungeon door rattled open. Seamus disappeared in a puff of smoke, taking on his hideous demon form just as the executioner lurched into view.

"Here now, what are you doing? Nobody's supposed to be here."

Though wearing the hunched form of a demon, Seamus hunched lower. "Sorry. I got lost."

The executioner snorted, which appeared to be his favorite thing to do. He frowned, revealing rows of pointed teeth that up to now had remained hidden behind other rows of pointed teeth.

Seamus shrugged. "Uh . . . I'm new."

"You'd better come with me."

The goblin transformed into a giant sabercat in a puff of blue smoke. Seamus pounced, sinking his fangs into the executioner's throat. A snap of powerful jaws severed the head from the shoulders, and the incident was over before the demon could utter a cry, and where a normal sabercat would've howled its victory cry, Seamus was deathly quiet. He was sabercat enough to swipe a few bloody gashes across the demon's corpse.

The prisoner chuckled. "That's a very neat trick indeed."

Seamus returned to his natural goblin shape and gagged, wiping the blood from his lips. "Remind me not to do that again."

The door rattled.

"I'll be back, sir," said Seamus. "With help."

Ned hadn't even raised his head to watch the executioner's death. "Whatever."

Seamus disappeared into a yellow puff. When the smoke cleared, it appeared as if the goblin had vanished entirely. Only the most alert observer would've noticed the jet-black scorpion scampering into the darkness.

A new executioner demon, identical to the last save for boils on his belly, trudged in. "Come on now, what's keeping you?" He stumbled over the corpse, which he puzzled over for a moment. He glanced at Ned, securely chained to the wall. Then to the body, well out of Ned's reach.

"How did you do that?"

Ned kept staring at the floor. "Evil eye."

The executioner turned to the other prisoner. "No, really. How did he do that?"

"Just like he said." The prisoner's eye squinted, turning an amused pink shade. "Evil eye. One glance is all it takes."

"There's no such thing," said the executioner.

"Oh, no?" Ned raised his head a few degrees. "Look me in the eye and say that."

The demon stepped back, slipping on the pool of his comrade's frozen blood. The executioner, whose hood covered his own eyes completely, still shielded them with his hands.

"Hey, now, I'm just doing my job. No need to get violent."

"I think I'll melt your bones in your skin," said Ned. "Painful way to die. Believe me. I know."

The executioner, palm clasped firmly over his face, fumbled with the cell door. Once on the other side, he opened the slit to peek inside at Ned. But when Ned raised his head, the slit quickly shut.

Ned laughed. He never would've guessed demons to be superstitious. They already were the stuff of nightmares. But he supposed that it was hard to deny the powers of darkness when you were already in their ranks.

He had no idea how long one mysteriously executed demon would keep the others at bay. Not long, he imagined. And certainly not long enough for Seamus to get back to Copper Citadel, for Ogre Company to overcome years of lax discipline and mount a rescue effort. None of that mattered to Ned, who was beyond hope. Instead, he did what men without hope who have not quite given up yet have done since the dawn of time.

He waited.

TWENTY-EIGHT

THE GOBLINS STRUGGLED to get the roc from the pens. The giant birds were almost supernaturally stubborn. When they were supposed to be in their pens, they always wanted out. And when they were supposed to be out, that was the only time they'd stay in. One team of goblin handlers pulled on a rope around the roc's neck, while two more teams prodded its backside with long spears.

Regina buckled on the last bit of her armor. "I don't have time for this."

Ace puffed on his pipe. "Trust me. If we're going to do this, we're going to need a bird that's broken in."

The roc used its tail to sweep the prodders away. They went flying in various directions, but a new team immediately sprang into action.

"You call this broken in?" asked Regina.

"He's just being persnickety. Once we get him saddled, he'll be more agreeable."

While the handlers inched the roc from its pen, step by arduous step, Regina paced. Her armor rattled loudly, which did nothing to soothe the roc's mood.

"I still think this is a bad idea," said Ace.

"Then why are you going?"

"Because you're going to need the best pilot if it's going to work. Not that it will. I doubt we'll even find Ned. And if we do, we'll have that whole swarm of demons to deal with. The way I see it, either we're wasting our time or this is a suicide mission."

"If you're afraid, you don't have to come."

"I said I thought it was a bad idea." He chuckled. "I didn't say I didn't like it."

Goblins didn't know fear. The closest they came was the concept of panic. The species lived under the shadow of death, having a lifespan that measured in months. Ace was three years old and somewhat embarrassed by his advanced age. Goblins considered a high risk of death and dismemberment a prerequisite for any worthwhile endeavor. Since Ace had yet to meet his end, it was assumed by many of his kin that he was more devoted to staying alive than living well. This would've been the one and only sin in the goblin religion if goblins had bothered with religion.

"We'll find Ned," said Regina.

"What makes you so certain?"

"Because we have to."

"I don't see why," said Ace. "The Legion will just send us a new commander."

"This isn't about commanders," replied Regina.

"Then what's it about?"

She stopped pacing. She wished she knew the answer to that.

"It's about Ned." Though siren vocal cords were resilient, Miriam's voice hadn't quite recovered from the Final Note. It was rough and dry. "And demons."

Regina whirled on the newly arrived siren. Miriam wore her own armor, lighter and quieter than the Amazon's.

"What are you doing here?" asked Regina.

"I'm going with you."

Regina scoffed. "I don't need your help."

"That's good," said Miriam, "because I'm not coming along to help you."

The women locked stares, something they'd been doing so often lately that this time it was mostly a habit.

Miriam said, "Archmajor, this isn't a debate. You're thinking the same thing I am. Those were demons abducting Ned. And there's no good reason for that. Unless maybe he was telling the truth."

Ace stood between the women. He was far too short to block their stares, but the noxious cloud from his pipe did make their eyes water. The smoke clung to their drying eyeballs, but both refused to blink.

"You aren't telling me you believe him? About destroying the universe?" asked Ace.

Miriam replied, "I don't know. But if it's true, if even some small part, then we have to try. And even if it's not, which it can't possibly be, I can't just stand by while you two rush off to your glorious deaths. I owe Ned more than that."

"You don't owe him anything," said Regina coldly.

"Oh, no? If I recall correctly, Ned is mine."

Regina scowled. "He's not yours. Not until you've won him by rite of combat."

"I thought I already did."

"We didn't get a chance to finish." Regina's hand went to her sword.

"Oh, leave it in your scabbard, ma'am," said Miriam. "We'll settle the matter once we've rescued Ned."

"Can't hurt to have backup," added Ace, "and you gotta admit, she's not bad with a sword."

Regina had to admit no such thing. Not aloud anyway. But she had gained a grudging respect for her rival. She didn't want Miriam coming along, but short of beating Miriam to death, which the Amazon was confident she could do in a pinch, there was no other choice.

"Just don't expect me to save you if things get hairy," said Regina.

By now, the roc was out of the pen. The goblins scurried over the monstrous bird, reminding Regina very much of giant green fleas. Saddles were strapped on for the pilot and passengers in no time at all, and the roc calmed a bit as Ace promised. The pilot climbed up the roc's neck to sit on the saddle just behind its head. He lowered his goggles. His scarf fluttered in the wind. Neither Regina nor Miriam commented, but the light of the evening sun cast a soft halo around the goblin, giving him a heroic glow. There was something dashing about twenty-five pounds of goblin determination perched atop eight tons of irritated, unpredictable bird flesh.

The handlers threw down a rope ladder for the passengers to ascend, and they hesitated. It was one thing to admire Ace's guts, quite another to place their lives in his hands.

"Coming, ladies?" asked Ace.

Both grabbed hold of the ladder at the same time.

"Permission to come along, ma'am?" shouted Corporal Martin out of the blue.

The roc twisted at the sudden outburst and would've stepped on Miriam and Regina. Ace prevented the accident with a yank of the reins, thus spurring some confidence in the women.

The ogre twins Lewis and Martin stood before them. Ogres rarely bothered with armor. The cost of outfitting their massive bodies was prohibitive to the bottom line of Brute's Legion. They were already notoriously thick-skinned, and getting stabbed was a general nuisance rather than a life-threatening event. But the twins were ready for action, each carrying his weapon of choice. Lewis favored a massive stone club, while Martin preferred a slightly less massive club embedded with iron spikes.

Martin saluted casually as a proper salute would've ended with him bashing his brother in the face. "Begging your pardon, ma'am, but I heard about what you're planning, and I was hoping to come along."

Regina asked Lewis, "And you, private?"

Lewis shrugged his half of their shoulders. "Honestly,

ma'am, I'm not as keen on the notion as my brother, but we should do something. One doesn't allow demons to abduct an officer."

"It simply isn't done," said Martin.

Regina glanced to Miriam, who nodded. The goblins were already throwing on another saddle, this one large enough for a one-headed ogre and barely large enough for a two-headed one.

"Fine. You can come." Regina sighed. "Now can we get on with this?"

"They might have something to say about it, ma'am," said Lewis.

Behind the twins, a mob of soldiers came from Copper Citadel. Frank led. Having been thrown through a wall, he was bruised and battered, but relatively unharmed. He'd broken a few bones but stubbornly refused to pay them any mind. Ogres broke bones so often, particularly in their terrifying and awkward adolescence, that unless one was sticking out of their skin, they hardly noticed.

Regina put her hand on her sword. "Don't try and stop me."

Miriam stepped forward. "Stop us."

Frank said, "We're not here to stop you. We're here to help."

"Yes, we like Ned!" shouted Sally loudly enough to spit a ten-foot gout of flame in the air.

The soldiers grumbled in agreement.

"You do?" asked Regina. "But what about the training?"

"That's just part of the job!" shouted an orc.

"And the dragon?" asked Regina. "And the demons? And the talking roc? You don't blame Ned for that?"

"Sure, we do!"

"But at least it's not boring around here anymore!"

The mob roared, raising their weapons in the air.

Ward added, "Anyway, if we don't get him back, management will just send down another asshole! And we don't want another asshole!" He raised his fists high. "We want Ned!"

"Never Dead Ned!" shouted one soldier.

"Never Dead Ned!" repeated another.

The air filled with the chant. Some of the more inspired soldiers clanged their weapons against their armor in time with the beat.

Regina marveled at the loyalty inspired by Ned. He hadn't done much of anything. But that had been the strength of Ned's command, she supposed. He hadn't tried to make Ogre Company into a crack military unit. He'd just tried to get by in a bad situation, like the rest of them. He was the first commander who truly belonged in the company. He was one of them.

Frank limped over on his broken leg. "Guess we'd better saddle up more rocs. We'll have to send out search parties in a spread pattern until we find some sign of him," said Frank. "And hope we find him before it's too late."

A pigeon landed on his shoulder. In a puff of smoke, Seamus sat there in its place. "I think I can help you with that, sir."

TWENTY-NINE

RUCKA SAT UPON HIS Throne of Skulls, which was actually made of cedar. But the infernal emperor enjoyed giving his things appropriately horrific names. The chair was perfectly sized for his slight proportions. Despite his diminutive stature, Rucka was supremely confident in his power. A larger throne might've been more impressive, but not so impressive as roasting flesh with a withering glance.

Six demons dragged Ned into the throne room. "Here he is, Your Majesty," said an executioner.

"Why does he have a bag over his head?" asked Rucka with his dark, squeaky voice.

"To keep his evil eye at bay, sire."

Rucka chuckled. "Remove it."

They pulled the bag off Ned's head, and all the demons looked away. Except Rucka. All of his eyes—except for those on his back and ass—gazed up at Ned. Ned's eye fell upon the tiny Emperor of the Ten Thousand Hells, and he wasn't terribly impressed. But he wasn't in the frame of mind to be impressed by much of anything. And he wasn't foolish enough to equate size with power.

Rucka's throne room was a large chamber atop his tallest tower. There was no decoration, unless one counted a few bones scattered absently. Half a skull leered up from Ned's feet. There was a painted glass window with an image of a giant demon with four arms standing atop a mountain of carcasses. The demon was covered with eyes, just like Rucka, and there was a passing resemblance. But the work struck Ned as unimaginative and unremarkable. It was just the kind of horrible image of carnage he would've expected in a demon's throne room and thus rendered terribly unimpressive.

Rucka commanded the executioners to leave, and they were all too eager to comply. No demon wished to stay in Rucka's presence, where death was just a moment of annoyance away, or risk Ned's evil eye. The massive iron doors were shut, and Ned was left alone with the emperor.

The demon smiled. "Let me apologize for not coming to fetch you personally from your little citadel. I have some trouble crossing into the world of mortals. Too much power within me, you see. I could leave this fortress, but it would violate certain age-old treaties. More trouble than it's worth.

"And my Iron Fortress itself can't cross running water, even that little trickle of a river below. Don't ask me why. Design flaw. I had the engineers killed for it, but I suppose it would've been wiser to wait until they'd corrected the problem. Oh, well, kill and learn. That's what I always say."

He dangled a pendulum. "Do you know how long I've searched for you? You have no idea how difficult it's been with only these to guide my scouts. These stones are the only thing that can detect your true essence. Come from the sacred rock that was part of the transformation rite. Won't bother you with the details. Some very special magic was used, the kind that comes along once every three ages, if that. Worked so well that even now, standing in this room with you, I don't see anything but a mortal man. Not the slightest hint of the awesome power just waiting within you."

The pendulum twitched in Ned's direction so slightly that

it might just have been the wind. But the stone glowed with a soft, red light.

Rucka said, "I won't tell you how much trouble they were to get in the first place, how many troublesome gods I had to kill, how many rival demon lords I had to slaughter, or how many souls I devoured in this quest of mine. My only consolation is I enjoy killing, slaughtering, and devouring. Hardly seems like any work at all, to be honest."

Rucka's four small wings beat like a hummingbird's, and he shot off his throne and hovered before Ned. The pendulum glowed brighter, and its tilt was undeniable as it pulled toward Ned.

"Have you ever tried searching the world by pendulum?" asked Rucka. "They're a devil to use and not nearly so sensitive as would be helpful. Not to mention there's only nine of these. Which is why it took so long to locate you. I've come close a few dozen times over the eons. But you've always wandered off before I could get my hands on you."

"Sorry," said Ned.

"Think nothing of it, old boy. I always knew I'd find you. One of the advantages of being an immortal. Time is always on my side. I'm surprised though that your troublesome guardian hasn't interfered."

"The Red Woman?" said Ned. "She's dead."

"Impossible."

"She died saving me."

Rucka stared Ned in the eye. "Really? How odd. Why should she sacrifice herself for an illusion? Disappointing. I was hoping to kill her myself. But seeing as how she died protecting you, I can at least take comfort in the futility of her sacrifice."

Rucka touched the stone to Ned's cheek. The pendulum flared, though it still wasn't much of a light, and the heat seared Ned's face without actually hurting him. He smelled smoke, but didn't see any. His bad left arm tightened, and he worried it might take a swing at Rucka. But he stopped worrying. Punching Rucka wouldn't accomplish anything, but it couldn't get him in any more trouble.

Something, some Thing inside Ned, stirred. The Void. Maybe it was the concentrated evil of Rucka and his Iron Fortress. Maybe it was the closeness of the sacred stone. Or maybe it was just the pressure, the maddening sense of futility, the impatience. But the Mad Void was awake. Somewhere deep inside, it roused. It didn't arise. Rather, it shifted restlessly, like a deep sleeper troubled by a mosquito buzzing in his ear.

It'd always been there. Always. Buried so deep Ned couldn't sense it. Forgotten. A burden, a weight carried over a thousand lifetimes by a thousand different men and women, all just illusions. A cage of dreamed flesh and false mortality and unknowable magic. Nothing else.

That was all Ned was. Nothing. So why the hell did he care? Whether Rucka succeeded in usurping the Mad Void's power or not, whether the illusion of Ned died or not, he saw no reason to give a damn.

But he did.

Rucka had been speaking while Ned, internalized, oblivious to the outside world, hadn't heard a word.

"Excuse me," said the all-powerful demonic emperor. "But am I boring you?"

"A little."

Rucka snorted. Acidic snot dripped from his nostrils and sizzled holes in the floor. "What is your name? Not your true name, but the name this shell carries?"

"Ned."

Rucka raised the thorny ridge that served as his eyebrow. "Would that be Never Dead Ned?"

"You've heard of me?"

"I've heard tales. Now and then, here and there. I even considered looking you up once. But the Mad Void hidden in the body of an immortal? Honestly, it seemed too obvious. But I guess that's the trick of it, isn't it? Draw attention to yourself, instill doubt, hide in plain sight. Very clever."

Rucka fluttered back to his throne. "Tell me, Ned, how much do you know about this business?"

Ned grunted. "Enough."

"Then you know I intend to take that power you conceal for my own."

Ned nodded.

"And you know there is nothing you can do to prevent it."

Ned nodded again.

Rucka leaned forward. "But do you know how I plan on taking it? Do you know where all that power rests?"

Ned shrugged. "Inside me. Somewhere."

"No. Not somewhere. Your power, that power, lies in the same place all great demons hold their might." Rucka's countless eyes burned. "Do you know where that is?"

"No," replied Ned absently, only half listening.

"Think about it." The room darkened, and every one of Rucka's eyes shone.

"Their horns?" ventured Ned.

"Don't be absurd. Too obvious. I'll give you another guess."

The emperor opened his jaws and sucked all the light from the throne room. All that shone in the pitch black was his hundred malignant, shimmering eyes.

"Stomach?" said Ned.

Rucka belched the light back into the air. He sat on his throne, his short arms folded across his tiny chest. His child-like face twisted into a pout, and his long tail thrashed. "Oh, come on. You're not even trying."

"Yeah. Uh, sorry, but I'd rather you just get it over with and kill me."

"Oh, I'm not going to kill you, Ned. In the first place, you're not really anything but an illusion, so you can't truly die. In the second, if I do . . . kill . . . this illusion, it will only awaken the Mad Void, and I've no desire to unleash all that power until it is firmly in my grasp."

Rucka shot across the throne room and grasped Ned by the hair with tiny, painfully strong hands. "No, Ned, I'm not going to kill you. I'm going to pluck out your eye." He laughed. "Of course, the spell will break then, and I suppose you'll die. In the sense that there will no longer be any need for you and you'll fade away. And then I shall insert that eye, the Dark Eye of the Mad Void, here." A socket opened in the middle of his forehead. "And I shall claim my rightful title as most powerful demon in this or any other universe."

Rucka tossed Ned away. He fell on his back to lie on the floor. The fall banged his head and bruised his elbow. The leering demon emperor hovered over him.

"You can beg for your life now. It won't do any good, but feel free."

"No, thanks."

Ned's bad arm shot up and seized Rucka by the throat. It squeezed without any effect. Rucka dug the claws of his hands and feet into Ned's forearm, lifted him high in the air, and spun around once before hurling Ned across the room, where he landed atop the Throne of Skulls, smashing it to bits.

Ned suspected he might've broken a bone or two. He played it safe by not moving. He was beyond pain now. Not that he didn't hurt. He hurt like hell, and a shard of armrest dug into his spine unpleasantly. But he'd gained acceptance of what was coming, and he no longer cared about such trivialities as agony. He was only an illusion in the end. By extension, so must have been his pain. And his worry. And everything else. That made them easy to ignore.

Rucka groaned. "Well, this isn't any fun. If you're not going to cower properly, I guess we might as well get on with it."

"Guess so," replied Ned as casually as if commenting on the bricks of the ceiling he was staring at.

The throne room doors opened, and seven demons stepped in. They wore hooded cloaks that concealed their bodies except for their large orange wings.

"I could pluck the eye out right now," explained Rucka. "Though I'd enjoy the vulgarity of it, some of the Void's power might slip away. And I want it all." He chuckled. "Every . . . single . . . drop."

It took longer than Regina would've liked to saddle up all of Ogre Company's rocs, but if she was going to face a horde of demons, she knew it was only sensible to have as many able-bodied soldiers behind her as possible. There were thirty-three rocs in the stables. On average, each could carry three full-grown ogres. The most capable warriors were selected for the mission. There weren't enough saddles for all of them. Most of the ogres held on to the feathers with one hand while carrying their massive club or giant sword or whatever absurdly huge weapon they favored in the other. At least another three hundred goblins, all too eager to rush headlong into oblivion and unwilling to be left behind, clung to the rocs' undersides, legs, necks, wings, and any other free space. Regina, Miriam, Sally, and Ace (along with a dozen goblin hitchhikers) led the flight.

The bulk of the company had remained behind at the citadel to prepare for the worst, whatever that might be. Frank had been one of them. Regina found herself wishing him by her side. She couldn't think of any other soldier in Ogre Company she would've preferred. But he was hurt. Even hurt, he was probably the toughest grunt in the company. Possibly as fearless and deadly as she.

She caught herself smiling and wiped the grin from her face.

Rocs filled the sky. The pilots had managed to get the monstrously ill-tempered birds into a tight V formation. From the ground, thought Regina, they must have been an impressive sight. One hundred airborne ogres, give or take, hurtling headlong toward certain doom, possibly about to begin a battle for the fate of the universe.

"There it is!" shouted Ace.

The Iron Fortress came into view. It was smaller than Regina expected, and its obsidian bricks were difficult to pick out on the dark horizon. But the glittering jade and the soft glow of its tallest tower made it obvious enough once her eyes adjusted.

Regina grinned. And this time she couldn't stop smiling. She so loved a suicide mission.

The moment the Iron Fortress appeared, she anticipated a great host of winged demons would pour from its every opening. She expected, with some grim Amazonian dream of glory, to be swept away in a tide of knives, gnashing teeth, and cruel claws. It would be a beautiful death, the kind an Amazon could be proud of.

But nothing of the sort happened. Not one demon, not even the littlest imp, came forth. The Iron Fortress just stood there. One of its tremendous legs absently pawed the earth, but in no way did it exhibit the slightest acknowledgment of Ogre Company's approach.

"Shouldn't they be doing something?" asked Miriam.

Regina agreed. Some response was expected. Even courteous. There couldn't be a legendary last battle for the fate of the universe if the Forces of Darkness refused to show up. It was extremely poor form. After all, the demons had to notice the mighty fighting force just moments from their doorstep. Did the residents of the giant, walking castle not consider them a threat at all? Were the hideous creatures within so powerful that the company wasn't even worth a minimal response? She found that hard to believe. More likely, she decided, the fortress had other defenses, dark underworld sorceries gathering now to swat each and every roc from the sky before the battle could begin. Green and orange lightning flashed all around the tallest tower, a sure indication that some demonic magic was at play. Yet she carried on fearlessly.

"Maybe they haven't noticed us!" yelled Ace above the whipping winds.

"Don't be ridiculous!" Regina shouted back, her pride stinging a bit.

It'd been a long time since anyone had dared lay siege to the Iron Fortress. Its long legs made scaling its walls an impossible feat. Those same legs also allowed it to crush any army stupid enough to dare the impossible, and should a force prove immune to even this deterrent, the fortress could always amble away at its leisure from more bothersome attackers.

Inside the castle itself, within its malign walls, a great swarm of terrible demons waited to unleash themselves upon anything foolish enough to challenge them. They would've gladly joined in battle against Ogre Company had anyone been on watch. But the Iron Fortress had no watch because it'd been a long, long time since it'd had need of one. And demons, being generally lazy and irresponsible, had ceased keeping up the duty.

Technically, there was a watch at work, but they were either drunk on elf blood, fornicating, or engaged in a rousing game of competitive skull juggling. Consequently, the only residents of the Iron Fortress to catch a glimpse of the trouble heading their way were a couple of gargoyles chained to a parapet. Since neither cared much for either chains or demons (and weren't particularly fond of parapets either), neither spoke up, but instead shared a good chuckle and wink. Regina knew none of that and assumed she was rushing into an ambush. It didn't deter her. If anything, it made her more determined. It'd been too long since she'd enjoyed the bloodlust. She'd forgotten how sweet it tasted.

"Where do you think they'd be keeping Ned?" asked Ace.

"There." Miriam pointed to the tallest tower, sheathed in crackling supernatural energies, casting an eerie red glow in the twilight that made the dusk as bright as a new dawn. "That would be my guess."

Regina shook her head. "Too obvious. Besides, this is Ned we're talking about. He's probably still locked away in some pit."

"I told you we should've brought Owens along."

"He's always been bloody useless," said Regina. "And what could he do anyway? Hear Ned's location?"

Ace whipped the reins, and the rocs broke into a power dive toward the fortress. The formation followed suit.

The hooded demons chanted. The Void stirred again inside Ned. It bubbled in his throat, tasting like rotten maple syrup, thick and clumpy.

Rucka flicked over and grabbed Ned by the shirt. The small demon casually tossed him into the center of the throne room. The sorcerers continued their chant as they formed a circle around Ned. Their pendulums shimmered, casting delicate strands of light that reflected off each other and bent in the air like silver threads. Still droning, the sorcerers pulled away their hoods to reveal faces they didn't have. No mouths. No ears. No noses. Only three eyes arranged in a triangle upon their foreheads.

Rucka leered. "It won't take long, Ned. The bindings that hold the Void in this shell are too powerful to be destroyed by anyone but the Void himself, but we only need loosen them a bit. The rest will come from within. And when he rises, when he can no longer sleep, at that one moment when he is at his full power yet too groggy to realize what is happening, I shall pluck out your eye."

The emperor salivated. Drool dripped from his lips to puddle beneath his hovering body.

Strangely, Ned didn't sense anything else wrong with him as the magic did its work. His pain faded, and the Void continued to rumble within him. But despite the awesome magics being unleashed (to be honest, this was just a guess since Ned knew nothing of minor magic much less the awesome type), Ned didn't feel anything else. There was only one explanation. He was fading away, and because he wasn't real, he couldn't even sense it.

He didn't want to die. And not just because his death meant the end of the universe. There was more at stake. Less, actually. But for the first time in as long as he could remember, Ned wanted to live. He didn't know why. His life had been a remarkably dull affair up to now, excluding the last few days of dragon wizards and demon emperors. But maybe that was his fault. Or maybe he was just destined to live a boring, eternal existence. And maybe one day he'd be sick of it. But not today.

Damn it all, he was Never Dead Ned, and if there was one thing Never Dead Ned was good at (and as far as he could tell there was only one thing), it was not dying. Actually, he was pretty good at that, but staying dead was another matter. And after all this time yearning for the icy whisper of true and lasting oblivion, Ned decided he wasn't so keen on end-

ing his days after all. He had to do something. At the very
least, he had to try.

The sorcerers' voices blended together into a low rumble
that vibrated the throne room and, indeed, the entire fortress.
The Mad Void grumbled, though only Ned sensed it, and even
he wasn't so sure about that anymore. There seemed every
possibility that what he thought was awakening unspeakable
evil was nothing more than a hearty case of indigestion.

Ned wondered if a mistake had been made. He didn't feel
all-powerful. Nor did he feel as if he was fading away after
all. He felt . . . well, he felt like Ned. But it didn't seem
likely that the Red Woman, the sacred stones, and the
demons could all have been wrong.

The chant reached its crescendo. The lights of the pendulum gathered into a swirling cube over his head that settled
on his body, and for a second Ned thought he might throw up.

Rucka pounced. The demon forced Ned to the floor and
pressed tiny, sharp claws to Ned's face.

Ned belched.

The light faded.

Rucka's smile vanished. He pulled back his empty hand
and squinted at Ned. "What's this? Where is it?" He hopped
to stand on Ned's chest and glare at his sorcerers. "Where is
the power?"

The sorcerers lowered their pendulums but dared not
speak. With a grunt, Rucka blasted a fireball out of his nostril that slowly and painfully incinerated one of his minions.
The sorcerer writhed in twisted agony, screaming and begging for mercy.

Rucka seized another by the robes. "Please, speak up."

The sorcerer's voice sounded muffled and distant, logical
given his lack of a mouth. "Forgive us, oh dreaded lord, but
we do not know. It should've worked."

Rucka disintegrated this sorcerer in an instant, discarding
the gift of agony usually granted to those who failed him. He
had more pressing concerns than such infernal civilities.

The remaining sorcerers cowered as Rucka stalked toward
Ned. "I felt it. For the briefest of moments, I sensed . . .

something. Something inconceivable, even to my intellect. Yet it remains hidden."

He clasped his hands behind his back and paced twice around Ned. "I see now that I must settle this affair personally." He turned to his sorcerers. "You're dismissed."

"Thank you, oh merciful dark lord," said one.

"Think nothing of it." Rucka waved a hand. The floor opened up beneath them, and they tumbled down into the depths, into the literal bowels of the Iron Fortress itself.

Rucka's many eyes glowed with blue flames. He made no move toward Ned, just stared at him. The demon picked up a pendulum and channeled his dark powers through it. The stone burned a murderous red, bathing Ned in a crimson spotlight as Rucka's magic clawed at the illusion of flesh, striving to tear it away, to strip away the chimera of mortal bone and blood. Ned blurred around the edges for just a moment. His lack of reaction surprised the emperor, but he kept this to himself. A cruel grin remained across his face as he pushed more of his awesome power against the ancient spell that was Never Dead Ned.

There were few external signs of the invisible magics. Shafts of unholy fire poured from Rucka's eyes. A single drop of sweat formed on Ned's forehead, and he felt kind of itchy. But he didn't scratch. He didn't want to give Rucka the satisfaction.

Scowling, Rucka hissed a rancid, orange mist that wrapped around Ned. His itchiness grew, and that stinging indigestion stirred again, much like the sensation triggered by the sorcerers but a little stronger. Ned stifled a gag. He scratched his nose and wiped the tears from his eye. But that was the worst of it.

Rucka grumbled. He'd expected Ned to melt away. The magic at work was more complex than he'd first imagined. Unmaking such spells demanded subtlety and patience, but he'd never been very good at these. Instead he poured more of his dark magic through the sacred stone and into Ned's false mortal shell.

Ncd's indigestion roared, though by the time it crawled

out of his belly and up his throat to push its way out his closed mouth, it was barely a dull snarl. Some alien presence rose in his guts and lashed out at the bothersome nuisance of the First and Greatest Emperor of Hell.

Rucka exploded.

For such a little demon, there was a terrible mess left behind. Slimy goop covered the walls. Ned was splattered with the malodorous stuff. He would've thrown up, but he didn't have the energy. Rucka's many eyes littered the floor. Each and every one glared at Ned. It was a good indication that the demon wasn't dead, though he was clearly very annoyed. Ned couldn't blame him. Rucka's might was beyond understanding, yet the Mad Void had swatted him away as casually as if the terrible demonic emperor were some easily swatted away thing. Ned didn't have the energy for metaphors right now either.

The Void settled back into its slumber. Although it hadn't really awoken. If it had, the universe would probably be ash by now. Except the stuff that was already ash. That would probably become some lesser class of ash. Dust, thought Ned. Or soot. He wasn't sure which, and it seemed largely irrelevant. What was relevant was that the Mad Void was a very deep sleeper and had little interest in waking up. That was good.

However, it had also crushed Rucka with the barest flex of its metaphysical might. Which meant if it ever did wake up, even against its will, there would be no force capable of putting it back to bed. Rucka didn't understand that, and he'd keep poking the Mad Void with a stick. The results could only be disastrous to the entire universe, including Rucka. The goop that was the emperor was slowly but certainly drawing himself back together. And that had to be bad since Ned doubted the exploded emperor had learned his lesson.

The throne room doors flew open, and in rushed a squad of demon soldiers. Ned could identify them as soldiers by their gleaming black armor and wicked scimitars. He could identify them as demons, though their armor covered them almost completely, because it was a safe bet that almost every resident of the Iron Fortress was a demon. Even him, when he thought about it.

"Forgive us, great and merciless lord," said the lead soldier, "but the fortress is under—"

The slimy remains of his master interrupted his report. He slipped on a bit of intestine and fell flat on his back with a resonating clang. Two others followed his example, sliding across the floor. The remaining three learned from their example and didn't cross the threshold.

The soldiers, those not trying to rise to their feet, took in the scene. Ned couldn't see their faces behind their closed helmets, but he assumed their expressions were of awe. It appeared as if he'd destroyed their fearsome leader. He didn't see any reason to correct the assumption.

"I guess I'll be leaving now," he said, "if that's okay with you."

Rucka's minions were so used to bowing before omnipotent masters that they lowered their scimitars without hesitation and stepped aside to let Ned pass. He didn't know how long it would take Rucka to reform, but the more distance between the emperor and Ned, the better. The trickiest part would be crossing the throne room without ending up sprawled helplessly across the floor. Before he could begin the delicate journey, a shadow fell across the window.

Ned turned just in time to see the painted glass shattered by a shrieking roc. The bird planted its feet in the slime and skimmed forward, driven by its momentum. Ned barely managed to dive to one side as it coasted by him and crashed against a wall. The moment's stop was enough to allow it to dig its claws in the floor to gain some stability, though it was a stiff breeze away from toppling over. A dozen goblins dropped from the roc's feathers and charged the demon soldiers. In other circumstances, the experienced demon warriors would've slaughtered their foes, but there were few opponents as wily and unpredictable as a squad of greased goblins.

The sounds of a battle raging outside reached Ned's ears

as he gingerly pushed himself to his knees. He spat out some goop. Not surprisingly, Rucka tasted horrible.

"I told you he was in this tower," said Miriam.

"Yes, yes." Regina threw down a ladder. "Ned, we've come to rescue you."

"Thanks." Ned smiled as he crawled his way toward the roc. A rescue at this point was a trifle late, but it was still the thought that counted.

Ace struggled to keep his mount steady. Not easy with the slippery floor and the roc's natural inclination to pace around. But it would be extremely bad form to have the giant bird fall on Ned in the middle of the rescuc.

"What the hell happened here?" asked Ace.

Ned grabbed the ladder and began the ascent. "Nothing much. I just exploded a demon emperor."

"You?" asked Regina as she helped him to his seat between Miriam and her.

"Sort of." He smiled sheepishly.

The pile of muck that was Rucka had managed by now to pull itself together enough to form a misshapen head, a lump with eyes and a crooked mouth. "This isn't done, Ned!" bellowed Rucka. "I will destroy you! I will have your power! I will—"

The roc, slipping and sliding its way toward the window, squished Rucka and his threats underfoot. Twice the bird lost its footing, but Ace's superior skills kept it from rolling over and crushing its riders.

Ned picked out ogres, goblins, and demons swarming on the Iron Fortress. The glow of the fortress itself bathed the battle in a green and red luminescence. It wasn't so much a grand battle as a warm-up clash. Right now, Ogre Company was winning by virtue of first strike, but each passing moment more and more demons were appearing.

"Sir?" asked Miriam.

"What?" replied Ned.

"Your orders?"

Again he'd forgotten he was supposed to be in charge.

Now that he remembered, he still didn't have the experience to be good at it.

"What would you do?" he asked Regina.

"I'd order a retreat back to the citadel, sir. Might give us the advantage."

"Right, right. Do that then, Archmajor."

Regina nodded to the goblin bugler clinging to the roc's tail. "Sound the retreat."

The bugler blew the call. Ogre Company remounted its birds with surprising discipline. There were a few stragglers eager to get in a few more licks, but the company was soon in the air, sailing back toward Copper Citadel.

The slime-coated goblins battling the demon soldiers skated effortlessly across the slippery throne room to climb back onto the roc, which Ace spurred out the window. The bird plummeted downward until Ace yanked its reins hard enough to remind it to start flying. Screeching with great irritation, as if it'd much rather hit the brick below, the roc flapped its majestic wings and soared off. The slime covering Ned sloughed off to stay behind in the fortress.

The bugler continued to sound the retreat as the rest of the reptilian birds launched themselves. By now, the demons had managed to get their brimstone cannons out. They fired a few volleys of sulfurous flame that went wide except for one that struck a roc's side. The bird wobbled but wasn't greatly bothered.

The Iron Fortress shrank slowly in the horizon. It stomped its great feet in an earthshaking temper tantrum.

"You came for me," said Ned.

"You are our commander, sir," said Regina.

"And we were worried possibly about the fate of the universe," added Miriam.

"Oh, yeah," agreed Ned. "I suppose that's important."

Ned glanced back at the fortress again. A few parting shots of stinking fire soared through the air, but were well short of the flight. There weren't any demons in pursuit. Probably in disarray without their emperor, Ned decided.

But once Rucka reformed, there was sure to be an army of the damned coming.

Ned weighed his options. He could order Ace to keep flying and hope to outdistance any pursuers. There was no shame in running away. But he doubted that would work. He might be able to put them off for a while, but hiding would be a lot harder now. The demons knew who he was. So did he. So did a few hundred soldiers. True, they didn't know exactly *what* he was, but close enough that obscurity would be difficult to find in the long run.

At least in the citadel he was surrounded by several hundred soldiers. They might not be the best of the best, the greatest collection of warriors, but they were a damn sight better than striking off on his own. He didn't know how many demons might be coming, but a few hundred ogres at his side meant he'd have some chance. Circumstances left him no other choice.

Ned shuddered. He didn't have much confidence in Ogre Company. And even less in their commander.

A goblin tugged at Ned's leg. "Did you really blow up a demon, sir?"

Ned didn't feel like offering clarifications of things he didn't truly understand himself.

"Yes. Yes, I did."

THIRTY

THE CITADEL CAME INTO view far too soon for Ned's liking. He would've preferred more distance from the Iron Fortress. He couldn't help but count every inch of every mile between him and an army of demons. It didn't make much difference, but it would've made him feel better just the same. The bulk of rocs put down in the pens on the other side of the citadel, but Ace put Ned's flight down in the courtyard. The courtyard was bustling, but Ace managed—impressively—to not squash anything in the landing.

The riders disembarked, and Ace spurred the roc back to the pen. Frank limped forward to greet Ned and company. The Ogre held a tree trunk across his shoulder. He saluted, the gesture without a trace of sarcasm.

"Any trouble, sir?"

"Nothing we couldn't handle."

"Good to have you back, sir."

"Good to be back, Lieutenant. And it's Ned. Just Ned."

Frank smiled. "If you insist, Ned."

"I do. I think we both know I'm not the right man to be in charge."

Regina cleared her throat behind Ned, who shrugged.

"Right *person*," he hastily corrected.

"Can't disagree with you there, Ned," said Frank, "but you are in charge. To be honest, I've seen worse commanders."

"I find that hard to believe."

"Look at it this way, Ned. Most horrible commanders don't know how horrible they are. You've got that on them."

Frank put his hands on Ned's shoulders. The gesture was meant to be comforting, but it reminded him how easily Frank could flatten the delicate human skull with a casual squeeze.

"This is all very nice," said Regina, "but we can probably expect a demon horde any moment now."

Frank waved his tree trunk at the soldiers running around. "We're almost prepared. As much as we can be. The citadel isn't designed to resist a full-scale assault. The gate's good and strong, but it won't amount to much defense with these crumbling outer walls. That one gap is large enough for a phalanx to march through."

"Won't really matter. Most, if not all, the demons can fly. A breach is to be expected."

"Good." Frank, like most ogres, preferred his warfare direct and to the point. A protracted siege would be far too dull.

"How are we doing for armaments?" asked Regina.

"Not nearly well enough," replied Frank. "We don't have a full complement. Just enough for training purposes."

"We'll make do," said Regina, "but the darkness will put us at a disadvantage."

"Ulga said she might be able to do something about that."

While Regina and Frank shared strategies, Ned stood to one side. They had things well in hand, and he didn't have anything constructive to offer, neither the experience nor the skills to be of great use on the battlefield. It was better, just plain smarter, to leave this war to others. If the mark of a good leader was the ability to delegate authority, then Ned wasn't just good. He was great.

He didn't feel great. He felt helpless. He might contain the most powerful force in the universe, but it didn't change the fact that he himself was practically useless.

Miriam tapped Ned on the shoulder. "Everything all right, Ned?"

"I guess."

She held out the speaking staff. "Some of the soldiers found this. Thought you might need it."

He didn't. The staff had no magic, and even if it did, he didn't know how to use it. He took it just the same. It was comforting to have something solid to hold.

"It'll be okay, Ned," said Miriam.

"I know."

He didn't, but he was commander. He couldn't afford to show fear or weakness or uncertainty. That was part of the job, damn it. He could fake it if he had to.

Miriam put her hand on his shoulder. Unlike Frank's meaty mitt, hers seemed a small reassurance. "Don't worry. We're professionals. Fighting is what we get paid to do."

Ned realized he wasn't as good at faking confidence as he'd hoped. Yet another basic leadership skill he lacked.

"We should really get you under cover," said Frank suddenly from beside Ned.

Ned sighed. The battle of the universe was about to commence, and he'd be stuck in some dank hole. It made perfect sense. His life was what this was all about. It'd be plain stupid to have him join in the melee. He was sure to be killed within minutes (if not seconds). He knew all this, but it didn't change his distaste for it. If he was to die today, he wanted to meet oblivion face-to-face, not cowering in some basement waiting for death to come to him. Especially since it always found him in the end.

"Private Lewis and Corporal Martin have agreed to serve as your personal bodyguard," said Frank.

The massive ogre twins saluted.

"It's an honor, sir," said Lewis.

"And a privilege, sir," added Martin.

"Right." Ned looked up at the towering brothers. They

only made him feel all the more insignificant. Ironic, considering how the fate of the universe was so indivisible from his own.

An orc watchman in a balcony blew the alarm on his horn. It was blasted dark now, but orcs had excellent night vision.

"They're coming." Frank wrapped his hands around the tree trunk and took a few practice swings. "Get him out of here."

"Right this way, Commander," said Lewis as he ushered Ned toward the pub basement.

"Good luck, Frank," said Ned.

The ogre lieutenant didn't hear him; he was too busy scanning the darkened sky for the first signs of the enemy. On the way to his hiding place, Ned passed Ulga as she began conjuring burning balls of light and launching them into the air in rapid succession. They bathed the citadel in a soft glow. They lit the night like small, very near stars. The light of an artificial dawn cast through the pub. Ned paused, staring out the window. He held tighter to the speaking staff.

Some unseen monster shrieked in the distance. Then another. And another. Ten million demon voices filled the air with their shrill, fearsome war cry.

"How many are there?" Ned wondered.

"Too many," replied the staff.

Somewhere, someone in Ogre Company had found a bone horn and blew the battle ballad of Grother's Death Brigade, a company of orcs famous for killing a dragon tyrant by cramming themselves down the tyrant's gullet until she choked to death. The soldiers raised their weapons and roared in one voice. The ogres, with their deep, bellowing voices, dominated the song. The demon's war cry and the company's song mixed together into an off-key miasma of glorious determination.

It hurt Ned's ears. It also simmered his blood. For the first time ever, Ned grasped in some vague sense the strange nobility of charging down a dragon's throat with a sword in your hand and a smile on your lips. For the first time ever, he wanted to step out onto the battlefield and do his part.

The twins opened a trapdoor behind the bar. "We should get you below, sir," said Martin.

"Right this way," said Lewis.

Ned sighed. Unfortunately, hiding was his part of this battle. He walked down the cellar stairway with some strange, foreign reluctance. The twins closed the door, dulling the horrible, enticing dirge of war.

Owens sat on a barrel. He turned his head as they entered. "Hello, sir."

"What are you—"

"Blind, sir," the oracle replied. "Hearing the future isn't much good in a fight."

Ned stood in the middle of a cellar surrounded by kegs of mead dimly lit by a single candle. Only it wasn't a candle.

"Is your staff glowing, sir?" asked Martin.

The staff cast a soft light. It also felt slightly, almost imperceptibly warm.

"Why are you glowing?" asked Ned.

"I'm glowing?" replied the staff.

Before Ned could ask it another question, he noticed the howls of the demons and bellows of the company had faded away. In their place was a deathly, all-consuming silence, so complete that even the cellar was seized in its grasp.

Demons settled on the walls of Copper Citadel, yet none entered its grounds. They perched like leering vultures, whispering and chuckling among themselves. And Ogre Company waited for the signal to attack. Both sides remained still as if fate itself dared not play out this final battle.

The first to step into the citadel was a terrible beast of slime and fangs, with the body of a cat, the wings of a buzzard, and the head of a cyclopean gnome. Its rider was a muscular warrior of a demon in black, spiky armor with a long blood-red cloak. The rider carried a wicked barbed lash. The demon spread iron wings and cackled. She pulled back her hood to reveal a face that, while not soft or delicate, was vaguely feminine.

"Who's in command here?" she asked with a delicate, gossamer voice.

Frank stepped forward. He adopted a proper smashing stance. "I guess that would be me."

Spear in hand, Regina stood beside him. "That would be us."

The demoness narrowed her glittering silver eyes. "My master, the Glorious and Dreaded Rucka, First Emperor of the Ten Thousand Hells, has sent me to negotiate. Listen well. Surrender Ned to us, or perish horribly beneath our unforgiving wrath."

Frank tightened his grip on his tree trunk. "And if we do?"

The demoness snarled and smiled at the same time. "Then perish slightly less horribly beneath our reasonably more forgiving wrath."

The demons cackled until the demoness quieted them with a thunderous crack of her whip.

"Tonight you will die, and I'll not insult your intelligence by lying. But to gain even the slightest degree of mercy from Rucka's minions is a charity anyone should be grateful for."

The demons cackled again.

Frank chuckled. Regina joined him. Then Miriam. Soon every soldier in Ogre Company was shaking with laughter. The stymied demons fell silent and glared. They were unaccustomed to such behavior from their victims.

"What foolishness is this?" shouted the demoness.

Frank wiped his watering eyes. "Sorry, but I thought this was supposed to be a battle, not a debate."

"You dare mock the legions of Rucka?"

"Oh, no. You're a very fine legion," explained Regina. "It's just that ogres don't really go in for that prefight posturing."

"It's true," said Frank. "We're less talky, more smashy." He thudded the earth with his club. "And we haven't had a decent fight in a very long time. So you'll have to excuse us if we're a bit impatient."

The demoness nodded. "Very well. If that's your wish, then let your blood soak my lash!"

Her weapon shot out toward Frank's throat. He blocked it

with his arm, and the whip wrapped around the limb. They stood there a moment locked in a brief tug-of-war. The spikes pierced his thick flesh, and blood dripped from the wounds. The lash drank the blood, turning darker as the demoness laughed.

Frank shifted his weight and yanked her off the beast. Her mount roared and charged. Its jaws weren't quite large enough to swallow Frank in one bite, but it was willing to give it a try. Frank smashed it across the face with his club. The monster staggered. He struck again. Blood and slime spewed through the air. Frank wrapped his arms around the stunned beast's neck. He called on every ounce of his ogre muscle, and the monster's spine cracked loudly. It collapsed, wheezing, still alive, but limp and broken.

The demoness drew an ax and rushed at Regina. Regina sidestepped a swing meant to split her in half, and struck with her spear. The demoness made no attempt to evade, having absolute faith in her dark armor. But there was a small hole just below her armpit that none had ever noticed before, much less been skilled enough to strike. But Regina's spear found it. The demoness howled as blood gushed from the fatal wound. She turned and took three defiant steps before falling to the ground dead beside her beast.

The citadel was deathly quiet once more.

"That wasn't so hard," said Frank.

"Two down." Regina took in the hundreds of unholy eyes perched on the walls. "How's your arm?"

The wounds pierced deep into the muscle, and even a thick-skinned ogre had to feel that pain. "It's nothing."

"Just be careful, Frank."

He smiled down at her. "I was wondering, Archmajor. I don't know if you'd be interested or not, but do you want to maybe get a drink after all this is over?"

The charge of the swarm drowned out her reply. In one instant the air was thick with demons, an unholy fog of screams and claws and blades. The horde came in many forms. Small imps more annoying than dangerous. Great warriors astride monstrous mounts. Some were armed with swords or whips or spears. Others were armed only with their gnashing teeth and slashing talons. But every demon, in all their infinite variety, shared one thing in common with Ogre Company.

They were spoiling for this fight.

Frank and Regina fought side by side. The ogre swung his club in wide, sweeping arcs that swatted demons from the air. Regina's spear slashed with brutal efficiency, slicing down scores of opponents. Within moments, the formidable pair stood on a small hill of dead demons. A fat underworld warrior jumped on Frank's shoulder and bit into his flesh. The jagged fangs drew blood, and Frank couldn't reach up to dislodge the beast. Regina speared it. The demon fell away, taking her spear with it.

It was far too loud to hear anything except the roar of battle. Frank nodded appreciatively to Regina. She drew her sword, nodded back. And before turning to face a new wave of attackers, she did something he'd never seen her do: she smiled.

He'd seen her smile before. But not like that. Not at him. Like maybe it meant something.

Regina neatly beheaded three demons with one stroke. She continued the motion effortlessly to stab a fourth stealing up behind her. Screaming, she hurled herself fearlessly into another cluster. They could've torn her to bits, except it was the last thing they were expecting. Before they could gather their wits, she'd already killed them. The blood of demons, a vibrant paint of deep reds, thick yellows, chunky greens, and shiny purples, stained her beautiful armor and even more beautiful face.

It was then that Frank knew he loved her.

A pair of demons, foolishly thinking the smitten ogre had dropped his guard, found themselves crushed beneath his club. A winged enemy swooped in to strike Regina from behind. Frank seized its wings, plucked it from the air, and squeezed its skull until three of its four eyes burst. Regina nodded to him. And it was his turn to smile.

A giant beast, like an ape made of equal parts mud and

discarded fish guts, lumbered forward as its rider prodded it with a trident. Regina and Frank raised their weapons and, screaming as one, charged.

The skirmish raged throughout Copper Citadel. Elmer battled with suicidal abandon against a gang of flaming gremlins. He would've been scorched to ash save for Ulga's quick thinking. She conjured a personal stormcloud over his head. It poured torrential rains, but even a wet treefolk wasn't completely fireproof. Most of his leaves smoldered, and bits of him smoked.

Ulga threw bolt after bolt of conjured lightning, blasting demons into blackened corpses. One or two bolts went astray and killed a few of her fellows. But friendly fire was to be expected in a battle of this chaotic nature, and most of the soldiers were either elves or goblins, generally considered expendable.

Sally's fiery nature was ineffective against most of the enemy host, and she relied instead on claws, teeth, and sword. But whenever an ice demon presented itself, she'd melt it with a fireball. Steaming puddles covered the ground around her before the frosty creatures learned to steer clear of her.

A half dozen of the company's strongest ogres encircled Miriam, compelled to protect her. She couldn't control the effect, couldn't switch off her innate siren's aura. She wanted to soak her sword in demon blood, but few demons were able to get within her reach. She had to settle for unleashing her enchanted song in tightly knotted notes that disintegrated enemies in small bunches.

Seamus had strained his shapeshifting abilities to their maximum. He'd become a huge lumbering minotaur, three times the size of an ogre. He swept his fists from side to side, batting aside his foes. He crushed others beneath his hooves and gored them with his horns. Swords and spears pierced his flesh, and green goblin blood dripped from the wounds. But he kept charging.

Ace and his squad of rocs soared through the darkened skies. The birds' talons shredded demons while they slurped down others. Soon, their appetites sated, the groggy rocs ground their opponents in their beaks before spitting them out. Hundreds of clinging goblins formed a crawling, living armor on the rocs, and the demons had a hell of a time getting to the vulnerable, reptilian flesh beneath. And when they tried, three or four goblins would leap from the roc. The boarders gleefully cheered as they and their unwilling ride plunged fatally to the earth. Several of the rocs lost their pilots, yet they carried on slaughtering whatever annoyed them, mostly demons. But two rocs did start tearing into each other amid the confusion. Great winged stags soared forth, spitting fire and roaring like lions. Ace, grinning, whipped the reins and led the squad forward.

Soldier for soldier, the army of the damned was little match for Ogre Company. There were few demons large enough to tackle an ogre, and fewer still who could take the physical punishment that an ogre could withstand. Ogres battled with broken bones and shattered jaws and half their blood pouring from vicious gashes. Some would die soon. Many were mortally wounded, but simply too stubborn to die until the battle was over.

The other species held up almost as well. As a matter of pride, the orcs were determined not to fall before the last ogre, and the humans were a tenaciously difficult breed to exterminate despite their lack of any particular strength or talent. The trolls weren't very dangerous, but anything short of beheading just slowed them down. More than one demon dashed about the battlefield with a limbless troll clamped to its throat, butt, or some other conveniently dangly bit. The goblins perished in droves, but at a rate of twenty goblins to one demon, that was a losing proposition for the underworld minions. Even the elves made a decent show of themselves. They died quickly, but demons loved the taste of elven flesh. Few demons possessed the will to keep their full attention on the fight while a flavorsome corpse lay nearby, and many a demon died with a mouthful of elf after turning its back on an opponent.

But the horde kept coming, pouring from every window and gate of the Iron Fortress. An unlimited supply of soldiers was at Rucka's command. The fortress itself was a portal to the underworld, and whenever a demon died, its body soon dissolved as it returned there fresh and renewed and ready to rise from the bowels of the Iron Fortress to continue the relentless assault on Copper Citadel.

Rucka's victory was inevitable. The Emperor of the Ten Thousand Hells stood in his throne room, gazing down at the endless stream of demons washing over the besieged citadel in the distance.

And he waited.

Ned hated waiting. While the battle raged noisily above, he sat there in the cellar with Martin and Lewis, Owens, and the faintly glowing speaking staff.

It seemed like he'd been waiting his whole life. Waiting to die. Waiting to not die. Waiting for his time in Brute's Legion to end. Waiting for his fate to be decided by everyone but him. But worse than the waiting was the knowing.

He knew it was all pointless. Ogre Company was formidable. Even without proper discipline and adequate armaments, these were dangerous soldiers. It was why the Legion had been reluctant to dismiss them. And Ned could imagine them to be one of the greatest arms of the Legion. With the right leader. Too bad he wasn't that leader. Too bad they were all about to be senselessly slaughtered. Too bad Rucka was going to wake the Mad Void. Too bad everything was going to end.

Just too bad.

Ned glanced to the trapdoor, expecting it to fly open and a tide of demons to come sweeping down and fill the cellar. They didn't, but they would. In ten minutes. Or twenty. Or half an hour. Maybe longer. But sooner or later.

He wished he could do something.

His bad left arm tightened its grip on the speaking staff. The staff glowed brighter. Martin and Lewis said nothing, but they did take a step back. Even Owens seemed to sense something and stood a little farther away than before.

"Why are you glowing?" Ned asked.

"I'm not glowing," replied the staff.

"Yes, you are." Ned shook it. "Don't you know why?"

"I'm not glowing. If there is light coming from me, then I'm not the origin of it."

"But you're still glowing," said Ned. "What does that mean?"

"Must mean there's magic running through me."

"The Red Woman," Ned hoped aloud. She wasn't dead. She'd just gone off to gather her power. She was coming back with an army of gods or angels or something like that to wipe out the underworld horde.

Ned slouched. He had to stop hoping for miracles. They weren't coming.

All that power inside him, and he was helpless.

The veins on Ned's bad arm throbbed. The flesh reddened and cracked. The staff itself changed to match the shade and texture so that it was indistinguishable from his hand. It glowed brighter still. And somewhere inside him, the Mad Void rumbled. The sound filled the cellar.

"Sir, are you okay?" asked Lewis.

Ned nodded, but he felt it coming. Rucka's magic must've awoken the Void after all. It was just slow to rise. He swallowed it down, even as an inner voice told him to let it out. It was the only way to stop the demons, the only way to save himself and the company. If he just let it out a little, if he just opened that inner cage the smallest crack. It wouldn't take much. The Mad Void could obliterate Rucka and his minions without a second thought.

Ned would never get it back in. It would destroy the universe.

And if he didn't, Rucka would let it out, and the universe would be destroyed anyway.

Something pounded on the trapdoor. The ogre twins positioned themselves at the bottom of the stairs.

"You'd better hide yourselves, gentlemen," said Martin.

"We'll handle this," said Lewis.

Owens drew his sword and used it to feel along the floor

to stand beside the twins. "If it's all the same to you, I'd rather die not hiding."

"Glad to have you by our side, sir," said Martin.

The trapdoor splintered inward, and shining eyes gazed inside.

Either way, Ned was going to die. Either way, the universe was dying with him. Ned was tired of waiting. He was tired of hiding. He was tired of being Ned.

The door shattered. Demons rushed in. Martin, Lewis, and Owens raised their weapons to make their final stand. The twins clubbed two demons, and the blind man managed through sheer luck to stab a third in its throat. But the rest overwhelmed them and were an instant from tearing them to pieces.

Ned held out his staff. Red bolts blasted from its tip to strike every demon in the cellar. They disintegrated in a flash, not just slain but obliterated. Wiped from reality into utter, irreversible nothingness, denied the endless return from the underworld.

"What happened?" asked Owens. "What's going on?"

The twins didn't answer. They saw in Never Dead Ned something they had never seen before. Something no creature in a thousand other devastated universes had ever seen and lived to tell. It wasn't an obvious transformation. Other than his bad arm going from gangrenous to blood red and the shining staff in its hand, he still looked like Ned.

But he wasn't Ned.

Silently, the thing that had been Never Dead Ned passed Owens and the twins without acknowledging their presence. It ascended the stairs. Demons started screaming.

THiRtY-ONe

DEMONS COVERED THE citadel, and Frank knew this was a fight Ogre Company could not win. He'd never been one for heroic last stands. When the odds were impossible and victory unachievable, there was nothing wrong with a strategic retreat. That wasn't a choice.

The more improbable the chances of survival, the more determined Regina became. She moved like a slaughtering whirlwind, with a broken sword in one hand and a demon's jawbone in the other. Frank could easily envision her as the last soldier of Ogre Company standing atop a mountain of demon corpses. The battle lust seized her, and she was both horrifying and dazzling at the same time. She smiled and laughed as she killed and killed and killed until only the strongest, most fearsome demons dared engage her. The rest gave her a wide berth.

The signs of imminent defeat were everywhere. Piles of demons covered the soldiers so thickly as to smother the most stubborn warrior. Roc screams filled the sky above as strange underworld beasts finally began wounding the birds enough to knock them from the sky. Four of the great birds littered the citadel, having crushed warriors beneath their stiffening corpses. There seemed now as many demons as goblins. Perhaps more.

The company hadn't given up quite yet. Sally and Elmer fought side by side. The wet treefolk smoldered beside the salamander. Miriam, having drained all the enchantment from her voice, now relied solely on her sword and her ability to inspire. The soldiers fighting at her command felled demons with supernatural fury. Ward fought with incredible zeal, and the vulture perched on his shoulder squawked but refused to abandon its master.

There were still more shrinking pockets of resistance.

Unable to maintain anything larger, Seamus now wore the shape of an ogre, and it suited him as he swung a club with admirable talent. Ulga had apparently run out of lightning bolts and was now conjuring sticks and stones to throw at the demons. Ace's roc was too wounded to fly now, but he spurred it to stomp its way across the battlefield.

Frank, beside Regina, had never been prouder. And if he was going to die a pointless death, he could think of no better company than Ogre Company.

Frank had done his best to protect the pub, but demons swarmed over it like everything else. The demons cackled with delight. Ned was probably dead, realized Frank, and very likely permanently so this time.

A bolt of red blasted through the pub's ceiling. Demons disintegrated so quickly that they had no time to even utter a cry. Streaks of red erupted, blowing holes in the pub, destroying more of the enemy. Frank was so taken with the sight that he was nearly stabbed in the back by a demon, had it not been for Regina's alertness and quick broken sword.

Regina kicked away the corpse. She shouted a warning to be more watchful, but he couldn't hear over the chaos, and he was too distracted by this new occurrence to notice. She was more focused, and it took some time for her to spot the deep red glow emanating from the pub. Its crumbling walls distorted outward in slow motion. The earth trembled.

Frank grabbed Regina, pulled her tight to him, and put himself between whatever dark magic was about to be unleashed.

With a flash of crimson and a stifled boom, the pub exploded. The building was reduced to freezing ash that rained down from the sky. A few small bits of demons—a hand, an eye, half a horn—pelted Frank.

He gazed down at the Amazon in his arms, whom he quickly released. "Sorry, Archmajor. I wasn't trying to imply I thought you were weak or delicate or needed my protection or anything. It's just I'm a lot bigger than you, no offense, and it only made sense." It dawned on Frank that all the noise had left the battlefield or else he wouldn't have been able to hear his fumbled apology.

Regina wasn't listening. She was too intent on the scorched earth where the pub once stood.

Ned stood in the middle of it. The staff in his left hand crackled and shimmered. Streaks of energy lanced outward to obliterate any demons foolish enough to stray within thirty feet of him. Most cowered just outside that range.

He'd changed. And it wasn't just his left arm with its graying flesh and strange, spiky protrusions growing from its shoulder and elbow. There was no way to describe it, to quantify exactly what was different, except for a certain cold disinterest in his eye, a disturbing calm in his expression.

Ned raised his staff. Bolts of magic shot outward in every direction, leaping from demon to demon, burning them into the same icy ash the pub had become. One came directly at Frank, only to veer away at the last instant and destroy a fat incubus. The bolts zipped through Copper Citadel, obliterating demons but avoiding the soldiers of Ogre Company. The magic killed a few dozen of the horde before returning to the point of Ned's staff. He lowered it, and the bloody aura around it dimmed.

Nobody did much of anything for a moment. Ogre Company and the demon horde alike gaped.

A huge green demon warrior, braver than his brethren, stepped forward. He put a shield glowing with unholy magic between him and Ned and then charged, intent on braining Ned with a single smashing strike of an ebony morning star. Ned thrust his staff through the impenetrable shield and into the demon's heart. The warrior's flesh and blood sloughed off into nothing. His bones clattered to the ground, shattering like crystal into powder. Ned looked bored with the entire affair.

Demons fled in horror. Those who weren't instantly destroyed by Ned's magic. The staff glowed brighter and brighter, and soon demons disintegrated without being struck by the red lightning. It was merely enough to stand too close to his dreadful radiance.

Ogre Company stood quiet. Victory was theirs. Never Dead Ned had become a living god of destruction, and every man could feel Ned's cold, unstoppable power. And every soldier knew there would be a price.

Miriam drew nearer. She approached within fifteen feet but dared no closer. It was all she could do to not turn and run at that distance.

"Sir?" Her voice, taxed by the battle, was barely a whisper.

Ned didn't look at her. "One second."

He held high his staff and emitted a single blinding burst of light. The distant retreating survivors of the demon horde disappeared. Just like that. This time there was no fire or ash left behind. Only an emptiness that caused even the trees to tremble.

"Sir?" asked Miriam.

"Almost finished," he replied.

He stamped his staff on the ground, and it launched a pinpoint of magic that shot across the night sky. It reached the Iron Fortress and opened a sucking vortex. The fortress tried to run away, but the pull was inescapable. Brick by brick, the Iron Fortress struggled, but soon enough it and all its inhabitants were consumed. All save one. A single tiny underworld emperor had enough strength to slip free, but no one noticed.

The brilliance of Ned's staff slowly dimmed until it shimmered with the faintest hues.

"Sir?" said Miriam.

This time he turned his head in her direction, though not all the way. He merely cocked an ear as if trying to hear a distant sound. The calmness on his face should've been comforting, but there was something alien about it. It wasn't so much calm as disconnected coolness. The serenity of a madman. A madman with the power to annihilate a horde of demons.

"Are they gone?" asked Miriam. "Is it over, sir?"

"They are. It is."

"Then you've saved us. Haven't you, sir?"

"Saved you?" He smiled then, very slightly. "For the moment."

Somewhere high in the sacred heavens, immortals cowered under their beds and discovered the hollow comfort of futile prayers. Every soldier of Ogre Company stepped back from Ned. Except for Miriam who dared step closer until she was within his reach. The staff's light glinted off her golden scales, turning them a coppery red: the color of old blood.

"It's okay. It's done. It's all done." She reached for Ned's hand.

He grabbed hers suddenly. His burning touch overwhelmed her. The siren screamed, and every soldier in Ogre Company was knocked off their feet. Ned released Miriam. She fell to her knees, clutching a fresh red wound sizzling on her arms. He regarded her agony with a pinch of curiosity. He no longer understood pain, save for a distant memory. He remembered he didn't like it, and being reminded of that filled him with contempt for this weak thing cowering before him. He would destroy it, and he would forget again. And then he would destroy it all. It was the only way to forget it all, the only guarantee he'd never be reminded of any of it.

"Sir?" Miriam covered her eyes as his staff flared. "Ned?"

He stopped. Something about that word made him pause. It reminded him of memories he wasn't sure he possessed.

Part of him wanted to destroy her for her weakness, but another part of him remembered the uncertainty that came with being a little thing in a grand cosmos.

He moved toward her, but she recoiled.

"It'll be okay." He held out his hand. "Here. Let me help you up."

She hesitated.

He pushed down his power. It took more concentration than it'd taken to destroy an entire demon horde, but he managed. He took her hand in his, and while his touch was hot, it didn't burn. He helped her to her feet.

"It'll be all right." He smiled. "Everything will be all right."

Rucka crashed into the courtyard, sending shudders through the ground, knocking everyone but Ned off their feet again.

"Oh, no, Ned. It will not."

The tiny emperor grew into fifteen feet of seething demonic fury. He spread his four tremendous black wings and growled. Rucka had never unleashed his full might for fear of breaking ancient treaties with old powers. But his army was gone, his fortress destroyed. And there was nothing quite so dangerous as a demon driven to madness, boiling with all the enraged, accursed fury of the Ten Thousand Hells. Even the boundless might of the Mad Void might hesitate in the face of that.

Rucka pounced, but a bolt from Ned's staff ripped through the demon's chest, blowing a hole through him. He fell to one knee and gasped, but it wasn't enough to destroy him.

Ned pushed Miriam away from him. The staff flared as he grew to match Rucka's size. The grayness in Ned's left arm grew lighter and lighter until it was a translucent white that spread from his shoulder to cover his entire body. His many scars turned into a gruesome black lattice across his flesh, and beneath that skin lurked not muscle and bone, but an ocean of lights, of colors and shapes that didn't belong in this universe, held behind a fragile illusion of mortal tissues.

The staff in his hand grew and changed along with him.

It twisted into a spiky gnarled stick, squirming with a life of its own.

"You can't defeat me, Rucka," said Ned. "Even the unbridled egotism of a demon emperor must surely see the pointlessness of this."

Rucka's wounds closed. He stood and sneered. "Oh, but I know your weakness."

He launched himself into Ned. The force of his charge carried both of them across the citadel to crash into the barracks. The building collapsed, burying them in a mountain of rubble. A blast of power disintegrated most of the debris, but some pieces shot out with dangerous velocity. They bounced off the ogres, but a few elves and humans were knocked off their feet to lie dazed and bleeding on the ground. One particularly large chunk hurtled at Frank. The ogre deflected it with his fists. His fingers broke audibly, and he grunted.

"Frank, are you okay?" asked Regina.

"It's nothing."

Ned and Rucka stood locked in a deadly embrace. They wrestled over the staff as it crackled with power, seeming to draw strength from both of them. Rucka dug two of his clawed hands into Ned's throat, and Ned fell to one knee.

Miriam drew a sword from a convenient corpse. "Come on," she grunted with her worn voice. "We have to help him."

Frank and Regina readied their own weapons.

A column of crimson mist rose in their path. It spoke. "No. You can't help him any more than you already have." The mist solidified into the Red Goddess. She wasn't the same gnarled, old creature she'd been. She was now tall and youthful and strikingly long and angular. "It's time to find out if Ned is ready."

"Ready for what?" asked Regina.

The Red Goddess smiled. "Ready to be his own keeper."

The Void roared. The staff burned brighter, and Rucka was sent hurtling, screaming, blazing into the air. The demon emperor howled all the way until he hit the ground in the woods a mile or two outside the citadel.

The Mad Void glanced down at the Red Goddess. "I see you've remembered what you are." There was an absence in his voice, a certain lack of Nediness that was hard to define but still missing.

"The cosmic counterbalance that bound us both to slumber has broken. You remember what you are, so I remember what I am. You awake. I awake. That is the way of things, the nature of this ancient magic."

"I remember," said the Void. "Just as I remember that even your power is no match for mine."

She nodded. "You are the supreme destroyer. There is no equal."

The Void frowned. Without saying another word, he soared off into the sky after Rucka.

"He's going to win, isn't he?" asked Miriam.

The goddess nodded. "There can be no doubt."

"Then why am I worried?" asked Regina.

The continent quaked as Ned collided with the earth, and the roar of clashing gods threatened to shake Copper Citadel to ruins. What little of it that wasn't reduced to ruins already. Many soldiers of Ogre Company were knocked off their feet again, and most had the good sense to not bother getting up anymore.

"Because to do so, Ned might very well have to become a greater monster than Rucka could ever be."

"Can't you help him?" asked Frank.

"No one can help Ned but Ned now. Even the gods must sit this one out." And so the Red Goddess did sit, looking quite indifferent as the sky darkened and cracks appeared in the earth.

"We have to do something," said Miriam.

"Then by all means, rush to his side if you must." The Red Goddess waved her hand. Miriam disappeared in a scarlet flash.

Regina stepped forward. "Excuse me, but could you—" She vanished with another wave.

Frank, his broken hands hanging limply at his side, approached. He didn't even have to ask, and she teleported him away.

Ace, Elmer, and a small band of goblins were next, but the goddess lowered her hand.

"Well, if this is how it's going to be, I suppose it'll be easier to do you all at once," she remarked. "Everyone who wishes to have a good view of the end of all things, please raise your hand."

The destructive powers of the Mad Void and Rucka were nearly without limits. Each sought to annihilate the other, but they regenerated from every wound. They disintegrated each other over and over again, only to reform instantly. Each rebirth burned away some of their boundless might, and the loser would be the godlike entity that was depleted first. But godlike entities had a lot of energy to burn, and it could take a century or two to find a winner—providing the universe wasn't destroyed in the process.

Reality itself was far more delicate than either of these titans. It began to crumble around them. The speaking staff held between them became the focus of their struggle. It radiated twisted energies. The forest withered around them. Small birds and beasts were consumed by invisible flames. A blizzard of black snow fell from a red sky even as the air grew hot and sticky.

Rucka belched a toxic cloud. It dissolved the Void, the grass, and nearby stones. The dirt began to boil and churn. The Void reformed and blasted a lance of power from his eye that sliced Rucka's head in half and burrowed into the earth. A torrent of magma gushed from the world's wound as the demon emperor's skull knit itself back together.

Grinning, Rucka tore at the Void's side with his two free hands. The demon sank his fangs into the Void's neck. Rucka's long, barbed tail speared his opponent through the chest and pulled out the Void's malformed heart. The organ continued to beat even as Rucka devoured it, laughing.

The gulped heart erupted in a spiky mass. It filled Rucka's throat, stomach, and bowels. Thorns tore at his flesh from the inside out. Pain wracked his body. The Void's heart blazed with such unnatural darkness that even the Emperor of the Ten Thousand Hells must shrink from its touch.

Rucka collapsed into a spasmodic heap. He shrieked, foaming at the mouth, tearing at his own guts. It was only temporary. If necessary, Rucka could rip himself apart to extract the heart and still regenerate.

The Void stood over the demon and considered how to rid himself of this nuisance once and for all. The answer was obvious. He must call down enough of his power to end this. One blow with sufficient strength of the Mad Void behind it would destroy anything. It could destroy everything.

The staff in the Void's left hand churned with power; like a miniature sun, it cast aside the night in its blinding light. The world beneath his feet quaked and whimpered as the Mad Void readied to deliver the strike that would obliterate the demon emperor and this small corner of the universe.

And then he saw them. All about him. Little things. Insignificant, unimportant. Not even worth noticing. Yet he noticed them as they stood in the stinking, blackened snow, so deep that it came to an ogre's waist. The soldiers of the company looked on, their faces etched in confusion and quiet terror.

His gaze fell across Regina and Miriam. He couldn't quite remember them anymore. There was nothing to remember. They were but particles of dust. They mattered not at all.

"Then why do you remember their names?" asked the Red Goddess, standing suddenly by his side.

He turned to her. "It's nothing, an empty memory from a man who never was." He looked at Rucka, still writhing in quiet agony beneath the Void, still struggling to remove the heart he'd so foolishly swallowed. All the light in the staff faded into a blackness that consumed the night in an ebony fog so thick that only the Void, Rucka, and the Red Goddess could still see.

"Are you a god who dreamed he was a man?" asked the goddess. "Or are you a man who dreams he is a god?"

The Void smiled grimly. "I am. And I shall always be. But

these things beneath me will pass away. As will their world one day. Today or tomorrow or the day after tomorrow, when does it matter to me? It is all but a moment in eternity."

Rucka had nearly succeeded in extracting the heart. There was but a handful of seconds left for the Void to take advantage of the demon's weakness. Otherwise, the titanic struggle would renew.

The Mad Void raised his staff to plunge it into Rucka.

The goddess leaned close and whispered in the Void's ear. "It matters. If not to you, Ned, then to them."

The Void hesitated. Not long ago, by his measure of time, he would've destroyed Rucka, this world, these specks, and countless others, and the entire universe as well without a second thought. But things had changed. He'd lived as a man, as many men. The exact memories eluded him, and he could only recall Ned's life.

Even measured by the insignificance of mortal lives, it had been an exercise in absurd futility, a complete waste of time, a struggle against fate to find a place in a world that cared nothing for one more mote crawling upon its surface. But there was some strange dignity in it, and in all these little things. And though they didn't mean anything and their lives or deaths meant even less, the Void saw them as oddly beautiful in a way he'd never before imagined and couldn't completely understand.

He lowered his staff. The darkness faded, and the night returned.

He smiled. At Miriam. At Regina. And Frank. And the whole of Ogre Company. The blizzard ended. The snow turned white, then faded away.

The Red Goddess held out her hand. "Give me the staff, Ned. You don't need it. The power lies within you. It always has. You've chosen not to use it before. You can choose not to again."

Rucka sprang. He threw the Void's own heart at it, and the blackened organ wrapped around its former owner. Rucka knocked the staff from the Void's hand, seized him by the throat, and before the Void could recover from the surprise, the demon reached into the Void's head and plucked out his eye. The Void slumped on the ground. His body shrank into Ned's proportions.

The Red Goddess moved to stop Rucka from inserting the eye into his empty socket, but his barbed tail sliced her into quarters. Rucka put the eye in its place and cackled.

"It's mine!" he screamed triumphantly. "The power is all mine!"

"No," said Ned.

The demon whirled on the little mortal creature below him. Ned looked completely normal except his eyes had grown back and his left arm remained red with its patchwork of blackened scars.

Rucka raised his heel to crush the speck. He slammed down his foot, but one touch of Ned's red fingertips pushed the demon off balance. He crashed to the earth.

"But I have your eye!" shouted Rucka.

"But my power lies elsewhere." Ned's left arm sparkled for an instant. "You were looking in the wrong place." He clenched his fist as Rucka tried to rise, and the demon fell as if bound to the ground.

"You can't hold me forever!" said Rucka. "I'll break free. Even if I have to tear the world apart to do it!"

"I know."

"And I'll come back! Again and again, I'll come back! As many times as it takes!"

"I know."

And he would. And each time he would fail. And each time Ned would have to call upon the Void's power to defend himself. And a little piece of his humanity would disappear until it all disappeared, until he became the Mad Void again.

"There's only one way to stop me! But you haven't the strength for that. Because all these worthless mortals mean something to you. And to destroy me, you'll have to destroy them all. They're your weakness. It'd be laughable if it weren't so pathetic." Rucka laughed anyway.

Ned gestured with his left arm, and still laughing, Rucka was raised into the air and shot up and out of sight.

Ned floated a few feet off the ground. He turned to Miriam, Regina, and Frank. "I'll be right back." He streaked after the demon.

The two hurtled out of the atmosphere, into the darkness of space, past the sun and planets of the solar system and onward. Physics twisted beneath Ned's will, and a billion billion miles passed by in moments. They continued onward, out of the galaxy, past the next galaxy and the next, until they reached a portion of the universe that fit Ned's needs, a corner filled with lifeless planets and dying stars.

Rucka whimpered, his misty breath visible in the airless emptiness. "No, no! I didn't mean it! I submit! I surrender!"

Ned said nothing. Whether Rucka meant the words or not, it didn't matter. He was too ambitious a demon to not try again.

"You can't do this," pleaded Rucka. "I have a purpose in this universe. I belong here. Not like you. What right do you have to destroy me?"

"I have every right," said Ned sadly. "I'm the Mad Void. And you made me remember, so I don't think you can complain."

Rucka, seeing his pleas fail, came to his last resort. "But to destroy me, you must destroy yourself. Are you willing to do that?"

"If I could've destroyed myself, I would've done it long ago." Ned laughed bitterly. There was only one thing the Void could not annihilate, and that was the Void itself.

Ned laid his hand on Rucka's chest, and a galaxy disappeared in a flash. There was no death rattle, no final gasping spasm for this empty portion of the universe. It was just gone, winking out of existence, dissolved into nothingness and then beyond nothingness.

A lone piece of charred, blackened debris fell from the emptiness. It was a man, but not a man. Dead, but not dead. Supernatural guidance took hold of it and gently steered it across the cosmos to an inconsequential ruined citadel on an inconsequential planet. The comet streaked downward to strike the world with devastating force, but the Red Goddess cushioned the landing so that it touched the ground without disturbing the dust.

Ogre Company circled the thing, barely recognizable as Ned.

"He'll come back," said Miriam. "Won't he?"

The goddess smiled. "He always comes back."

THiRtY-twO

NED AWOKE IN a tent. It was a nice tent, just large enough to hold a cot, a table, a chair, and a glowing heatstone. It was the wrong time of year for heatstones, and Ned wondered just how long he'd been dead this time.

"Just over five months," said the Red Goddess, sitting in the chair. Her raven sat on her shoulder.

Ned pulled up the heavy blankets. "Took you long enough."

"Don't blame me," she replied. "You were in the center of an obliterated galaxy. Takes a while to recover from that, and even I don't have enough power for it. But I'm not the one who brought you back this time. I don't do that anymore."

"Oh, really? Who has the responsibility now?"

"You, Ned."

"But I thought if I brought myself back, I'd come back as—"

"I think you've finally grown out of that."

"But what about the Void?"

"What about it?" She stood. "You know it better than anyone. So why ask me?"

Ned concentrated. Deep, deep inside he sensed the ancient, unstoppable evil as it slumbered. This wasn't the forced, uneasy doze of old, but a content, relaxed nap. The Void couldn't change its nature, nor could it ever be destroyed, but it could sleep. And it might sleep forever, or at least until the natural end of this universe.

"Once it was held by a spell," said the goddess, "but that was never a lasting solution. The only power that could ever hold the Mad Void in check was the Void itself. And now it does.

"That was the original intent of this business, you see. The spell was merely part of the process. As was each and every life it lived. A crash course in what it means to be mortal, to see the world in the way gods and demons never can. And you are the final result of that spell, Ned."

"Me?" Ned sat up. "But I'm not very good at anything."

"Exactly. You have no particular talents, no greatness, no exceptional skills or abilities. You can't even keep yourself alive. You are incompetent and inconsequential, and I can think of no being in this universe farther removed from godhood."

"Wait a minute." Ned mulled this over. "You're saying I'm supposed to be an idiot?"

"If it makes you feel better to think of it like that," said the raven.

"You aren't an idiot," said the Red Goddess. "You're just mortal. Very, very mortal. Perhaps too much so." She put her hand on his cheek and smiled. "But that is your burden, Ned. Bear it well. The universe depends on it."

She moved toward the tent flap. "If you'll excuse me, I must return to my mountain. There are more threats to this world than just you, and I still have my duties. Take care, Ned."

She stepped out of the tent, and Miriam stepped inside a moment later. Ned didn't ask if she'd seen the Red Goddess leave.

Miriam's fins raised. "Ned, you're back."

"I'm back."

He stretched and noticed the absence of so many aches and pains that he'd grown used to carrying. He threw aside the blanket to reveal his naked body. His scars had vanished. His left arm remained a tad greenish, and his right eye was still missing, but everything else seemed in working order.

Miriam averted her gaze. "Sir?"

He jumped to his feet, grabbed her by the shoulders, and gave her a long, long kiss. The gesture surprised her, but she wrapped her arms around him and kissed him back.

He pulled back suddenly and started getting dressed.

"Ned, are you okay?" she asked.

"Great. I'm a boob. A complete, utter screwup. But I'm supposed to be, so that's the good news."

"I don't understand."

"Don't worry about it." He pulled on some breeches and grabbed his shirt. "But do you want to know something else?" He gave her a peck and ran his tongue across his lips. "I think I'm beginning to like the taste of fish."

He exited the tent, and smiling, she followed him.

It was cold outside, but he didn't seem to notice. He strolled briskly through the citadel, grinning and waving at everyone. Many of the soldiers didn't recognize him without his scars, but they waved back. Most of Ogre Company was working to fix the damaged citadel, which had to be rebuilt from the ground up after its last siege.

A woolly ox pulling a cart of stones stopped and nodded in Ned's direction.

"Good to see you too, Seamus," replied Ned.

The ox snorted and continued on its way.

Ned stopped suddenly. "Oh, no. The deadline. Did I miss the deadline?"

"Don't worry, sir. The Legion decided we weren't such a waste of resources after all, once we filed a report on the doomsday battle with the demon army. They didn't believe us at first. Until we had a goddess testify on our behalf. Even upper management couldn't argue with that."

They passed Elmer, who seemed to be deriving excessive pleasure from driving nails into boards. So much so that he didn't notice Ned. But Ulga paused conjuring nails and waved at him. Lewis and Martin busily stacked stones in a large pile, but the twins still took the time to salute, and Ned saluted back.

Miriam held out his coat. "Aren't you cold?"

He slipped it on. "Thanks."

"No problem, Ned."

He leaned in to kiss her again.

"Excuse me, sir," said Regina.

Ned froze mid-lean. "Archmajor, how are you?"

"Very well, sir," the Amazon replied, "and you?"

"Pretty good."

Frank appeared. His hands were bandaged. Ogre bones were slow to heal, but they'd mended enough to allow the use of his fingers. He had a black eye and a fresh purple bruise on his shoulder. He carried a club in one hand, a spear in the other. "Hey, Ned."

Ned bobbed his head in Frank's direction. "Hey, Frank."

"Good to have you back, sir." He tossed Regina the spear. "Are you ready?"

"Sure." She nodded at Ned. "Take care, sir."

The ogre and the Amazon walked away. Frank put his hand on her back, and she didn't seem to mind.

"Are they dating now?" asked Ned.

"About four months," said Miriam, "if you can call it dating. They mostly just beat the hell out of each other, and have drinks after. But Frank should best her any day now. Then they can get on with it."

Ned wasn't so certain of Frank's victory. He was a formidable warrior, but no one could match Regina when it came down to sheer stubbornness. But one day after her fierce Amazon pride had been satisfied, she'd let him win.

"Maybe after he gets that promotion to commander," thought Ned aloud.

"But you're commander, sir," said Miriam.

"Not anymore. I'm through with it, through with soldiering. I can't make up for everything the Void's done, but I can at least put aside my sword. Besides, I was always a terrible soldier. Frank is the best one for the job. He's good with the men, and he's big enough to keep their respect."

"Regina isn't going to like that."

"She'll get over it."

The citadel was a jumble of tents now, but one building had been rebuilt. The new pub was not strictly up to code. The ceiling was a little low for ogres, and the structure leaned a bit to the left. It might collapse in a month or two, but it appeared safe for now. And Ned was thirsty.

Stepping inside the darkened building, he was immediately greeted with a round of cheers. Ward slapped Ned across the shoulder, sending Ned sprawling across the floor.

"Whoops," said Ward. "Sorry about that, sir." He helped Ned up. "What kept you?"

"Exploding galaxies takes a lot out of a guy," replied Ned.

"In that case, sir," said Ward, "let me be the first to buy you a drink."

Nibbly Ned shifted on his perch on Ward's shoulder. The vulture stared Ned right in the eye. Ned stared right back, and Nibbly blinked first. The bird tucked his head under a wing.

They bellied up to a bar that, though just right for ogres, was a little too high for humans. Owens and Sally were working behind the counter. The salamander roasted various cuts of meat, while Owens tended bar. He presented Ned with a smile and a drink.

"What is it?" asked Ned.

"It's what you want," replied the oracle. "Trust me, sir. And that steak you planned on ordering is on its way. How's it coming, Sally?"

"Almost done." She eyed the piece of meat she was breathing on. "You wanted it rare, right?"

"Medium rare," answered Owens. "Right, sir?"

Ned actually wanted it well done, but he didn't feel like contradicting the oracle. Anyway, who was to say that he didn't want it medium rare? The oracle might know something he didn't.

"So what do you hear for tomorrow?" asked Ned.

"Oh, nothing much, sir. Death, destruction, chaos, strife, and conflict. Business as usual." Owens tilted his head and listened. "And a spot of rain."

Goblins had to take turns standing on each other's shoulders in stacks of three to place their orders. Ace balanced atop an unsteady pole of drunken goblins.

"To Never Dead Ned," toasted Ace. "Nobody dies better."

The soldiers smashed their mugs together, shattering most of them. Ace's tower toppled, but he managed impressively to land on his back without spilling a drop. He jumped to his feet and downed the drink just before a wave of goblins jumped on his back and started shouting their orders.

Miriam tapped her glass gently against Ned's. "But if you're not going to be a soldier anymore, what are you going to do?"

Ned shrugged. "I'll figure out something."

She moved closer and took his hand.

He frowned at the burn scar on her wrist where the Mad Void had touched her. "Sorry about that."

"Don't worry about it." She smoothed his hair. "You know, Ned, you don't have to be a soldier to stay here. I hear there's an opening for a gardener."

"Is that so?"

"So how are you at gardening, Ned?"

He took a long draft of ale and slammed the mug on the counter.

"Absolutely terrible."

Turn the page for a preview of

A NaMELESS WiTCH

by A. Lee Martinez

Available May 2007
in Hardcover and Trade Paperback

0-765-31868-7 (Hardcover)
0-765-31548-3 (Trade paperback)

I WAS BORN DEAD. Or, to be more accurate, undead. Not that there is much difference between the two. It's just a matter of degrees really.

When I say undead, I do not mean vampyre, ghoul, or graveyard fiend. There are many versions of unlife. These are only the most common. My state was far less debilitating. Bright lights bothered me to some noticeable degree, and I preferred my meat undercooked. Once reaching adulthood, I'd become ageless. Most means of mortal harm could not truly hurt me, and I possessed a smattering of unusual gifts not known among the living. Yet all these advantages came at a high price.

Exactly how I came to be born undead is a long, complicated story not really worth telling in detail. It involves my great-great-great-great-grandfather, a renowned hero of the realm, and his conflict with a dark wizard. This wizard, his name is lost to history so I just call him "Nasty Larry" for convenience's sake, had raised an army of orcish zombies to ravage the land. Now everyone knows orcs are terrible things, and zombies aren't much fun either. Mix the two together and you get an evil greater than the sum of its parts. Naturally, a legion of heroes was assembled, and the requisite last stand against doomsday was fought and won by a hair's breadth. My great-great-great-great-grandfather slew Nasty Larry, cleaving his head from his shoulders with one sweep of a mighty broadsword. Nasty Larry's head rolled to his slayer's feet and pronounced a terrible curse as decapitated wizard's heads are prone to do.

"With my dying breath, I curse thee and thy bloodline. From now until the end of time, the sixth child of every generation shall be made a gruesome abomination. A twisted, horrible thing that shall shun the light and dwell in miserable darkness."

That bit of business finished, Nasty Larry died. According to legend, he melted into a puddle, the sky turned black, and—if one could believe such tales—the land within a hundred miles turned to inhospitable swamp. That was the end of Nasty Larry's small, yet noteworthy, influence on my life.

I often wondered why my parents chose to have a sixth child, being forewarned as they were. They had many excuses. The most common being, "We lost count." Second common, and far more acceptable in my opinion, was "Well, none of our family had ever had six, and we thought it might not have taken." Perfectly reasonable. Not all curses grab hold, and one couldn't live one's life fretting over every utterance of every bodiless head one ran across.

Being undead was not all that horrible a curse. Unfortunately, this was not the end of my worries. For besides being made a thing born to dwell in darkened misery, I was also made, in the infinite wisdom of fate, a girl. These two conditions taken individually were minor handicaps, but toss them together, and you would understand the difficulties I experienced growing up.

There are kingdoms where a woman is prized for her mind, where she is more than a trophy or a poorly paid housemaid. Kingdoms where the chains of a thousand years of chauvinism have finally rusted away. I was not born in one of these kingdoms.

I was not very popular amongst the male suitors of my village. It was nothing personal. Husbands just prefer living wives, and I met so few potential spouses locked in my parents' basement. At the age of eighteen, I was already an old, undead maid sitting in a darkened cellar, waiting to die.

Of course, I don't die. Not like normal people. Certainly, old age wouldn't accomplish the task. So I settled in for a very long wait. I figured it would be another fifty years before my parents died, and one of my brothers or sisters would inherit caretaking duties of their poor, wretched sibling. One of their children would take over next. And so on. And so on. Until one day, they either forgot me, or all died, or maybe, just maybe, an angry mob would drag me from the shadows and burn me at the stake. Not much to look forward to. But no one is master of their fate, and my lot was not all that terrible in the end.

All that changed with the arrival of Ghastly Edna. That wasn't her real name. I never learned it. I just called her "Ghastly Edna" because it seemed a proper witch's name. She was a grotesquely large woman, bear-like in proportions, with a pointed hat, a giant hooked nose, and a long, thin face. Her skin, while not truly green, possessed a slick, olive hue. Her nose even had a wart. Ghastly Edna's only flaw, witchly speaking, was a set of perfectly straight, perfectly polished teeth.

The day I met Ghastly Edna changed everything, and I remember it well. The basement door opened. I scrambled to the foot of the stairs to collect my daily meal. Instead, she came lumbering down. Her bulky frame clouded the light filtering behind her. She placed a callused hand under my chin and smiled thinly.

"Yes, yes. You shall do, child."

Ghastly Edna purchased me from my parents for a puny sum. I'm certain they were glad to be rid of their cursed daughter, and I couldn't honestly blame them. My new mentor whisked me away to her cottage in the middle of some forsaken woods far from civilization. The first thing she did was clean me up. It took six long hours to wash away the accumulated filth of eighteen years and cut the tangle of hair atop my head. When she finally finished, she stood me before a small mirror and frowned.

"No, no, no. I do not like this. I do not like this one bit."

The effect this had on my self-esteem was immediate and crushing. I'd always known myself to be a hideous thing. Yet Ghastly Edna was no prize beauty herself, and to evoke such a revolted tone could only mean that Nasty Larry's curse had really had its way with me.

"You're not ugly, child," she corrected. "You're quite—" Her long face squished itself into a scowl "—lovely."

I had yet to dare looking in the mirror for fear of being driven mad by own hideousness. Now I chanced a sidelong glance through the corner of my eye. It was not the sanity-twisting sight I had expected, but still a far cry from lovely.

"But what about these?" I cupped the large, fatty mounds on my chest.

"Those are breasts," Ghastly Edna said. "They're supposed to be there."

"But they're so . . . so . . ."

"Round. Firm." She sighed. "That's how they're supposed to be. Ideally."

I found that hard to believe, but I wasn't about to argue with the person who'd rescued me from my solitary existence.

"And that bottom of yours," she mumbled. "You could bounce a gold piece off it."

"But the skin is pale," I offered, trying to please her.

"It's not pale, dear. It's alabaster." She circled me twice, looking more disappointed each passing moment. "And I don't believe I've ever seen eyes quite that shade of green. Or lips so full and soft. And your hair. I washed it with year-old soap, and it's still as soft as gossamer." She drew close and sniffed. "And it smells of sunflowers."

"What about my teeth? Surely they're not supposed to look like that."

She checked my gums and teeth with her fingers. "No, dear. You're quite correct. They're a tad too sharp. But it's not an obvious flaw, and besides that, they're nice and white. Good gums too. The tongue has a little fork in it, but only if you're looking for it."

She ordered me into a seat, still naked and slightly damp from the bath.

"Are you certain you spent all your life in that basement?" I nodded.

"No exercise. Dismal diet. Dwelling in filth. Yet somehow you come out like this. Not even half-mad as far as I can tell."

"You mean, I'm not cursed, ma'am?"

"Oh, you are cursed, child, and undead. That much is certain. Curses come in many forms, however, and not all are as bad. Especially death curses. It's tricky enough to cast a decent spell when you're still alive. But throwing one out as you're expiring requires a certain knack. Apparently, the wizard who cursed your family was not as in control of his magic as he should've been. The undead part came through, but the hideousness element didn't quite make it. The magic must've had a better idea, as it sometimes does."

She handed me a towel. "Cover yourself, dear. I can't bear to look upon you anymore."

I did as I was told.

"That's the thing about death curses. One really shouldn't employ them unless one feels they can pull it off. It just makes the rest of us look bad."

She spent several minutes rocking in her chair, mulling over the situation. A dread fell upon me. I didn't want to be sent back to my cellar if I could help it. Given no other choice, I'd accepted my fate. Now my universe was filled with other possibilities, and I didn't want to lose them.

Ghastly Edna snapped up from her chair.

"Well, dear, the magic called me to you. Far be it from me to contradict it. Your loveliness just means you'll have to work harder at your witchery. A handicap yes, but not an insurmountable one." She peeled the wart from her nose. "False, darling." She winked.

She proceeded to wipe the greenish makeup from her face to reveal skin that, while rough and haggard, was not especially hideous. She removed six layers of clothing to show that her hunch was nothing more than an illusion of well-placed fabric. When she removed her hat, I realized that Ghastly Edna was a large and ugly woman, but not at all witchly without her full outfit.

"We all need a little help, dear. You just need far more than I. Now let me see what I have here that might do the trick." She began digging through various moldy trunks filled with equally moldy clothing.

My heart leapt with joy.

Ghastly Edna spent the next six months acquainting me with the ins and outs of witchly wardrobe. Wearing just the right outfit was fifty percent of a witch's business, she explained. She was not exaggerating. It took a great deal of work to make one look as bad as was expected. Especially for me, my mentor pointed out, as I was afflicted with a form most unsuitable for a witch.

Once I'd mastered the art of looking witchly, she proceeded to teach me the black arts: necromancy, demonology, the forgotten language of unspeaking things, and forbidden nature lore. The powers of magic that had drawn Ghastly Edna to me had not been mistaken, and in due course, I mastered the craft of the witch.

And for a while, I was happy.

Until the dark day when they finally killed her.